6/15/17

To Lynn,

Thank you so

East of Mecca

Sheila Flaherty

much for your
support!

Be brave!

Sheila

REVISED EDITION
Copyright © 2015 Sheila Flaherty
All rights reserved.

ISBN: 1490315233
ISBN-13: 9781490315232
Library of Congress Control Number: 2013910295
CreateSpace Independent Publishing Platform
North Charleston, South Carolina

Publisher: Pink Orchid Publishing
Evanston, Illinois

Praise For
East Of Mecca

"*East of Mecca* offers a deeply engaging narrative on the brutality waged against women and the bonds that unite them. The vivid and powerful scenes illuminating this story will stay with you."

—David Finch, author of New York Times bestseller *The Journal of Best Practices: A Memoir of Marriage, Asperger Syndrome, and One Man's Quest to Be a Better Husband*

"Brilliantly captures the everlasting ties of sisterhood, the struggle of the forsaken, and a mother's resolve to protect her family in the face of grave danger. If you're somehow able to set this book down, it will probably take you a moment to remember you're not actually living the story."

—Kristen Finch, Life Coach

"*East of Mecca* is an elegant balance of cultural nuance and moral inquiry, well-told with precise detail and emotional impact. It is an important story for our time."

—Mark Bryan, founding member of Oprah Winfrey's Change Your Life team.

"This is an important story that is written so well that you won't be able to turn off your bedside lamp until you've turned the last page. Sarah is a woman that most of us can relate to and will feel a kinship with as she faces the many challenges that come with being a woman in Saudi Arabia."

—Janeen Halliwell, Founder & Director of We Move Forward International Women's Day Conference

"This would make an excellent companion piece to A HOLOGRAM FOR THE KING. But while Eggers novel highlights the absurdities of life in a conservative, oil rich kingdom, Flaherty deals with the horrors of a dogma that considers women little more than property. The story is riveting, and Flaherty's prose is elegant and powerful. This is definitely a book not to miss."

—Eric Diekhans, Screen Writer and Television Producer

"This is a cautionary tale of good intentions gone wrong, of the skewed power dynamics that couples are likely to confront, both within and outside their home, if they choose to pursue the American dream overseas in a society that denies women basic human rights."

—Mary Trouille, Professor of Women's Studies, Illinois State University

"Sheila Flaherty is a gifted writer. Her compassionate words paint the picture and touch the reader's heart. Her descriptive language and knowledge of the country is convincing and believable. The brutality also forces the reader to look closely at their own beliefs and search for the truth of Godly love. This message makes the book a must read!"

—Carl Ray Copeland, Retired Haltom H.S. Football Coach, Texas

"It is the kind of book you have to talk about once you're done, so you'll bug your friends to read it, you'll make your book club pick it."

—Ellen Maddy

"Flaherty captures the exotic magic of the Middle East and with vivid imagery, transports the reader to this faraway land where you can almost feel the oppression of the desert heat and the extremist regime. Incredible story that is beautifully written!!"

—Diane Moore

"Every detail, characterization, plight, physical and psychological, rings true. Written in first-person, Sarah holds the reader close while she journeys through the maze of Saudi, Ocmara, family relationships and feminism, hers and Saudi women's."

—Anne Lamas

"East of Mecca will capture your interest and heart within ten minutes. Just be ready to stay up late reading."

—Zazapen, reader on Goodreads.com

"This is a story for both men and women -- especially those who want to explore the under-belly of a sex-separate society as it goes about its daily routines."

—Paul Fields, Retired Attorney

"This book has changed the way I look at woman garbed in the traditional dress of the Middle East. The characters still linger in my consciousness, the sign of a great piece of writing."

—Sarah Thurber, Managing Partner, FourSight LLC

"This was a FABULOUS book!! It was difficult to put down, the author draws you in and doesn't let go! My Book Club read this and the author, Sheila Flaherty Skyped in with us to discuss the book! She loves to connect with her readers! Buy this book ASAP!!!!"

—Tracy L. Cook

"I will await the movie version, as in addition to great dramatic conflict, this is also a highly visual, even cinematographically, compelling work."

—Brian Smolens

"East of Mecca is a beautifully written story! From page one I was hooked.

—Jason Sarna, author of *Night Burger*

"Could not put this book down, the story is fascinating. It's been many years since I stayed up half the night reading but this one did that. I felt like I was living the part and felt withdrawal when the book ended."

—Amazon Customer

"The account written about in East of Mecca is moving and draws you into the lives of the characters. It is well written and has an important message to convey to its readers."

—Michael Wall, CPA

"I could not put this book down! It was gut-wrenching, haunting, enlightening, angering, thought provoking, exciting, sad, loving and more.......a compelling "read" that I am highly recommending to everyone!"

—Amazon Customer

"Very interesting book....I finished it near 3 in the morning - could not stop. If I had seen this fifteen years ago, I would have thought it a nice story but nothing like reality. But after reading more about the Saudi culture and traditions including the religious police and honor killings and intolerance, I see where most of the incidents could have been lifted out of a news report or hospital entries."

—K. S. Rude, Shamanic Practitioner, Environmental Advocate, Author

"Written in a first person perspective point of view, the main character tells her unique story of living in an Islamic country, where women are treated much, much differently than they are in the United States."

—Wayne Reinagel, reader on Goodreads.com

"Sheila did a wonderful job of portraying the plight of victimized women in a Saudi Arabian company town without attacking religion but by uncovering the true cause of the disparity. Well written and thought provoking."

—Melissa Heisler, Stress Reduction Expert, Author

This book is dedicated to the memory of Mary Siewert Scruggs,
to the women in Saudi Arabia who entrusted me with their stories,
to the spirit of Yasmeen,
and to all women who long to be free.

Life without liberty is like a body without spirit.
~Khalil Gibran

Prologue

It was the last box. Wrapped tightly in packing tape with "Saudi" written on the side in black marker, it sat alone in the middle of the living room floor. Everything else was gone. It was a time of moving on and letting go. I'd sold the battered Victorian house and closed on the new, minimalist condo. I could have chosen to cart the box with me, settled it into the far corner of the storage area, and left it unopened. But the move would have made that a deliberate act. Not that forgetting isn't sometimes a deliberate act.

For the past eighteen years I'd known where the box was. On some level I was always aware of it, shoved deep into the recesses of the hall closet— lying in wait like a repressed memory. I couldn't open it, but I couldn't throw it away. For the past few years, it had been getting harder to ignore. I couldn't turn on the news or open the paper without a nudge, a reminder. Fleeting glimpses of a black shadow. Dark eyes above a mask. The box lived on the periphery of my mind like the forgotten words of a song, or the remnants of a disturbing dream. And then the news coverage of the Girl of Qatif, a young Saudi rape victim sentenced to jail and 200 lashes, made the memories too loud to ignore.

When I dragged the box out of the closet, I was surprised by how light it was. I set it on the floor and walked around it for a week. It waited in silent reproach. Now, all else was gone except an old boom-box that kept me company while I cleaned. Finally, it was time. All other distractions and demands had been silenced or met.

Even then, I circled, restless and reluctant. I poured myself a glass of red wine. On bare feet I padded quietly into the living room, bringing the bottle with me, just in case. The house was still and slightly chilly. It was early evening and the windows held the diminishing glow of daylight. I dimmed the overhead light and lit several candles.

I sat cross-legged on the ancient hardwood floor and took a sip of wine. Using a serrated knife, I sawed through the tape and opened the box. Immediately I was hit with the lingering smells of smoke and desperation. Underneath, and more subtle, I caught the sweet scent of henna, sandalwood, frankincense, and myrrh—the perfume of the Middle East. Wadded pieces of newspaper, covered with Arabic calligraphy, formed a protective layer. I tossed the paper into the empty fireplace. Now, everything in the box was dark, swaddled in black cloth.

Reaching in, I pulled out the first thing I touched, immediately recognizing the dense familiar weight. Wrapped in a scarf was my Nikon EM. I examined the camera and took off the lens cap. Peering through the viewfinder, I looked out the windows into the darkening night. After setting the Nikon on the floor, I took a swallow of wine and picked up the scarf.

The scarf was long and black, scalloped edges embroidered with red and gold silk thread. Green and red sequins formed the shapes of flowers. I smoothed the scarf across my lap and traced the flowers with my fingertips. The gauzy fabric was ripped in several places. I wound the scarf around my neck.

Digging deeper, my fingers closed on black silk. I gathered my *abaya* into my arms and buried my face in the soft cloth, breathing in the odors of incense, blood, freedom, and fear. Suddenly I saw blood billowing through water—a maroon river swirling down a drain. In that moment I felt the first sting of tears. Awash with emotions and memories, I sat on the cold hard floor, rocking gently, keening. When I finally lowered the cloth, the sky was black. I slipped my abaya over my T-shirt and jeans, finding comfort in the warm damp silk. I finished my glass of wine and poured another.

The only thing left in the box was a small, light blue backpack. I lifted it onto my lap, unzipped it, and looked in. On top was an audiotape labeled with one word handwritten in black ink: "Belly." I smiled and set the tape on the floor. Next up was a crumpled burgundy and gold box of Dunhill cigarettes. As I lifted it to my nose, I smelled the faint, sweet scent of tobacco. I set the cigarettes beside the tape.

Rummaging deep in the bag, I found a cowry shell with minute pink speckles scattered across the rounded top. The opening on the flat white bottom had tiny tooth-like edges. Touching it to the tip of my tongue, I tasted the sea.

I pulled a blue airmail envelope out of the backpack. On the front, *SHUKRAN* was printed in red ink. I took a swallow of wine and a deep breath. As if tucked hastily into the envelope, a small photograph crookedly faced away. I knew what it was without looking. I turned the picture over and saw a woman's face, bruises and torn skin barely visible beneath a thick layer of makeup. Her solemn dark eyes stared straight into the camera—straight into mine. I stared back for a long time.

With trembling fingers, I picked up the Dunhills and pulled out a crumbling cigarette. Specks of tobacco scattered like confetti. I lifted a candle and put the tip of the cigarette into the flame. The brittle paper flared quickly. I inhaled, choked, and exhaled. Holding the cigarette loosely between my fingers, I watched the curling smoke. I took another drag, gagged, then threw the cigarette into the fireplace and watched as it smoldered. The wads of newspaper caught, smoked, began to burn. The flames quickly consumed the paper and the fire was out.

I put the picture back into the envelope and as I slid the envelope into the backpack, I heard a faint jingle. Reaching in, I felt along the bottom of the bag and pulled out an ankle-bracelet. Intricately hammered from dull silver, it was lined with dozens of tiny bells. *Khalakhil,* I heard her say. Holding both ends, I shook it. The bells made a sweet soft music. *Be brave.* I fastened the bracelet on my ankle.

After putting the camera, shell, and cigarettes into the backpack, I stood and stretched. I tossed the empty box into the corner and finished the glass of wine. Then I put the tape into the stereo, pushed play, and stood in the center of the room, waiting. Soon, Middle Eastern music filled the air, the rhythm slow, faster, slow again. Eyes closed, I stood in my abaya and scarf, swaying until muscle-memory took over—the placement of a foot, the undulation of the belly, the shimmy of a hip.

As my body moved to the beat, I felt the weight of the khalakhil and heard the chime of bells. I surrendered to the music and the memories. When I smelled the sweet and bitter scent of Clementines, I opened my eyes. The candles flickered and threw long shadows against the bare walls. The windows cast back my reflection. And, as if she had been conjured, we moved in unison—together again.

1

I startled awake early this morning, long before the alarm, heart pounding as I sensed her presence. Sitting up, I looked around. It was that time just before dawn when the light is a darker shade of grey—before a white thread can be distinguished from a black thread. Sunrise in Saudi Arabia is the exact moment those threads become distinct—when the first of the five daily calls to prayer begins.

Slowly, almost imperceptibly, shapes become clear. Soft edges sharpen. Shadows darken and colors appear. There is the bed, the dresser, the chair, the lamp. Heart still pounding, I got up and walked through the condo. After switching on the coffeemaker, I opened the drapes and watched the horizon lighten—going pink with the promise of the day.

Outside my window I can see Lake Michigan and the park. During summer months, the park is filled with Arab families. Children play while their parents lounge on blankets, talking and laughing. Men tend smoky grills full of beautiful food. Women wearing *hijabs* stand on rugs and bow to the east at sunset. Middle Eastern music fills the air—mournful, full of longing and desire unfulfilled.

These many years later, Saudi is not done with me. The Middle East can do that to you. It settles in like a virus, lying deep and dormant, flaring without warning. Triggered by a sight, smell, or sound, it sets off a fever of profound yearning—like the ache of a torrid love affair gone wrong. The memory of old wounds, loss, and grief resurfacing.

Since I'd opened the box, her presence grew stronger every day. I took the blue backpack from my closet. After wrapping the scarf around my neck, I fastened the khalakhil on my ankle, put music on the stereo, and poured my coffee.

When I finally settled at my desk with paper and pen, Bette Midler was singing *I shall be released*. I pinned the photograph of the woman on the wall and stared into her eyes. The truth is, I blame myself for what happened to her, and her spirit is haunting me. Now, like Scheherazade, the only way I can save myself is to tell the story.

One night early January 1987, my husband Max met me on the porch when I got home from work. He wore sweats and slipper-socks the kids had given him for Christmas and smiled as he watched me stomp snow from my boots. Max took my briefcase and purse and held the door for me. In the entryway, I looked at him while I pulled off my gloves and hat, unwound the scarf from my neck.

"What?" I asked. "You look happy."

Max shrugged as he hung up my coat. He was still smiling. Max had a beautiful smile, but it had been awhile since I'd seen so much happiness behind it. He leaned down, grabbed me, and kissed me hard on the mouth.

"You'll see." Taking my hand, he led me toward the kitchen.

As we passed the dining room I saw the table was set. Lit candles surrounded a vase of long-stemmed red roses. In the kitchen, our daughter Kate sullenly pulled boxes out of a bag from Pita Inn, a local Mediterranean restaurant. She barely glanced at me, but Kate had just turned eleven and this was not unusual behavior. What was unusual was the food. I cooked most nights, and on the rare occasions we ordered in, it was pizza. We'd never eaten Mediterranean food.

"What's all this?" I asked as Max handed me a glass of red wine.

At that moment our son Sam thundered down the stairs. He bounded into the kitchen, grabbing me in a fierce hug. "Mom! We're moving to Saudi Arabia!" Sam, at eight, was nothing if not exuberant.

As I held my glass high to keep wine from spilling, I looked into Max's smiling blue eyes. His gaze steady, Max lifted his glass to mine, nodded, and grinned. "I got the job, Sarah. We're going."

Max had applied for the job at Ocmara months before when a head-hunter called to tell him about an opening for an engineer. The biggest oil company in Saudi Arabia, maybe the world, was automating its control systems to keep up with production demands.

Max had struggled with his career for years. Perennially unhappy, he bounced from job to job, always feeling underpaid, underappreciated, and bored. He was forever sending out résumés and query letters. Now his job-hopping had paid off, giving him a résumé filled with diverse experiences. Suddenly, Ocmara was wooing him.

Not only was the job prestigious, the compensation package was more than we'd ever dreamed. The $70,000 base salary was double what Max was making in the States and additional bonuses and benefits made the actual total much higher. There was a housing allowance, hardship pay, travel, and vacation expenses. Free medical and dental services. No taxes are required on the first $70,000 earned when living outside the United States, and there was a sign-on bonus of 25 percent of his base salary. It felt like we'd won the lottery.

The company sent us *Ocmara, Saudi, and the Middle East,* a glossy coffee-table book, and a company manual entitled, *Ocmara: A Good Place to Work.* Colorfully illustrated and reading like a travel brochure, it told us what our lives would be like in Saudi. It promised safe communities free of alcohol and drugs, with excellent schools, grocery stores, libraries, recreational facilities, and leisure activities like tennis, snorkeling, sailing, and horseback riding. Max and I looked at each other. *When had we last had time for leisure activities?*

"Look." Max pointed to a picture of a couple walking on the beach holding hands. "That could be us." On the back of the manual was a picture of windswept sand dunes. The Kingdom of Saudi Arabia felt like the Promised Land.

"We'll be living the American dream," Max exclaimed. "In Saudi Arabia!"

The American dream had become increasingly elusive for us. We lived in Evanston, a suburb north of Chicago. Neither Max nor I came from money and neither of us knew how to manage it. Living with two kids in the midst of affluence, we struggled to keep up. Our Victorian house, built in 1865, was in perpetual need of repair and currently in peril of foreclosure. Our ancient VW van and rusty Toyota were constantly breaking down. We paid the minimum on our credit cards and the balances kept growing.

While we fought to hold it together, the cost of living was rising and the economy was on the verge of collapse. Max was unemployed for months before being hired by an engineering firm. But the project he was on was nearing completion and there were rumors of layoff. We had no cushion, no savings, nothing put away for the kids' college. And Kate was already in fifth grade.

The job at Ocmara offered us hope. We would go for the three years of Max's contract and be home before Kate was in high school. The sign-on bonus would save the house from foreclosure. We'd rent it out, letting tenants cover the mortgage. For the first time in our lives we could pay down our debt and build up savings.

There would be opportunity for travel at the end of each year. Travel was something Max and I had once done with abandon, but kids and responsibilities had ended that. When Max's contract was over, we'd pick up our lives in Evanston, but meanwhile we would be expatriates! Moving to Saudi would be an amazing antidote to the static, desperate lives we were living.

While Max was always searching for the next best thing, I'd spent six years working in the children's unit of a Chicago hospital. My job as social worker was rewarding, but also sad, exhausting, and overwhelming. I felt dangerously close to burnout, but had no choice except continue. Every day I commuted 60 to 90 minutes on the el—each way. I got there by nine and on good days I could leave at five. Most nights I brought work home with me. I encouraged Max to apply for the job in Saudi.

If Saudi Arabia had become the Promised Land, the rigorous application process made us long to be the Chosen People. Even after Max accepted the offer, we were told it was conditional. There were extensive background checks, including certification of our religious affiliation. We could not be Jewish or have traveled to Israel. We had to get passports and apply for visas.

The process of waiting had the psychological effect of making us want it more than anything. The bureaucratic wheels of Ocmara turned slowly. Months dragged by as we waited for the phone call or the envelope to arrive. As the dream felt more elusive, it became more desirable. Living in the Kingdom had become, in our minds, our only hope for salvation.

"Maybe this week we'll hear something," became our mantra.

Meanwhile, our financial situation became more desperate. Max received notice he would be laid off in a matter of weeks. The Toyota needed brakes. Our credit cards were maxed out from Christmas. Just as all seemed lost, Max was given the job. I'd never seen him so excited.

That night in early January, bathed in candlelight, we ate food we'd never tasted—*shish kabob, hummus, baba ghannoush, tabbouli,* and *falafel.* The words made Sam giggle and his laughter was contagious. When Kate became tearful at the idea of leaving her friends, we promised her horse-back riding lessons in Saudi. We promised Sam a new bike. As Ocmara had wooed me and Max, we wooed our children—with promises.

Later, after the kids were asleep, Max brought out the bottle of Dom Perignon he had hidden in the refrigerator and champagne flutes. We giddily stumbled upstairs to bed, lit candles, toasted our future, and made love.

2

The wheels that turned with agonizing slowness while we were awaiting redemption sped up once everything was in order. Max and I were required to attend a three-day orientation at Ocmara's US headquarters in Houston the first weekend in February. From there, Max would leave for Saudi with other new-hires.

Max was bursting with excitement, but I panicked. The nitty-gritty logistics of a move to Saudi Arabia had never been part of our fantasy. There was a mountain of work to be done and I was afraid I couldn't do it alone.

"Can't you tell them you need more time?" I pleaded. "Even a month?"

The tentative inquiry Max made into delaying his start-date met with such resistance that he backed down immediately. There was no choice but for Max to go on ahead.

During orientation weekend, we sat in an auditorium watching presentations about the do's and don'ts of Middle Eastern life. They bombarded us with information about acceptable clothing, the weather, and the strict prohibition against alcohol. It was impossible to absorb everything. Between presentations, I huddled in a phone booth talking to my mother, making sure the kids were okay and the house was still standing.

That weekend, Max and I were also fed expensive dinners and transported by limousine to upscale gallerias. The sheer luxury of it all heightened our anticipation of what life in Saudi Arabia would be like.

The last night in Houston, I couldn't sleep. Sometime near dawn, I slipped out of bed, walked across the soft carpet, and eased open the sliding glass doors leading to the balcony. There, I looked down at the swimming pool glowing fourteen floors below. Holding the railing, I closed my eyes, resisting the pull. The next day Max was gone and I was on a plane back to Chicago.

Max and I decided the kids and I would join him three months later. School in Saudi was on a yearlong trimester system with a month off between trimesters. A new trimester was beginning the first week of May. The kids would miss the end of the Evanston school year, but it would give them a smooth start in Saudi.

Back from Houston, I talked with my mother. Although it was too late to jump off the speeding train that had suddenly become my life, I needed her blessing.

"What do you think, Mom?" I asked. "Really?"

We were in a booth at The Lucky Platter, our favorite lunch spot.

"I think you should go, honey. See the world." Mom reached across the table and took my hand. "I never got the chance."

Tears filled my eyes. I'd miss her terribly. "It's so far away. What if something happens to you?"

"Don't worry, I'll be fine." She smiled. "Ruth will make sure I eat right!"

We laughed. Mom's roommate cooked broccoli and salmon twice a week, whether Mom wanted it or not. Ruth was divorced, and they had shared her house for six years, allowing Ruth to pay the mortgage and Mom to cut back hours at her bookkeeping job.

"Besides, it's a great career opportunity for Max." Mom hesitated. "It'll be good for him to carry the load awhile and for you to have a break."

Mom had been a perfect role-model, a working mother who enjoyed her job. She had never interfered in our marriage, but I'd seen the concern in her eyes whenever Max was out of work.

"Thanks," I whispered. "When we get back, we'll be in a much better place financially. Then you'll be able to take a break." I felt less guilty about leaving if it meant I could help her.

"That's sweet," Mom said. "But I'm doing okay as long as Ruth doesn't kick me out."

Over the next three months I collected school and medical documents, made the necessary financial arrangements, sold the cars, scheduled movers, and rented the house. I decided what to discard, what to ship, and what to leave. Every night after dinner I did whatever I could toward the move, took a bath, then collapsed into bed. One night Sam woke me soon after I'd dozed off.

"Mom, what about Mimi?" Sam's blue eyes were wide with fear. He cradled the black and white cat we'd gotten as a kitten when Sam was four.

Oh, God, how could I have forgotten about the cat? "Oh, sweetie, don't worry. Of course Mimi's coming with us." Even Mimi needed an entry-visa to be allowed into Saudi. And she had to be declared disease-free a week before arrival.

In March, I gave two months notice at the hospital and began handing over my caseload. The last week in April, I said goodbye to the children, families, nursing staff, and medical team I'd become close to over the years.

Amidst all the hard work, I had a few lunches and dinners with friends I would truly miss. My best friend Lara spent an entire weekend accompanying me on errands and helping me pack. The kids had sleepovers with friends, so Lara and I made dinner and stayed up late drinking wine, talking, laughing, and crying. We'd become best friends in graduate school. Both social workers, we spoke the same language.

"Am I making a mistake?" I asked in the middle of a boozy, teary spell.

"Probably," Lara said, without hesitation. "But it's an interesting mistake."

We laughed and opened another bottle. I could always count on Lara to tell me the truth and could tell her anything without fear of being judged. We did that for each other. I'd miss her the most.

Max and I had never been apart and keeping in touch was difficult. We exchanged a handful of letters, but even airmail took weeks. Because of the nine-hour time difference, we only talked once or twice a week—brief, urgent phone calls. I'd call at 10 p.m. when it was 7 a.m. in Saudi. But I'd be tired and Max would be going to work, so there was no time for real conversation.

"It's wonderful over here," Max reported during one call. "Our house is 125 steps from the beach! Yesterday I took a swim after work."

"Nice," I said. "It snowed ten inches today, so I had to shovel the sidewalk after I got home from work, before I fixed dinner for me and the kids."

The most arduous and emotional task was taking apart our home of nine years. Katie was two when we'd moved in. This had been Sam's only home. If I'd allowed myself to stop and feel, I would have been heartbroken.

The night before the movers arrived, we had our favorite deep-dish pizza delivered for dinner. Our suitcases and carry-on bags were packed.

Mimi's carrier was lined with a blanket, her documents taped on top. The kids were asleep and the house was quiet when I finished working at midnight.

Before turning out the lights, I stood in the living room and looked around. Catching my reflection in the mirror over the fireplace, I was startled by how gaunt and pale I looked. Strands of blonde hair had escaped my ponytail and hung around my face. I walked to the mirror and stared into my own grey-green eyes. It was the first time I'd been still in months. Suddenly I missed Max and felt more alone than ever before in my life. I watched as my eyes filled with tears then bent over and sobbed. When I was too empty and exhausted to continue, I went to bed.

I was finally able to relax during the last leg of the interminable journey to Saudi Arabia. The months of anticipation and preparation had melded into the kind of fugue usually reserved for the mornings after nights of restless dream-filled sleep, and storms before the calm. The days leading up to our departure were a hazy blur of activity, witnessed through the gauze of fatigue and tears.

I came to in the quiet hum of a British Airways jet. The last leg was seven non-stop hours from London to Dhahran. The first-class cabin was dark and most passengers were asleep. Kate and Sam were sprawled across the aisle from me, wrapped in blankets, and wearing blue eye masks. Moments after boarding Sam had unzipped his leather flight kit.

"Look, toothpaste! Socks!"

Kate initially acted like a nonchalant seasoned traveler, but was soon won over by Sam's exuberance. They bounced around in their seats, exploring all the buttons and gadgets at their fingertips and laughing. Despite annoyed looks from other passengers, I was too tired to care. We took off our shoes and pulled on our new socks. Kate and Sam put on their headphones and stared at their tiny screens, watching movies and eating until they were comatose.

The first-class cabin was only half full, so I slipped across the aisle and sat by the window. The seat beside me was empty and I luxuriated in the extra space. I, too, had let myself be pampered by the lavish amenities and crisply attentive flight attendants. When the last cart had rolled away and the lights dimmed, I reclined my seat, snuggled under my soft blue blanket, closed my eyes, and listened to classical music—allowing myself to relax and breathe.

Greed, it occurred to me, has a smell. It smells like the scented oxygen pumped into first-class cabins on European airlines, soft leather seats, fancy food on fine china, champagne, and aged Scotch. Greed smells like "more."

When I opened my eyes again it was dark. Frozen in time and space, suspended between what had been and what was to be, I allowed the hum of the engines to have their mesmerizing effect. Images from the past weeks moved through my mind—wrenching goodbyes and promises to keep in touch.

Pushing back a wave of sadness, I looked at my sleeping children. Kate initially protested the move, but soon became a celebrity among her friends. That appealed to Kate's sense of drama, and she became a tragic figure—dressed all in black. With her late November birthday, Kate was younger than most her classmates and less precocious. I was delighted that she still galloped pretend horses on the playground, while other girls dressed like rock stars and saddled up to boys. It disturbed me when Kate traded her little girl clothes for black Metallica T-shirts, black Converse sneakers, and black jeans.

Kate was a young, female version of Max. She had his straight, thick black hair with red highlights that only appeared in sunlight—Black-Irish, Goth-girl hair. When Kate stopped wearing a ponytail, the hair framing her face emphasized her pale skin and startling blue eyes. Suddenly I saw the beautiful woman she would become. Now Kate slept curled on her side, face pressed against the palm of her hand. Her thumb just a hair's breadth away from her open mouth.

Sam lay sprawled on his back. He'd missed Max terribly and had been wildly excited about moving to Saudi. Sam lived so full-out in the moment that he never sensed the possibility of loss until it happened. Only after we'd said goodbye to the friends who'd taken us to the airport and were boarding the plane did Sam turn to look at me, tears streaming down his cheeks. It took most of the first flight to calm him down. Now he slept peacefully, his straight blond hair scrunched beneath his mask. Never a slave to fashion, Sam wore baggy sweat pants and a Chicago Bull's T-shirt with a stain that nearly obliterated Michael. As I watched, he stirred then settled into a deeper sleep.

I relaxed into my seat, pulling the blanket around my shoulders. It was chilly in the cabin and I was too cold to go back to sleep. According to the tiny plane on the map on the screen in front of me, we were getting close. I knew we were already in Saudi airspace because the attendants had announced the suspension of liquor service in deference to Islamic law.

We flew low over the vast *Rub al Khali* for almost an hour. The largest desert in the world, it's also known as the Empty Quarter. Looking down from the small, oval window, it looked just that—empty. White sand illuminated by moonlight stretched out in the distance beneath a black star-studded sky. All that was left behind felt truly remote and much farther away than the eight-thousand-something miles I'd traveled to reach this place.

We arrived in Saudi in the middle of the night. Despite the long flight, arrival felt abrupt, like a wake-up call. Lights came on, the pilot made announcements, and passengers struggled into upright positions. Suddenly we were on the ground and the aisle was crowded with people wearing dazed expressions and sleep-wrinkled cheeks.

"Hey, Mom!" Kate whispered loudly.

When I turned, she widened her eyes and nodded toward the aisle. I looked up to see a line of women covered in black who seemed to have materialized out of nowhere. The women, also first-class passengers, had obviously only pulled out their abayas, veils, and hijabs when the wheels touched the runway. It was hard not to stare.

Nothing could have prepared me for the blast of oppressive heat that greeted us as we stepped off the plane in Dhahran. Even at midnight, the air was hot and heavy, thick and still. Almost tangible, it wrapped around us like a cloak. Noxious airplane fumes hung in the air.

Weighted down with carry-on luggage, I descended the stairs and walked across the sticky tarmac, Kate and Sam trailed close behind. Following the other passengers, we entered the international terminal building, filing past uniformed soldiers holding rifles.

Inside, the enormous arrival room of the Dhahran Airport teemed with masses of bedraggled travelers. As planes arrived from around the world, a constant flow of Westerners, Asians, Pakistanis, Arabs, and Indians entered the room. Babies cried and toddlers shrieked. The low murmur of the crowds intermittently swelled to a deafening hum. Speakers blared announcements in Arabic, English, French, and other languages I couldn't identify.

And it was so hot. Whatever air-conditioning there was could not keep up with the current of steamy air rushing in whenever the doors opened. Within moments, my hair was matted to my scalp. Sweat covered my face and trickled down my back.

Pushing through the crowd, I was acutely aware of my own smell and that of those around me. Sour breath, sweat, spices, and perfumes filled the air, along with nervous excitement and an undercurrent of fear. I was struck with the realization that most of the other people were in Saudi for the same reasons we were—and that desperation can smell like curry or Chanel.

Holding the kids' hands, I struggled to keep us together. Ahead, I saw people forming lines leading to Passport Control. We joined the end of a line and shuffled forward as it moved with agonizing slowness, before stopping completely. Following the example of those around us, we made seats of our hand-luggage. Sweat-drenched, tired, and miserable, we waited and watched.

In the next line were four women covered in black, indistinguishable except for their shoes. Two sat on suitcases and two stood. A tiny boy in white pants and a robe clung to his mother's abaya. Suddenly an Arab man joined them. He wore a long white robe and a red-and-white checked scarf encircled with a black cord. Leather sandals slapped his bare heels as he walked. After speaking to the women in Arabic, they gathered their luggage and followed him to the only line that was moving—for Saudi nationals.

"I've got to pee," Kate whispered.

"Can you wait?" From her expression, I knew her answer.

"Sam, do you have to go, too?" He shook his head.

For an agonizing moment I wondered what to do. I didn't want to leave Sam alone. A woman behind us heard what was going on.

"Not to worry," she said in a British accent. "We're not going anywhere." She rummaged in her bag and handed me a pack of tissues. "You'll need these." She pointed across the room. "It's there, where the sign says *hammam*."

The bathroom was crowded with abaya-clad Saudi women and their children. Kate and I waited in line, sweaty and uncomfortable. When it was our turn, we pushed open the door and stepped into the large stall. As I locked the door, Kate swiveled to face me.

"Mom, I can't." Kate gagged and covered her nose.

There was a hole in the floor surrounded by oval-shaped porcelain embossed with footprints. The floor was wet and there was no toilet paper, instead, a hose hung on the wall dripping water. It smelled worse than an outhouse.

"Oh, sweetie, I'm sorry. But if you've got to go, this is the time."

Kate glanced nervously at the hole. "You first."

I placed my feet in the footprints, hiked up my skirt, and squatted. Holding my breath, I pulled my underwear aside, and aimed. While I managed to be discreet, Kate had to pull her jeans down, exposing her white bottom as she squatted. I held her hands to keep her from falling. She tried to hold her breath, but instead let out an explosive gag. She let go of one of my hands to cover her nose, almost lost her balance, and frantically grabbed my hand.

Once she was steady, we looked at each other and were suddenly overcome with laughter. When she finished, we took a moment to regain our composure before opening the door. We washed our hands in a trickle of water at the sink, avoiding each other's eyes. Back in line we exchanged thankful glances with the woman who'd given us the tissues.

After an hour, we reached Passport Control. The desk was elevated, so I had to look up at the two unsmiling Saudi officials behind it.

"Documents." One man held out his hand.

I dug our passports, visas, and a letter from Ocmara out of the small blue backpack I'd bought especially for the trip. He opened the letter and read it aloud in Arabic while the other man typed into a computer. He did the same with our visas. One by one he opened our passports, studied them, and scrutinized us—comparing pictures with faces. The men conferred in Arabic. The first official reexamined my passport and visa, and reread the letter from Ocmara.

"Mrs. Hayes," he said, looking down at me. "Where is your husband?"

"Here, he's already here, in Saudi." I pointed to the Ocmara letter. "Working for Ocmara. He's picking us up." I realized I was talking loudly and sounded like I was lying.

The officials conferred again. The kids crowded closer, shooting me nervous glances. I gave them what I hoped was a reassuring smile. We waited another agonizing minute before the first officer loudly hand-stamped our documents, pushed them across the desk, and gave us a dismissive wave.

"Next," he bellowed.

I grabbed our documents and we rounded the corner to baggage claim.

"Dad!" Sam screamed and took off running.

Max was across the room by the luggage carousel, our bags already lined at his feet. Even in a crowd, Max filled the room. Hearing Sam, he turned toward us and grinned. He held up the cat carrier to show us Mimi had arrived safely then set it down just in time to catch Sam in a hug.

Kate, too, ran across the room, joining them in the embrace. I stood watching my family. Then Max looked at me, his blue eyes gleaming, a shank of black hair falling across his forehead, and I felt the same pull I'd felt the first day we met. He let go of the kids and I walked into his waiting arms. Max nuzzled my neck, ears, and hair—smelling me, holding me tight. I squeezed him back. Feeling the strength of his body against mine, I felt safe.

3

After baggage claim we went through customs, where officials stood behind long tables. Max lifted the suitcases, and the kids and I surrendered our backpacks and carry-on luggage. The pile we created was enormous.

"You look like you've just arrived from Bombay," Max teased.

"Open your bags," an official demanded.

While the kids squatted beside Mimi's carrier, rubbing her nose and talking to her, Max and I opened every bag. I watched the men ransack all the things I'd carefully folded. Contents of the smaller bags and backpacks were dumped onto the tables.

At O'Hare I bought a *Cosmopolitan* magazine, a rare indulgence, and had barely leafed through it. After a perfunctory glance, the official tossed it into a trash bin, where it landed among other confiscated magazines like *Sports Illustrated* and *Glamour.* It was a small loss and I was too weary to protest.

Meanwhile, another official had emptied my cosmetics case and was systematically going through everything. He opened the compacts of eyeshadow and blush, smelled them, and touched the powder. He opened every bottle and smelled the contents. I watched with horror as he stuck his little finger into my new bottle of Clinique moisturizer then smelled his coated finger, leaving a yellow drop of lotion on the tip of his nose.

Suddenly a child began to wail. Looking down the row of tables, I saw an official holding an Ernie doll. A little girl, about three, struggled in her mother's arms, reaching for the doll. I recognized the family from our flight. The mother was making soothing noises, but the child wept inconsolably. The man holding the doll consulted with another official in Arabic. My children moved close to me—watching.

The child's crying escalated. Her cheeks were flushed and wet, sweat matted her wispy hair. Her mother rocked her, while her father talked to the officials, trying to make sense of what was happening.

"Not allowed," the second official told the father.

"I don't understand." The father reached out to touch his daughter's head with one hand, while imploring the official with the other. The child yanked away and shrieked.

"Dolls are not allowed in the Kingdom," the official said loudly.

"What?" The father was incredulous. "Why?"

The child stretched out her arms for Ernie then arched her back and screamed while her mother struggled to hold on. Sam leaned against me and Kate's arm snaked around my waist. They looked scared, transfixed by the drama. I pulled them close.

"Statues forbidden by the Koran," the official yelled.

In orientation they discussed the Islamic prohibition against human or animal statues, but they never talked about dolls. For a moment I worried about Kate's dolls and Sam's action figures. *Thank God, I put them in the shipment.*

The child's shrieks had reached new decibel levels and showed no signs of stopping. Suddenly the frustrated official snatched the doll from the other's hands and shoved it at the child. The little girl grabbed Ernie and hugged him. She shoved a thumb into her mouth and her body relaxed with a shudder.

I smiled with relief.

By 2 a.m. customs was finally finished with us. An eager Filipino man piled our luggage onto carts and Max and I pushed them through the exit doors. The kids followed, Kate lugging Mimi's cat carrier. Outside, we were greeted by a wall of stifling heat and an army of third-world entrepreneurs. Pakistani and Indian boys and men swarmed, begging to carry our bags. Vying with each other, they pushed and shoved while grabbing for the carts. Kate shrieked as a man lunged toward the cat carrier.

"*La! La!*" Max yelled. The man withdrew his hand and the others backed off. Pulling a wad of *riyals* from his pocket, Max chose two of the men then nodded toward an Ocmara van waiting at the curb, lights flashing. While the bags were loaded, the kids and I collapsed into the backseat, Mimi's carrier at our feet. It was a relief to have Max handling everything, and I was impressed by how confident he seemed. Max got into the front passenger seat and we took off into the night.

The ride from the Dhahran Airport to Al Hassa seemed endless, despite the fact that the van was traveling at breakneck speeds. I leaned forward and looked at the speedometer where the needle hovered at 200 kilometers. Squinting, I could see the inner circle of smaller numbers: 125 miles per hour. With a bolt of fear, I sat back.

It was cool, dark, and quiet inside the van and the kids fell asleep immediately. I tried to look out at the rapidly passing countryside, but in the blackness of the night, my attempts were futile. I saw only a dim reflection of my tired face bathed in the green glow of the van's panel lights. Just beyond the headlights, I caught fleeting glimpses of flat pale desert. My family slept as we barreled through the darkness. I sat watch, resisting waves of drowsiness, until the vibration of the wheels lulled me to sleep.

I awoke as the van turned off the highway. We drove down a short road enclosed by tall chain-link fences topped with rolls of barbed-wire, then passed under an archway reading: Al Hassa, Seaside Community. At the first of two guardhouses, a man in a military uniform stepped out and gestured for the driver to stop. He was holding a small machine gun. Max and the driver presented their identification along with the papers and passports for me and the kids. The guard peered into the van, matching our sleepy faces with photos, then opened the rear door and looked over our bags. Satisfied, he slammed the door and motioned for us to move forward. We went through the same process at the second guardhouse.

At 3 a.m. the van turned into a driveway, headlights sweeping across a two-story townhouse with an attached garage. A porch light illuminated a single short, sturdy, palm tree in the middle of the front yard. Max looked back at us with a proud grin.

"Welcome home."

I managed a feeble smile. *You are my home.*

The next morning I surfaced slowly, awakening to Max gently brushing my hair from my face. Although his lips were warm and soft when he kissed my forehead, I shrank deeper, resisting the pull to consciousness. Max persisted, rubbing my back, whispering my name. I felt like I was swimming underwater in slow motion, pulling my way through water that resisted every stroke—water that fought back. Max's hand, heavy and strong, pulled me to the surface.

I awoke curled on my side clutching the sheet. My arms were sore from whatever struggle I'd engaged in as I slept. I was cold and my throat felt sore. A vent across the room blew chilled air toward the bed. Living in a Victorian house, I wasn't used to air-conditioning. I was wearing one of Max's white T-shirts, the one I'd pulled from the hamper before he left for Saudi. I'd worn it every night we were apart, comforted by his scent. It had kept me warm through the deepest part of a Chicago winter, but was no match for manmade Saudi chill.

"Time to wake up." Max was gentle, but insistent.

Fighting waves of fatigue, I opened my eyes. Max smiled down at me. His hair was neatly combed, his face freshly shaven, and he wore a crisp white shirt and khakis.

"Morning, beautiful. Going to sleep all day?"

"Mmmmm." I nodded, closed my eyes, and burrowed into the pillow.

Max laughed and pulled the pillow away. "Hey, that wasn't a suggestion." He playfully smacked my butt. "It's late, time to get moving. I brought you coffee."

"What time is it?" My mouth was dry.

"Almost ten, I let you sleep as long as I could."

Only 1 a.m. at home—the middle of the night. I opened my eyes and rolled onto my back. When Max leaned down to kiss me, I looped my arms around his neck and pulled him close. His body felt warm, his shirt damp with perspiration. I smelled his skin, the scent of his aftershave. We held a long, sweet kiss. He nuzzled my cheek and neck then looked into my eyes.

"Tonight," he whispered.

I smiled, suddenly shy.

He kissed me again before standing up.

"I'll get the kids ready while you dress." He lifted my suitcase onto the bed. "Don't be too long, I have to get back to work."

I yawned, stretched, and sat up. Every muscle was sore, as if I'd been holding a heavy weight for three months and suddenly set it down. "Where are we going?"

"To get your IDs and get the kids registered in school," Max said.

"God, I'm so tired." I rubbed my face. "Why do we have to do it now?"

"New student orientation is today. They have to have IDs and be registered to attend."

Leaning against the headboard, I looked around my new bedroom. There was a dresser and mirror, bedside tables with matching orange ceramic lamps, a white chenille bedspread, and gold blackout curtains. It looked like a cheap motel room—everything uniformly unremarkable.

Max unzipped my backpack, took out our passports, and blew me a kiss as he left the room. I heard him moving down the hallway, calling to the kids. As I sat in the quiet, dimly-lit room, exhaustion washed over me and I knew I was in trouble if I didn't move. I sat on the edge of the bed and took a sip of coffee. It was bitter, tepid, obviously instant. A wave of nausea roiled through me. I put the mug down and got up. Stretching as I walked, I crossed to the window and opened the curtains. A beam of intense white light slashed across my face.

"Jesus!" I closed the curtains.

Rummaging through the jumbled contents of my suitcase, I found my cosmetics bag and went into the spacious, brightly lit white-tiled bathroom. I started the shower, opened the bag, and reached in to find a sticky mess. The tops to all my bottles of shampoo, cream rinse, lotions, and makeup were loose. The toothpaste cap was missing and a gummy rope of hardened peppermint hung from the tube.

"Shit," I whispered, shuddering with revulsion. Grabbing shampoo and cream rinse, I got in the shower, let the hot water pour down on me, and closed my eyes.

When I heard Max knocking on the door, I realized I'd been lost in reverie. Suddenly in a hurry, I pulled my wet hair into a ponytail and moisturized my face—fighting images of the customs official's finger. A brush of mascara, lip-gloss, and I was done.

At orientation we'd learned women had to wear modest loose-fitting clothing at all times in Saudi—high necks, sleeves that covered elbows, baggy pants or calf-length skirts. In preparation, I'd bought a wardrobe of light-weight knits from the clothing line they recommended. I dug through my suitcase and found a matching long-sleeved grey blouse and skirt, both wrinkled after being crammed into the suitcase at customs.

After dressing, I examined myself in the bathroom mirror. I'd never been a slave to fashion, but before now, I had at least looked like I cared. My small gold cross gleamed in the bright bathroom light. Another "don't" in Saudi was wearing religious symbols. The necklace had been a confirmation gift from my parents when I was thirteen and I never took it off. I tucked the cross inside my blouse, grabbed my backpack, and went downstairs.

Looking rumpled and sleepy, the kids leaned over bowls of cereal. Max sat at the head of the table staring at me. "Holy crap, babe, what are you wearing?" At that moment I came undone. The kids watched as Max rushed to console me. "Shhhh, baby, you're beautiful." Max held my face in his hands. "It's okay, it's all okay." He hugged me as I cried.

I didn't have the energy to explain it wasn't about the outfit. I just let myself be held. When I pulled myself together, a half hour had passed and the kids were asleep on the sofa. Max woke them while I went upstairs and rinsed my face. My skin was blotchy, my nose and eyes red. After blotting my face, I put on more moisturizer and lip-gloss. I didn't bother with mascara.

Walking outside was like opening the door of an oven and being hit with a blast of heat that makes the gold necklace you're wearing burn your neck. The sun was high and intense in a cloudless sky. Squinting through swollen eyes, I remembered I'd forgotten sunglasses. It was sweltering inside the Ocmara car waiting in the driveway and sweat instantly coated my face. It was a small consolation—makeup would have been useless.

As he drove through the streets of the compound Max pointed out the houses of people he knew. The kids and I sat in dazed silence. We could easily have been in Arizona or Texas. Cookie-cutter houses lined the curving streets with scraggly brown lawns that looked like they were fighting a losing battle. Some, like ours, had palm trees. A few had colorful flower beds, but all were parched under the relentless Saudi sun.

At the Passport Control Office they called the kids first—Sam, then Kate. They were fingerprinted and had their photos taken while holding a placard with Max's employee number. I looked at Max and he was watching me. There was something about his forced smile, the guarded look in his eyes. *He's hiding something.*

"Just company policy," he said, glibly. His smile didn't make it to his eyes. *What isn't he telling me?*

While the kids sat rubbing their smudged fingertips with paper towels, it was my turn. The uniformed Saudi official took my hand in his, pressed my thumb on an inkpad, and rolled it on a piece of paper. I pressed down too hard—smearing the tiniest bit—deliberately.

I was led to a wall, turned to face a Polaroid camera, and given the placard to hold. I felt like I was guilty of something and didn't even know what it was. The camera flashed in my face.

Outside, the kids examined their new IDs, laughing and poking each other. "You all need to memorize the number," Max said. "You'll need it everywhere you go."

I looked at the picture on my ID—hair pulled back, skin pale and blotchy, traces of mascara beneath my swollen eyes. With Max's employee number across my chest it looked like a mug shot. As I tucked the card into my backpack, I remembered.

"Wait! Where are the passports? We forgot our passports." As I turned back toward the office, Max grabbed my hand.

"The company keeps our passports while we're in the Kingdom."

I felt panic rise in my throat. "But what if we need them? What if we need to leave?"

"I apply for exit-visas then we get them back." Max grinned. *There it was again.*

Are you fucking kidding me? "You have to get them back? Are you saying I can't do it?"

"Relax, baby. It's all okay." He turned to the kids. "Come on, guys. Let's get you to school."

I froze, watching Max usher the kids into the car. *How do I get to the airport? How do I get out of here?* Sweating under the brutal midday sun, I frantically weighed my options. With a wash of horror, I realized I had none. I took a deep breath and got in the car.

The school was a one-story, modern building with flowers and lush green palm trees planted in front. The principal was welcoming and reassuring. After giving me quick hugs, Sam and Kate wandered off without a backward glance. I watched them walk down the long, beige linoleum hallway, feeling like I had years before, when they entered kindergarten.

Back at the house, Max gave me a key. He cupped my face in his palms and kissed me. "Get some sleep. I'll pick the kids up after work and we'll be home about four."

Sheila Flaherty

I stood in the driveway as Max drove away, watching until the car disappeared around a corner. Sweat trickled down my face and the back of my neck. The air was still, and so thick with heat that it was hard to breathe. I looked up and down my new street. It was lined with identical beige-stucco townhouses and looked deserted. Nothing moved. It was eerily quiet.

As I walked to the door I examined the palm tree in the front yard. With the sun directly overhead, the fronds cast only a meager lattice of shade on the brown lawn. Closing my eyes, I imagined the cool deep shade of our immense ancient catalpa back in Evanston, green lawns, colorful Victorians. Opening my eyes, I looked down the barren street. *I can't do this. I have to get out of here.*

Suddenly I heard a noise in the distance. It began as the faint, electronic static of a loudspeaker. Slowly it became an intense hum. Soon the air was filled with a man's voice.

"Allah akbar! Allah akbar!"

"Allah akbar! Allah akbar!"

The words repeated, followed by others sung in a mournful, achingly beautiful chant. I was hearing my first Islamic call to prayer. Inexplicably, the sound filled me with a sense of longing and profound grief. I listened until the final echoes died away. Then I wiped the tears and sweat from my face and unlocked the door to my new home.

4

The house was dim and quiet except for the faint hum of air-conditioning. I kicked off my shoes and walked down a long hallway, stopping inside the combination living/dining room which stretched across the back of the house. Outside in the searing heat I'd become soaked with sweat, but I was shivering after a minute in the chilly room. I bumped the thermostat from 65 to 80 degrees. Hugging myself for warmth, I leaned against the wall and looked around.

In the living room area were two brown plaid sofas, a matching chair, a coffee table, end tables, and orange lamps like those in the bedroom. Sliding glass doors opened to the backyard. There was a picture window in the dining area, and a brass chandelier hung over the center of the table. All the windows were covered in floor-length ivory drapes, walls were off-white, and the carpet was a worn gold-shag. It looked like a still life from the 1960s.

"Dear God," I said.

Luggage lay in the middle of the floor overflowing with clothes and shoes. Cereal bowls filled with puddles of watery milk, empty juice glasses, and a coffee mug waited to be cleared from the table. Stepping over the mess on the floor, I walked to the sliding doors where a beam of sunlight streamed between the closed drapes. I pushed them open and looked outside.

"Oh," I whispered. "Lovely."

The backyard was like a secret garden. It was enclosed with white adobe walls, lined with bushes and laced with green vines and dark pink flowers. A tree with a smooth white trunk and feathery leaves stood in the middle of the yard. Crepe myrtle, frangipani, bougainvillea, and oleander thrived in the Saudi heat. There was no grass, just sand. In the far corner of the fence was a wooden gate. The backyard was the prettiest thing I'd seen in Saudi.

Off the dining area was a galley kitchen with "Harvest Gold" appliances, dark wooden cabinets, and fluorescent lights. A jar of Nescafé instant coffee and a tin of powdered milk sat on the counter. Louvered doors led to a small room with a table and washer and dryer. I opened the drapes, letting light flood the room. A picture window faced the front yard.

"Nice." I imagined turning it into a cozy breakfast room or home office. Pictures on the walls would make it inviting, and I'd be able to watch passing traffic. Leaving the drapes open, I continued exploring. Back in the front hallway, there were doors leading to a powder-room, hall closet, and garage. Inside the garage, another door opened into a large storage room.

Absently rubbing my tight shoulders, I climbed the stairs and wandered through the kids' rooms, and another bathroom. Passing Kate's room I heard a sad mewing and found Mimi hiding under the bed. After some coaxing, she finally came out.

"It's just you and me, Mimi," I crooned, carrying her downstairs to the kitchen. In the refrigerator, I found eggs, butter, bread, orange juice, bottled water, and a can of evaporated milk, two triangular holes punched in the top. With my free hand, I searched cabinets until I found dishes. *How odd to be a stranger in my own kitchen!*

I poured milk into a saucer and set Mimi on the counter stroking her until she began to drink. It was then I noticed my black fingertips. *My passport!* Panic surged through me and my hands trembled as I turned on the faucet. I squirted dish soap onto a sponge and scrubbed until my skin was red and sore, but the ink wouldn't come off.

Suddenly thirsty, I filled a glass with water from the tap. My first sip left me with a mouthful of salty chemicals. I gagged and spit into the sink then poured some orange juice. As I drank, I thought back to orientation. There was a mention of Ocmara holding our passports—a casual aside, like a footnote, or fine print. *Jesus, I could kick myself for not paying attention.*

To keep panic at bay, I tackled the chaos in the house. Fueled by frenetic energy, I put clothes and belongings away, and stowed the suitcases in the upstairs hall closet. I made beds and washed dishes. Max had obviously straightened up before our arrival, but I realized the kitchen and bathrooms needed serious scrubbing.

Finally overcome with fatigue, I lay on the sofa, Mimi curled into a ball beside me. Pushing back the looping anxiety about my confiscated passport, I took calm deep breaths—until I dozed off.

From somewhere deep in sleep, I became aware of a sound. Mimi leapt down and raced upstairs. I heard it again and opened my eyes. When the doorbell rang a third time, I sat up.

I opened the door to a woman holding a tote-bag and smiling broadly. Her tan cheeks were flushed with heat and her short brown hair dripped with sweat. A bicycle was parked on the sidewalk behind her.

"Hi, Mrs. Hayes, I'm Sissie Vaughn. I'm here to officially welcome you to Al Hassa." She had a friendly Southern drawl.

I stood speechless, squinting into the light. *A welcome woman? Really?*

"May I come in?"

"Sorry." I smiled and backed into the entryway. "I feel drugged."

"Jetlag! You'll have it awhile." She walked in and glanced around. "Depressing, isn't it? Such ugly furniture and it's everywhere you go."

As my smile faded, she touched my hand. "Not to worry, Mrs. Hayes. When you get your shipment, it'll feel just like home."

I looked around the room, trying to imagine it feeling like home.

"Please, call me Sarah."

As Sissie sat on the chair, I folded the blanket I'd been sleeping under and sat on the sofa. Then I remembered my manners.

"I'm sorry. Can I offer you something?" *Bad instant coffee?*

"No, thanks, but I have something for you!" She pulled a large bottle of water from her bag. It still had condensation from the cold.

"Oh, thank you so much." I liked this woman already. "What's the deal with the water?"

"A lousy desalination plant. Don't drink it. Don't even cook with it. It'll make you sick. You can buy plenty of bottled water at the commissary."

That explained the water in the refrigerator, I wished Max had remembered to tell me. I went to the kitchen and when I returned with glasses, there was a plate of homemade cookies on the coffee table. Pouring water, I again noticed my smudged fingers.

"Sorry. They're clean," I said.

Sissie laughed. "I know, ink. It'll fade soon."

"I was surprised they fingerprinted me."

"Just company policy," she said with a shrug.

"They kept my passport," I said.

"It's okay." Sissie smiled. "Your husband can get it back whenever you need it."

I need it now! I felt panic lurking just beneath the surface, but I smiled and nodded.

Sissie took some papers from her bag. "Maps, phone numbers, everything you need to know about the compound. I'd like to show you a few things on this map. These are houses." Her fingernails were bitten to the quick, cuticles swollen and bloody. "Here's your house."

I looked where she pointed. The tiny square meant nothing to me yet.

"How many people live here?" I asked.

"About five thousand, but that doesn't include those living off-camp," Sissie said. "Did you notice the housing just outside the main gate?"

"No."

"Well, that's where the Pakistanis, Sri Lankans, and Filipinos live. They do maintenance work and keep the beaches and compound clean."

"Oh, I see." *A caste system.*

"Here are the swimming pools, tennis courts, bowling alley, restaurant, library, and riding stables. Here's the golf course." She laughed. "They're called browns over here because they don't have grass. They spray oil on the sand then pack it down. Do you play golf?"

"No." I shook my head.

"Oh, well." Sissie looked disappointed. "Here's the school, the yacht club, and the beach."

"Where's the beach?" I was suddenly interested. As she drew her finger down the shoreline, I placed it in relationship to the tiny square that was my home.

"There's going to be a welcome coffee at the next meeting of the Women's Club the first Wednesday in June. Here's a flyer." She smiled. "Please come. It'll give you a chance to meet other newcomers as well as ladies like me who've been here much longer."

Sissie looked so eager, so happy to include me and make me feel welcome. I felt both reassured and uneasy. "I'm sure I have no other plans," I said. "How long have you been here?"

"Eight years."

"Wow. I can't imagine."

"That's what I thought, too. That's what everybody thinks, at first." Sissie gathered her things and stood. "But after awhile you get used to it. There's so much to do."

"Well, thank you for coming."

"You're most welcome." She smiled. "You're going to love it here."

Sissie paused at the door. "By the way, I noticed the drapes were open in your front room."

"Yes?"

"You need to keep them closed. Tightly closed."

I felt a chill. "Why is that?"

"Ocmara security guards patrol on foot and in cars, day and night. Orange cars. You'll see them everywhere. They're watching all the time to see if you're doing anything illegal."

"Like what?"

"Drinking alcohol, playing poker or chess," she said.

"We aren't allowed to play games?"

"Not if they involve dice, poker chips, or cards. Gambling is illegal and Saudis consider almost any game to be gambling," Sissie said. "They also make sure no one is out past curfew."

"We have a curfew?" I asked incredulously.

"Kids have to be inside by 10 p.m. For adults it's not well-defined. But if they see you out too early or too late, they might pick you up for questioning." She shook her head. "It's gotten worse since Ocmara started hiring *matawain* to work security. At least that's the rumor."

Suddenly it felt like Sissie was speaking another language. "I'm sorry, I'm not following you. What are matawain?"

"Religious police. Watch out for them when you go into Saudi towns. Out of nowhere a *matawah* will show up with a whip. You'll recognize them because they wear short *thobes* and have wild beards streaked with *henna*." Face flushed, she seemed worked up.

"Thobes?"

"Those long white dresses Saudi men wear." Sissie sighed as if she had exhausted herself.

I stood in the doorway, squinting in the sunlight while Sissie mounted her bike. She waved as she rode off. When she disappeared, I felt a wash of loneliness. Back inside, the house seemed far too dark, quiet, and empty. *The beach. I'll go to the beach!* Within minutes I'd closed the drapes in the front room, left a note for Max and the kids, and headed out the sliding doors and across the backyard.

Outside our back gate was a grassy field with a path. I followed the path as it wound behind a row of houses and across a street, to a bank of sand dunes dotted with sparse dry grass. From there, I saw the Arabian Gulf stretching infinitely toward the eastern horizon. I made my way down to the beach, took off my shoes, and walked across the sand to the water's edge. Lifting my skirt, I waded into the water and let the gentle waves lap against my winter-white thighs.

The water was warm, heavy with salt, and so clear and beautiful it could break your heart. It changed colors as I watched—turquoise to green to blue to lavender. Over time, I would see it go from silver to gunmetal to black. I stood swaying, staring out at the horizon. Eventually, the call to prayer began to echo in the distance. But it was only when I heard Max and the kids calling me, that I turned and reluctantly waded back to shore.

5

My skirt dragged in the water, clinging to my legs, making each step a struggle. In the distance a woman covered in black stood at the edge of the ocean, a pair of white running shoes dangling from one hand. It looked like she was gazing at the horizon as I had been, but I couldn't see her eyes behind her veil. It was just how she stood—stock-still, facing east. I watched her as I emerged from the water.

"I was afraid of that," Max said, looking at my face. He settled a baseball cap on my head and kissed the tip of my nose. "You're sunburned."

"Look, Mom." Kate held a delicate white seashell.

Back home we'd collected smooth, opaque pieces of colorful sea-glass from the shores of Lake Michigan, depositing them in a bowl in the entry-way. I smiled at Kate.

"Let's start a collection," I said.

"Mom! I found out how to get a bike." Sam tugged at me. "Garage sales!"

Kate and Sam vied for my attention, chattering about their classes and kids they had met. As we walked along the shore, I turned back, searching. The Saudi woman was gone.

"Look at all this!" Max gestured grandly at the ocean and beach. "I knew you'd love it."

"You were right."

Max touched my cheek, suddenly serious. "I missed you so much."

"I missed you, too."

Sam darted in and out of the surf and Kate searched for shells as Max and I walked down the beach holding hands—just like the couple in the Ocmara brochure. We passed a row of houses with backyards facing the beach.

"The second house from the end." Max pointed. "That's where the Mitchells live."

"Who?"

"Bobbi and Ray Mitchell," Max said. "Ray's my supervisor."

"I thought that was Mohammed."

"Mohammed's the big boss. Ray is my immediate supervisor." Max stopped and studied the house. "That's what you get with seniority and job status, a house on the beach." He squeezed my hand. "That'll be us someday."

Startled, I took a step back. "Whoa! Wait a minute. Don't forget we're only here for three years. I doubt you'll get enough seniority for a beach house."

"You're right. I guess I have to go for the promotion." Max laughed, but there was something serious in his expression. He started walking, but when I stood still, he looked back at me.

"You said so yourself. We're only 125 steps from the beach. I counted."

"You did, did you?" He grinned.

"Yes, I did. The house is perfect." I smiled.

"Oh, I forgot to tell you, the house looks great. I can't believe you got it cleaned up so fast." Max grinned again. "You even made cookies."

Wow, he does think I'm superwoman. As we walked, I told him about Sissie's visit. But the mention of cookies made me realize I was hungry.

"What are we doing for supper?" A question I'd often heard, but seldom asked.

"It's covered." Max said. "Bobbi stopped by with everything we need for tonight. She was hoping to meet you."

"That's nice," I said. "I'm sorry I missed her."

"You'll meet her next weekend. They're having a party so everybody can check you out."

"Check me out?" I felt a flush of anxiety.

"Relax." Max squeezed my hand. He knew I was shy and easily over-whelmed meeting new people. "It'll be fun. They're excited to meet you."

I did want to make new friends'and hoped Sissie would be there. "Sounds good."

We gathered the kids and started home, still holding hands like the couple in the brochure.

That night we ate dinner together for the first time in months. Bobbi had brought salad and a Mexican-style casserole with layers of meat, tomatoes, corn tortillas, and cheese. It was perfect. Less successful was the milk I made for the kids from the tin I'd found on the kitchen counter.

"What's this?" Kate scornfully examined her milk.

I'd mixed the powder with bottled water as instructed, but there was a skim on top that wouldn't dissolve. I knew I would have to experiment with proportions until I reached a formula that resembled milk the kids were used to, but that night both refused it.

Later, after the kids were in bed, Max and I were finally alone in our room. I was tired, but curiously awake. My internal clock was still nine hours behind so it felt like early afternoon.

Max set the stage with candles and wine glasses. Smiling seductively, he "uncorked" a green bottle with a ceramic top sealed with wire and a rubber gasket, then poured me a glass. The chilled liquid was pale yellow.

"What's this?"

At orientation I'd learned that sparkling apple juice—"Saudi Champagne"—was the beverage of choice for festive celebrations in Saudi. This didn't smell like apple juice.

"Taste it," Max said.

I took a tentative sip. "Wine?"

Max nodded with a big smile.

I took another sip. It was definitely wine, but unlike any I'd tasted before. Good, but different. "Where did you get it?"

"It's from Bobbi and Ray's private cellar. They made it." He took a sip. "It's some of the best in Al Hassa."

I was confused. Possession of alcohol in Saudi Arabia could result in arrest and deportation, even jail. I enjoyed a glass of wine or a margarita, but Max had a tendency to overindulge. I'd realized early on that for me, part of the appeal of Saudi was the prohibition on alcohol.

"Isn't it illegal?" I sounded prudish.

Max laughed. "That's why the moonshine industry is alive and well in Saudi."

As I stared at my glass of wine, I noticed traces of ink in the whorls of my fingertips. I remembered the flash of the camera while holding Max's employee number. I thought about my children sleeping down the hall and felt a flash of fear. *Oh great. They have my passport and now there's booze.*

"Hey, baby, don't worry." Max hugged me. "We don't have to make wine. I'd never do anything to put you and the kids in danger."

I looked at him.

"Come on, relax. We're safe here." Max took another sip.

After a moment, I did too.

"Besides," he whispered, his breath warm against my ear. "We can get it anytime we want it." When he kissed me I tasted wine on his mouth.

Between sips, Max and I settled in. Kissing, touching, and reconnecting. At first we were shy and awkward. I felt like a teenager on the verge of giggles. Our bodies were known to each other, but time and distance had added a veil of mystery. I had lost weight while Max had become fit and rugged. But his chest was still pale, much lighter than his neck and arms. I traced the tan lines with my fingers. *Farmer's tan.*

I was wearing a new white cotton nightgown. Max fumbled with the tiny mother-of-pearl buttons at the bodice then pulled the nightgown over my head. He pressed his body hard against mine, skin against skin. Suddenly we were lost in touch, taste, and smell—lost in each other.

I lay in the darkness watching the digits on the clock turn toward dawn as Max slept beside me. Finally at 2:30, I slipped out of bed. No stranger to insomnia, I knew staying in bed would only make it worse. I put on my nightgown and went into the bathroom. Digging into the cosmetics bag I'd stashed under the sink, I pulled out a package of cigarettes that had miraculously made it through customs only slightly crushed.

Max and I both quit smoking when I was pregnant with Kate. Eventually I'd picked it up again, but only on occasion. Before smoking was banned in hospitals, nurses' stations were the place to go for indulgences like candy, cookies, strong coffee, and cigarettes. It was there, writing process-notes or consulting over tragic cases, that I first allowed myself an occasional puff. Then I started having one during drinks with coworkers on Friday nights—and so it goes. I never shared this with Max. Maybe I didn't want him to have an excuse to start smoking again. Maybe I didn't want to make it too easy for myself. Maybe I just liked having a secret.

I went downstairs, slid open the doors, and stepped outside into the dark, quiet night. The air was still and balmy. I lit my cigarette, inhaled deeply, and stared up at the vast black sky above me. Leaning against the adobe wall, I closed my eyes and imagined I could hear waves lapping on the beach—only 125 steps away.

6

The second day in Saudi, Max's alarm woke me at 5:30 a.m. Max encircled me with his arm and snuggled against my back. My head was pounding from the wine and I felt a familiar ache in my thighs. As Max nuzzled my neck, I scooted back to meet him. Before leaving for work, he reset the alarm and I was in a deep sleep when it went off again.

I made toast and eggs for breakfast, a safer bet than cereal with unperfected milk. The kids sat listless and yawning, picking at their food until the eggs were cold. I couldn't blame them. I would have liked nothing better than to crawl back into bed, but the cure for jetlag was staying awake during the day.

"Mommy, I want to stay home with you," Kate whined, regressing to about five.

"Why do we have to go to school on Sunday?" Sam asked. Mimi was curled on his lap.

The Muslim holy day is Friday, the workweek Saturday through Wednesday. Expatriates like to say, "TAIW"—Thank Allah it's Wednesday. Expat humor, I would learn, ranged from ridiculous to clever obscure references no one would understand if they had not lived in Saudi.

"Because Friday is the new Sunday." I stroked Mimi. "You have to pretend it's Tuesday."

"I'm tired of pretending," Kate said, and for a moment I saw the ache in her eyes. Then the mask came down and she was back to being a sullen preadolescent.

I smiled and started stacking dishes. "Your dad said we can look for garage sales this afternoon and see if we can find some bikes. Maybe a TV." Bribery never hurt.

When they left, I stood outside watching them trudge down the sidewalk and around the corner. In that short time, I felt the sting of the sun. Still, I stood a while longer, looking for signs of life. Nothing moved. When I went inside, sadness enveloped me. I took a deep breath, closed my eyes, and leaned against the door. My head was throbbing. *I woke up Sunday morning, with no way to hold my head that didn't hurt.*

Words and melody of a favorite song came unbidden. *There's nothing short of dying, half as lonesome as the sound, of the sleeping city sidewalks, Sunday morning coming down.* I was aware of the pull of a deep well. I could choose to fall in, I told myself. Someday I'd dive in head first—but today I had to resist the pull.

I stopped beside a Sunday school and listened to the song they were singing. We weren't regular churchgoers, but there's much to be said for having the option. Soon I'd find out about secret services held in the school gymnasium—for those who dared to go. Bleachers turned into pews.

The song played in my head as I went upstairs and got dressed. Still pink from the day before, I slathered on sun-block, slipped on a long-sleeved shirt, and put on a baseball cap. I walked to the beach, looking for the Saudi woman. But the beach was deserted so I went back home. *There's something in a Sunday that makes a body feel alone.*

That afternoon, Max borrowed a car and drove us to the community center. There were few cars on the road and the parking lot was almost empty.

"Where is everybody?" I asked. "Why is it so quiet?"

"It's the first week of Ramadan. Lots of people are gone."

During Ramadan, Islam's holiest holiday, Muslims fast all day. Stores and restaurants are closed and all services suspended while the devout stay home and sleep. At sunset people flood the streets to shop and eat. Non-Muslims were technically exempt from fasting, but could be punished by matawain if seen eating or drinking. Expatriates stayed inside to avoid being caught, or left for the month.

"Here's our mailbox," Max said. It was empty.

"Let's look at the bulletin boards," I said. As we jotted down garage sales, I saw a list of jobs and decided to come back and check them out. Then we went to the commissary.

At first glance, it looked like a US grocery store, except staffed entirely by Indian men. But as we pushed a cart through the aisles, I felt a growing alarm. The shelves were nearly bare.

"Jesus, Max, there's nothing here," I said. *How am I going to feed my family?*

Since there were no deliveries during Ramadan, the commissary—which I would discover was never well-stocked—became even less so. Longtime expats knew to stockpile ahead of time.

"I'm sorry." Max shrugged. "Let's do the best we can."

We got what we could from my list: pasta, tea, brown sugar, herbs and spices, and cake mix. There was no fresh produce so we bought canned corn, peas, tomato sauce, pineapple, and juice. In the meat department I tossed a football-shaped lump of frozen chicken breasts into the cart.

"Mom, what's mutton?" Kate pointed at ominous cubes wrapped in Saran Wrap.

"Sheep." It was the first time I'd seen mutton.

"Like with mint jelly?" Kate endured lamb once a year on Easter.

"No, that's lamb. Mutton is full-grown sheep. Want some?"

She pretended to gag.

At checkout, Max paid the clerk with riyals and pushed our cart outside into the blistering heat. After dropping the groceries at home, we went to The Surf House, one of several restaurants on the compound. Surrounded by other Americans, we ate hamburgers and French fries in a cafeteria so bland we could have been in Iowa.

"Next week I'm taking you guys to Rahima." Max smiled.

"What's Rahima?" Sam asked, dragging a French fry through a puddle of ketchup.

"It's the closest town," Max said. "Then you'll get to see what Saudi Arabia is really like."

Thursday night, Max and I went to the Mitchell's party. The kids were invited to sleepovers and eager to be off with new friends. I'd agreed after talking to the parents and finding their houses on the map. When I put the Mitchell's phone number and address in the kids' backpacks, Sam didn't mind, but Kate was offended.

"I've been going to sleepovers since I was six," she muttered. "I'm eleven," she informed me, as if I'd forgotten.

"Yes, but I've always known your friends. Their parents were my friends, too." I heard the catch in my voice and felt a sudden pang of loss.

"Well." Kate smiled and patted me on the head. "Time to make new friends." Unable to resist teasing me, she spoke in a voice that sounded alarmingly like my own. "Then maybe you'll get invited to sleepovers."

At 8 p.m. Max and I walked around the corner to a house identical to ours. Max wore jeans and a blue shirt, long-sleeves rolled to reveal tan forearms. I thought he looked handsome. I wore black slacks and a white blouse, modestly accessorized with silver hoop earrings and a bracelet. Since I was still sunburned, lip-gloss and mascara were all I needed for makeup. It was dark, but the air was thick with heat. I felt sweat collecting under my arms. *So much for my crisp blouse.*

Max carried Bobbi's Pyrex dish refilled with my specialty—pineapple upside-down cake. It had been my father's favorite. He'd died soon after Kate was born, so the kids hadn't known him. But once a year I baked the cake to celebrate Grandpa's birthday.

As Max pressed the doorbell, we heard conversation and music. One booming voice got louder, and a tan heavy man in his fifties opened the door, highball glass in one hand. He glanced up and down the street then motioned us in and locked the door.

"Glad ya'll could make it!" he bellowed in a Texas drawl.

"Sarah, this is Ray," Max said.

Like Max, Ray wore jeans and a long-sleeved shirt rolled at the cuffs. But he also wore a gold Rolex watch, a huge college ring, and a thick wedding band.

I offered my hand, but Ray pulled me close and kissed my cheek.

"Very nice!" Ray winked at Max. "Keep her covered-up or the Arabs will get her." He pronounced Arabs with a long A.

Max grinned proudly as Ray headed toward the living room. "Come on back. Join the party."

Widening my eyes, I wiped my cheek to signal disgust. Max just shrugged.

The Mitchell's living room was decorated with Middle Eastern and travel souvenirs, and filled with clusters of Americans talking and laughing. Classic rock blared from a stereo. Ray gestured for attention, sloshing brown beverage over his wrist.

"Hey, everybody, I want ya'll to meet Sarah. Max's better half."

People crowded in to greet me, shaking hands and smiling. The men dressed like oil workers with jeans, big belt buckles, boots, and Rolex watches. The women had big hair, heavy makeup, tight revealing clothes, and flashy gold jewelry. Most spoke with Southern accents and everyone had the kind of tans suggesting golf, tennis, and long afternoons by the pool.

After the quiet solitude of my days, I was overwhelmed with all the noise and visual stimuli and felt myself shutting down. And for the first time I felt like I was in a foreign land—but it wasn't Saudi Arabia.

A fifty-something faded redhead, clinging to the illusion of youth, approached. Her miniskirt and plunging neckline showed off good legs and slick tan cleavage. Black mascara caked the lashes of her hazel eyes. Her orange lipstick was just a little too bright. But under the flash there was something delicate about her, a slight bird-like tremor.

She took Max's arm and smiled up at him. "Hey, handsome, I'm so glad ya'll could come." She kissed Max's cheek, leaving a greasy orange smudge, then turned to me.

"I'm Bobbi." She didn't fit the Mexican-casserole image I had of her. "So nice to finally meet you." Bobbi surprised me with a warm hug. Her body felt fragile beneath her silk blouse.

Max handed her the cake. "Sarah made dessert."

Bobbi grinned. "Aren't you sweet? I told Max you didn't have to bring anything. You've only been here a week!" She gave the cake to a Filipino houseboy who'd appeared at her side. "Put this with the desserts."

Still smiling at Max, Bobbi took my arm. "Excuse us while I introduce Sarah around." She pulled me away, chattering in a drawl like you'd hear on the television show *Dallas*. "Your husband is the sweetest thing, but I've got to tell you, he talks about you all the time. We've been dying to meet you." It sounded so sincere I felt myself melt with pleasure.

In the dining area, Filipino houseboys bustled back and forth, replenishing hors d'oeuvres, clearing dirty dishes. Large carafes of wine sat on the table.

"Honey, what can I get you, red or white? It's all *chez* Mitchell. Max told us you liked the white. Want to try some red?"

"Please," I said.

"Oh, wait." Bobbi pointed to a carafe filled with brown liquid. "We make great *sid*, too. Want a *sid* and coke?"

"Sid?"

"Short for *sidiqui*. It means 'friend' in Arabic." She smiled. "Hundred proof moonshine!"

"Red is fine. Oh, and thanks for the casserole, Max didn't know to stock up for Ramadan."

"That's a man for you, honey." Bobbi leaned close. "Let me know if you need anything and I'll get it for you." Her breath was a warm mix of mint, tobacco, and alcohol.

For awhile I stood on the edge of a group of women. I hoped Sissie would show, but she never did. The men gathered across the room, Max the center of attention.

"Dinner everybody!" Bobbi called, pointing to the chairs. "Boy, girl, boy, girl—no spouses together!" I sat between Ray and a man in a cowboy shirt.

While houseboys served salad, vegetables, rice, and grilled fish, conversations centered on vacations, shopping, and money. Shy in the best of times, I answered a few questions then just listened, letting the red wine relax me. I watched Max gesture extravagantly as Bobbi and another woman laughed. Max caught my eye, winked, and lifted his glass to me.

Ray saw Max's gesture, put his arm around me, and pulled me close. Leaning down, he whispered in my ear, "Thank God you're finally here. He's been miserable without you." Ray smiled. "One more week and I might have lost my best engineer."

Max was once again lost in conversation. In college Max had always been the big man on campus, but the years had kicked the shit out of him. I was happy to see him back in true form. It felt like we'd made a good decision for him.

I looked around at the gold jewelry, the travel souvenirs, and the houseboys bustling attentively. The drapes were closed, but I knew the beach was just outside the sliding doors. Suddenly I understood the seduction. It all felt so sexy. That night Max and I made love again, and it was more than just having been apart. I was attracted to him all over again.

7

My second Sunday in Saudi, I was on the beach at dawn standing thigh-deep in the warm water. As the sun rose, the horizon turned vivid neon-pink. By the time the last echoes of call to prayer were fading, the sky was bleached pale by the intense sun and I felt the heat.

I'd grown up Methodist, the least conservative branch of Christianity, attending Sunday morning services and earning babysitting money in the church nursery. I went to Methodist Youth Fellowship (MYF) meetings for the dances, hayrides, and boys. Church was always a backdrop in my life. By high school, Max, who was raised Catholic, preferred sleeping off hangovers to attending mass. When we married Max was happy to convert to Methodism, and while we made the kids attend Sunday school, Max and I were inconsistent in our own practice.

We weren't prepared for how much religion would dictate our lives in Saudi Arabia, the most fundamentalist of all Islamic nations. The mosque in Rahima had loudspeakers in the minaret from which a man called a *muezzin* broadcast call to prayer five times a day—sunrise, noon, mid-afternoon, sunset, and nightfall. Following the call, the entire prayer service was broadcast. Saturday through Thursday, it lasted 30 minutes, but could go for an hour on Fridays.

"La Ilah illa Allah!" No God but Allah.

Call to prayer became the soundtrack playing in the background of our lives in Saudi.

During Ramadan, the muezzin also set off a cannon to announce sunrise and sunset.

"I heard it!" Sam barreled into the living room where Kate and I waited.

We rushed outside to the company car where Max had the air-conditioner running. It was our first trip off Al Hassa since we'd arrived two weeks before—our first venture into the real Saudi. If we left quickly we'd have almost an hour in Rahima before the next call to prayer. At nightfall we planned to have dinner at a Chinese restaurant.

Timing was everything. When shops closed for prayer, everyone had to leave and no one could reenter until prayer was over. Restaurants were different. Once prayer began, no one was permitted to enter, but if you were already inside, you were allowed to stay. The trick was to get inside before prayer began.

As we approached the main gate, Max joined a line of cars. I could see the first of two guardhouses manned by uniformed guards, rifles slung over their shoulders. As each car pulled up, a guard peered inside then walked around the car, inspecting wheel wells and the trunk before waving it through.

When it was our turn, Max gave his ID to the guard who looked at the kids in the backseat then at me. "Her ID," he told Max, pointing at me.

I was confused.

"Give him your ID," Max said.

After fumbling in my backpack, I smiled nervously and gave the guard my ID. The guard closely examined both our IDs before handing them back to Max and motioning us forward.

"What was that all about?" I asked.

Max watched the rearview mirror as we neared the second guardhouse. "I'll tell you later."

"Tell me now," I said.

"They're making sure we're married to each other," Max said quietly. "It's against Saudi law for men and women to be together if they're not married."

"But we're not Saudis," I said.

"Doesn't matter."

The second guard examined our IDs, then circled the car holding his rifle like he expected us to make a break for it. He rapped on my window and motioned for me to roll it down, then studied my face before moving toward the back of the car. In the side mirror I saw him gazing at Kate for what felt like too long.

Max faced straight ahead, but I knew he was watching the guard's every move. Finally, Max was given the IDs and motioned forward. As he shifted into gear, I heard him exhale.

"That was scary," I said.

"Just routine." But I saw the muscle working in Max's jaw, like it always did when he was angry. He patted my leg and gave me a tight smile. "Don't worry. It's all okay."

The evening air felt charged as we walked the narrow streets of Rahima. Middle Eastern music blared from shop radios, intermingling with sounds of laughter and language. Carpet sellers stood in the doorways of their shops, holding glasses of tea. Baskets of rice and spices rested on sidewalks and racks displayed abayas and thobes.

"All the shopkeepers are men, but they aren't all Saudis," Max said. "Some are Lebanese or Egyptian, Turkish, Syrian. Most are Indian or Pakistani."

I looked around. "How can you tell which ones are Saudis?"

"Their clothes. That one's Saudi." Max nodded toward a man wearing a thobe and a red-and-white-checked scarf. "His scarf is called a *gutra,* and that black cord holding it on is an *igal*. The other shopkeepers wear slacks and shirts."

"What's that?" Sam pointed to a vertical cone of meat on a rotisserie over burning coals.

"*Shawarma,*" Max said. As the meat turned, the vendor shaved off slices, piled them on thick bread, and ladled red or white sauce on top.

"What kind of meat is that?" I asked.

"I think it's a combination of stuff." Max shrugged.

"Oh, yum," Kate said. "Mystery meat."

One vendor offered us samples of *falafel,* the Middle Eastern hush puppy. After one taste we had no choice but to order a bag full. Farther down the sidewalk, we stopped to watch a baker spin and stretch balls of dough like pizzas. He slammed them inside a beehive-shaped wood-burning oven where they cooked on the walls.

"Two, please," Max said. Using metal tongs, the baker pulled two rounds of bread from the oven, slipped them into bags, and gave them to Max. "Shukran," Max said, handing over riyals.

Max tore one round in half for the kids and we shared the other. "It's called Arab bread."

It resembled pita bread, but was soft and puffy with brown spots where the dough had blistered as it cooked. I tore at the chewy bread, widened my eyes at Max, and smiled.

"Mmmmm, this is great," Sam said.

"Like it, Katie?" Max asked.

Kate nodded, her mouth full.

Max bought us Oranginas, citrus soda in pear-shaped bottles, and we sipped while we walked. Kate's eyes widened as a group of Saudi women walked by in head-to-toe black. None of their eyes were visible—all wore black veils draped over their heads.

"I wonder what that feels like," Kate whispered, taking my hand.

"I do too."

"Look," Max whispered, glancing across the street. "A matawah."

Following his gaze, I immediately recognized the matawah from Sissie's description. A man with a red-streaked beard and short thobe stood in the middle of the sidewalk, surveying the crowd. He held a long stick, as if poised to strike. Foot traffic flowed around the matawah like water around a boulder in a stream. Everyone avoided eye-contact as they hurried past.

"His job is to make sure we behave ourselves," Max whispered.

I was suddenly aware of how much we stood out in the crowd and glad we were across the street. Max was in his work clothes, but the kids wore T-shirts and jeans. I had on a long skirt, long-sleeved blouse, and a scarf around my neck. Not being Arab, I wasn't required to cover my hair, but I kept an extra scarf in my backpack, just in case.

I paused outside a shop resembling an old-fashioned apothecary—cool and fragrant, with colorfully wrapped bars of soap and yellow boxes of Jean Naté.

"Come in, lady!" An Indian man smiled and motioned to me.

Inside, I was drawn to flat blue tins of the Nivea cream my German grandmother had used, then I remembered I didn't have money. I stepped outside to get riyals from Max, knowing we needed a system. It wasn't going to work for me to constantly have to ask Max for money.

While the merchant rang up my purchase, a Saudi woman walked into the store, selected a few items, and joined me at the counter. She looked at me and nodded. I stared at the black veil covering her face, making out the faintest suggestion of eyes. I smiled, nodded, and turned back to the merchant, trying to mask my discomfort. *What's it like not having others see your eyes?* After taking my package, I smiled at the woman again before joining Max and the kids.

Outside, the night was sultry, the crowds suffocating. Sweat coursed down my face and back. Thinking about the Saudi woman, I imagined having my face covered in the oppressive heat and felt a wave of panic. I grabbed Kate's hand and stepped off the curb. After a few steps, Max noticed we weren't following. When he turned and saw the wild look in my eyes, he led us off the main thoroughfare and down a less crowded sidewalk. Suddenly we found ourselves across the street from the mosque.

"Look." Max nodded. "There's the mosque."

"It's like our church," I told the kids.

In front of the mosque, old Saudi men sat on rugs talking and drinking coffee from handle-less demitasse cups. Other men washed their hands, faces, and feet in low-set basins then disappeared into the door of the mosque, leaving behind a pile of leather sandals.

We gazed at the white adobe building. The minaret was tall and slender, like a church bell tower. On top, a gold crescent was silhouetted against the darkening sky, like a new moon.

"That's where they broadcast call to prayer." Max pointed to loud-speakers in the minaret.

As if on cue, the nightfall call to prayer began and Saudi men moved toward the mosque while Westerners and Saudi women moved away. Shopkeepers hung signs reading "Closed for prayer" outside their doors.

"Let's go," Max said.

We followed him as he hurried down the sidewalk to the Gulf Royal Chinese Restaurant, a favorite among expats. It had good food and an area screened off from the main dining room where families could eat together. Restaurants without family sections would not serve women.

After placing our orders with the smiling Chinese waiter, Kate whispered, "I have to pee."

Remembering our experience in the airport hammam, I smiled. "I'll come with you."

The green-tiled hammam was enormous with a Western-style toilet, bidet, and two pedestal sinks all in green porcelain with gold-plated handles and faucets. Rumors had it that the restaurant had been remodeled in anticipation of a visit from the Saudi royal family. Despite the ornate fixtures, there was no soap or toilet paper. The flusher handle was missing from the toilet.

"If it was gold, maybe someone stole it." Kate giggled.

"Maybe." I turned on the water in the sink then shrieked as water poured on my feet. We laughed as water streamed from the bottom of the sink into a drain in the middle of the floor.

Our food arrived soon after we returned to the table, and it was delicious. At some point, the Chinese waiters delivered a cake to a nearby table and sang "Happy Birthday." For the remainder of the evening a mixed tape of every birthday-related pop song ever recorded blared through the restaurant speakers—*They say it's your birthday! Happy birthday, Baby!*

The kids laughed as they sang along. It felt like being in Disney World, with Epcot's samplings of artificially created cultures. It was another reason why expats loved this cheesy Chinese restaurant. It felt familiar and safe, and could have been anywhere but Saudi.

Ramadan turned out to be a blessing for us. The school curriculum was loose and special after-school activities helped the kids make new friends. Garage sales provided bicycles, a TV, and other household items. Max worked 6 a.m. until 3 p.m., so every night we went to bed early. Alone all day, I cleaned and organized. When Max and the kids got home we went to the pool or the beach. It was like being on vacation in some all-inclusive resort, only I was cooking.

One afternoon Max surprised us with snorkel equipment. There was a reef a few yards offshore and I swam out looking for it, leaving Max with the kids. The water was warm and clear. I saw a sandbar beneath me and followed a large fish, hoping it would lead me to the reef. When I suddenly realized I was in deep water, I turned and started toward shore. Once I could touch bottom, I stood and took off my mask.

Just then, a wave crashed over me, knocking me off balance and throwing me against the bottom of the ocean. I felt sand ripping my skin as I was tumbled until I lost all sense of direction. The pounding surf was loud as thunder. Saltwater burned my nose and throat. Suddenly I was being swept rapidly along in an undertow. Kicking and pulling with my arms I'd just broken the surface, when I was sucked back under. In that split-second I heard my kids' horrified screams. I still fought, but I was exhausted. For a moment I had the urge to surrender and let the current pull me out to sea, then I felt a hand grab my wrist.

Max pulled me to the surface, gagging and coughing. He wrapped his arm across my chest and swam hard, towing me toward shore. My body relaxed as I realized I was safe. Close to shore, Max carried me out of the water and laid me on the sand. The kids touched me while Max blotted my face with a towel. When I could stand, we slowly walked home.

8

The alarm painfully pierced me awake from the place where dreams turn to nightmares—shackles on my ankles, waves washing me to sea. I fought damp tangled sheets to hit snooze. The clock wasn't there.

I rolled over, burrowed under the pillow, and willed the alarm to stop. But it persisted—just as I'd intended when I put the clock on the dresser across the room. Rising up, I squinted at the time: 9:30. I was asleep less than an hour. The alarm shrieked increasingly louder as I struggled to get up. I smashed the off-button, stumbled into the bathroom, and started the shower.

This was my guilty secret—I'd been going back to bed every morning after Max and the kids left. I collected Mimi on my way upstairs and she snuggled beside me while I slept. With the drapes drawn, lights off, and thermostat set low, the room was dark and cold. Perfect.

Sometimes I slept until 11 or noon. Then I got up, cleaned, baked cookies, and started dinner. At night I lay in bed staring into the dark long after Max was asleep. I had been in Saudi for a month, but the monotony of my routine made it seem much longer. One day faded into the next and I'd begun to lose track of time. Not only was I sleeping during the day, it had become increasingly difficult to leave the house. Today I'd set the alarm to make sure I got up. It was the morning of the Women's Club welcome coffee.

I pushed back waves of fatigue as I dressed. I'd carefully planned what to wear. Since I was riding my bicycle, it needed to be sweat and wrinkle resistant. The compound dress code was "activity appropriate"—swimsuit and cover-up for the pool, shorts and T-shirt for tennis, loose, modest attire for public areas like the library, commissary, and restaurants.

After putting on a white blouse, black slacks, green scarf, and sandals, I went into the garage to get my bike. By the time I'd pulled the garage door shut, I was already feeling damp. A deep sleep-wrinkle creased my cheek.

Biking down the street, I passed a golf cart with two women. Grocery bags filled the back. "Good morning!" They called, waving cheerily.

"Morning." I waved back. It reminded me of an ad for Sun City. Women could drive golf carts and the family car on the compound, but outside Al Hassa it was illegal. Bicycle riding was also prohibited for all women off the compound. Saudi men were obviously still fearful of allowing women any mastery over their own lives, not to mention the adaptations in clothing it would require for Saudi women to straddle a bike.

I pedaled through the quiet streets, trying not to break a sweat. I knew where I was going. By the end of the second week in Saudi I'd explored the entire compound on my bike, taking pictures and locating the destinations Sissie had marked on my map. By the third week the novelty had worn off and I'd started sleeping late.

Housed in a cinderblock building, the Women's Club sign read: "Welcome to the Della House" with a painting of a *della*— an Arabic coffeepot the sensuous shape of a woman. Inside, dozens of women gathered, talking in excited voices and laughing. *Life!*

"I'm so glad you came!" Sissie rushed to hug me.

"Me, too." Already I felt more energized and hopeful.

"Sign in and fill this out." The nametag had "newcomer" across the top. "Then make yourself at home. I'll catch up with you later."

I put on my nametag and looked around. The room was furnished in the same dark wood and brown plaid as my house. I spotted Bobbi across the room chatting with some women. When I waved and started toward her, she gave me a quick smile then turned away. Laughter erupted from a woman in the group and I felt an old familiar flush of fear that it was about me.

Instead of continuing across the room, I walked to a table laden with coffeecakes, pastries, and coffee urns. I filled a Styrofoam cup full of coffee, adding cream and sugar. It was strong and delicious, the best I'd had in weeks. I went back for refills until caffeine tingled in my arms.

Wandering about, I noticed an absence of Arab women. Judging by the accents, most women were from the US South, some from Great Britain, a few from other European countries. Everyone spoke with an accent. I wondered what mine sounded like to them.

I'm shy by nature—okay one-on-one and in small groups. But if a group is bigger than some magic, arbitrarily changing number, I become tongue-tied. I'm accustomed to being the wallflower, the one both wanting and dreading to be asked to dance. The one who annoyingly clings to whoever brought her to the party and, once seated, will stay in one spot all night. I find mingling with strangers shatteringly painful.

Tight little cliques formed around the room as women caught up on vacations, family news, and gossip. I hovered on the edges, wishing I belonged. Thankfully, my nametag highlighted my status as newcomer and most women were welcoming. After 20 minutes, I got another cup of coffee, filled a plate with pastries, and found a place to sit.

A woman sat down beside me, smiling and rocking to a tune playing in her head. I smiled at her, but she seemed oblivious to my presence. Slowly I realized she was humming, but so quietly it felt more like a vibration. She looked in her mid-thirties, curly blonde hair going grey. Her blue eyes darted around the room. She seemed popular, but in a weird way.

Whenever anyone approached and spoke to her, she smiled and launched into gracious discourse. "How are you? How's your family?" And she'd listen intently to the response. When they walked away, she slipped back into humming. After awhile I noticed a pattern. The other women circled, approached, interacted, and backed away. They were kind, but wary. Like with a stray dog that seems friendly, but you don't know if it is going to cower at your feet and pee, or go for your jugular. The tune she was humming was familiar. *Just on the tip of my tongue.* I glanced at her and she smiled.

"Biblical," she said.

"Sorry?"

"We've both got biblical names." She pointed to her name tag: "Rebecca."

I smiled. "Yes, we do."

But Rebecca had already retreated inward. She got up and wandered away.

Sissie slipped into the vacated seat. "I see you've met Rebecca," Sissie whispered, nodding knowingly. "She's married to a doctor." She leaned close. "Rebecca's whacky under the best of circumstances, but they just got back from repat so now she's full-out loony."

"Repat?"

"Repatriation vacation," Sissie said. "She's been gone a month." Sissie gazed at Rebecca who stood alone, smiling and rocking. "We're all a bit loony when we get back from repat."

I nodded, but wondered whether Rebecca had a more serious psychological problem. Already, I understood why she would be depressed returning to Saudi after being away a month. I ran my fingertips over my cheek, feeling for the sleep-wrinkle. To my relief, it was gone.

While Sissie continued to watch Rebecca, I surveyed the room. "I notice there aren't any Saudi women here. Do any belong to the Women's Club?"

"Oh, no," Sissie said. "Ocmara frowns on that kind of thing."

"Why?" I asked. "I've seen Saudis on the compound."

"Oh, they live here, but they keep to themselves," Sissie said. "Saudi women aren't allowed to spend time with Westerners."

"Is it illegal?"

"Not illegal, just not done. Saudi men don't want them learning our bad habits." Sissie laughed. "Besides, who wants them? I'd be afraid to say a word if I thought it might get back to Ocmara management. They control us enough as it is." Sissie stood up. "Come on, I want to introduce you to the other new ladies."

She introduced me to Amy, a fair, soft-spoken woman in her late twenties from Louisiana. Amy was so happy to be there she glowed. "My husband is an Ocmara Brat."

I must have looked blank.

"Mark grew up in Dhahran," Amy explained. "His dad retired a few years ago. Mark has wanted to come back to Saudi his whole life."

"Why?" I asked.

"He was so happy as a kid. It's the best place to raise a child. Safe. Great schools."

It sounded like propaganda from the Ocmara brochure, yet I felt reassured.

"Do you have kids?" I asked.

"Two little ones, a boy and girl. And the company benefits are great." Amy was wide-eyed with enthusiasm. "Mark wants to stay here at least ten years."

The other woman, Bonita from Texas, was much less effusive. Tall and lanky with long red hair and green eyes, she smiled politely as Amy talked, but she was clearly still on the fence.

"Steve and I don't have kids. We're only here for the money," Bonita said. "I'm going to be working, too, as soon as my work-permit is processed. Part-time office work. Not interesting, but it pays okay."

I perked up. "Is it hard to get a work-permit?"

"Once you're here, it's almost impossible," Bonita said. "I started the process in the States."

"Oh." I wished I had known.

A woman walked to the front of the room, rang a bell, and the room quieted. She introduced herself as the president of the Women's Club.

"Welcome back, everybody. Before we start the video, I want ya'll to know about the next shopper's bus to Khobar. We'll be passing around a sign-up." She waved a clipboard. "All you new ladies will want to be sure and come. You'll get to visit some authentic Arab *souqs,* but even better, you'll get to go grocery shopping at Safeway!"

The audience cheered and clapped. *What kind of people applaud going grocery shopping?* When the clipboard got to us, Bonita, Amy, and I signed up.

"Ladies, get ready for a treat!" The president shot us an enthusiastic smile. "This video will give you a good idea of what's in store for you!"

Lights dimmed and the TV lit up. "Valentine's Tea" flashed on the screen. The camera panned a room where women dressed in red lunched at tables decorated with hearts. I already recognized some of the women. There was a close-up of Bobbi.

Next was "Mother's Day Tea." The same women, wearing red and white corsages, were eating and laughing. "Ice Cream Socials" preceded shots of women scooping ice cream into bowls and piling on toppings. In the segment "Variety Shows," a mother and daughter danced in matching sequined outfits. The girl was about Kate's age. The mother, fortyish and overweight, was wearing heavy makeup and a frozen smile. She looked too scared to be having fun.

Each segment evoked rounds of applause and laughter. As the lights came up, the applause continued. Amy looked enchanted. I struggled to keep my expression neutral, but almost laughed aloud at the horror on Bonita's face.

After the meeting, it was such a relief to walk into the cool quiet sanctuary of my house that I knew it would be tempting to stay there forever. But I sat down and leafed through the schedule of classes offered by the Women's Club. Most were crafts—cross-stitching, découpage, quilting, crocheting, tatting doilies. *Like hell!*

I looked around at the obsessive orderliness of my living room. The rest of the house looked the same. Even that morning, I'd made the bed, cleaned the bathroom, and washed the breakfast dishes before I left. A foil-wrapped plate of homemade chocolate-chip cookies was on the counter. Max caught the company bus every morning at 6:45. It dropped him off at 5 p.m. The kids were out the door at 8:30. With afterschool activities they seldom got home before Max. Every day I was alone for eight hours, much of the time spent cleaning and cooking.

Something was nagging me. Nagging me like the tune Rebecca was humming. As I absently played with my cross, I had images of television shows I'd grown up with. With a flash of clarity I understood June Cleaver's tremulous expression as she nervously fingered her pearls. Or was that Donna Reed, in her shirtwaist dress, lipstick too bright? Did the father who knew best even have a wife? Did Harriet stare up at the ceiling or get up in the middle of the night to smoke, or have a drink? It was my life now—in black and white.

I buried my face and laughed aloud, aware of the maniacal edge. *What was it called?* Suddenly I remembered from my feminist studies. Betty Friedan, *The problem that had no name.*

When Max got home he found me sitting on the sofa. The kids had already checked in and I'd given them a handful of riyals to bring back hamburgers for dinner from the Surf House.

"Well? How'd it go?" Max had been eager for me to go to the Women's Club meeting.

"It was interesting." I searched for the right words. "Informative."

Max looked pleased. "Was Bobbi there?"

"They were all there." I took his hand. "Listen, I want to talk about something else."

"What's wrong?"

"Nothing's wrong," I said. "I've decided I need to find a job."

"What are you talking about?" Max looked stunned.

"I met a woman named Bonita who told me about a work-permit, and..."

"Wait a minute," Max interrupted. "You're not getting a job." When I looked stunned, Max touched my cheek. "Come on, babe, you just got here. Things are going great."

I shook my head. "Max, I'm bored. I need more to do. I'm like a freaking housecat. For the last month you and the kids coming home has been the highpoint of my day."

He actually looked pleased. "That's why you're joining the Women's Club. So you'll have more to do." Max stroked my hair. "You don't have to work anymore. I make enough money to support us. Besides, you used to complain about work all the time. You were miserable."

Was I? I gazed across the room. I'd loved my work at the hospital. It was raw and real and urgent. I'd loved the kids, the families, my team. Over the years, I'd saved every letter, note, or picture I'd ever received from a patient or the family of a patient. They were in a pink accordion folder in the middle of the ocean with the rest of our shipment. But Max was right, I had complained about the commute, long hours, paperwork, and exhaustion. *Why had I thought work was the problem?*

Now, looking around the tidy living room, I realized it had been much safer to complain about work than the domestic responsibilities and financial problems waiting for me at home. It wasn't work I'd struggled with—it was the combination of all of it. *How do I tell Max I wasn't miserable at work, I was miserable at home?*

After dinner, the four of us went for a walk on the beach. It was the quiet hour before nightfall. We were past the last of the houses, where a long strip of beach separated the ocean to the east from the desert to the west.

"Mom, look!" Kate pointed.

Ahead of us three Saudi men walked onto the beach leading a sheep by a rope. There was a red X painted on its side. We stopped as the men crossed our path and led the animal to the water's edge. As one man lifted the sheep's head, another slit its throat with a knife.

Kate shrieked and covered her mouth with her hand.

Wild-eyed, the sheep thrashed as blood gushed from its neck.

"Gross," Sam said, unable to look away.

Kate gagged then vomited in the sand.

I buried my face in Max's chest. He held me while watching the writhing sheep over my shoulder. Suddenly the words to the song Rebecca had been humming popped into my head. *Why don't they let me go home? Let me go home? This is the worst trip I've ever been on. I feel so broke up... I want to go home.*

Later, we sat with the kids and Max tried to explain the three-day feast following Ramadan.

"Ramadan is like Lent and Eid al-fitr is like Easter." Max reached back into his Catholic childhood. "Like when you get to eat chocolate on Easter after giving it up for Lent."

The kids stared blankly. They only associated Easter with bunnies and baskets.

"Jesus is called the Lamb of God," Max continued. "We eat lamb on Easter."

I touched his hand. "I don't think that's helpful."

"What?" He shrugged. "Muslims just sacrifice animals instead of a person."

"That's horrible." Kate's eyes filled with fresh tears.

I squeezed Max's hand. "I know we don't understand it," I said. "But we have to respect the culture of others. Especially because we are the foreigners here and they are our hosts."

"Isn't that what you said mutton is?" Kate asked. "Sheep?"

I nodded, remembering the dark meat in the commissary.

"That's it," she said. "I'm becoming a vegetarian."

I hugged Kate, exchanging a look with Max over her head.

"Time for bed, buddy," Max said to Sam. They went upstairs, leaving Kate and me alone.

"I want to go home," Kate wailed, unaware she was echoing Rebecca's song.

Kate was inconsolable for hours, but I was more disturbed by Sam's indifference. Despite our rules against violent television and movies, he'd clearly witnessed too much bloodletting. Or maybe it was just a "guy" thing. Max hadn't flinched while the sheep wrestled against death.

9

I had become ambivalent about the night. I longed for sleep, but my legs tingled, muscles twitched, my hands were in fists. Random thoughts and images looped through my mind, feelings of anxiety and fear. Every night I willed my body to relax. But as soon as I concentrated on breathing, it seemed I no longer could. Suddenly I fought for breath. Chest tightening, body flooded with the adrenaline of impending doom, I slipped out of bed and fled into the night.

In the backyard I huddled in shadows and smoked. The night gave me solace, the blanket of stars my only witness. Under cover of darkness I felt safe. The air was cooler at night and after I finished my cigarette I filled my lungs. When I finally felt on the edge of a doze, I crept upstairs and back to bed. Max never noticed I was gone. Eventually I surrendered to the restless, tormented sleep that carried me till dawn. I had dreams I could never remember.

It was Thursday, our new Saturday. Max was working out and running errands and the kids and I had slept late. Rumpled and still in pajamas, the kids shared a sofa. I lounged on the other sofa too lazy to get up for more coffee. The drapes were drawn and the room was cool and quiet.

"Hey, Mom." Sam looked up from petting the cat. "Mimi is wearing her abaya." I smiled. The top of Mimi's head was black, with a band of white across her eyes.

"Good thing you're not a sheep," Kate crooned to Mimi.

The front door slammed and Max charged into the room. "Everybody get dressed. We're going out." When the kids and I didn't move, Max crossed to the window and opened the drapes. Sunlight slashed across the room. "Come on. Let's go."

"Where are we going?" Squinting, Sam stood, displacing Mimi.

"It's a surprise." Max looked pleased with himself.

"What should we wear?" I asked.

"Compound casual for you and Kate," Max said "Sam, you can wear a T-shirt and shorts."

Kate and I exchanged worried glances.

"Don't worry, it'll be fun," Max said.

Twenty minutes later we were driving through the gates in a Land Rover Max said he'd borrowed from a coworker. At the highway, we turned south toward Dhahran. Everyone was quiet, watching the desert passing by.

Max was a good driver, but it had been awhile since he'd driven on a highway. He studied the instrument panel, adjusted mirrors, and played with the air-conditioning controls. When he pushed in the audiotape, Bruce Springsteen filled the air.

"Nice sound system." Max nodded along to *Born in the USA*.

There was little traffic and no posted speed limit. Cars either flew by us or puttered along. Saudis were notoriously bad drivers since there were few requirements for getting a driver's license besides being male. Debris from accidents littered the shoulders. Max navigated around slower vehicles and moved out of the way of a Mercedes flying past.

"Nice car, isn't it?" Max smiled, settling back. "Smooth ride."

"Yeah, it is." I'd never ridden in a Land Rover before. "Whose is it?"

"Guy named Bob. He's a Brit working out of Jubail."

"Hey, look! Camels!" Sam pointed to the side of the highway where a lone shepherd guided a herd of camels, their heads nodding back and forth with each step. "Cool!"

Max slowed so we could look, then sped up again. "So, what you think?"

"They're wonderful." I smiled.

"Not the camels." Max laughed. "What do you think about the car?"

Immediately I realized we were on a test drive. "I thought we weren't going to buy a car."

"Relax. I'm just thinking about it."

I looked around the sleek interior. "This has got to be expensive."

"It's an '86, almost brand new." Max looked smug. "But it's a steal. Bob's going home next month and he's desperate."

"How much is a steal, exactly?"

Max stared ahead. "We haven't worked that out yet."

We drove up behind a Toyota pickup chugging along with goats packed in the bed. Max gunned the engine and maneuvered around it.

"Feel that? Turbo-engine." Max grinned. "Man, this car handles great."

I felt duped. "Is this what we're doing today? Buying you a new car?" I kept my tone even.

Max looked wounded. "No, I told you I have a surprise."

"The car is not the surprise?"

"Don't be like that, babe. I'm taking you guys someplace I thought would be fun." He smiled. "Besides, I'm getting the car for us."

I felt a flash of anger. "What do you mean *us*? You take the bus to work and I can't even drive over here." My heart pounded and I pushed back tears. *No more tears!* The kids leaned forward and I felt their breath on my neck.

"You can on the compound," Max said. "I know it's hard grocery shopping on a bike."

There was no arguing that. Grocery shopping on a bicycle in 100-degree heat was a bitch. I filled my backpack, the front basket, and the rack behind my seat. Sometimes I also dangled bags from the handlebars. The only consolation was that the commissary sold cigarettes.

On the highway we passed signs for Dhahran and Dammam. The last sign was for Half Moon Bay, which sounded promising, but we flew past that exit. I had no idea where we were. After half an hour of chilly silence, we pulled into a crowded parking lot.

"We're here!" Max pointed to a sign: Prince Mohammed Bin Fahd Amusement Park.

"What is it?" Sam asked.

"It's like Six Flags, buddy," Max said.

"Cool!" Sam loved Six Flags.

As we passed through the gates I looked at my watch: one o'clock. Max had timed it perfectly. We'd missed the noontime call to prayer and would get to enjoy three hours under the scorching sun before the mid-afternoon prayer. I resisted sarcasm.

The park was nothing like Six Flags. There was no attempt at grass or flowers, just acres of asphalt, food stalls, and rides. Max bought a string of tickets. "Let's check it out!"

The kids were excited, so I decided to be a good sport. I smiled at Max and he relaxed. He was trying so hard to make us happy.

"Anybody hungry? Thirsty?" Max stopped at a kiosk and bought bottles of Zam Zam water for us and cups of juice for the kids. Kate barely suppressed a gag at the sight of platefuls of rice with cubes of mutton. We opted for roasted nuts, popcorn, and cotton candy.

As we wandered through the park, I tried to take Max's hand, but he pulled back. At first I thought he was still mad then remembered we couldn't hold hands in public.

Saudi families milled about, groups of veiled women trailing men. Saudi girls about Kate's age and younger wore colorful dresses. Boys wore thobes and gutras, miniature versions of their fathers. I worried about Sam's shorts, but saw other American boys dressed the same.

Kate nudged me and nodded at two Saudi men strolling in front of us holding hands. Homosexuality was punishable by death, but Saudi men often held hands with friends or other male family members. Occasionally, women held hands, but never men and women or boys and girls. Not even married couples.

"Why don't you hold hands with Dad?" Kate grinned at Sam, who looked disgusted.

"Hey, there's no line for the Octopus!" Sam shouted. He and Kate tore up the ramp, laughing as they scrambled into an empty car. Max and I were halfway up the ramp when the attendant, a Pakistani man, stormed over to the kids.

"You," he shouted, pointing at Kate. "Get off. Men only." He looked at me. "You, too. Off."

We were too stunned to move. Slowly, realization dawned. The cars were filled with boys and men. I looked down the ramp where girls and women lined the fence. One woman gestured to me, beckoning me back.

"Katie," I called. "Come with me." Flushed with embarrassment, Kate hurried over. The attendant gestured for Max to get in with Sam. "Go ahead," I told Max, pulling Kate away.

Joining the other women, we watched as the Octopus arms lifted and the chairs spun. The ride gathered speed and the Saudi men laughed as their red-and-white checked gutras flew about their heads. They called out to each other and waved to the women waiting below.

Kate wrapped her arms around my waist and leaned against me. I saw tears on her cheeks and kissed the top of her head. When the ride ended, the males filed off and women and girls took their places. Kate was reluctant, but I pulled her with me. We took our turn with the other women, waving down at Max and Sam who stood with the men. As the cars spun I saw the laughing faces of the young Saudi girls. The women's faces were invisible, but I heard shrieks of laughter from beneath their veils. When the ride was finished, Max and Sam were waiting.

"For a minute I was worried you and Kate wouldn't be able to go on the rides," Max said. He wanted us to have a good time, but I knew he was uncomfortable on the male-only rides. His smile was self-conscious and his walk had a macho swagger.

Fair and tall, I stood out in the crowd and drew curious stares. At one point, I felt my hair being touched. I moved away and tied my scarf over my head. It was more Hepburn than *hijab*, but I felt less conspicuous. Kate's humiliation lingered throughout the afternoon while Sam acted like he'd never had more fun. He eagerly boarded every ride, happily demonstrating fearlessness.

But on the bumper cars, I saw a crack in Sam's happy veneer. He was alone in his car, laughing as he bumped and was bumped. When he rammed into a Saudi boy's car, the boy rammed back. Both were laughing. It continued until the Saudi boy suddenly lost control of his car. Even then, Sam continued to back up and smash forward until the boy's gutra was askew and his expression dazed. Sam, no longer laughing, didn't stop until the ride was over.

The sarcasm I'd stifled earlier bubbled out when call to prayer began blaring at 4.

"Thank God, we can go," I said. "Or should I thank Allah?" My tone gave me away.

Max shot me a stony look as we joined the crowds moving toward the exit. We piled into the Land Rover, rolling down the windows to let heat escape while stuck in the stream of cars trying to leave. In the backseat, Sam was unusually quiet. Kate leaned forward.

"I've got to pee."

"Jesus, Kate, you should have gone before we left the park," Max snapped.

Kate flopped back into her seat with a grunt. I knew how she felt.

"We're going to have to stop somewhere. I have to go, too." I stared at Max. His jaw was clenched and tiny veins pulsed at his temple. "You know we couldn't go there."

"It was gross," Kate said.

We had tried to use the women's hammam at the park, but couldn't get past the wall of stench at the door. It was worse than the Dhahran airport.

"You're going to have to get used to it," Max said.

"Yes, but we haven't yet." I kept my tone level.

We had been walking around with full bladders and now the blast of air-conditioning increased the urgency. I felt queasy and my arms were covered in goose bumps. On the highway back to Al Hassa, Max pulled into a gas station. Kate and I jumped out and ran into the restroom.

"Oh, Mom, I can't." Kate was crying as she backed out the door. It was worse than the park.

"Here, sweetie." I pulled the extra scarf from my backpack, wrapped it around Kate's nose and mouth then did the same with mine. It helped block most of the smell.

When we came out, a truck was parked by the pumps. Kneeling in the back of the truck was a full grown camel. It was tied down with bungee cords and had a green cloth bag covering its head. I pulled out my camera and took a shot.

"Don't do that!" Max snapped when I got in the car. He threw the car into gear and sped out of the station, watching the rearview mirror like we were being chased.

"Why not? It was a camel."

"I don't know." He shrugged. "Because they don't like it."

Photography was discouraged in Saudi, but the reasons and rules were vague. Taking pictures of women was illegal, even covered in veils, but Saudi men usually posed when asked. Once, I'd seen a sign with a red X superimposed over the image of a camera. I snapped a picture of the sign. How quickly you learn to disobey when held to rigid obedience.

I took a picture of Max's scowling face then put my camera away. We drove home in silence.

Back home the kids dashed off and Max and I tore into each other. The cool house was a welcome refuge after the blistering heat of the amusement park, but it wasn't peaceful or quiet.

"You're just looking for reasons to hate it here. All your talk about respecting different cultures and you haven't stopped complaining since you've been here." Max paced around.

I looked up at him from the sofa. "That's not true. I'm just having a hard time adjusting."

"That's why I wanted us to have a good time today," he screamed. "Good family time." Max sat down and stared at me. "You read everything about Saudi. You knew what it would be like."

"I read about it," I said. "But I didn't know how it would feel to live this way."

"You talked to people at orientation. What did they say?"

"They said what they're supposed to say, 'How great it is.' That's what everybody says."

"It is great!" Max screamed.

I took a deep breath and tried to switch gears. "Today at the park, Kate was humiliated when she was kicked off the ride. And I'm worried about Sam. It's not like him to be so aggressive."

"What the hell are you talking about?"

"On the bumper cars," I said.

"He was just having fun," Max yelled.

"No, he wasn't. He was angry and he was being mean," I said.

"It was the bumper cars, for Christ's sake." Max jumped up. "They're supposed to be aggressive." Max looked down at me. "I know it's different for girls." He pantomimed slow, cautious driving and giggling with his hand over his mouth. It was pure ridicule.

"I'm just saying I think Sam is hurting and I'm worried about him," I said quietly.

"Why do you always have to read so much into everything? You're not a fucking shrink!"

His words stung as much as if he'd slapped me. Max stormed off, the front door slammed, and I sat in the sudden silence. I had always dreamed of getting my doctorate in psychology, but was never able to make it happen. We earned too much to qualify for financial aid and too little to afford tuition on our own. Two kids, a mortgage, and a restless husband made it impossible. Every time I'd been about to sign up for a class, some monetary crisis prevented it.

The next day the kids left early—I suspect to avoid more "family time." Max and I resumed our standoff. First, we fought about the car.

"I agree it would make shopping easier," I said. "But a Land Rover? We're here to save money. Why don't we get an older, cheaper car?"

"Oh, babe, I can't drive a beater in my position!" Max puffed with pride.

"What about maintenance?" Back home we'd kept our local mechanic in business for years.

"It's still under warranty," Max said.

Warranty was something I knew nothing about, never having owned a new car. Max acted like a spoiled child being denied a toy. We went round and round until I gave up, like an overindulgent parent unable to tolerate another scene.

Right then I decided I would never drive the Land Rover. Even for grocery shopping. Remembering the intricate role the bicycle had played in the Women's Suffragette movement, I decided that it if a bike had been good enough for Susan B. Anthony, it was good enough for me.

Max and I also fought about packing up and going home. I'd always believed that if it didn't work, we could change our minds. Max had never had a problem quitting a job he didn't like. He ran upstairs to our bedroom, came back with his briefcase, and pulled out his contract.

"Here, you look at it," Max said. "See if you can find a loophole, because I sure can't."

I stared at him. It was the first time I'd heard Max even hint that he might be unhappy. *What had I missed?* Although Max worked in Al Hassa, I'd never seen his office. I knew his project involved Ocmara's control systems. Other than that, I never understood what he did. When I'd pressed for details, Max said, "Can't tell you. I signed a confidentiality agreement." Not sharing was new for us and I felt sorrow in that loss.

"Did something happen?" I asked, quietly. "Is something wrong?"

Max looked at me with the most vulnerable expression I'd seen in years. "We've just been assigned an enormous project. There's going to be a lot of pressure. Everyone says I'm so great, but I've never worked on any-thing like this." He stared at his hands. "I don't know if I can do it, but I don't think I have a choice."

As I studied his contract, it became clear the terms were different than we'd understood. First, Max wasn't making as much money as we thought. Ocmara deducted money for rent, utilities, and "hypothetical tax," a figure based on what he would be paying if we lived in the US. It negated the tax benefit of working abroad.

If Max broke his three-year contract, we would have to repay the signup bonus and moving expenses. We'd used the signup bonus to pay the mortgage arrears, pay down credit card debt, and get the house ready to rent. When our renters informed us the hot water heater had broken, the whole damn thing needed to be replaced. The credit card was maxed out again.

I set down the contract and looked at Max. He was right—we had no choice but to stay. This time I was the one who got up and walked out. I went to the beach and stood at the water's edge. I gazed at the horizon and thought about surrender.

10

The sun was still low on the horizon, white and intense in a cloudless blue sky. The pink of dawn had faded. I made my way through the dunes, across the sand, and to the water's edge. I hadn't run in years, so I decided to ease into it with a light jog on the beach. I quickly abandoned that idea when the heat was already oppressive at 7 o'clock.

That time of morning was peacefully quiet. The last notes of call to prayer had faded and the only sound was the gentle motion of the tide as foamy waves washed over my feet. As always, being close to water soothed my soul. I walked north, continuing past the houses to where the dunes flattened into raw desert.

Gradually the topography changed. The desert rose to form a wall of sand, rock, and driftwood. I found an area with half-buried boulders and large flat stones. Rivulets of water ebbed and flowed between the rocks with the rhythm of the tide. It was the farthest I'd walked and it was getting late. I knew I should turn back, but something compelled me forward.

As I rounded a curve I saw her. Twenty feet above me, on the edge of a rocky promontory, she stood overlooking the water. Her abaya swirled around her calves in the ocean breeze. Running shoes dangled from one hand and with her other hand she held her veil off her face. Above the black mask covering her nose and mouth, her dark eyes gazed out at the horizon. She was still, lost in thought.

I stood frozen beneath her. It was like coming upon an animal in the wild. I was afraid I'd startle her and she would run away. We stood like that for several moments until she stiffened, as if picking up my scent. She looked straight at me, dropped her veil, and stepped backward, out of sight. I heard the rustle of gravel, then only the sound of the ocean and my pounding heart.

Sam was sleepily spooning cereal into his mouth when I swooped in and hugged him from behind. He was dressed, but hadn't combed his hair. It stood in blond spikes.

"I've got a great idea for your birthday!" Sam would be the first to have a birthday in Saudi. He'd be nine in two weeks.

"Yuck, Mom." He pulled away. "You're all sweaty."

Kate assessed me over the rim of her juice glass. "Yeah, you're pretty gross."

My T-shirt and shorts were damp, my face red, and my hair was plastered to my scalp. I could smell that my deodorant had failed me.

"Thanks, sweetie, I love you, too." I reached to hug her and she shrank away with a shriek.

We laughed and for a moment everything felt normal. After seeing the woman I'd run most the way home. It was the first time I'd moved my body in months and I felt giddy, almost happy.

"What's your idea?" Sam's eyes widened over the freckles dotting the bridge of his nose.

"Bowling! You can invite your whole class and we'll have pizza." Surfside Bowl had a snack bar, party room, and twelve lanes. I smiled at Kate. "You can bring friends to help out." I looked at Sam. "It'll be fun!"

I knew he'd like it. I'd thought of it the night before. Once I'd realized going home wasn't an option, something shifted inside me—suddenly I was open to possibilities. After a brief deliberation Sam nodded, then jumped up when he realized he had to start spreading the news.

"Gotta go!" He grabbed his backpack and started to leave. Then he stopped and hugged me. "Thanks, Mom." He and Kate ran out the door.

I looked at Mimi. "Wow. That went well." Mimi seemed to be waiting for me to take her back to bed. Instead, I cleared the table and started washing dishes.

I wondered where the woman on the beach had come from. I was accustomed to seeing Saudis at the community center, but there were so few living in Al Hassa, it was always startling to see one in the residential area or on the beach. Al Hassa was so Western it was as if Saudis were the foreigners.

The encounter on the beach thrilled me, but I also felt wary. There were no clues as to what lay underneath her veils, except the fleeting glimpse of her eyes. I wondered if she was the same woman I'd seen on the beach my first day in Saudi. She too had been holding running shoes. For all I knew they all had running shoes.

After getting dressed, I sat down with a calendar and the Women's Club information. The days were long and I had lots of hours to fill. Sipping coffee, I leafed through the schedule of activities. There were bake sales and "Fungo," which was really Bingo, but couldn't be called Bingo because of the prohibition against betting. Yoga was mysteriously outlawed and I hated aerobics classes. I circled basic Arabic and Middle Eastern cooking.

I also discovered there was a photography lab on the compound. Photography had been my second major in college and my creative passion. Early on I'd sold a few prints and hoped to make it a career before real life intruded. My Nikon EM resided in my closet, ever hopeful.

Several hours and another pot of coffee later, I had a to-do list and a grocery list for the Safeway shopping trip. I yawned and stretched, resisting the urge to take a nap. Despite all the caffeine, I was sleepy. I thought it was because of my new schedule and the early morning exercise. But there was something else nagging me, just beneath the surface. *Something lost or forgotten.*

All afternoon it haunted me, while cleaning house, doing laundry, baking cookies, chopping vegetables for salad, and stirring spaghetti sauce. It was as if I'd walked into a spider web that clung to me, persistent and sticky.

When Max and the kids got home the house gleamed, the table was set for dinner, and the sweet smell of spaghetti sauce permeated the air. I'd changed into a sundress, dabbed on perfume and lipstick, and brushed my hair. When Max walked in, I greeted him with a kiss and a hug.

"This is wonderful." Max smiled as he took a second helping of spaghetti.

"Yeah, Mom, it's the best." Sam hunched over his plate, shoveling in pasta. Even Kate contentedly swirled noodles onto her fork.

"Everybody wants to come to my party." Sam grinned.

"Can Lizzie and Amanda spend the night?" Kate asked. "After they help?"

"Fine with me." I looked at Max.

Max nodded and Kate beamed. Everything was perfect—except for the uneasy feeling.

After I washed the dishes and the kids were asleep, I put on my nightgown and got into bed. Max rolled to greet me. "You look beautiful tonight." He touched my cheek. "Glowing."

It's the sunburn. I smiled. Max kissed me softly then with increasing urgency. I bit his lip and he moaned. As we made love, I glimpsed my reflection in the dresser mirror, my eyes staring over Max's shoulder. I flashed to the woman on the beach and suddenly had the sense of a presence in the room—watching.

Later, after Max was asleep, I slipped on my nightgown and went downstairs. The night air was cool as I leaned against the wall and smoked. Suddenly I heard a voice. It was muffled, as though speaking from behind a veil. *You putting Saran Wrap on that list?* I laughed aloud, aware of how crazy I'd have looked if anyone was watching. *Maybe what I've lost is my mind.*

I took another drag of my cigarette. For my women's studies classes in college, I had to read a book called *The Total Woman,* a backlash to the feminist movement advocating subservience to your husband to get whatever you wanted. To cook, clean, worship, adore, and obey him, and to spice up your sex-life by greeting him at the door wearing nothing but Saran Wrap.

As I thought about the woman on the beach, it occurred to me—even though there are degrees of choice involved, a woman *being* wrapped in black and a woman wrapping *herself* in Saran Wrap—really amounts to the same thing. Suddenly I knew what had been missing all day. I had misplaced myself.

11

The Women's Club shopping bus turned onto the highway, heading toward Al Khobar. At both checkpoints, the armed guards stepped on the bus, glanced down the aisle, then got off. They apparently didn't consider a busload of women in baggy clothing much of a threat.

Amy, Bonita, and I planned to spend most our time exploring the traditional Arab souqs before going to Safeway. We had been told to bring coolers to store perishables for the ride home, so I bought a small Igloo at a garage sale. I noticed the other women had enormous coolers and wondered if I should upgrade for the next trip.

Almost everyone else had boarded when I got on, so I walked down the aisle feeling like the new kid on the bus. Amy and Bonita were talking to the women's club president. Sissie smiled and waved, but she was sitting with someone.

I passed Bobbi, who nodded, but kept talking to her seatmate. "Can you believe how fat she's gotten? Soon she'll need a jumbo-sized abaya." They laughed.

The only empty seat in the first half of the bus was beside Rebecca, who clutched a tote-bag and stared out the window—smiling, rocking, and humming. I hesitated. Rebecca obviously needed help, but I didn't think I could sit beside her for an hour. Feeling very un-Christian, I hurried on before she noticed me and took a window seat in the back.

The Mercedes bus had plush seats with crisp white cloths covering the headrests. The over-chilled air and tinted windows made the bus feel like a long cave on wheels. As we picked up speed, I watched the desert rush by. When we passed a herd of camels I thought of the disastrous trip to the amusement park. It had been just the week before, but seemed long ago.

"Camels have the right of way, you know." Bonita was in the seat beside me. "They're like royalty over here. It costs thousands of riyals if you hit a camel. Look!" She pointed out the window and I saw a triangular sign with a picture of a camel: Camel Crossing.

The bus passed a truck filled with sheep bearing red Xs. *The sacred and the sacrificed.* I didn't want to think about the sheep on the beach, so I looked at Bonita. "How's your job?"

"It's okay. Today's my day off."

"How does that work, exactly?" I asked. "Your job."

"I'm called a 'casual.' Anybody married to an Ocmara employee is a casual, even a teacher or a dentist," Bonita said. "I have no benefits and make practically nothing."

"That doesn't seem fair," I said.

"It's not. If I was doing hair or decorating fucking cakes I could write my own ticket."

"Why's that?" I asked.

"Because women's home businesses are considered hobbies and don't require work-permits." Bonita shrugged. "They can charge as much as they want."

"Really?" I wondered what I could do out of my house.

"And the gals running classes sponsored by the Women's Club don't need work-permits, either. But if it's a real job, you have to have one."

I vaguely recalled something from orientation. If a spouse was caught working without a permit, the employee could be admonished for his wife's misdeeds, or he could be fired. There was a psychologist on Al Hassa who worked illegally out of her home without a work-permit. Fortunately, she left before she was discovered.

"My job sucks, but I'd go nuts over here doing nothing." Bonnie saw my tight smile. "Oops."

She examined the ends of her red ponytail then nudged me. "How *do* you do it?"

"Not very well." I laughed. That had always been my answer when I worked full-time. Now it felt like the only hard work I did was trying not to go crazy.

"Seriously? What do you do all day?"

I ticked off activities on my fingers. "Clean house, do laundry, bake cookies, cook dinner, supervise homework, and adore Max." I smiled. "I've found total fulfillment."

In truth, every day I struggled out of bed before dawn to jog on the beach. Before Max came home I made myself pretty. My days were a mind-numbing vacuum. All week I'd tried to talk myself into feeling happy. It was crazy-making. *No wonder I didn't want to sit beside Rebecca.*

"All that domesticity gives me the creeps," Bonita said with a shudder. "The only thing domestic about me is that I live in a house."

I laughed.

"Seriously," she whispered. "I saw you watching that awful video at the welcome coffee. Why don't you look for a job?" Bonita glanced around. "It makes all this more bearable."

I shifted uncomfortably, ashamed to admit Max was holding me back.

"And it's nice to have my own money. I couldn't stand being given an allowance."

With that she hit the mark. Max left riyals on the dresser so I could just take what I needed and never made me explain where it went. Being the sole breadwinner was salve for Max's wounded ego after years of under-employment. But I hated being dependent.

"I plan to look for a job as soon as we get our shipment." I smiled, hoping Bonita wouldn't see how pitiful I felt.

"Good." Bonita nodded like she had accomplished something important—saved a housewife.

I'd seen postings on the bulletin board for crossing guards and receptionists. Once, Max saw me looking and pulled me away. I looked back— like a child in front of a pet store longing for the puppy in the window— knowing the answer was "No."

Once parked in the Safeway lot, we filed past the Filipino driver and stepped off the bus, blinking in the sun. Heat radiated from the pavement and noxious fumes filled the heavy air. Amy was waiting with an eager smile, a red backpack on her shoulder, blonde hair in a ponytail. With her big black backpack, Bonita looked like she could be hiking the Andes. I had my blue backpack, automatic camera tucked inside.

Together, we crossed the parking lot toward the marketplace. Entering the Al Khobar souq felt like stepping into a hole and falling into a foreign world. Tiny, dimly-lit shops lined a maze of narrow alleys. Male shopkeepers hawked their wares while Middle Eastern music blared from radios. The souq teemed with Saudi men and women. We three were clearly in the minority.

Sheila Flaherty

I pulled out my camera and surreptitiously snapped pictures. Peering through the lens, I suddenly saw a matawah with a whip surveying the crowd. I nudged Amy and Bonita. "Matawah sighting." They followed my gaze.

"Let's go the other way," Bonita whispered.

We turned, trying to be inconspicuous, and hurried through the textile souq, where bolts of colorful fabric lined the shelves. In the kitchen souq, stalls displayed brass pots, dellas, spice and coffee grinders. Amy examined what looked like thick wooden spoons.

"What are these?" she asked the shopkeeper.

"Molds for *mamool*." He smiled. "Cookies made with dates."

Next were the spice merchants, displaying fragrant baskets of cardamom pods, cinnamon sticks, and cloves. I picked up a heavy muslin bag. On the front was a woman's hand decorated in intricate designs.

"Henna," said the shopkeeper, a young Saudi man. "Smell it."

I breathed in the sweet aroma. "Very nice."

As Bonita and Amy took turns smelling the henna, I noticed baskets filled with small pieces of wood and rough little lumps that looked like resin.

"What are these?" I asked.

"*Ouda*, also called sandalwood," he said, touching the wood. He pointed to the lumps. "The darker of the two is myrrh. The other is frankincense."

"Frankincense and myrrh!" Amy said. "What's it for?"

"It's incense." He held up a wooden and brass container. "This is a *mebkhara*." He dropped a piece of frankincense into the brass bowl and lit it with a match. As it burned, it had the sweet scent of a campfire. The shopkeeper smiled as he waved the smoke into the air.

I took a deep breath. "Sure beats patchouli."

The shopkeeper filled three small bags with sandalwood, frankincense, and myrrh and gave one to each of us. "For you to try at home."

"Thank you," we said.

"You are welcome." He smiled.

"Frankincense and myrrh would make great Christmas presents," I said.

"So would gold!" Amy smiled. "Let's find a gold souq."

Bonita rolled her eyes. I noticed she wore only a Casio sports-watch and thin gold wedding band. Her ears weren't even pierced.

"Oh, come on," I said, nudging her. "It'll be fun."

76

Waving goodbye to the shopkeeper, we continued down the alley until we found a store selling bright yellow 18- and 22-carat gold jewelry. Ropes of gold chains hung from the wall and two Saudi men sat on stools behind a glass display case.

I took out my camera and gestured tentatively. "May I take your picture?" The men straightened and smiled—proud to be captured on film in the midst of their treasures.

"Here's what I want," Amy said. "It's a gold necklace with your name in Arabic."

There were many styles—thin and delicate, thick and heavy, teardrop-shaped pendants that looked like paisley spun from gold. After Amy tried on several necklaces, she picked the one she wanted and had the merchant write it down.

"Makes it easier for Mark to surprise me," she said with a grin.

Continuing down the alley, we found shops devoted to women's clothing and stopped to look at a display of abayas and veils.

"God, I love this," I said. It was exciting to touch what seemed so untouchable. I thought about the woman standing on the ledge in her abaya. I wanted to know how it felt.

Bonita held a veil over her face. "What do you think? Can I pull it off?"

"We'll need abayas, you know," Amy said. "For some trips off the compound."

Abayas were open in the front or had zippers or buttons. Most hit mid-calf, but some were ankle-length. Prices varied widely according to style and material—stiff rayon or polyester, supple nylon or silk. My fingers closed on an abaya that felt seductively soft and I slipped it on. Running my hands over it felt like heaven. It was silk, made by Christian Dior, and 500 SR.

"That's beautiful." Amy stroked the sleeve. "You should get it."

"You think?" Even at US $133, I wanted it.

"Definitely," Amy said. "It's gorgeous."

"What do you think?" I asked Bonita. "Too expensive?"

"Not for a silk Christian Dior." Bonita grinned. "Depends on what you're going to use it for."

We burst into giggles.

"I'll use it for my robe." I imagined how luxurious the silk would feel against my bare skin.

I gave the abaya to the shopkeeper, along with a handful of riyals. Amy and Bonita chose inexpensive nylon abayas, and at the last minute I got one, too—for everyday.

As we were leaving, three Saudi women walked in wearing abayas, hijabs, and masks, but no outer veils. Their dark eyes were exotically lined with kohl.

Bonita nudged me and whispered, "Should we buy you some kohl?"

After dropping our packages at the bus, we went to the Safeway. It was vast as an airplane hangar, air-conditioned, and brightly-lit. Shelves overflowed with food imported from all over the world. Meat counters were filled with beef, chicken, mutton, and camel. There was shrimp, grouper, snapper, pompano, and fish I'd never heard of. Immediately I understood why the women had applauded. We pushed our carts through the store, scratching items from our lists.

In the baking aisle I stocked up on flour, sugar, bags of chocolate chips, and candles for Sam's birthday cake. I wanted to try making his cake from scratch, but bought boxes of cake mix and icing—just in case.

At check-out, I was suddenly afraid I wouldn't have enough riyals, after my extravagant abaya purchase, and relieved to see credit card emblems. I paid with my Visa. Back at the bus, we filled our coolers and settled into seats.

As the bus rolled north to Al Hassa I stared at the desert and thought about the day—the souqs and the Safeway—making new friends. Being with Amy and Bonita had been fun and easy. I was tired, but almost happy.

That night I slipped the silk abaya over my naked body and presented myself to Max.

"Whoa, babe." He patted the bed. "Come here."

The cool silk caressed my body as I walked across the bedroom. I felt exotic and sexy, and had a fleeting image of dark eyes above a mask. *Maybe I should have bought kohl.* Later, I went outside wearing only the abaya. As I leaned against the garden wall in the darkness and smoked my cigarette, I felt truly invisible.

12

The week before Sam's birthday party, I was consumed with preparations. We couldn't take possession of the Land Rover for a month, but one night Max borrowed it and drove us to Rahima for party decorations. Inside a variety store, we passed shelves holding everything from sewing machine oil to cotton balls, before finding party supplies.

"Hey, look at this." Kate held up a greeting card.

It was a picture of an Arab woman in a hijab and mask—head tilted seductively, dark eyes heavily outlined with kohl, "Greetings from Saudi Arabia" garishly printed in gold. It was disturbing on so many levels. I flashed to the women in the souqs and wearing my abaya to bed with Max. *What was I thinking?*

"I want these." Sam held up yellow and blue balloons. They were the colors of his Pele Stars soccer team back home. Sam blinked back tears and I reached out to him, but he turned away. Something in the way he held his shoulders—the rigidity of his thin pale neck—broke my heart.

Midweek, I went to the library, checked out dessert cookbooks, and pored over cake recipes until I found one that looked good. After carefully following the directions it turned out flat and dry. So, using the mixes I'd bought at Safeway, I made a devil's food sheet-cake with white icing. With food coloring and sugar, I created blue and yellow sprinkles to put on top.

At the party, one mom stared down at my cake. "I'll have to give you Sue's number. She had her own bakery back in the States."

"Oh." I felt embarrassed. "Are her cakes nice?"

"They're wonderful and beautifully decorated."

"Are you talking about Sue?" a second mom asked.

"Yes, aren't her cakes amazing?" the first mom replied.

"Sue is amazing! She cleans up!" the second mom said. "There's a waiting list, you have to pay up front then she turns her profits into gold."

"And her cakes are delicious!" the first mom insisted.

"You'll recognize Sue when you see her," the second mom told me. "She's covered in gold jewelry." Sue sounded like a rock star.

Despite my cake, Sam's party was a success. All twelve classmates attended—seven girls and five boys. After bowling, the kids filled the party room where Sam unwrapped GI Joes, a Saudi Monopoly game, a bootleg "Top Gun" video, Match Box cars, and sporting gear. Everyone feasted on pizza, and the cake and gallon of chocolate ice cream were polished off.

Kate and her friends were capable helpers. It was the first time I'd spent with Amanda and Lizzie and I noticed they were borderline precocious—nothing as obvious as heavy make-up and Madonna-style clothing—just the kind of attitude you sense as a parent.

"Anything else we can do, Mrs. Hayes?" Amanda smiled obsequiously.

Amanda was clearly the alpha-girl, already well-developed and wielding the power of her body. Lizzie was determined to emulate her. Throughout the day they exchanged knowing smirks and whispered secrets. I worried about Kate being third wheel.

Sam pulled me aside at the party's end. "Dad said it's okay with him if it's okay with you."

"If what's okay with me?"

"For me to have a sleepover? Just the boys?" Sam's cheeks were flushed with excitement.

"Where are we going to put all of you?"

"They'll go get their sleeping bags!" He clenched his fists under his chin. "Please?"

I smiled. "Of course it's okay."

"Thanks, Mom." Sam ran back to his boys and they let out a whoop.

Late that night, I lay in bed listening to whispers and giggles coming from the kids' rooms. I didn't care if they kept me awake. It was the first night of laughter since we'd been in Saudi—the first full night of normal.

The next day a box arrived for Sam. It had been opened and resealed with tape, our first experience with personal mail being opened.

"Wow, look at this," Sam said, holding up a Garfield shower curtain. "Cool!"

Mom had also included an Evanston T-shirt for each kid, which they pulled on. Then Kate dug through the box, disappointment clouding her face. Mom always sent the other sibling a gift, but there was nothing else for Kate. Tossing the box, I shuddered at the idea of strangers rummaging through presents my mom had lovingly packed. Then it hit me—the visceral certainty something was missing.

"Let's hang it up!" Sam ran toward the bathroom the kids shared.

"Mom, it's so orange," Kate said. "And it stinks!" She was right, the thick vinyl was smelly.

"Well, it certainly brightens things up." I hugged Kate, knowing she felt left out.

Later that night we called Mom. After Sam talked, he gave Kate the phone.

"Thanks for the T-shirt, Grandma." As Kate listened, I knew my gut had been right. "What horse? There wasn't a horse." Kate's eyes filled with tears and she handed me the phone.

"Hi, Mom." I pulled Kate close. "What were you telling Kate?" Not wanting to upset her, I'd never told Mom about our experiences with customs. I kept conversations and letters breezy and upbeat. Now I struggled with what to say. "Don't worry," I said to Mom, while smiling at Kate. "It probably got separated in the postal center. We'll check on it." But my instincts told me the horse was gone forever, and I began to worry about our shipment.

After Sam's party I biked to the library to return the cookbooks.

"Did you enjoy the books?" The woman at the desk had a European accent.

"Yes, but I wound up using cake mix." I laughed.

She glanced at the check-out slip. "Sarah, my name is Andrea. I'm the librarian."

"Did I meet you at the Women's Club?"

"No, we haven't met. I don't go to the Women's Club." Andrea's eyes twinkled behind her glasses and her smile spoke volumes. "Come, let me show you around."

As Andrea gave me a tour, I learned she was from Greece and married to an Ocmara engineer. Even in her position as librarian, she was classified as a casual.

"I would do it for free," she said. "I love the challenge."

Andrea stocked the shelves with the most recent titles, no easy feat with Saudi censorship. I told her about our experience with Sam's birthday package.

"How did Garfield get through, when Kate's horse was confiscated?"

"It's often a mystery." Andrea shrugged. "And shows how arbitrary Saudi censors can be."

The library became one of my sanctuaries. The modern, two-story building was cool and quiet. I could count on Andrea for interesting conversation and good book recommendations. Sometimes, I just read magazines. Issues were a couple months behind, but there was an impressive collection of sports, news, travel, decorating, and women's periodicals.

Magazines went through rigorous examination by a censorship department. There were strict regulations against sexual content and political topics, especially about Saudi. Pictures and ads with too much skin were inked over, or the entire page ripped out.

Sometimes censorship was so extreme it was actually funny. When Max bought an inflatable raft for the beach, the people in bathing suits on the outside of the box had been covered in black marker, making it look like three abaya-clad women were floating on a raft.

During our second trip to Al Khobar, Bonita, Amy, and I wandered into a bookstore in a mall. Leaving them in fiction, I explored the stacks. In psychology and health, I found a medical textbook on gynecological diseases with pages of descriptions, causes, and treatment—each with a close-up photograph of a vagina. Every vagina had been blacked out with magic marker.

Holding the book against my chest, I crept up to Amy and Bonita. "Look," I whispered. I flipped the pages and we started to laugh.

"If your hoohah ain't covered in black marker," Bonita gasped in a Texas twang, "Your doctor won't recognize your disease!"

Flushed with embarrassment, Amy laughed so hard she snorted.

As we continued leafing through the book, we laughed harder. Disapproving looks from male salesclerks only made it impossible to stop. As one clerk started toward us, I quickly re-shelved the book. We fled the store and hurried down the marble hallway to the ladies hammam. Safely inside, we howled out loud, before finally pulling ourselves together. For the rest of the day, it took only a suggestive glance to lose it again.

13

I thought of her as *the woman on the beach*, and mentioned her to no one—she was my secret. I began to think of us as in a relationship, but it was more like the relationship you'd have with a feral cat than with another person. Every morning I left through the sliding doors, slipped out the back gate, and walked to the beach. In the predawn light I ran north along the hard sand at the edge of the surf, turned around at the end of the beach, and ran back.

All the while, I looked for her. Sometimes I sensed her nearby, or felt the intensity of her gaze. I'd slow to a walk, collecting shells or pretending to watch fish in the shallows. Once, I caught her reflection as I kneeled, examining crustaceans at the bottom of a tide-pool. She stood high on the ledge where I'd first seen her and was reflected in the water like a tiny black bird perched on my shoulder. I watched until she backed out of sight.

Like approaching an animal in the wild, I let her become accustomed to my presence— avoiding sudden movements or direct stares. Gradually we closed the gap. One morning I rounded the curve to see her standing on the beach near the water. She watched as I approached, stood motionless as I passed. She was gone when I ran back, but I was happy. It was a start.

Weeks passed when I didn't see her, and I worried. Then, one day, she was walking south as I ran north. I slowed to a walk and she continued toward me. Up close, I saw the slender outline of her frame under her abaya and noticed she wore an ankle-bracelet lined with tiny silver bells. Her wrists were delicate and she had long thin fingers, the hands of a young woman.

"Hello." I smiled.

She nodded, but didn't speak. We passed each other and kept going.

Although I ran the same time every morning, she appeared only randomly. I was always happy to see her and greeted her—"Hello." "Good morning." "Hi." But she just nodded and never said a word. I wondered if she spoke English. After I said, *"Marhaba,"* and she only nodded, I wondered if she spoke at all.

I wondered what she looked like under her veil. I longed to see her face and talk to her. The longer that eluded me, the more seductive it became. I hungered for her friendship. She seemed a loner, like me, and I convinced myself we could be allies. *She's going to help me make this work.*

Within Al Hassa, a constant flow of people left for short holidays, repatriation vacations, and for good—while a steady stream of new employees and their families moved in. Although I was welcomed by the Women's Club when I first arrived, I was quickly forgotten when other new women came along. Like small towns everywhere, a new face provided fodder for gossip and speculation. I wasn't unique or outgoing, so my novelty wore off quickly.

"You're going to have to try harder," Max chided as he rubbed my back.

We were in bed after I'd had a particularly hard day. The urge to sleep overcame my determination to run, and I'd paid the price with despair and self-loathing. All afternoon I played sad music on the stereo and wallowed in misery. *Sunday morning coming down.*

"Easy for you to say," I mumbled against his chest.

After two months in Saudi, I still had only Amy and Bonita as friends. We went on shopping trips and to Women's Club events and made pool, beach, and lunch dates. But Amy had young children and Bonita had her job. That left lots of lonely space. Sam's party had given me temporary focus, but when it was over I felt even more adrift.

"Why don't you just call some of the other women from the Women's Club?" Max asked.

During our years together, we'd been at this empathic impasse many times. Having always been outgoing, Max didn't understand my shyness. I'd never been popular, but always had deep, meaningful friendships. Like most introverts, I required a great deal of solitude to replenish my soul. But in Saudi I had more solitude than my soul could bear, and there was no one deep and true to turn to.

"Why don't you call Bobbi and ask her to lunch?" Max suggested.

"Because Bobbi has no interest in being friends with me." I'd told Max about the awkward moments at the Women's Club meetings and on the bus.

"Come on, babe, you know she likes you."

It was true Bobbi could be charming and effusive, but I figured that was a Southern thing. There were advantages to being a silent observer with a social work background. Hovering around the edges, I heard conversations and witnessed the exchange of meaningful glances. It wasn't intentional data collection, it unfolded naturally. As I watched the interactions, I recognized a number of different social systems at work.

First, there was the Southern culture. Since most of America's oil industry is in Texas, Louisiana, and Oklahoma, the majority of American employees were from the South. My mother, born and reared in Georgia, taught me that graciousness doesn't guarantee inclusion. Southern systems are notoriously tight and can be impossible to break into. Bobbi was a Southerner through and through. Her welcome casseroles were superficial gestures, instead of genuine acts of friendship.

The Brits and other Europeans had their own cliques. Women mingled at the Women's Club, but true friendships were rare across cultural lines, especially Western and Arab. But the most pervasive system was based on status. Like military wives, we were identified by our husbands' rank at Ocmara. A woman could become part of a social network because of her husband's position, but that only guaranteed inclusion, not friendship.

I understood why we were invited to the Mitchells' social events, but I was not included in Bobbi's gang. As a supervisor's wife, Bobbi belonged to the high-status club. It was not a club I wanted to join, because the dues were too high. We would have to stay in Saudi for much longer than three years, a prospect I couldn't imagine. Max, on the other hand, desperately longed to be part of that club. When we were invited to Bobbi and Ray's July 4th barbeque, Max was atwitter.

"I don't get it." Max stopped rubbing my back "You don't even want to make more friends."

"You're right!" I pushed away. "You don't get it."

I wanted more true friends like Amy and Bonita. But the more I knew, the less likely that seemed. At the Women's Club I heard vicious gossip about women who never left their homes, prescription drug abuse, infidelities, domestic violence, rampant alcoholism. A lot of crazy shit went on in Al Hassa. Although I ached with loneliness, it felt safer to have an imaginary relationship with the woman on the beach, than attempt a real one with someone I couldn't trust.

Sheila Flaherty

July 4th was our first holiday in Saudi. It wasn't outlawed, like Christmas and Easter, but it wasn't promoted. Being in a foreign country as fundamentally oppressive as Saudi Arabia made us realize what Independence Day is really about. Not only does it commemorate our country's founding, but it celebrates the God-given right to freedom of religion and self-expression.

All day, our family was overwhelmed by homesickness. We missed our hokey hometown parade with marching bands that never failed to make me cry. We missed sitting on blankets watching fireworks reflected in Lake Michigan while *Stars and Stripes Forever* played on portable radios. We missed the company of family and friends.

"I want to go home." Sam lay on the sofa petting Mimi while cradling a soccer ball. He wore his soccer uniform—blue shorts and a blue-and-yellow striped shirt with number 5 on the back.

Every year the Pele Stars participated in Evanston's Fourth of July parade. With coaches and parents walking along, the kids passed soccer balls back and forth down Central Street, showing off fancy foot-work or head-butting balls to teammates.

"Me, too." Kate echoed from the other sofa.

Even Max moped around, looking like he didn't know what to do with his hands. Back home Max manned the grill in our backyard, feeding the hungry multitudes after the parade.

It had been a lazy morning. We'd slept in and eaten pancakes at home instead of waffles at the Surf House. The July heat held us hostage. No one wanted to ride our bikes in temperatures in the high 90's. It was late afternoon by the time the four of us went to the Mitchells' barbeque, where the party was already in full swing.

"Happy Fourth!" Ray boomed, sid and coke in hand. He planted his customary kiss on my cheek. I knew it was coming, but shuddered with revulsion when I felt his cold wet lips.

Bobbi greeted us wearing a low-cut white blouse and blue miniskirt, a red scarf tied patriotically around her neck. "Why, aren't you sweet!" she said, upon seeing the cupcakes I'd decorated with red and blue sprinkles. She gestured to a houseboy who whisked them away.

Red, white, and blue balloons hung from the dining room chandelier and cubes of cheese were speared with American-flag toothpicks. Hamburgers, hot dogs, baked beans, and potato salad lent an air of authenticity.

"Come here." Bobbi beckoned. "I want you to meet our son, Billy."

Billy was a tall, sullen, 16-year-old with Bobbi's red hair. Acne competed with the freckles splashed across his face. He was heading toward the backyard with a bottle of cola when Bobbi called out, "Billy, wait up. I want you to meet the Hayes family."

"Hi, Billy." Max held out his hand. "Nice to meet you." Billy shook Max's hand with a studied expression of boredom and disdain.

"Billy's home from boarding school for the summer." As Bobbi touched his shoulder, Billy jerked away.

"Where do you go to school?" I asked.

"Switzerland." Billy gazed longingly toward kids congregated in the yard. "I have to go."

"Nice to meet you," I called after him as he headed out the door.

"All the returning students are out there," Bobbi said.

Since Saudi schools went only through ninth grade, "Ocmara Brats" attended boarding school starting sophomore year, returning for Christmas and summer vacations. This created a premature empty-nest syndrome that broke the hearts and spirits of many mothers in Al Hassa.

"Ya'll go on out there," Bobbi told Kate and Sam. "Kids' party is in the back." Looking relieved, the kids followed Billy.

"Help yourselves to food and drink," Ray said. "We've got plenty."

As I was spooning potato salad on my plate, one of Bobbi's friends sidled up to me. I couldn't remember her name, so I just smiled.

"I see you met Billy," she said.

"Oh, yeah."

"Too bad about all that." She filled her plate. "Isn't it?"

"All what?" I asked.

"Bobbi didn't tell you?" She tilted her head. "Billy's in trouble for bad grades and drinking. He's on probation and they're worried the school won't take him back." She frowned and shook her head. "Poor Bobbi, she's at her wit's end with that one."

"I bet she is," I said. "That's terrible." I suddenly wondered if the bottle Billy was carrying had alcohol in it. From the panic I felt, I was sure of it.

"That's the problem with boarding school." The woman sighed. "Too little supervision. Are you worried about your kids?"

I peered out the back window. *Was Billy drinking?* I couldn't tell.

"My kids are still little," I said. "We'll be gone before they have to go to boarding school."

I resisted the urge to run into the backyard and grab Kate and Sam.

"How are you settling in?" she asked.

I was confused by the abrupt shift in topic, but then I understood. Bobbi was standing beside her. "Oh, fine," I said. "Our shipment arrives next week. We're excited."

"Good luck with that." The woman and Bobbi exchanged glances.

"What?" I asked.

"Oh, nothing," Bobbi said. "Here, have some baked beans." She dumped a pile on my plate.

I looked out back again, checking on the kids. They seemed fine, so I went to find Max.

Throughout the evening, I had a glass of wine, then another. As the hours passed, I grew more homesick. Everything felt forced, like we were trying too hard to celebrate Independence Day in a country where we were anything but. I was standing by the sliding doors looking out into the night sky when I felt a heavy arm across my shoulders.

"Your cupcakes were a huge hit." Ray's breath was hot on my cheek.

Startled, I looked into his bloodshot eyes. "Oh, thanks."

"They're all gone," Ray said, swaying.

"I'm glad people liked them."

"I hear you're a runner," he slurred, clearly sloshed.

"Yes, I am."

"It's not safe to run in Saudi," Ray said. "They'll arrest you for sure."

"Really?" I felt a bolt of alarm.

"Well, there was this guy? An expat?" Ray grinned and I knew he was starting a joke. "One day he was running and a Saudi security guard stopped him." Ray paused, waiting for a reaction.

"What happened?"

"The guard screamed, 'What are you doing?'" Ray yelled in a bad Arab accent, getting everyone's attention. The crowd closed in. Max appeared at my side.

"'Running,' the expat said." Ray took a dramatic pause. ""Ah, ha!' the guard handcuffed him. 'What are you running from?'"

Laughter erupted, though it was clear most people had heard the joke before. I stared at Ray.

"Get it?" he asked.

I smiled. "Isn't it about the scarily arbitrary nature of the Saudi legal system?"

There was a long silence.

"You're cute," Ray said, squeezing my shoulder. He looked at Max. "She's cute."

Max grinned proudly. "Yes, she is."

Pulling away from Ray's grasp, I pushed through the crowd. My chest tightened, my hands and face were sweating, and I couldn't breathe. I rushed toward the sliding doors. In the backyard I took deep gulps of air and collected the kids.

"Oh, Mom, can't we stay longer?" Kate pleaded.

"You've got school in the morning." I ignored her exasperated sighs and rolled eyes. She followed as I hustled Sam toward the door.

I found Max in the middle of an adoring crowd. "We need to go." I tugged on his arm. "It's late and I'm not feeling well."

Max looked annoyed, but threw his arm around me and acted the dutiful husband. His voice had grown loud, a clear sign he'd overindulged. And as the four of us walked home in the dark, Max wove and stumbled, talking loudly. The kids were in front of us and I could tell by their rigid backs that they knew Max was drunk. I felt an old mix of rage, shame, and sorrow. When an Ocmara security car approached, my heart pounded with fear. I gave Max a warning look.

"Shhhh," I whispered. "You're too loud." Max's eyes flashed angrily, but he caught himself and the car drove off.

At home, the kids went to bed while I washed my cupcake plate. When I got to the bedroom Max was sprawled on the bed in his underwear, one foot firmly planted on the floor. He was pale, eyes bloodshot and glassy. I dressed for bed, keeping the path to the bathroom clear. Soon Max was in there vomiting and it continued throughout the night. He was finally done at dawn, just in time to get ready for work. Before leaving, he sat on the bed smiling sheepishly.

"I'm sorry." His eyes filled with tears. "It won't happen again."

"Okay," I said.

At the door he looked back at me. "I'm done. I promise."

I nodded and smiled. We both knew how many times he'd promised that before.

When the kids left for school, I went back to bed, but couldn't go back to sleep. The night's events looped through my head until I pulled on running clothes and went to the beach. It was too hot to run, so I walked in the surf. Even in a baseball cap and sunglasses, I squinted in the sun's glare. I dripped with sweat, my skin burned, and I was furious with Max.

Drinking was a fundamental part of growing up in Chicago, with reputations built or ruined around tolerance for alcohol. There were those who wound up crashed on other peoples' sofas and those who wound up crashed into trees. Sometimes, capacity was identity.

"I'm Irish," Max said, proudly. "Therefore, I drink!"

I'd partied with the best of them only stopping when pregnant with Kate. Suddenly, the smell of booze made me gag. Once, after a night out with friends, Max passed out in our bed. He was stinking drunk, but I was the one throwing up.

When Kate was born Max bought champagne. I drank one flute and he finished the bottle. The additional eight months I abstained while nursing Kate turned me into a "lightweight," wasted after one margarita. Half a martini put me under like a "roofie." While I usually stuck with a Corona or glass of wine, Max drank whatever was being poured.

Max occasionally tried cutting back. After a particularly embarrassing binge, he even tried sobriety. He attended a few AA meetings, but came away convinced he wasn't alcoholic because he'd never "hit bottom."

"I can stop anytime I want to," Max declared. He just didn't want to.

When Max drank he started happy, got progressively louder, and if he had too much, he became angry and irrational. I never knew when he would cross that line. When I was young and stupid, this made him seem dangerous and sexy. When I got older it just made him dangerous.

As I waded in the surf, I caught a flash of orange. A security car was parked in the desert, just yards from the beach. The two guards were talking and didn't seem to be watching me. I resisted the urge to freeze and look suspicious, but I was afraid. *What if they're following me?* I forced myself to breathe while wondering if I should make a run for it—then I remembered Ray's stupid joke. Casually, I turned and walked down the beach and home without incident. But my heart raced, my muscles were tensed, and my sweat had the pungent stench of fear.

Once home, I decided to call Bonita and Amy instead of wallowing in misery. When Bonita was off we'd sometimes get together at one of our homes or have lunch at the Surf House. It was too hot to play tennis. Gulf water temperature was 85 degrees, so ocean swimming was like taking a warm bath inside a sauna. We chose to meet at the pool, which had chilled water.

Mid-afternoon we were the only ones there. Wearing conservative bathing suits and hats, we sat under umbrellas with bottled water and snacks. That day the sun burned with extra intensity. Sweat slicked our bodies and swarms of moisture-seeking flies buzzed our wet skin and eyes, keeping us in constant motion— blinking, flicking, and waving.

"Where the hell are these flies coming from," Bonita asked. "A rotting carcass?"

"Yeah, did somebody sacrifice something for the Fourth?" Amy asked.

"Only our independence," I said.

Amy stared into space. "I didn't know I'd feel so sad."

"Me either," Bonita said. "I keep humming *America the Beautiful*."

I started to sing, "Oh, beautiful, for spacious skies."

Bonita joined in, "For amber waves of grain." She pointed at Amy.

"For purple mountain majesties, above the fruited plain." Amy's voice was surprisingly powerful. We sang the rest together, clapping at the end.

"Check for matawain." Bonita looked around. "Three half-naked women singing *America the Beautiful* will be arrested for sure!" We laughed, but knew it was true.

"Ya'll ready for your shipments?" Amy asked. Our shipments must have come on the same boat, because they were all scheduled for delivery the next week. "It's like Christmas in July!"

"Yeah, it's about time," Bonita said. "Stuff's been here since early June."

"I can't wait," I said.

"Me either," Bonita said. "But I'm worried about our washer and dryer."

In orientation we'd learned that "boycott laws" prevented Ocmara from telling new employees in advance that Saudi boycotts numerous brands of appliances and other items. They were vague about the list, but it included everything with any relationship to Israel—Zenith, RCA, Ford, Firestone, Coca-Cola, and Sears—and hundreds of others. Whatever fell under Saudi boycotts would be confiscated and we'd be reimbursed a percentage of the value for replacement. Bonita and Steve had a Kenmore washer and dryer.

"I hope they come through." Amy patted Bonita's arm.

"Me, too," I said. Thankfully, I'd attended the orientation before packing up the house. We'd planned to leave our old washer and dryer for our tenants and buy a new set for Saudi—at Sears. Instead, we included a washer and dryer in our monthly rent.

"I still can't believe they didn't tell us until after everything was gone," Bonita said.

"What do they do with all the stuff they confiscate?" Amy said.

"I bet they take them home," Bonita said. "The houses of customs officials are filled with brand new appliances. They're making Israel work for them!"

"Their home libraries are extensive, with books, art, and magazines," I said.

"They watch videos on new VCRs and TVs!" Amy said.

Bonita laughed, but still looked worried. Amy and I were worried for her. Meanwhile, the assault from the flies had intensified. They landed on our lips and eyes, crawled into our nostrils. We were in constant movement, twitching like cattle.

"Jesus, God! This is making me crazy!" Bonita jumped up and took a running dive into the pool. She surfaced, dark hair slick like a seal.

I walked down the pool stairs, the contrast between hot air and chilly water making for a torturous descent. When water reached my waist I took a deep breath and made the plunge. After the initial shock it was pure pleasure to glide through cool, clear, sunlight-dappled water.

Amy stood on the deck looking down at us. Then she backed up a few steps, took a running leap, and cannon-balled into the middle of the pool.

Whenever we tried to get out, we were swarmed by flies, so we spent the rest of the afternoon as three talking, laughing heads—staying in the pool until our fingers and toes were wrinkled, our lips blue, and we were shivering.

"Let's go to my house." Amy's teeth were chattering. "I'll make hot chocolate."

We biked to Amy's and shut off the air-conditioning until we warmed up. The day felt uniquely carefree. We'd covered many topics, but there had been no gossip or mean speculations about other women. Our friendship felt real and true. We were in the trenches together and had each others' backs. It had been our best time together—we had no idea it would be our last.

14

Max and I were waiting by the front window when the movers arrived. Max had the day off so he could receive the shipment and sign the documents. My signature meant nothing in Saudi. The moving-van backed into our driveway and three men hopped out. Then an Ocmara passenger van pulled up with six more men. All were Pakistani.

"Mr. Hayes?" The man who was boss held a clipboard while the others opened the truck and formed a human conveyor-belt. We'd had an allowance for the US movers to pack everything, and Saudi customs required a content description on the outside of every box. The boxes were numbered and a master-list created. Max and the boss stood in the meager shade of the palm tree checking numbers off the master-list as each box was unloaded.

Inside, I tried to direct boxes to the proper rooms. But the movers were fast and spoke little English. After running up and down the stairs for an hour, my thighs were quivering. I gave up and let them put boxes wherever they could. Meanwhile, I showed them where to place our few pieces of furniture—a small blue table, Kate's electronic piano, a mirror, and bookcases.

After everything was delivered, we were told to unpack, noting anything missing or damaged. An agent would return in a week to collect trash and make sure everything was okay. Max signed off and the men left. The house was strangely quiet after all the frantic activity.

"Where should we start?" Max was flushed and sweaty.

It was hot inside the house. My clothes and hair were soaked with sweat. I bumped up the air-conditioner, poured us water, and got two sharp knives. "Start opening boxes. Let's unpack the downstairs first."

With the first box I had an uneasy sense of what was to come. The contents had been unwrapped and tossed back into the box—like our suitcases the night we arrived in Saudi. "Oh, God," I said. "Look at this mess."

"Same here," Max said.

We moved box to box, cutting tape, opening flaps. Everything had been rummaged through. Kitchen items survived the best. Plates, bowls, and mugs remained wrapped in paper, but a crystal decanter was shattered. *Was it broken because it was for liquor?*

Lamps shades were dented, picture frame glass was cracked. CDs were loose in a box, some out of their cases and scratched. Our stereo, VCR, video-camera, and typewriter made it through unscathed. Tennis racquets, soccer and basketballs were intact, but our Yahtzee game, checkers, and playing cards were gone. When the kids got home, boxes with their things were in their rooms, ready to unpack.

"Hey guys, look at this." Sam pointed to a spot on his globe. "They marked something off." We stared until it registered.

"They marked off Israel," Max said

"Why would they do that?" Sam asked.

Max and I exchanged a cautionary glance, hesitant to shatter Sam's innocence. Many friends back home were Jewish.

"It's complicated, sweetie." I smoothed his hair. "We'll talk about it later."

"I wonder what they did to the atlas," Sam said. Sure enough, maps of Israel were ripped out. Index pages were intact, but Israel was marked off wherever it appeared.

Kneeling on the kitchen floor, unpacking cookware, I pondered what powerful hatred it takes to pretend another country doesn't exist.

"Mommy." Kate was crying. "Is there another box of my stuff?"

"What's wrong?"

"All my horses and dolls are gone." Kate no longer played with dolls, but had a Barbie and treasured baby-doll. I remembered the screaming child reaching for Ernie at the airport.

"Maybe they're in another box." I stood up and called to Max. "Honey, I need you. Kate can't find her dolls or horses."

"Oh, shit," he said.

We searched everywhere, but the dolls were gone. As was Kate's collection of model horses and stuffed animals. "I'm so sorry, sweetie," I said, then suddenly saw the soft floppy sock-monkey flattened at the bottom of a box. "Wait. Here's Smiley!"

Smiley once had buttons for eyes and a big red-yarn smile, but an eye was missing and the smile had been kissed away. Smiley had been loved into anonymity and therefore had probably gone unrecognized as being of animal form. Kate wrapped the monkey in a hug.

"I'll check with the movers tomorrow to see if they forgot any boxes," Max said, squeezing Kate. But he didn't look hopeful.

It was a hard night. Max and I tried to explain the globe and atlas without sounding bigoted. We tried to reassure and comfort an inconsolable Kate. Late that night, I found Kate clutching Smiley as she slept, thumb in her mouth. It was heartbreaking.

I unpacked over the next few days. All our books had been thrown into one big box, and surprisingly, my tiny Bible made it. But I was shocked as I leafed through my one art book. Page after page was torn or defaced— Rodin's *The Kiss*, Botticelli's *The Birth of Venus,* Picasso's *Mother and Child*— arms, necks, and breasts violently slashed with black marker. What Amy, Bonita, and I had found hilarious in the bookstore was no longer amusing.

Knowing Christmas decorations were banned in Saudi, I'd packed only a small box with unsentimental ornaments. The box was gone—as was my pink folder. I sat crying in the darkened living room. The idea of hands and eyes going through our personal belongings— destroying or throwing them away without a thought—was unbearable.

Most heartbreaking was the loss of our home-movies. We knew not to ship commercial videos, but assumed home-movies were okay. Had customs officials viewed them, they'd have seen kindergarten graduations and birthday parties. Max submitted a claim, but weeks then months went by. Whenever Max followed-up he was told, *"Enshallah"*—God willing. But we never got them back. To this day I regret putting them in the shipment. I wish I'd known not to.

Two days after our shipment arrived, Amy was at my door, her eyes red and swollen.

"I can't believe it," she cried.

All afternoon Amy mourned what was lost. Dolls, teddy bears, and videos were missing. They'd also lost home-movies and photo-albums. I was grateful I'd brought only an envelope of family photographs that some-how made it through airport customs. Our personal losses were great, but Amy and I ached for our children. We consoled each other over homemade cookies and cups of hot tea. The next morning my phone rang.

"Goddamn, fucking Arabs," Bonita screamed. "I followed their god-damn stupid rules and the fucking bastards still took all my shit. Our stereo and new washer and dryer are gone. Fuckers!"

"I'm so sorry," I said.

"Fucking assholes!" Bonita slammed down the phone.

Amy and I handled our losses with tears and cookies, Bonita handled hers with a stream of enraged phone calls. All afternoon and the next day whenever she found something missing or broken she'd call and loudly berate "fucking Ocmara," "fucking Saudi Arabia," and all the other "fuck-ers" that had "fucked with" her stuff.

I took a break whenever Bonita called. Her rants were so extreme they were funny. And hearing her scream what I was feeling was cathartic. Between Bonita's calls, Amy and I checked in with each other.

"Have you heard the latest?" Amy asked.

"Yeah, I'm thinking we need to make an intervention," I said.

"Cookies?"

"Might take more than cookies." I laughed.

Mid-afternoon Bonita's calls stopped. I was calling her when Max walked in early from work. "Hi, babe," I said, hanging up.

Max looked angry. "We have to talk."

"What's wrong?" I felt a wash of fear.

"Who've you been talking to all day?"

"Just Bonita and Amy," I said. "Why?"

Max put an audiotape in the stereo and Bonita's voice filled the room ranting about her ruined photograph album and her hatred of "fucking Ocmara" and "fucking Saudis." Occasionally I heard my own sympathetic response. Max hit stop.

"Where did you get that?" I asked.

"Mohammed gave it to me."

I stared at Max, sensing I was in trouble, but feeling the adrenalin rush of a bigger, more terrifying truth. "Our phones are tapped?" I glanced around the suddenly alien space in which I'd been living and felt my breath go shallow. "Please don't tell me you knew about this."

I looked into Max's eyes and instantly felt the shift.

"Oh, my God, you knew." My body shook and from somewhere I heard Max's voice, but it was drowned out by the roar in my ears. He walked toward me and I backed away. "Don't touch me," I screamed, flailing my arms.

Max froze and I turned and ran out the front door into the blinding afternoon sun. My feet were bare, but I was only vaguely aware of sizzling pavement and sharp stones ripping into my flesh. I hit the beach and ran by the water. Call to prayer howled in the distance and I caught a flash of orange out of the corner of my eye. *Let the fuckers catch me. Just let them try.*

I ran until I reached the tall wire fence at the end of the beach. Wrapping my fingers through the metal, I stared up at the rolls of barbed-wire and screamed. I shook the fence as a prisoner shakes the bars holding her captive. I shook until my arms ached and my fingers bled. Finally, pressing my face against the wire, I clung to the fence and cried. When my legs gave out, I let go and lowered myself to the ground.

Gradually, I caught my breath. In the quiet I heard the gentle lapping of waves on the beach, my heartbeat, and my ragged breath. When nightfall prayer began I slowly limped home, letting warm saltwater wash over my feet and soothe my torn soles. Walking under the ledge, I caught a fleeting glance of the woman standing high above me. When I looked up, she was gone.

The phone woke me at ten the next morning. The ringing stopped when the answering machine picked up, but resumed a minute later. I stared at the phone, willing it to stop. It stopped and started a few more times before the house descended into quiet. Sitting up sent a wave of pain throughout my body. Bruises and angry cuts crisscrossed my palms. When I stood, searing pain shot through my feet. I immersed myself in a warm bath, soaking and refilling for the next hour.

Early afternoon the doorbell rang, followed by pounding. "Sarah, it's me!" I limped to the door and opened it. Bonita stood holding a cardboard box. "Jesus, what happened to you?"

"Max beat me up." At her alarmed expression, I smiled. "Just kidding."

Over glasses of iced tea we recounted our stories from the day before.

"Ocmara gave Steve a choice whether to stay or leave," Bonita said. "But I didn't. We don't have kids or debts. There's no reason for us to stay. The money isn't worth it."

I was sad, but not surprised. I wished I was that free to go. "When are you leaving?"

"Tonight. It's a voluntary deportation, so I get my exit-visa immediately. Steve will stay another week to repack the boxes." She smiled and stood.

"I'll miss you." I already felt the loss. "Please keep in touch."

"I will," Bonita said. "But I won't call."

We hugged and she was gone. I opened the box she'd left and found her abaya. Gathering it to me, I remembered the day she'd bought it. And I thought about what she whispered to me while we were hugging goodbye.

"Get out of here, Sarah," Bonita said. "Before it kills you." I wish I'd been able to.

Friday night, Max rubbed my back as we lay in bed.

"I'd heard rumors about phone-taps," he said, "Nothing for sure."

"You should have told me," I whispered.

"I know, I'm sorry," Max said. "But I thought they were just rumors like all the others."

"What others?"

"This guy on the compound was trying to call a friend living in Israel," Max said. "Every time he dialed the number he was cut off, so eventually he gave up. Then his phone rang and a man with an Arab accent asked if he was trying to call Israel."

I rose on one elbow. "What happened?"

"When the expat said, 'Yes,' the Arab yelled, 'Stop it!' and hung up."

"Is it true?" I asked.

"Who knows?" Max shrugged. "What kind of idiot would try to call Israel from here?"

The kind who doesn't know the phone is tapped. "What other rumors did you hear?"

"A guy was called into his boss's office to talk about his marital problems," Max said.

"Mohammed's office?" I asked.

"Maybe, I don't know." Max sounded impatient. "Anyway, when the guy denied having marital problems, his boss popped a cassette into a tape-player and hit play."

"And then?"

Max looked at me. "The employee heard himself on a phone call fighting with his wife."

We stared at each other. I didn't ask why he hadn't investigated the truth behind these "rumors." It didn't matter anymore. We knew the truth.

"It's alright, babe." Max pulled me close. "We don't have anything to hide."

With Bonita and Steve's departure, I'd been "forgiven" by Ocmara for taking part in "inflammatory" conversations defaming Arabs, Saudi Arabia, and Ocmara. Nothing was said about Ocmara's right to tap our phones. But by that time it was clearly established—as expatriates living in the Kingdom, we had no rights.

I was out of my mind for awhile. The first week my feet hurt too much to walk, so I stayed home. But I felt terrified. *If they opened our mail and tapped our phones, wasn't it possible our home was bugged with microphones and hidden cameras?* Whenever the phone rang I let it go to the machine. It was usually Max or Amy, but when the caller hung up without leaving a message, I shivered with fear. *Who was it? Were they checking to see if anyone was home?*

I kept doors locked and drapes pulled tight. I examined light fixtures and smoke-alarms for surveillance equipment. I suspected the bathroom mirrors were two-way. When not stealthily looking for bugs, I tried to create order, but felt like I was being watched. And everything I put away was a reminder of something lost. My moods were complex tangles of grief, anger, and paranoia. I lived in a constant state of high alert.

Max was kind and contrite, patient when I cried or refused to leave the house. He tried to act sympathetic, but didn't understand. The tapping meant nothing to him, besides a threat to his job.

One day I heard a knock on the door and saw Bobbi through the peephole. I almost tip-toed away, but since she was married to Max's boss, I opened the door. Bobbi smiled and held up a foil-wrapped plate.

"I made cookies. Not as good as yours, but I thought you might like them." Bobbi's skin was pale and splotchy without makeup, red hair faded and dull. She wore a white polo shirt, khaki pants, and blue Keds.

Bobbi sat on the sofa while I poured iced tea and unwrapped the cookies. She smiled awkwardly as she looked around the room and seemed nervous. I wondered if this visit was her idea. "It looks nice with all your stuff."

Bookshelves housed the stereo, CDs, books, and mementos from home. The mirror hung over Kate's piano and family photographs lined the top. The blue table in the entryway held a big bowl for seashells and the kitchen counter was crowded with a toaster-oven, coffeemaker, and crocks of wooden spoons and whisks. There were potholders, cookbooks, magnets on the refrigerator. It didn't look exactly like my home, but it looked like someone's home.

"I heard you've been having a hard time," Bobbi said.

"You could say that."

"I should have told you about the phone taps." Tears sprung to her eyes. "I didn't do a very good job of welcoming you."

"You did a lovely job." I suddenly felt compelled to comfort her. "I just wish someone had told me and Bonita about the phone." Since our husbands didn't work together, Bonita had never been included in Bobbi's events. I wasn't sure Bobbi even knew who Bonita was. "Tell me, how do you deal with all this without going crazy?"

"All what, dear?" Bobbi looked alarmed.

"Security prowling around, being locked in the compound." The list felt endless. "Ocmara keeping our passports, being fingerprinted."

Bobbi shrugged with practiced nonchalance. "There are things you have to accept when you live in another country. This is your first time living abroad, and you've only been here, what, three months?"

I nodded. *Three long months.*

"You'll get used to it." She smiled.

It felt condescending. "How did you get used to the phone taps and having your mail opened?"

"Well, unless you have something to hide, you don't have to worry." She sipped her tea then spoke quietly. "For example, on the phone, you never say 'wine' you say 'juice.' They have no idea what you're talking about." Bobbi leaned forward and whispered, "And you never speak ill of the company or the Kingdom. It can cost you dearly. Max could have lost his job."

I looked at Bobbi, wondering if she knew how crazy it was to tell me I had nothing to worry about then proceed to tell me how to protect myself. Now, I was certain Ray made Bobbi visit me. Ray didn't want to lose his best engineer.

"It takes awhile to settle in." For an instant, Bobbi's expression changed—a light faded in her eyes. Then, as if a switch had been thrown, she smiled. "But it's such a small price to pay for all the benefits."

All I could do was stare. I was sick to death of hearing about the benefits.

Bobbi tilted her head. "Now, what can I do to help? How about being my guest at the next Women's Club luncheon? We'll get you so busy you'll never want to leave!"

"Okay." I would agree to anything to make her go. When Bobbi whispered, I wondered if she was wearing a wire.

I was walking her to the door when Bobbi stopped and looked at me. "I'm so sorry about Bonita. It's sad to lose a good friend. This is a lonely place without one." Bobbi gave me a hard hug and suddenly I felt truly comforted. When she left I wondered what had just happened.

15

While I tried to regain sanity by creating warmth and order in our house, Max took delivery of the Land Rover, devoting hours to washing and waxing the already spotless car. On Thursday we decided to drive to Al Khobar, have lunch, and go to Safeway. I made a list and filled two coolers with ice. The ride down was comfortable and cool. I'd forgotten about the great sound system and plush interior. It even had that "new car" smell.

We had a late lunch in a "broasted" chicken restaurant, drawn in by delicious aromas and a family section. Then we went to Safeway.

"It's huge!" Max said.

"I told you," I said.

Max pushed one cart while I followed with another.

"This is great," Max said, tossing frozen pizzas into his cart.

"We'll never be hungry again," I deadpanned.

"Seriously," he said. "If we come every few weeks we'll always have everything we need."

Being Thursday, Safeway was filled with Western and Saudi shoppers—families on an outing to the grocery store. We had never grocery shopped together in the States.

"Let's get this." Sam held up a box of Cocoa Puffs. "Please?"

"Oreos!" Kate said.

I seldom allowed the kids sugary cereal, processed foods, cola, or anything else I referred to as "crap," but we had all felt deprived for so long I let them go nuts.

Max examined a box of taco shells. "We haven't had tacos since we've been here.

I added cheddar cheese and ground beef to my list. Tacos sounded good.

"Let's have them tonight!" Sam said.

I bought fresh produce in Rahima, so we only needed avocados for guacamole. For meat, I selected ground sirloin, three whole chickens, a beef brisket, and a chuck roast. Kate boycotted the meat aisle, choosing to look for bath products.

"These okay?" Kate held up scented soaps and bubble bath. "They smell so good."

"As long as you share them with me," I said.

Our last stop was the ice cream section.

"Everybody gets their favorite flavor," Max said, choosing butter pecan. I picked coffee, Kate chose strawberry, and Sam, of course, picked chocolate.

Our Safeway purchases were rarely or never found in Al Hassa. The commissary stocked export-quality food, like that sent to Third World Countries. It was sadly enlightening to be on the receiving end. By the time it got to us, produce was moldy and rotten, expiration dates long expired. Whenever word got out that there was good stuff in the commissary, there was a run on it. By the end of the day it was gone. People bought as much as they could then hoarded. Over time, I hoarded herbal and decaffeinated teas. I always felt ashamed of myself, buying all the boxes, but I did it anyway.

After two hours in Safeway, we started back to Al Hassa. Leaving the city took forever because of traffic and wrong turns and by the time we reached the highway it was dark, our headlight-beams the only light.

"There's a map and flashlight in the glove box," Max said.

I'd just found our location on the map, when we hit a roadblock. Barricades stretched across the highway diverting cars onto an exit ramp. We slowed to a stop.

"Get your ID," Max said.

Two Saudi policemen approached the car, shone flashlights on our IDs and faces, then on the kids in the backseat. Sam was wearing his Goofy hat, a souvenir from our only Disneyland vacation. Goofy's face was on the cap, long black ears hung on either side. I held my breath while the light lingered on Sam's face. *Please don't let them take his hat.* Then the light was off and Max was told to open the back of the car. The police rummaged through our groceries before waving us through.

Past the barricades, it was pitch-black. We followed the curving frontage road, but it soon became clear we were no longer near the highway. There were no other cars in sight.

"I don't know how I missed the on-ramp," Max said. The dashboard's glow illuminated his worried expression. "Look for a place to turn around." But the narrow road cut through light desert sand. There were no shoulders and the sand looked soft.

"I see cars!" Sam pointed toward distant red taillights on a road parallel to ours.

"Good job, buddy," Max said. "We must be going the right way."

I played the flashlight over the map. "I can't tell where we are." Suddenly our car was lit from headlights behind us.

"Where'd they come from?" Max studied the rear-view mirror.

I turned to look and saw Sam's Goofy hat in silhouette. Smiling, I turned back.

"They're passing us," Max said.

A Toyota pickup truck swerved in front of us. Brake lights flashed, forcing us to stop. Two men jumped from the truck-bed as the driver got out. All three were Filipino, wearing shorts, sleeveless T-shirts, and white bandannas around their foreheads.

"What the hell?" Max unrolled his window.

When the driver approached, we saw his machinegun.

"He's got a gun!" I said.

"They all do," Max said.

The driver pointed his machinegun at Max, shouting something in Arabic.

"I don't understand." Max instinctively raised his hands.

Suddenly we were surrounded by three more vehicles, one on each side and one in back. Bright lights filled our car from behind. Doors slammed, but we could only see the truck in front of us. The driver exchanged words with a man behind our car then resumed yelling at Max, punctuating each word with a menacing gesture with the gun.

In a surprising adrenaline surge, I waved the map and screamed, "Al Hassa! Al Hassa!"

The driver leaned down and stared at me. Heart pounding, I held my breath. After a long silent moment, he spoke again with the unseen man. The gun remained pointed at us. As Max and I exchanged a glance, I snaked my arm between the seats. The kids grabbed my hand. I held tight and looked back at their scared faces.

Outside, doors slammed and the vehicle to our right slowly drove forward. It was a military jeep, desert-camouflage beige. Soldiers crouched in the back, rifles leveled at us. When the Filipino driver slammed his hand against our car, we all jumped and Kate shrieked. He walked toward his truck, gesturing for us to follow. The other two Filipinos climbed into the truck-bed and kneeled, pointing their guns at us.

Max shifted into gear and began to roll forward when the driver screamed, pointed his gun in the air, and fired off a round. The shots were deafening—as were our screams. Max slammed on the brakes and sat with both hands gripping the steering wheel. His face was pale and his heart was beating so hard I could see his body move with each beat. We sat frozen.

Once the jeep pulled past the Toyota truck and onto the road in front of it, the Filipino driver backed the truck next to us. Again he gestured for Max to follow.

"Let's try again," Max whispered.

As we followed the Toyota, the two other vehicles followed us. Led by the jeep, our caravan moved slowly down the road. The men in the Toyota kept their machineguns leveled at us. Outside the headlights, the desert was completely black.

I looked at the kids. Their faces were in shadow, but they still clung to my hand and I felt their trembling. I sat like that for what seemed like forever, glancing at Max, the men in the truck, the silhouettes of my children. We drove in silence.

Looping through my mind were stories I'd heard of people massacred on desolate roads in remote places around the world or after making a wrong turn in a city ghetto. Families shot or hacked to death. I'd felt queasy at the horror of what it must be like to know you were helpless to prevent the death of your children. To know you were going to die. *How did they feel?* Driving through the blackness of that Saudi night, I knew the answer. I alternated between feeling frozen with fear, and plotting survival moves. And I prayed.

The Toyota stopped. A door slammed behind us and a Saudi soldier appeared in our headlights. He called to the Filipino driver then walked to the side of the road and shone a flashlight on the ground. The driver got out of the truck and approached our car. He pointed the gun at Max and barked an order in Arabic.

"I don't understand," Max said, in a voice I'd never heard before.

The driver gestured toward the soldier. *Oh, God, oh, God, oh, God.* I clasped my hand over my mouth. Max looked at me, his face white with fear, then he opened the car door.

The driver fired another round and we all screamed. Max dove toward me as I lunged for my children. We held each other for a long terrifying moment.

Grunting impatiently, the driver slammed Max's door. He gestured at the soldier and yelled another command. The soldier walked up an embankment then played the flashlight over a stretch of barbed-wire fence flattened on the ground. Just as the soldier pointed up the embankment, a car flew by above us.

The Filipino driver stepped back and pointed upwards, toward the highway. "Al Hassa!"

As understanding dawned, Max turned the wheel, gunned the engine, and we raced up the embankment, over the fence, and onto the highway. After a minute, the kids loosened their grip on me and I relaxed into my seat. Max grabbed my hand and squeezed it so tightly I gasped in pain. After driving five minutes we saw the sign: AL HASSA 25 Km.

Safely in our garage, Max turned off the car. All was quiet except for the engine ticking as it cooled. I'd reached for the door handle when Max boomed out, "Well, kids, this was one for show and tell, wasn't it?"

"I'm never going anywhere with you guys again," Sam said, running into the house.

"Me, either." Kate sobbed as she disappeared through the door.

I looked at Max, astonished by his stupidity. The ticking sounded like a bomb about to go off. "What the fuck?" I got out, slammed the door, and followed my children into the house.

The kids were so exhausted they just wanted to sleep. After getting them settled, I took a long shower. Max was waiting when I walked out of the bathroom.

"I brought the groceries in." His voice had a pathetic, eager-to-please tone. He looked so broken I felt sorry for him.

"Thanks." I got into bed.

"I put everything away."

Jesus, what do you want? A medal? I felt like I was coming out of my skin. "That's good," I said evenly, closing my eyes. I heard Max breathing— waiting.

"Look, about earlier...," Max said.

"Please, not tonight." I looked at him. "Just come hold me."

As Max hugged me, I pushed my body close to his. A moment later Sam and Kate rushed in. It had been years since they'd slept with us, and they were so big we barely all fit. But I wanted them to stay, reassured by the warmth of their bodies and the sound of their breathing.

While my family slept, I lay awake reliving the terrifying night. Although the trigger-happy driver was ultimately showing us the way home, during those dark moments I was changed forever. I learned what helplessness really means, to have totally surrendered our lives with no guarantee of safety. It was no longer about freedom, it was about survival.

I dozed off after first call to prayer. Sometime later, I felt Max getting up. Leaden with fatigue, I sank back into oblivion. The kids and I slept all morning. After I finally got up, I felt a surge of rage when I walked into the kitchen. Max's idea of putting away groceries was not the same as mine. Items were jammed into cabinets and lined on counters. Nothing was where it belonged. I looked in the refrigerator.

"Goddamn it!" It was crammed with all the meat I'd buried in the coolers to keep frozen until we got home. When I poked the Saran-wrapped chuck roast, my finger sank to the first knuckle. "Shit." All the meat had thawed.

While coffee brewed I put away groceries, resisting the urge to slam the cabinet doors. I started cooking the meat we wouldn't be eating over the next week so I could refreeze it. When Max got home at 2 p.m. the kids were up and lounging on the sofas. Sam was wearing his Goofy hat and Mimi was asleep on Kate's lap. Both kids were reading books assigned for school.

"Wow, something smells good!" Max said, appearing in the kitchen doorway.

I looked up from basting the chickens.

"Come in the living room," Max said. "I've got something to tell you guys."

I closed the oven and walked into the living room.

"I found out who those men were last night." Max looked excited.

"Who were they?" Sam asked. Kate deliberately studied her book.

"Secret police," Max said. "We were near a bay where drug and gun-runners try to come into Saudi by boat."

"Like pirates?" Sam asked.

"Yeah, buddy. Sort of like pirates." Max nodded. "Those guys in the truck hide out, waiting to catch them. When we got lost we drove into a trap."

Sam looked at Max then at me. I could tell he wasn't buying it.

"They were good guys," Max said.

"Then why did they shoot at us?" Sam asked.

"They thought we were pirates," Kate said dryly, never looking up from her book.

"They didn't shoot at us," Max said.

"In our Land Rover," Kate continued.

"They didn't shoot at us." Max sounded exasperated.

"Maybe your Goofy hat confused them." Kate glanced at Sam.

"They shot at us because they thought we were Pirates of the Caribbean!" Sam said.

"Stop saying they shot at us," Max yelled.

In the silence that followed, I started to laugh. Whether it was exhaustion, Max's irritation, the absurdity of the whole situation, or all three, I started to laugh and couldn't stop. So did Kate and Sam. Max was not laughing and as he grew increasingly upset, we became more tickled. It was three against one. We couldn't stop laughing, but Max had lost control.

When Max stormed from the room, we laughed even harder. But after a split-second, I ran after him. He was sitting on the bed in our bedroom, his face buried in his hands. When I put my arms around him, he resisted for a moment then grabbed me. He was crying.

I knew Max's "good guys" story was to minimize the danger we'd felt the night before, and our resulting hysteria had lightened the mood. But that night, after the kids were asleep in their own beds, Max and I talked about our options.

The first was go back to the States deeper in debt than when we'd left, with no home to live in and no jobs. The second was for me and the kids to go back, find an apartment and a job, leaving Max to finish his contract. The third was to stay in Saudi, hoping we'd already survived the worst. Since I had no intention of tearing our family apart—our only option was to stay.

"Oh, babe, I'm sorry it's been so hard," Max said.

We were in bed sharing a bottle of wine Ray and Bobbi gave us after hearing about our "misadventure." The wine broke Max's rule about no booze in the house and tested my paranoia, but we both wanted a drink.

Holding my face, Max kissed me. "If we can stick it out it'll be better, I promise. Ray said there's a huge project coming up. If it's successful, I'm next in line for promotion."

I pulled back and stared at him. "Don't even think about staying longer."

"No, babe." Max grinned. "If I get a promotion I'll make lots more money. We'll be able to get the hell out of here that much faster."

I wanted to believe him. The reasons why we couldn't just pack up and move home were sobering. That night of red wine and reckoning made it clear we needed a plan to pay off our staggering debt and start saving.

"Just six months, babe." Max emptied the bottle into our glasses.

"Six months?"

"Until our vacation," Max said. "Let's start planning." The three-week repatriation required by the Saudi government sounded incredible. People took trips around the world or went home and took care of business. Max's was scheduled for February.

"To our vacation." I held up my glass, imagining drinking wine in Paris.

"To us," Max said.

That night in late July, snuggled safely in bed and buzzed with red wine, Max and I focused on the future.

16

The kids were off school the entire month of August and it couldn't have come at a better time. Max worked and the kids and I did whatever we wanted. We slept late then snorkeled at the beach or joined Amy and her kids at the pool. The hottest part of the day we spent at the library or at home, napping and reading. Kate practiced piano. After dinner we all went bowling or to the movies. The kids had sleepovers with their friends.

Life in Saudi returned to normal in September. The kids went back to school and I was left home alone. Our food from Safeway was gone, so one day I biked to the commissary. Pushing my cart through the produce section, I caught the stench of garbage. When I picked up a tomato so rotten it dissolved in my hand, I knew I'd soon have to brave the Rahima shopper's bus.

Mid-October we heard about a company-sponsored trip to the town of Hofuf. The main attractions were a camel market, a limestone mountain, and an oasis. Even the kids were interested, so we signed up.

At 4:30 a.m. we sleepily boarded one of three Mercedes coaches. It felt strange to be out among people. In my self-imposed exile, I'd stopped going to the Women's Club. Other than casual encounters, I didn't interact with anyone outside my family except Amy. I suspected my breakdown at the discovery of the phone taps and Bonita's abrupt departure had become juicy fodder for gossip, so I felt self-conscious walking down the aisle of the bus. I avoided eye contact, but knew I needed to rejoin the others before long.

Once seated, the kids went to sleep. Max and I sat across from them, sipping coffee from travel mugs. Between Al Hassa and Dammam, Max squeezed my hand. "There it is," he said. The break in the fence looked unremarkable in the early morning light. Still, it was tangible evidence that what felt like a nightmare had really happened. My heart raced at the memory.

At 7:30 we pulled into a parking lot packed with tourist buses, pickup trucks, and Mercedes sedans. Stepping off the bus, we were hit with a tremendous wave of noise—hundreds of loudly bleating camels and voices of Arab men negotiating deals.

"Look!" Sam pointed to a camel speedily loping away, chased by its owner.

"Run!" Kate screamed. Delight etched her face as she cheered for the camel.

The camels were all sizes and colors—black, brown, beige. Females nuzzled nursing calves. Those outside corrals were tied with rope, their front legs hobbled together with black cords like igals. In caricature, camels are portrayed as sweet and cuddly—in reality they are not so adorable. They are foul-tempered and we were warned to steer clear of their mouths because they hiss, spit, and bite with enormous yellow teeth. Their matted coats were filthy and they stank. Raising their long rat-like tails, they released steaming streams of dung wherever they stood.

Constantly in motion, they chewed, swayed, and shuffled broad, flat, two-toed feet. Tails switched at flies. Saliva dripped from their mouths, and they were noisy, with all their hissing and bleating. The bleat was a loud, high-to-low pitched sound—drawn out and mournful.

If not adorable, camels are captivating. Huge brown eyes, deep with ancient intelligence, are fringed with a double row of long thick lashes. They are all curves, from their humps to the graceful arc of their necks. Heads are held high and aloof, and their faces wear wily, ironic expressions. Even the scruffiest stood majestically.

In a clearing, there was an Arab boy offering camel rides for 3 riyals. Holding a rope, the boy led a camel in a circle, switching its hindquarters with a thin whip. Tourists were lined up.

"Want to ride?" Max asked the kids.

Sam nodded eagerly, but was suddenly shy as he gave the boy riyals. Max aimed the video-camera as the Saudi boy tugged the camel into a kneeling position and Sam climbed on. "Cool!" Sam yelled when the camel stood. He grinned self-consciously throughout his ride.

When it was Kate's turn, she shrieked with laughter as the camel rocked to its feet, bleating loudly. Kate's face was flushed with pleasure when she dismounted. "Your turn, Mom!"

"Yeah, Mom," Sam said.

I hesitated, terrified of the beast towering over me.

"Come on, babe." Max videotaped my reluctance.

The kids wore such happily expectant expressions, I had to try. Straddling the camel, I held tightly to the saddle-horn. "Whoa!" I yelled, as the camel stood. The ground looked far below, but the camel's rolling gait made me laugh—I loved it! After dismounting, I thanked the boy in halting Arabic, "Shukran," and was rewarded with a smile.

"Your turn, Dad," the kids cried.

To my surprise, Max paid the boy and climbed on. He looked sweetly ridiculous perched on top of the massive beast and I recorded every second.

After our rides we walked past a truck with a tiny camel in the back. The owner, an old Saudi man, beckoned to us. "You can pet him."

We stroked the camel, its coat surprisingly soft.

"How old is he?" Sam asked.

"Ten days."

"Aw, he's so cute," Kate said.

"Only 1000 riyals." The man smiled, but didn't look hopeful.

As Sam stroked the camel's face, it sucked his fingers then bleated plaintively.

"Mom? Dad?" The kids wore silly, pleading expressions and for a moment I imagined having a spitting, hissing camel as a pet. We took a picture instead.

Within the market was a souq run exclusively by women. Men were allowed, but most preferred the livestock auction and men's souq. "You girls go ahead," Max said. "Sam and I are going to do some manly stuff. Let's meet by the bus at 9:30."

The path leading to the women's souq was neatly swept and lined with smooth white stones. As we left behind the noise of camels and men, it was truly like walking into another world. Blankets were spread on the ground in the shade of canvas tarps or large black tents. The melodious sound of women's voices and laughter filled the air—girl-chatter recognizable in any culture. Children laughed, shrieked, and played. Babies cried.

I squeezed Kate's shoulders. "Aren't you glad we came?"

She smiled and nodded.

The women were Bedouin and veiled differently than women we'd seen in Rahima and Khobar. Abayas were pulled casually over colorful dresses. They wore masks over the bottom of their faces and black hijabs covered their hair, but there were no outer veils. Wandering through the souq, I studied the women's eyes.

Most items were handcrafted by the women. Colorful balls of wool had been sheared from sheep, dyed with plant pigments, and spun into yarn. There were rugs and bags woven from wool, baskets woven from palm fronds. I examined a red woolen bag decorated with white mother-of-pearl buttons and seashells.

"What is it?" Kate shyly asked the woman selling the bag.

"A purse," she said.

"It's beautiful." I ran my fingers over the designs.

"I make," the woman said proudly. "Twenty riyals."

As she took my riyals I noticed her palms were discolored from dye, but her fingernails were painted bright red. I took out my camera.

"May I take your picture?" I asked.

"Yes." She stood tall and still, hands clasped in front of her, eyes smiling warmly.

Kate slipped the bag on her shoulder and we moved on. The Bedouin women acknowledged us with nods as they lounged on their blankets, chatting with each other. Some sold curvy dellas or camel-saddles made of wood and leather. There were pots and trays roughly hammered from copper and brass, hand-carved wooden bowls and spoons.

"What's this?" I touched a crudely carved wooden bowl with a small handle and the patina of age. Knotted wire mended a long crack.

"For milking camels and goats." Holding the bowl in both hands, the woman offered it to me.

The bowl was surprisingly light and sweetly aromatic. I laughed. "Smell this," I told Kate.

"Milk!"

Part of the souq was dedicated to selling spices and food. There were crocks of olives, baskets of cinnamon sticks, cardamom, and sesame seeds. October was peak season for harvesting dates and there were baskets full of the dark brown fruit.

"Please taste." The vendor offered us big plump dates. After biting into the waxy skin, delicious moist sweetness filled my mouth. The only dates I'd ever had before came in small flat boxes—tasteless dried tidbits ready to be mixed into fruitcake.

"Taste it, Katie," I said. "You'll love it. Careful of the pit."

Kate nibbled cautiously then grinned with pleasure. We bought a generous bag of dates.

"Shukran." The woman nodded, eyes smiling.

Women stirred pots and basted meat over smoking grills. I looked at Kate.

"Forget it, Mom." She grimaced. "It's probably camel."

As we bought Arab bread hot from a beehive-shaped oven, I saw a Bedouin girl about Kate's age, standing nearby. She was barefooted and wore a colorful blouse and long skirt. No veil or mask, just a hijab wrapped gypsy-style around her hair. She held a smiling, pudgy baby on one hip and absently swayed back and forth, watching Kate and me.

Holding my camera, I tilted my head in silent question. Smiling, the girl straightened, posing. I quickly snapped her picture and waved "thank you." As we walked on, Kate turned to look back at the girl and I thought of the woman on the beach. It had been months since I'd gone to the beach at dawn. I pulled Kate close, and promised myself I'd go back soon.

Our last stop was the tent of two women I sensed were mother and adult daughter. They were selling jewelry. One basket held ropes of fat amber beads, another had chains decorated with silver balls, colorful stones, and glass. Rummaging through yet another basket, I found a wide silver bracelet. As I examined it, the older woman took it from me, polished it on her abaya and clamped it on my left wrist—all in one smooth motion.

"Thirty riyals," she said.

Laughing, I admired the bracelet, a bargain at $7 US. I gave her riyals, appreciating what a shrewd business woman she was.

"It's beautiful, Mom," Kate said.

The women zeroed in on Kate. Chatting softly in Arabic, they pulled veils and hijabs from another basket and beckoned to her.

"What?" Kate looked nervous.

The women laughed and made friendly cooing noises. The younger tied a Bedouin-style mask on Kate's face. The older draped a hijab over

Kate's long dark hair, deftly arranging it to frame her face, then handed Kate a mirror.

Kate studied her reflection while the women watched smiling, nodding approvingly. When Kate looked at me I was startled to see her clear blue eyes above the black mask, her dark eyelashes and eyebrows emphasized by the hijab framing her face. She looked beautiful and exotic. Chatting and laughing, the women took the hijab and mask off Kate. *Dress up, I thought. This is how little Arab girls play dress up.*

Glancing at my watch, I was startled to see it was 9:20. "Come on, sweetie. We've got to get to the bus."

The older woman pulled a slim silver bangle from a basket, took Kate's hand, and slipped it on her wrist. Kate's face lit up as she looked at the bracelet and I reached for riyals.

"La, la!" Eyes smiling, the women shook their heads and hands—refusing money.

"Say thank you," I told Kate.

"Shukran," Kate said, softly and shyly.

There were peals of laughter and more pleased chatter. We backed away smiling and waving, then turned and hurried to the bus.

As soon as Kate and I sat down, Sam showed us what he'd found in the men's souq.

"It was so cool. Look at this!" Sam waved a curved knife in an ornate sheath. When he pulled it out, I was surprised at the razor's edge.

"Be careful, that's sharp," I said.

"Dad said I could start a collection."

I glanced at Max. *We'd never even let Sam have toy guns!*

"Look what Dad got," Sam said.

Max held up a container made from a brass artillery shell. It looked like a giant bullet. "Guy stuff." He smiled sheepishly.

"Look what I got." Kate showed them her bracelet. "Mom got one, too. And look at our bag."

Sam took a cursory look. "What was the girl's souq like?"

"It was good," Kate said. We smiled at each other, knowing it would be impossible to explain our experience. I pulled her close. So far, the day had been a wonderful respite from the homogeneity of the compound, and a powerful reminder of all I'd found seductive about Saudi.

Soon the buses began the short drive to Hofuf. On the way, the barren beige desert abruptly changed into a verdant forest of date palms. I studied the primordial green fronds. After experiencing the desert, I suddenly understood how an oasis could quench physical thirst—and the thirst in your soul.

That day we learned that Al Hofuf is the largest oasis in Saudi Arabia, with 2 million 100- foot palm trees, each producing over 200 pounds of dates. The ancient walled-city of Hofuf is in the middle of the oasis. Driving through the narrow streets we passed two mosques and a Turkish fort the color of mud. Residents of Hofuf are predominately Shiite, and since Saudi's ruling family belongs to the Sunni tribe, Hofuf lacked the wealth we'd seen in Khobar. There were no marble malls. Instead, Hofuf felt quaint, peaceful, and friendly. As Saudi women walked the sidewalks, their eyes were visible.

We had lunch at the Hotel Hofuf. After a hammam break, we were treated to a sumptuous buffet. Bowls of tabbouli, hummus, and baba ghannoush rested beside piles of Arab bread. There were sliced cucumbers mixed with yoghurt and mint, roast chicken, lamb-kabobs, vegetables, rice, and lentils. A dessert table held baklava, cookies, nuts, dates, and fresh fruit. There was hot tea and dellas of strong Arabic coffee.

I remembered the night Max announced we were moving to Saudi— how we'd celebrated with some of the same food. It seemed years ago. Suddenly, I was ravenous. While my family ate chicken and rice, I tried everything, enjoying the combinations of tastes and textures.

"Please try some of the other food," I said. "It's really delicious."

"You know how I feel about lamb," Kate said.

"There's more than lamb," I said.

"That other stuff looks yucky." Sam gnawed on Arab bread.

"I'm good," Max said.

I felt my enthusiasm draining away. It took so much energy to stay engaged when everyone else refused to. Kate must have sensed my disappointment, because she went to the buffet and came back with a plateful of pastries and dates.

"Try the dates," Kate told Sam. "They're delicious." She ate one to convince him.

Sam took a tentative bite. "Tastes like candy."

"Dad?" Kate smiled at Max.

"No thanks," Max said. "I don't eat dates."

To her credit, Kate tried everything on her plate. Sam and Max ate cookies.

After lunch, we were driven to an enormous limestone formation called Jabal al Qarah. It rose above the surrounding date palms like a pink flat-topped mountain. A path wound through deep, vertical fissures. Some were like canyons, with tall smooth walls. Others formed deep, cool caves. Signs warned against leaving the path—for danger of getting lost. Sometimes the path was so narrow we had to squeeze through, other times it was so spacious we could have danced. The path wound upwards, with steps carved out of the rock. At the very top was a plateau.

Looking out over the edge of the mountain was like looking at a green sea formed by the tops of the date palms. It was hot and windy, and we explored carefully, because scattered about were cracks open all the way to the bottom of the mountain. It would have been a perilous drop.

Just outside the caves, a potter was hard at work. His dusty foot pressed a pedal to spin the wheel, as he shaped simple pots the same pink color as the mountain. He affixed a handle and set the pots on a shelf to dry, but they were not glazed or fired. We bought one for a souvenir. Over time the pot softened and the handle fell off. During humid days it became sandy. Layers crumbled off creating a circle of pink dust around the ever-thinning pot. Eventually, it eroded like the mountain.

On the ride home, Max and the kids dozed off, but I was too happy to sleep. Caressing my bracelet, I gazed out the window, lost in thought. The Bedouin women haunted me—the accepting honesty of their eyes. I had felt so much more comfortable with them than with the women of Ocmara. It was as though the Bedouins were my tribe. *I have to get back to the woman on the beach.* Thirty kilometers outside of Al Hassa I saw the break in the fence and felt a twinge of anxiety. Almost fear. I took a deep breath and pushed it aside.

17

Feeling the intense heat on my face and arms, I knew sunburn would be evidence of my lingering. I sat on an enormous, smooth, flat stone close to the ocean's edge. Water lapped calmly near my feet and I felt wrapped in serenity. For a month I'd been running before dawn. My calves and thighs, dormant for three months, had become firm strong testimonies to muscle-memory. My arms, legs, and face were golden tan, and when I took off my silver bracelet, there was a wide white band above my left wrist.

Every day I ran to this spot, sat on the stone, and waited—hoping to see the woman. But there'd been no sign of her. I'd used the space and time to pray, meditate, or just be grateful, and in doing so I'd created a personal vortex of peace. It calmed me to sit there.

A glance at my watch told me it was time to go wake the kids. Reluctant to leave, I stared at the water. Suddenly I sensed her presence. She stood on the rocky precipice where I'd first seen her. Lifting her veil, she looked directly at me. I smiled and waved and she waved back. After a long moment, she dropped her veil, stepped back from the edge, and disappeared. I sat another minute—waiting. When she didn't reappear, I ran home.

After Hofuf I'd started going out again, renewing my effort to make life in Saudi a positive experience. I was tired of being lonely. The gathering of Bedouin women had made me long for community. I went back to the Women's Club for meetings, coffees, luncheons, and trips to Safeway. It was mostly the same faces, Bobbi and her crew, but I met more women over time.

At one luncheon the club president described an upcoming 3-day trip to Riyadh, the Saudi capital. "Your husbands will need to sign a permission slip for you to go."

"She's kidding, right?" I whispered to the woman beside me.

"No," she whispered. "She's not kidding."

I widened my eyes, hoping to engage in whispered discussion about how ridiculous it was that grown women needed their husbands' permission. But she turned away and her rigid posture discouraged discussion. I glanced at Amy, on my other side. She shrugged and smirked.

The woman's name was Margaret and we'd talked the first time that day. I'd remembered her from the Hofuf trip. After mentioning Hofuf, Margaret spoke at length about the historical significance of the Turkish fort and the battles fought there.

"Interesting," I said. "How do you know so much?"

"I was a history major," Margaret said. "It's my passion."

"Do you teach at the school?"

"No." Margaret smiled tightly. "I never finished my degree."

"Well, you should. You're good at it," I said. "How far did you get?"

Margaret hesitated. "I'm what they call ABD—all but dissertation."

"You're that close to your doctorate?" I asked. "I've always wanted a Ph.D. I'm impressed!"

"Don't be," Margaret said flatly. That should have been my cue.

"What's your dissertation about?"

"I'm not writing one," Margaret said.

"Why not?"

Margaret shrugged. "I thought I would when we moved here. God knows I had plenty of time, but I never could."

"Is it too late?" I asked.

"Not too late. I just don't care anymore." Her look told me the topic was closed.

I wanted to argue, make her care. But I resisted the urge as Margaret pointedly turned away. I found it inconceivable to be so close and just give up.

"Forget it, Sarah," Amy whispered. "That's your dream, not hers."

I looked at Amy, moved that she understood me so well. Glancing around at the other women, I wondered about their stories—what they gave up to follow their husbands to Saudi—what was hidden behind their smiles.

I haunted the library, and loved talking to Andrea. She was an excellent librarian—smart, insightful, and dedicated to stocking a current, diverse selection of books. In her lilting, no-nonsense voice, Andrea recommended books that I read voraciously. One day she gave me *The Handmaid's Tale* by Margaret Atwood.

"Heard of it?" Andrea asked.

"Yes, but I never read it."

"It's brilliant. I read it on repat last year and I've ordered it repeatedly. Customs always confiscates it." She shook her head. "It finally came through and I wanted you to have it first."

"Thanks." Leafing through, I saw a post-it. I looked at Andrea.

"I marked something for you." Andrea smiled. "You'll get it. You'll see."

That night, I settled into bed, into *The Handmaid's Tale,* and into a universe parallel to the one in which I was living. I read late into the night. At times I clutched the book to my chest, shot through with inarticulate grief and rage. *Nolite te bastardes carborundorum* was the passage Andrea had marked—"Don't let the bastards get you down."

The next day I mailed letters to friends in the States, asking them to read *The Handmaid's Tale,* so they'd understand what I was going through. Lara called two weeks later.

"Are you okay?" Lara was crying.

"The best okay I've been," I said.

"Come home," she insisted.

Taking the weekly shopper's bus to Rahima, I became a regular at the bakery and produce market, where I practiced basic Arabic. I learned how to buy small carpets, bargaining with merchants who offered me tea.

I settled into compound quirkiness having nothing to do with Ocmara. Every week an Arab man drove through Al Hassa selling fresh seafood from coolers in the back of his truck. After learning his schedule, I waited outside to flag him down. Then he'd sit under our palm tree cleaning the shrimp and filleting the fish I'd purchased.

Occasionally a small, wiry Filipino man came to shimmy up the palm tree and trim the fronds. And there was the tall thin Pakistani man with fearful eyes, who sometimes appeared in the backyard, asking in broken English if he could sweep the sand or prune the bougainvillea. I always said, "Yes," pressing riyals into his calloused hands.

Kate wanted to learn to ride horses. We biked to the Al Hassa stables, located in the desert north of the houses. We bought Kate lessons involving English saddles, helmets, boots, and posting. The lessons were in training rings, but there were also riding paths in the desert. Kate took lessons on an enormous brown Arabian horse called Mias. She was in heaven.

Hoping to share something with Kate, I tried a few lessons. Kate was a natural, instinctively calm and confident. "Like this, Mom." She held her hand palm-up with a bit of carrot or apple.

When I held out my hand, Mias sniffed the treat with his big velvet nose then took it gently with soft competent lips. "Good boy," I said.

"Good job, Mom." Kate giggled. She knew I was afraid he was going to take a finger.

The instructor was Lana, a deeply tan woman in her mid-forties. "Do it like this, honey," Lana said in a Texas drawl, demonstrating with a currycomb and brush. She was smoothly efficient as she lifted heavy hooves, picking out small stones lodged in the shoes. Lana taught us to saddle and bridle the horses. At least she taught Kate.

I tried to be calm and confident, but was afraid of being bitten or kicked. I was strong enough to lift the saddle across their backs, but scared to reach beneath their big heaving bellies to buckle the belts. I was terrified to bridle them, prying open their mouths to put in the bit. Their enormous snapping teeth and wild, white-rimmed eyes made me feel panic I'm sure they sensed.

"Come on, Mom," Kate encouraged, elegant in breeches and boots— tall in her saddle.

"Okay, here I go!" I'd awkwardly struggle up and grip the reins.

Kate and Lana exchanged amused glances. Posting up and down as I rode around the ring was great for my thighs, but felt like too much work. The helmet was hot. Sweat matted my hair and trickled down my face. Kate loved it too much to be uncomfortable. I was miserable and had to resist the urge to whine.

Most of the horses were retired race horses, put to pasture in Al Hassa. They'd been trained to be fast and first. Our third lesson, Lana took us on a desert trail. Going out was fine. I rode a docile grey mare called Baby. Lana led the way, Kate followed on Mias, and I pulled up the rear. Everything was fine until we turned back toward the stables. Suddenly the race was on.

All three horses took off, vying for the lead. I heard Kate's laughter as Baby surged to the front, leaving the others in our dust. It was both thrilling and terrifying. Terror won and I stopped riding. I just hung around the stables taking pictures while Kate had her lessons.

One day I found the photography lab. Commissioned by a member of the Royal family, it was extraordinarily well-equipped. After the Royal lost interest, it was rarely used. Quiet, dark, and cool, the photo-lab was my idea of heaven. It didn't take long to reacquaint myself with the process. I gathered my film, and spent the next few weeks developing pictures I'd taken since arriving in Saudi.

In the dimly lit room, I examined each print before hanging it to dry—the Bedouin girl with the baby, a woman's dark-stained hands with red fingernails, camels, horses. The picture I'd taken early on—the sign forbidding the taking of pictures.

In Rahima, I had taken pictures of the smiling men in the bakery holding platter-sized rounds of bread. Whenever I asked, the answer was "yes." Sometimes I just took pictures secretly. Over time I'd print in color, but in the beginning I used black and white. I bought black wooden frames in Rahima and hung the photos on our dining room wall.

When not at the library or photo-lab, I was in my kitchen trying new dessert recipes. I perfected my chocolate-chip cookies. Every day I made a batch of cookie dough, ate half, and baked half. At social gatherings I became famous for my fabulous desserts.

"And you never gain an ounce!" People cooed incredulously.

Running every morning helped. I also went to the gym and used weights. Amy gave me a bootleg exercise video someone had smuggled into Saudi. I did *"The Firm"* three times a week in my living room with beautiful people in leotards and tights. Sometimes Amy joined me, too.

"Looking good, babe," Max said when I wore my white nightgown.

And I did— with my sun-bleached hair and buff, tan body. It was like I was in boot-camp preparing for battle, except the battle already raged in my head. Every morning, I awoke depressed, anxious, or both. I'd awaken early, startled from a dream, heart racing, tears on my cheeks. I'd lay still, reassuring myself I wasn't having a heart attack, or the house wasn't falling down, or whatever other crazy thought had taken residence in my head. Breathing deeply and holding panic at bay, I dressed and went running. I feared if I didn't run, the thoughts in my head would kill me. So far I was winning the war—not letting the bastards get me down.

18

The end of November, I'd been in Saudi seven months. There was no rain the entire time, just the unrelenting, soul-numbing, monotony of sunny days. Some nights I dreamed of rain—wistful dreams that left me restless the next day. I remember it was the last day of November when it finally rained. *Oh, I remember.*

Thunder had rolled into my dreams—deep rumblings, flashes of light. I dreamt about the cannon signaling sunrise during Ramadan and awoke confused in the middle of the night. The patter of rain lulled me back to sleep. Max woke me soon after dawn.

"Hurry," he whispered, pulling me to my feet.

"Where are we going?" I stretched and yawned.

"To watch the rain." Max gave me my abaya and I slipped it over my nightgown. Leaving the kids sleeping, we tiptoed downstairs and into the garage.

By that time every other morning the sun was already bright. That morning was ominously dark. Backing out into the pouring rain, the head-lights played across the palm tree. Water coursed down the fronds, dripped from the pointed ends. The streets were swollen swirling torrents, like wadis—dried riverbeds come to life.

Rain hammered the windshield as Max navigated through the streets, past the houses, and north on the road running along the edge of the desert parallel to the beach—the road where I'd seen the orange security car. That morning there were no security cars, but there were cars moving slowly ahead of us, or already parked. Thirsty expats lured from their beds, seduced by the storm. Max found a space far from the others, close to the rocky cliffs overlooking the beach. We sat in our Land Rover in a row of parked cars all facing the same direction. It was like being at a drive-in movie—the Arabian Gulf playing on the screen.

The wipers made lazy, rhythmic swipes as we watched the storm-tossed sea below us. Most mornings the water was a placid, clear blue. That morning it was an angry, steely gray. The air smelled sweet and felt charged with energy. Thick, low-hanging clouds crowded the horizon. Occasional bolts of lightning flash-danced through the sky, followed by heavy vibrations of thunder. *We felt the lightning and we waited on the thunder.*

Max pulled me close and switched on the stereo. With the first notes I knew he'd set the scene. Bob Seger's *Night Moves* is one of the sexiest songs ever written—the kind of song that leaves you restless, like dreams of rain in the desert. I leaned into Max's warmth and looked into his eyes. When we kissed, I was lost in the taste, smell, and feel of his mouth on mine. Suddenly we were swept away. Max slid his hand inside my abaya, inside my nightgown, kissed my neck. My body reacted with fire and rain, a storm raging like the one outside. Together we fumbled, groped, and moaned—locked in our own world—locked in us. Later, we laughed at the fogged windows. Max drew a heart on the windshield, M + S inside. *Ain't it funny how you remember?*

The storm lasted an hour and was done. The sun came out and rain absorbed into the desert, disappeared from the streets. The only evidence left were colorful blossoms suddenly appearing on scrubby desert plants and the song running through my head. It was almost like I'd imagined the rain—or dreamt it.

Later that day Sam's soccer game went on as scheduled, the field dry enough to withstand 22 pairs of cleats. There was no soccer in Al Hassa before we arrived, so Max organized and coached a boy's team. Playing soccer was a great outlet for Sam.

That afternoon I watched from the sidelines as they played against Dhahran. Sam ran up and down, concentrating on making goals and assists. Max also trotted back and forth, yelling instructions and encouragement. His tan muscular legs flashed as he ran. Occasionally, Max threw me a meaningful grin.

"Wasn't that storm something?" Janet, another soccer-mom, stood beside me.

Startled, I couldn't reply.

"I thought I saw you and Max," she said. "In the Land Rover?"

"Oh, yeah." I blushed.

"I thought so." She smiled and waited. "Well?"

Well what?

"What did you think of the storm?" Janet asked.

"Oh, it was amazing." I held back a goofy smile.

Sam scored a goal and Janet and I cheered as the boys gave each other high-fives. Sam grinned at me. Max smiled and winked.

"It was great of Max to put this team together," Janet said, watching Max run by. "He's my son's personal hero."

Max looked so handsome with his clear blue eyes, black hair blowing in the breeze.

"He's a keeper." Janet smiled. "Hold on to him."

"Thanks." I felt fiercely proud. "I will."

The home team won that day—on all counts.

The next day December arrived with sunshine and humidity that made my run more grueling than usual. I was slick with sweat within minutes. The water lapped calmly as I dodged driftwood, tangled knots of fishing net, and other debris washed up by the storm. I found some large shells, but the Arab woman wasn't there. I slowed to stare up at the spot where Max and I'd parked the day before and finished my run lost in reverie.

Later that morning, Amy and I hit some garages sales. "Look!" Amy held a quilted, blue silk comforter. "It's perfect."

Amy's mother was arriving soon for a month-long visit. She'd spend Christmas and New Year's before flying back to Louisiana. Like mine, her mom was widowed, and Amy had gotten a special family visitation-visa. We were shopping for the guestroom.

I caressed the soft fabric. The blue was rich and deep, the color of the sky at dusk. If Amy didn't buy it, I would. "It's lovely, she'll like it." Suddenly I missed my mother. "What else do you need?"

"A lamp. Throw pillows. Coat hangers." Amy hugged the comforter.

"How about this?" I pointed to a brass camel with a light bulb sprouting from its hump. "Delightfully tacky," I whispered.

Amy laughed, adding the lamp to her haul. The garage sale culture was interesting. People leaving for good were ecstatic, bitter, sad, or scared. Those who'd lived in Saudi the longest were the most afraid. They were used to Ocmara providing everything and weren't sure they could make it in the real world.

Ecstatic people scared me the most. Now that I'd settled in, I didn't want to hear horror stories of what finally made them leave and I didn't want to feel the envy invariably stirred up. Mostly, I didn't want to see pity in their eyes when they asked how much longer I had to go.

"Sarah, look," Amy whispered, nodding toward a box of six silver Christmas ornaments. "We'll split them."

Already, it felt like we were rushing full-tilt into our first Christmas away from home. I was anxious, anticipating homesickness—the normal wife-and-mother pressure, compounded by being in Saudi. We'd be missing so many traditions—the school assembly, Christmas Eve candlelight service, Mom's corn chowder.

I was determined to create the best Christmas possible. Every week I scoured garage sales for gifts, collecting transformers and toys for Sam and sports equipment for Sam and Max. I found a silver bracelet with tiny horseshoe charms and a hot-pink feather boa for Kate. I found books, CDs, and videos—*ET, Crocodile Dundee, Cocoon*— for all of us. Most videos in Al Hassa were pirated copies and some had been filmed in movie theaters— silhouettes of heads and people standing up, leaving, returning to their seats. "Down in front!" we'd scream when that happened. We called it our "standing joke."

Two weeks before Christmas, I was at the library when Andrea motioned me over.

"Want to borrow our Christmas tree?" she whispered. "We'll be in Greece." Years before Saudi's ban against Christmas, Andrea and her husband's shipment had included a small artificial Christmas tree and two strands of tiny white lights.

The day I picked it up, Andrea disguised the tree in a black garbage bag and I carried it home on my bicycle. Pedaling furtively through the streets I thought about the contrasts—there I was smuggling a plastic tree while sweating under the Saudi sun—back home we bought fresh trees and carried them home in the snow. There wasn't a chance in hell that we'd have a white Christmas. That night we set it up.

After inserting the branches into the trunk and wrapping it in lights, Max placed the tree on top of a side table, hoping for an illusion of grandeur.

It didn't work. Fully assembled, the tree was four feet tall and blatantly fake. I hung the three silver ornaments.

"That's it?" Kate's voice trembled. "That's our Christmas tree?"

"I hate it." Sam stared angrily at the tree with clenched fists. He was fighting tears.

A few days later, trying desperately to create Christmas spirit, I insisted we make homemade ornaments. I assembled the materials—skinny red ribbon from Rahima and a bag of white seashells with holes. We put on a bootleg Perry Como Christmas CD and settled in.

"Are we going to string popcorn?" Kate asked, squinting as she poked ribbon through a hole.

"If I can find popcorn." The commissary was out and I wondered if it was deliberate.

After making shell ornaments, I brought out the rest of the materials. I'd found a recipe for bread-dough ornaments and collected cookie cutters—a camel, star, circle, and gingerbread man. Instructions were to roll out the dough and cut out shapes, using extra dough for decoration. Pierce the tops with a toothpick, and bake until hard but still pale. Paint ornaments, or brush with glue and sprinkle with glitter. Once threaded with ribbon, they were ready to be hung.

"Mom!" Kate laughed. "Look!"

Sam's gingerbread man sported a penis. As did his camel and snowman. It was enough to bring us to hysterics. Back home, Sam couldn't have hung his ornaments on the Christmas tree. That year it was okay.

The week before Christmas, the Women's Club held a luncheon and holiday bazaar.

"Hey, you!" Amy and her mom had arrived. Esther was a tiny, older version of Amy—light hair, brown eyes, quiet Southern drawl. I'd spent time with Esther when she first arrived, but since then they had been busy. I'd missed Amy.

I stood and hugged them. "I saved you seats."

We pinned on red carnation corsages. Sissie, Rebecca, and two other women were also at our table. Amy shot me a mischievous grin before introducing her mother.

"Hey, everybody, this is my mom Esther," Amy said.

Rebecca's eyes brightened. *Biblical names!* She smiled at Esther and held out her hand. "Nice to meet you, Esther, I'm Rebecca." There was no humming or rocking.

"Welcome to Saudi!" Sissie said. "I hope you're enjoying your stay."

"I am." Esther beamed. "It's been wonderful." Esther and Amy smiled lovingly at each other.

Suddenly and acutely, I missed my mom. My smile wavered and I fought tears. Throughout the luncheon I drifted in and out. I'd be seeing Mom in February, but that seemed a long way off.

After lunch we browsed the bazaar filled with items hand-crafted by women on the compound—paintings, ceramics, quilts, pies, cakes, and cookies. I'd contributed Christmas cookies, declining Sam's offer to help decorate.

"We have to buy Sarah's cookies," Amy said. "They're the best."

"I've got a tin for you at home," I said. "Come over this afternoon for coffee."

"Sarah, dear, you're so sweet!" Esther smiled. "Your mama must miss you like crazy."

Again I felt the sting of tears. My motives weren't entirely pure. If Amy and her mom came over it'd be like sharing the Christmas ornaments.

That day I paid an exorbitant amount of money for a miniature red poinsettia flown in by the Al Hassa garden club. Since poinsettias are tropical plants, Saudi customs didn't recognize them as Christmas decorations. I also bought four Christmas stockings made from red-and-white checked gutras—a tangible example of expat humor. Lacking a fireplace mantle, we hung them on the bookshelves.

Perhaps it was all the anticipation, but Christmas Day wasn't as bad as I'd feared. Max had a massive hangover from the night before. He'd been part of a squad of outlaw Santas wearing homemade Santa suits and driven around Al Hassa in SUVs. They crouched in backseats, hiding from Ocmara security. At designated stops they popped out to deliver toys to tiny Ocmara tots and imbibed Christmas cheer in the form of homemade wine and sid. I'd video-taped Kate and Sam stuffing a pillow into Max's Santa suit, straightening his cotton-ball beard.

"Dad's back!" Sam yelled, two hours later.

I video-taped Max stumbling in the door.

"Ho! Ho! Ho!" Max screamed, his beard askew and stained with red wine.

"How was it?" Kate asked.

"Did you bring us anything?" Sam asked.

"Ho! Ho! Ho!" Max headed toward the bathroom. "Santa's got to pee." He struggled with the buckle on his wide black belt while desperately ripping off his beard.

The kids and I laughed as I filmed the ensuing hilarity—until Max locked himself in the bathroom. Through the door we could hear him vomiting.

"Santa's not feeling well," I said, my amusement transformed into annoyance. "Time to get ready for bed." Kate rolled her eyes and Sam sighed loudly.

Thankfully, the kids were too old for the early-morning wake-up calls of Christmases past, so everyone slept late Christmas morning. I lit the tree and we lounged about drinking coffee and hot chocolate, eating scrambled eggs and homemade coffeecake. The drapes were pulled tight to shield against prying eyes and the fiery reminder that we were a million miles from home.

After breakfast we opened presents. Funny, how I remember the gifts from that year. Limited resources brought out creativity and we did just fine without a shopping mall. Everything came from Rahima or garage sales in a Middle East-meets-West kind of theme. Stockings were stuffed with candy, gum, and Saudi souvenir key chains. Max bought Sam a knife for his collection.

"Cool!" Sam inspected the sharply honed blade.

Kate wrapped the boa around her neck and admired her reflection in a sepia-toned mirror overlaid with Arabic calligraphy. "I am so beautiful," she said.

"Yes, you are," we told her.

My gifts were a *fleur-de-lis* shaped crystal perfume decanter, a blue ceramic pitcher, and a clock radio the shape of a mosque. It had a gold dome and two tiny minarets. The alarm was the call to prayer.

"I love it!" I laughed.

The kids gave Max a paperweight with real Saudi oil inside.

"Very nice," he said. "I'm putting it on my desk at work."

We also bought Max a "traveling" Islamic prayer rug with a compass glued on top. On this compass, Mecca was true north. Max laid the carpet on the floor and we watched the needle point west, confirming what we already knew—we were living east of Mecca.

When I went to start dinner, I was surprised when Kate joined me. "What can I do to help?"

"How about cutting up the celery and onions for the dressing?" It was what Mom usually did.

"Okay," Kate said, tying on an apron.

That day I taught her to make cornbread dressing, yeast rolls, and pecan pie. Suddenly at twelve, she was aware of the woman's role in holiday meals and wanted to be part of it. I loved having her company. We roasted a turkey—a gift from the Mitchells—and had canned cranberry sauce, candied yams, and peas. Kate was proud of her homemade rolls and pecan pie. Dinner was exactly what we would have had at home.

After dinner we called people in the States. It was still Christmas morning at home. We kept conversations light and cheerful and that night the kids went to bed exhausted and happy. Christmas had been a success. I was proud of our little family. Where there easily could have been pouting and tears, there'd been joy and laughter. We had made it through with grace.

Once the kids were asleep, Max and I snuggled on the sofa in the dim glow of the Christmas tree. We listened to Perry Como sing *Oh, Holy Night* while sipping homemade red wine, another gift from the Mitchells.

"One more thing." Max handed me a box tied with red ribbon.

"What's this?" It was long and slim, but weightless. There was no sound when I shook it.

Max laughed. "Just open it."

Inside the box was a folded piece of paper. I gave Max a questioning glance. The paper looked official, with signatures and stamps, but I couldn't read it. It was all in Arabic. When I looked at Max again, he was beaming.

"It's your mom's visitation-visa," Max said.

"Oh, my God!" I hugged him and started to cry.

"Merry Christmas," Max whispered.

It was the very best Christmas present he could have given me. I studied the paper then held it close to my heart. "Thank you," I whispered.

"You're welcome." He brushed my hair off my wet cheeks.

"Does Mom know?"

"Not yet. I wanted you to tell her." Max sounded excited. "We'll bring her back with us from repat. She'll spend a week with us in Paris then be here for a month."

"Mom's always wanted to see Paris!" I'd always wanted to see Paris. We'd see it together.

"Think she'll be willing to babysit a couple nights?" Max smiled suggestively. "So we can have some romantic time in the City of Lights?"

"I'd bet on it!"

Max kissed me. "Let's call her to make sure."

"Hello?" Mom sounded tentative when she heard my voice. Maybe she was afraid she wouldn't be able to remain cheery this time.

"Mom!" I was unable to contain my joy. "How would you like to spend a week in Paris with us then come back to Saudi for a month?"

"Oh, my God!" Mom echoed my words then yelled out, "Ruth, guess what? I'm going to Paris and Saudi Arabia!"

We laughed and cried. I watched Max grin as he told Mom the details. That first Christmas night in Saudi I slept safe and warm, happily at home in Max's arms.

19

Max thought of everything. Our vacation started mid-February—we'd spend a week in London on the way home, a week in Chicago, and a week in Paris on the way back. Weather in Saudi would be mild for Mom's visit and we'd accompany her through the Dhahran airport.

The vacation became a joyful project. Ocmara paid our airfare, so Mom's was our only expense. I poured over travel books in the library looking for inexpensive hotels and restaurants in London and Paris and collected travel tips from other expats. I hung a countdown-calendar in the kitchen beside a bulletin board with travel articles and pictures.

The call came at 4 in the morning on February 1st.

"Sarah, it's Ruth."

I knew immediately. Ruth's voice was strong in the way you make your voice when you have to deliver the worst possible news. I pushed against hearing. I looked at the clock, doing mental calculations.

"Honey, your mom had a heart attack. I'm so sorry, Sarah. She's gone."

We were 9 hours ahead. She died yesterday—already last month. I sat up.

"Where is she? Is she okay?" I'd heard, but I didn't hear.

Ruth was silent a moment. "She died, honey. She's dead." Ruth's voice crumbled. She'd only had the strength to tell me once and I'd made her tell me twice. I heard her crying on the other end of the line.

For the rest of that long night, Max comforted me the best he could. We cried in each others' arms. In the morning he helped me break the news to Kate and Sam. Both were stunned, saddened, and helpless in the presence of my grief.

In Saudi Arabia there was no just going to the airport and getting on a plane—there was red tape. Max had to get us exit-visas. It would be a week before we could leave. Max worked frantically every day trying to hurry the process and was frustrated at every step. Every night he stumbled into bed and fell asleep. I'd taken to haunting the night again, slipping outside to smoke in the deep shadows of our garden wall.

Grief is universal. The women in Al Hassa knew how to do grief. Anyone who'd lived in Saudi for a while had lost someone or knew someone who had. For an expatriate, loss is complicated by bureaucracy, distance, and time-zones. These many years later I'm still sometimes confused by the date I found out about Mom's death and when she actually died. *Was it the day before, or the day after?* That question can take up strange, determined residency in my mind until I'm forced to sit down and figure it out. As if it really matters.

Bobbi arrived with a casserole and a genuinely warm hug. Tears filled her hazel eyes. Sissie came and Rebecca, other women, too, offering food and comfort. I suddenly felt part of this community of women.

Amy sat on my sofa and cried uncontrollably. Esther had just left and Amy feared someday it would happen to her. She offered to take care of Mimi while we were gone. Again, I'd forgotten about the cat. I was grateful someone else took charge.

Even the woman on the beach seemed to hesitate at the sight of my grief-torn face. All those days waiting to leave I ran to push back sorrow— my running fueled by rage. Because it took so long, I gave Ruth permission to cremate Mom. I wouldn't even be able to see her to say goodbye. As I ran past the woman without stopping, I imagined her dark eyes filled with concern and sympathetic tears.

When we were finally allowed to leave, it took 31 hours to get home. I remember little of the endless flights, except drinking massive quantities of red wine and struggling with guilt. I hadn't seen Mom in almost a year and I'd never see her again. I remembered the day at lunch when she encouraged me to go—that helped ease my guilt, but not my pain.

Resting my forehead on the cool glass window, I stared into the black night sky, arguing with fate. Mom was just 63. My dad had died 8 years earlier at 58. It felt unfair to lose both parents so young. Now I felt a flash of anger—I'd already paid my dues.

It was freezing in Chicago and we were jetlagged, but it felt wonderful to be home. Friends who wintered in Florida loaned us their condo and car. That first night, many of our friends greeted us with hugs and food—the welcome-home party they'd planned turned into a Shiva.

Early the next morning, I took the car and drove north on Sheridan Road, winding through the ravines and tony villages along the shores of Lake Michigan. At first I was scared I might have forgotten how to drive, but after a few minutes I was fine. I cranked up the stereo and reveled in the exhilaration of freedom. I drove all the way to the county line, turned around, and drove back to Evanston.

Wandering the aisles of the grocery store, I was overwhelmed with all the choices. Waiting to check out, I looked around at other customers and employees. Everyone and everything looked the same as it ever had. But I'd experienced so much, I felt like a stranger.

The third day we held Mom's memorial service in our church chapel. Ruth helped us choose Mom's favorite hymns and flowers—daisies and a single gardenia blossom floating in a bowl of water. Mom's and our friends were there, but I was surprised and moved to see some of my hospital coworkers.

"So sorry," people said, hugging me tightly. At the end of Mom's service I was given a startlingly heavy pearly-gray box.

Late that night Max and I lay in bed. "How are you feeling?" He rubbed my back.

"Better." My grief had been soothed by the celebration of Mom's life. There is healing in rituals—I no longer felt as raw.

"It was nice seeing my workmates, but it made me miss my job." I smiled. "I think I'll look for a job when we get back to Saudi."

Max sighed and kissed my forehead. "Let's talk about it then."

We spent the next two weeks putting Mom's affairs in order—picking up death certificates, canceling credit cards, closing bank accounts, disconnecting her phone, selling her car, filing insurance claims—stuff you don't know you have to do until you have to do it. Mom's simple will left me everything. She'd even signed her car title, so it was easy to sell.

One day I spent hours at Ruth's house going through Mom's belongings. I found her suitcase in the closet, clothes neatly folded inside. Ready for a trip she would never take. Her passport was in her lingerie drawer and inside the front cover a brave, solemn picture—her last picture. I stared into her eyes. *Goddamn it, why couldn't you have waited?*

Mom's diamond engagement ring, wedding band, and silver watch were in the baby-blue jewelry box I'd given her when I was 10. I took it, along with her bible, family photographs, and mementos of my dad. Anything else Ruth didn't want, I'd donate to the local women's shelter. After her room was empty of everything but furniture, I changed the bed linens, dusted, and swept while Ruth watched from the doorway.

Ruth had always been athletic and robustly healthy, but now seemed small and frail. A thick line of silvery-grey roots zigzagged through her vibrantly red hair. Mom's death had clearly taken a toll. Ruth had lost her longtime friend and constant companion.

"I miss your mom," Ruth said quietly. "She was such a lovely lady."

"Yes, she was." Tears sprang to my eyes. On the floor was a sprig of silk daisies from a bouquet I'd given Mom years before. I dusted them off and put them in my pocket.

"I'm going downstairs to make tea," Ruth said. "Come down when you're finished, I want to talk to you."

Ten minutes later, Ruth and I were sitting at the green linoleum table in her kitchen. I'd spent so many hours at that table it felt like home.

"I've always loved your house," I said.

"Me, too." Ruth glanced around. "But I'm selling it. It's too big and lonely for just me and I can't afford it anymore." She studied me as she sipped her tea.

For a moment I wondered where Ruth was going with this. *Does she need money?* Then she pushed an envelope toward me. "Your mother wanted you to have this."

Inside were ten crisp one-hundred dollar bills and a $20,000 certificate of deposit—I was sole-beneficiary. I looked at Ruth.

"Where did Mom get all this money?"

"She saved every nickel. The cash was her traveling money." Ruth smiled. "How much is it adding up to with the CD, car, her bank accounts, and insurance? I figure about $35,000."

I did a quick calculation. Mom had a modest savings and a decent amount in her checking account. After her cremation and memorial service,

$5000 was left from insurance. We'd sold the car for $3000. "How'd you know?"

"Your mother told me everything, in case something happened." Ruth lifted her mug, stared at her tea, then set the mug down. When she looked at me, her eyes were dark with concern. "Sarah, you need to put all that money in an account in your name. Don't even touch it."

I'd immediately thought about paying down debt. Ruth had read my mind.

"Take it from me, you never know," Ruth said. "With $35,000 you can walk out anytime you want." I had only a vague sense of Ruth's story, but knew that after her divorce she'd struggled to raise three kids by herself.

"I'm not thinking about divorce," I said.

"I'm not suggesting you are. I'm saying your mother wanted you to have this money. *You*," she emphasized. "She told me to tell you."

I stared at the envelope. Paying down debt was seductive, but having a cushion was equally appealing. Mom had always worried that we had no savings.

"Thanks," I said. "I'll talk to Max."

Ruth covered her face then looked at me through her fingers. "I suggest you do it without telling him."

"I can't do that," I said.

Ruth gazed at me and sighed. "Whatever you have to do, just promise you'll put the money away like your mother wanted."

If part of our reason for going to Saudi was to finally have savings, why not create that with Mom's money? "Okay," I said. "I promise."

Max's eyes widened. "Wow! Think how far that will go." He sipped his Scotch.

"It's not going anywhere," I said. "I'm putting it in savings."

Both kids were at sleepovers with friends and I was making a salad in the condo kitchen. We'd ordered a pizza and were staying in to watch a rented movie.

"All of it?" Max frowned. "That's ridiculous."

"It's not ridiculous." I took a sip of wine. "It's what Mom wanted."

"How about we hold onto the CD until it matures and put the rest in checking?" Max asked. "We don't have to spend it."

"We both know if we put it in our checking account it'll be gone in no time." I felt a flush of wine and annoyance coloring my cheeks. "Mom wanted me to put it into savings in my name."

"Just your name?" he asked.

"It's what Mom wanted," I said slowly.

"Didn't she trust me?" Max sounded indignant.

"Don't even go there. You know how Mom felt about you."

"She didn't trust me and you don't either." Max was getting loud.

"That's not true." I stepped over and hugged Max. "She just wanted to take care of us. You know how frugal she was—always scared about money. She didn't want us to feel that way."

"Yeah, but not spend any of it? And put it all in your name? That sounds like she was scared of me." Max pulled away and poured himself another Scotch.

"I think she knew we'd both spend it if she didn't insist on it going into savings," I said.

"Well, I think that's bullshit." Max glared at me. "And after I did so much for her to come to Saudi, this is the thanks I get."

"Jesus, Max, what the hell?" I felt a surge of rage. "She worked her ass off her whole life and she didn't have to give us a damn thing."

"She didn't give it to us, she gave it to you," Max screamed.

"If she gave it to me, she gave it to us," I screamed back. "What's wrong with you?"

"What's wrong with you?"

Just then the doorbell rang. Max scowled as he went to answer the door. For a moment I wondered if the pizza guy had heard us fighting. My heart raced as I leaned against the counter. We were at an impasse. Max was right. Mom never would have said it, but she knew Max would spend it carelessly. I was right, too. Mom wanted to make sure I wasn't scared about money.

Max came back into the kitchen carrying a familiar red-and-white box and the room filled with the sweet aroma of Chicago-style deep-dish pizza. I smiled and held out my hand. "Truce?"

He hesitated, but the seduction of hot pizza won over. "Truce."

We ate pizza and watched a movie while lounging on the sofa— silently agreeing that the evening was too perfect to wreck with fighting.

"Don't you dare reconsider." Lara's brown eyes flashed indignantly. "That money will be gone in a heartbeat."

I was spending the night in the tiny, two-bedroom apartment Lara shared with her 8-year-old daughter Mia. Lara had arranged a sleepover for Mia so we could visit without interruptions. Now we were wearing flannel pajamas and reclining on the sofa. Lara lived on the 33rd floor of a downtown Chicago high-rise and the lights of the city twinkled below us.

Dinner was cheese and French bread, paté and olives. Dark bittersweet chocolate was dessert. We'd finished a bottle of champagne and were drinking red wine. It was a night for indulgence.

"But he's so hurt," I said.

"He's a big boy. He'll get over it," she said, tossing her dark brown ponytail.

"I hope so."

"Can you say 'codependent'?" Lara nudged me with her foot.

I laughed. *I love this woman.* Lara was the only person I knew who dared speak the truth, however painful.

"Ruth's right, you know." Lara peered over the rim of her wine glass. "With that kind of money you can leave whenever you need to."

I did know the story of Lara's divorce, and it wasn't pretty. And I'd told her about the fight with Max. Lara knew me better than anyone so there was no point denying I was unhappy.

"You might just want to leave Saudi," Lara said. "Ever since I read that book I've been worried sick about you. I told you it was a mistake to go."

"But you said it was an interesting mistake." I smiled. "You were right about that."

"Don't go back," she said.

"I wish I didn't have to." After reconnecting with my "real life" I didn't want to go back.

"Why can't you stay?"

"Max still has two years on his contract," I said.

"Let Max go," Lara said. "You stay here with the kids."

"We have no place to live. Our house is leased."

"Kick them out. Or come live with me and Mia," Lara said. "It'll be fun!"

We laughed at the impracticality, but I had to agree. "It would be fun."

"Rent an apartment." Lara smiled wickedly. "You have $35,000."

The next day I went to a bank, opened a savings account, and deposited $14,000. I also rented a safety-deposit box where I put Mom's jewelry, the cash, and CD certificate. I didn't mention it to Max and, surprisingly, he never asked.

The day we left Evanston, Max and I stopped by our house. We'd called just an hour before to ask if we could, and a woman had answered the phone. Her husband was at work, but she was at home and graciously consented.

"Feel free to walk through." The tenant was a young stay-at-home mother, her two daughters not yet old enough for pre-school. One straddled her hip, thumb in her mouth. The other was down for a nap.

"Thank you so much," I whispered.

"It's okay, really," she said quietly. She knew why we were home early. I saw sympathy in her eyes and gentle smile.

I felt uncomfortable walking through my house, acutely aware I was in someone else's home. The house looked odd with their personal belongings and furniture interspersed with what we'd left behind. Their dishes filled our china cabinet. Her pots and pans hung in my kitchen. Every room was immaculate, even with small children. She was obviously a much better housekeeper than I'd ever been before moving to Saudi. The house had a different smell—not bad, just unfamiliar. *Not my tribe.*

After we thanked her and left, I stood another moment looking at the house. Snow covered the yard and the lilac bushes on either side of the front porch. A lamp glowed warmly inside the front window. From the outside, it still looked like my home. But for the time being, it was lost to me. Just like my real life.

All the way to the airport I struggled against waves of panic. Even as we waited to board, I debated whether to get on the plane or grab my kids and run. In the end, it felt impossible to remain in Chicago. Teary-eyed and subdued, we began the long journey back to Saudi and made it through the Dhahran Airport with no problems. I'd left Mom's ashes in Ruth's care. I was afraid the customs agent would open the box and stick his finger inside—and I would lose my mind, leap over the counter, and beat him to death with my bare hands.

20

We arrived in Saudi the night of March 15. Amy had stocked the refrigerator and put flowers on the table. After her initial feline shunning, Mimi wove a welcome around our ankles. Nothing had changed and everything was different.

I felt buzzy with fatigue and my body ached. After putting the kids to bed I lay beside Max, but couldn't sleep. I stared into the darkness, too bone-weary to move. When the alarm rang at 6, I feigned sleep while Max got up and dressed for work. I finally dozed off and the kids and I slept all day. The next day was Wednesday and I kept them home from school. On Saturday Max went to work, the kids went to school, and I went back to bed.

It felt crazy to be back. I felt crazy. Women returning from repat were crazy in a way that looked like depression, rage, or both. Most became reclusive until jetlag and reentry shock wore off. I remembered Rebecca rocking and humming. *What was that song she was humming?*

I rummaged through our CDs until I found it—*The Sloop John B,* by the Beach Boys. I played it over and over. The lyrics filled the room and my head. *Let me go home, I want to go home. I feel so broke up, I wanna go home. I* sang along until I knew every word. *This is the worst trip I've ever been on.*

My mother was dead and strangers were living in my house. I wanted to go home, but didn't know where that was anymore. I found myself rocking and humming to the words repeating in my head. *Oh, my God. It's happening to me!*

For two weeks I never left my house. Amy stopped by, but after she and her family left on repat I was totally alone. I slipped out for groceries then rushed back home. When I occasionally thought about looking for a job, the idea made me tired. I slept most days and stayed up most nights. I'd become as nocturnal as a cat.

Max and I had just gone to bed one night when he handed me a gift-wrapped box.

"Open it."

Inside was a gold bangle-bracelet—a design twined around it like a delicate vine. It was beautiful, but not something I would have chosen. "It's lovely."

"It's your name in Arabic." With his fingertip Max found a point on the bracelet and traced counter-clockwise—and the indecipherable became distinct.

He can't take it back, I thought, as I slipped it on my wrist. My tan had faded—the white band from my Bedouin bracelet now just a ghostly suggestion. The gold bracelet looked out of place on my arm. "What's the occasion?"

Max shrugged and smiled. "No occasion." *Something feels off.*

"Very sweet of you." I studied the bracelet. When I looked at Max, I saw the nervous tugging at the corners of his mouth. "What did you get yourself?" I kept my tone light.

Max froze then laughed too loudly. He should have known I'd know. Max got a bag from the dresser then climbed back in bed. Obviously stalling, he looked in the bag then closed it again.

"Just show me." I swiped the bag from him, took out a box, and lifted the lid. Inside was a gold Rolex watch. "What's all this?" My tone was no longer light.

"Jesus, it's been such a hard time." Max sighed. "I thought it would make you feel better."

"You bought me a bracelet to make me feel better. Really?" I held up the watch-box. "Is this what you bought to make yourself feel better? A fucking Rolex?"

Max looked nervous. Like he thought I was going to throw the watch across the room. Maybe I was. He took it from me.

"Where'd you get the money for all this?" I asked.

"We had all that money we saved from not going to Europe."

I felt like he'd punched me in the gut. I stared at him.

"Come on, babe," Max pleaded. "There's money left. We'll keep saving and go to Europe next year."

"It's not about fucking Europe!" I screamed. "We had that money because my mother died." I pulled off the bracelet and threw it across the room.

"Ssshhhh, you'll wake the kids." Max reached out and I shrank back, batting his hands away.

Although Max hadn't used Mom's money directly, it felt tied together in a vulgar way. I rolled on my side and refused to be comforted. After Max was asleep, I pulled a pack of cigarettes from under the bathroom sink and crept outside for a smoke. I hadn't touched a cigarette since we'd left Saudi to go home, but that night I thought Mama would understand.

The third week in April, Max came into the bedroom while I was reading myself to sleep.

"I want you to do something for me," Max said.

"What?"

"My new engineer just arrived in Saudi. I need you to visit his wife and welcome her," Max said. "Her name is Jennifer Sanders. You have something in common."

"What's that?"

"You're both Yankees." Max grinned. "They're from Philadelphia."

"I can't." I covered my face with my hands.

"Yes, you can. You have to." Max pulled my hands from my face. "Ben graduated first in his class from MIT. He could go anywhere. I need him here."

I was silent.

"Baby, I need you to pull yourself together."

I closed my eyes and sighed. When I opened them Max was still staring at me.

"Ben has the expertise critical for this project. If it's successful I'll get promoted."

I stared at him. "I don't know even what you do. What is the project?"

Max hesitated. "It's classified." When I just blinked, he sighed. "We're computerizing the whole refinery and teaching the Saudis to run everything. The Saudi government wants to totally eliminate any dependency on Western engineers."

"So if you do your job well, you no longer have a job?" *At last, a beam of hope.*

"That's about right," he said.

"Then I guess it's in my best interest to make sure Ben stays."

The next morning I went for a run. My heart was broken and my body ached, but it was time to rejoin the living. Mom would have long grown impatient with my self-indulgence. My legs felt leaden and with every step I resisted the urge to turn back.

It was quiet on the beach—the ocean a dark still presence in the early morning light. Call to prayer echoed in the distance. As I rounded the curve, I saw the woman on the beach. She walked toward me, ankle-bracelet glinting softly. It was comforting to see her, as if we were picking up where we'd left off. She stopped when I neared. Without slowing, I nodded and wove around her. I felt her watching me as I continued to run.

Back home, I kicked off my shoes and went to the kitchen. I was pulling a baking sheet of chocolate-chip cookies from the oven when Kate shuffled in. She leaned sleepily into me, resting her chin on my shoulder. I suddenly realized she was taller than I was. *When had that happened?*

"Morning, sweetie." I kissed her cheek.

"You're stinky." Kate wrinkled her nose and pulled away.

"Thanks." I slid a spatula under each cookie. "I ran this morning."

"About time." Kate reached for a cookie. "Breakfast?" She nibbled gingerly.

"Your dad wants me to visit his new engineer's wife. I'm taking them to her."

"You?" Kate widened her eyes in mocking disbelief. "A welcome woman?"

I gave her an exaggerated, puzzled look. "Why not?"

"No reason." Kate shrugged, her expression suddenly serious. She reached out, wiped my cheek then showed me her thumb. It was coated with chocolate from the raw dough I'd consumed for breakfast. "Caught you." Kate popped her thumb into her mouth.

I laughed, but knew I had to work harder at looking okay. "Where's Sam?"

As if conjured, Sam walked in cradling Mimi. "Cookies!"

I pulled him close and kissed the top of his head. I liked having one kid still shorter than I was. Suddenly I remembered the summer I'd grown taller than my mom and started calling her "short ribs." I felt a wash of sadness and turned away before the kids could see my face.

While dressing, I tried to remember what helped me when I'd first arrived in Saudi about the same time last year. Ramadan had arrived earlier this year, so we were a week into our second Ramadan in Saudi. It seemed much longer than a year.

An hour later, I stood on Jennifer's porch wearing a determined smile. My face was sweaty, my blouse damp under the arms. I'd ridden my bike, balancing a foil-wrapped plate of cookies and practicing my welcome speech. My backpack was full of maps and cold bottled water.

When I rang the doorbell a second time, I wondered if I had the wrong address. Maybe the right numbers, but the wrong street. Everything looked so much the same it was still easy to get lost. I'd turned to leave when the door opened.

Jennifer stood squinting in the sunlight. She was barefoot and wearing a baggy T-shirt and sweatpants. Her short dark hair was matted against one side of her head and sticking straight up on the other. Sleep-wrinkles creased her cheek on the matted side.

"Hi, Jennifer. I'm Sarah Hayes." I smiled apologetically. "Want me to come back another time?" I felt intrusive and was eager to pedal away.

Jennifer shook her head. "No, it's okay. Come in." Her voice sounded froggy from sleep.

I followed her into a living room identical to mine. Clutter covered every surface and suitcases overflowed onto the floor. It was the house of a refugee. Stepping over piles, I perched on the edge of the only empty chair, setting the cookies on the coffee table.

Jennifer settled on the sofa into the nest of blankets where she'd obviously been sleeping. We sat silently for several minutes. Dust motes swirled in a sliver of light escaping from between closed drapes. I'd forgotten what I was going to say.

When she cleared her throat I remembered. I opened my backpack and pulled out the bottle of water. "I brought you this," I said. "The tap water is awful. Don't drink it."

Jennifer opened the bottle and took a long swig. "Thanks," she croaked.

"And I brought you a map of Al Hassa." I pointed to a spot on the map and tried to recite Sissie's speech. "I've circled your house. This is the beach. This is the postal center and commissary. Here are the pools and tennis courts." I smiled at Jennifer, but she was staring dully at the map. Jennifer was younger than I, maybe early thirties, and Midwestern pale. Her blue eyes had dark circles beneath them.

"And here's the Women's Club. There are meetings and teas and a welcome coffee..." I stopped when I realized how annoyingly cheerful I sounded.

Jennifer was unresponsive. We sat in total silence for five minutes before I zipped up my backpack. I knew all too well how it felt to have just arrived in Saudi. Now I also knew how hard Sissie's job had been.

"I should go," I said.

"Is that food?" Jennifer nodded toward the plate. Her voice, I'd learn, was naturally gravelly.

"Sorry! I baked you cookies." I unwrapped them.

Jennifer reached for a cookie, but froze mid-reach. Her fingertips were black. Jennifer lifted her hands and stared at them, her eyes hollow and frightened.

"They fingerprinted me. I can't get it off. And they took my passport." Jennifer's voice had an edge of panic moving toward hysteria. Now she looked at me with an expression so desperate I wanted both to hold and comfort her—and run for my life.

I took a deep breath, trying to remember what I was supposed to say. I shrugged and tried to sound casual. "That's just company policy." It sounded false, even to my ears. I'd just surrendered my passport again when we returned from repat. I knew what she was feeling and felt like a hypocrite.

"But what if I want to leave?" Jennifer asked.

Good question. Attempting a reassuring smile, I kept my tone confident and soothing while I lied to Jennifer. "Not a problem. Your husband applies for your exit-visa." Suddenly I understood why Sissie had made light of my concerns. I wondered if she'd felt as creepy and guilty when she'd lied to me, as I felt lying to Jennifer.

Jennifer leaned forward. "Can't I apply for the visa?"

"No, he's the employee."

Jennifer stared incredulously then buried her head in both hands. "Jesus, I can't do this." She looked at me. "I'm an engineer, for God's sake. I need to do something more meaningful than go to teas and bake cookies." Her voice was raised angrily. It was the most life I'd seen in her.

But I also felt like I'd been slapped. Stung and embarrassed, I kept the ridiculous smile plastered on my face. "Do you have a work-permit?"

Jennifer shook her head.

"Apply for one," I said.

Jennifer crossed her arms and rocked with agitation. She gazed at the floor with narrow eyes, chewing her bottom lip, shaking one foot. I could tell she was trying not to cry. Anger was hard for me to deal with, but this broke my heart. I leaned forward and spoke honestly.

"It's hard for everyone at first, but it gets easier. I promise." *Somewhat easier.* I refused to tell Jennifer she'd love it. But I realized how much I wanted her to stay and understood how much all the women of Ocmara wanted newcomers to stay.

Jennifer looked skeptical. "How long have you been here?"

"Almost a year," I said.

When Jennifer shook her head and looked even more panicked, I picked up the map and a pen. I wrote big numbers in the margin. "My phone number, you can call me." Then I remembered the phone taps, but knew I couldn't tell Jennifer about them just yet. I was afraid I wouldn't be able to handle her reaction.

"Wait, even better." I drew a circle around my house. "Here's where I live. Come by anytime." And, just to make sure. "If you call me, I'll come right over."

Jennifer looked at the map.

"Okay?" I asked.

When she nodded, I smiled again. "You'll be alright." I hoped I could make that be the truth.

Late that afternoon I went to the beach again. The kids were doing homework and Max was working late. Since we'd been back, he was putting in longer hours. I walked barefoot along the water's edge. To my left, the enormous red sun was setting over the desert, casting brilliant reflections on the sand, sea, and sky. It was unbelievably beautiful. When I was far past the houses, I waded into the warm dark water. My skirt caught in the gentle waves as I stared toward the horizon, listening to call to prayer.

It was there Max found me. I was startled by the sound of his voice. Suddenly I was aware call to prayer was long over, and I'd been standing, lulled by the warmth and the pink, for much longer than I'd realized. I'd lost touch with how calming the water could be. Night was falling and I hadn't even noticed.

I turned and saw Max waving. After one last glance at the darkening horizon, I waded back to shore. My skirt was heavy against my legs and the tide had changed. It took longer to reach the shallows. When I finally walked onto the sand, I smiled at Max as I wrung out my skirt.

"Katie told me you were at the beach. I was worried, I had no idea you'd be this far."

It was true, Max and I'd never walked this far north together. The closest we'd ever come was that morning in the rain.

"So how'd it go?" Max smiled eagerly as he took my hand and we started home.

"What?"

"Your visit with Ben's wife."

I felt a twinge of betrayal. It was my first real day out of the house in over a month and all he cared about was his new engineer. I waited an extra moment then nodded.

"It went great. I like her a lot." As soon as I said it, it felt true.

Max frowned. "I heard she's a nightmare. She gave them hell at processing."

Good for her. I realized that Jennifer reminded me of Bonita. "She's jetlagged. Her place is a disaster. She'll be okay."

"She better be. Ray's pressuring me and Mohammed is watching all of us." Max squeezed my hand. "We don't want anything distracting Ben from his job."

My smile wavered. "Like a wife who is pissed off about her phone being tapped? Don't worry. I'll take care of her."

I would tell Jennifer about the taps next time I saw her. If she didn't immediately bolt and run, she'd know to use code when talking on the phone. Either way, I wanted to protect her from the trauma Bonita had experienced.

Max kissed my forehead. "That's my girl, I'm counting on you."

The rest of that week I was up early, struggling and gasping as I forced myself to jog. Whenever I took time off from running, it was hard getting back. Each time was more difficult. Once again I promised myself to stay disciplined. As I jogged I scanned the beach and cliffs, but there was no sign of the woman.

And every day I helped Jennifer get settled. She recovered quickly from her initial trauma. On the second day, she was showered, dressed, and the ink had disappeared from her fingertips.

"How'd you do it?" I examined her hands. Her nails were clipped short and her cuticles were pink and raw. They looked like they hurt.

"Scrub brush and persistence," she said in her rough voice.

We chatted while I helped her put her house in order. I was nervous telling Jennifer about the phone taps, but she took it well.

"I don't think that'll be a problem," she said. "I'm not much for chatting on the phone."

We talked about the weekend coming up. True to form, the Mitchells were throwing a welcome party and Jennifer was understandably anxious. Except for the first day, she'd not left the house. Besides Ben, I was the only person she knew in Saudi. Jennifer had yet to meet Max and I hadn't met Ben. The four of us planned to go to the party together on Thursday.

This was my first party since returning to Saudi. I dreaded it, but remembered Bobbi's compassion when Mom died. During the nightmarish wait for exit-visas, Bobbi arrived every day with food and comfort. Remembering made it easier.

"What should I wear?" Jennifer asked.

"Dressy-casual." I didn't know how to prepare Jennifer for all the gold, miniskirts, and tan, crepey cleavage. "I'm wearing a skirt and blouse."

"Good, I hate dressy-dressy," she said. "I don't even own a skirt."

Jennifer made it clear she was not a "girly girl," but she was very pretty. She had delicate features and was so short and petite I felt enormous standing beside her. I couldn't imagine how hard it must have been for Jennifer to be taken seriously in the male-dominated field of engineering.

21

The night of the party I chose a modest V-neck blouse and I wore the gold bracelet for the first time. Max glanced at my wrist then gave me a long, tight hug. It felt good to be connected.

"You're beautiful," he murmured against my ear.

"And you're very handsome." His rolled sleeves showed off his tan muscular forearms and Rolex watch.

When Max insisted on driving Jennifer and Ben the three blocks to the party, I knew he wanted to impress them with what Ocmara money could buy. Max kept the Land Rover immaculate and it still had that new-car-panache. It was foreign, exotic—English Leather on wheels. I knew Jennifer wouldn't be impressed by a car.

Jennifer and Ben were wearing athletic shoes, khakis, and polo shirts. Ben's shirt was navy and Jennifer's baby blue. They looked like His and Her engineers. Ben had sandy brown hair, green eyes, and a pleasant smile. He was of average height and build, but Jennifer looked tiny and delicate next to him. They were cute together.

"You look nice," Jennifer said. "Pretty bracelet."

"Thanks." I was aware of Max's smile.

Someone besides Ray opened the door, so Max and I led Jennifer and Ben through the crowded room. It was the Mitchells' "adults only" party—oil-men, gussied-up women, moonshine, cigarettes, and small talk. Knowing the parties overwhelmed me, Max kept his arm around my shoulder while I carried my cake.

Jennifer looked at the cake. "Shit! I didn't bring anything. I'm an idiot!"

"No, you're not." I smiled. "You're new."

"And I'm totally dressed wrong," she said. "I'm way too casual."

"Stop it," I said. "You look cute."

People crowded in, thrilled to see Max. In the sudden crush, I wanted to disappear, but Max exuded his usual charisma and I felt the familiar pride that his arm was around me.

"Here are our host and lovely hostess," Max finally announced. "Jennifer, meet Ray and Bobbi Mitchell."

Ray grinned and slapped Max on the back. Then he kissed my cheek and smiled sympathetically. "Hey, babe, how're you doing?"

"Fine, thanks," I said, surprised at sudden tears. Tears clearly made Ray uncomfortable.

"Good, good." Ray stepped back, nodded at Jennifer then vigorously shook Ben's hand. "Our guest of honor! Glad you could make it."

While I blinked back tears, Bobbi, in a skimpy formfitting dress, reached out to Ben and Jennifer. "Nice to meet you both," she cooed. She smiled up at Max. "Hey, handsome."

But Bobbi's eyes went soft and damp when she turned to me. "I see you brought one of your fabulous desserts." Right on cue, a houseboy took the cake. Bobbi hugged me, then held me at arm's length and smiled. "You look marvelous, as usual." Bobbi grinned at Jennifer. "Sarah's desserts are to die for, but somehow she never gains an ounce."

After Bobbi moved away, Jennifer looked at me. "What's going on? Why did Ray ask how you're doing?"

"My mom just died." I willed myself not to cry.

"Oh, my God, I'm so sorry," Jennifer said. "Why didn't you tell me?"

"You've had a lot going on."

While Bobbi flirtatiously greeted another male guest, Jennifer whispered, "When do we swap keys?" I laughed so loud I had to cover my mouth.

As houseboys bustled about serving food and refilling glasses, men and women formed separate groups. Women gossiped and men shared stories. Jennifer and I were close enough to overhear a man named Bob.

"They used to give chits for bags of ice when you first arrived," Bob said. "The day after I got here I went to get my ice. The Saudi at the icehouse said my chit was for 'yesterday's ice.' I told him I couldn't make it yesterday and wanted my ice today. He said he couldn't give me today's ice with yesterday's chit." Bob grinned. "We pushed that damn chit back and forth."

"What'd you do?" Another man asked.

"I finally asked that stupid Saudi if he had any ice left over from yesterday," Bob said. "When he said 'yes,' I asked for yesterday's ice and he gave me a bag." The men laughed heartily, congratulating Bob on his brilliance.

"Really?" Jennifer whispered. "They think that's funny?"

I nodded. "They call them 'stupid Saudi stories.'"

Jennifer shook her head.

For an hour we nibbled on appetizers and drank wine. I introduced Jennifer around, trying to make her feel included. Across the room, Max was particularly animated, no doubt showing off for Ben. Max caught my glance, winked, and blew me a kiss. I smiled, still feeling the glow of being the popular boy's girl.

Jennifer and I were on the outskirts of a group of women when I noticed she seemed agitated. Her face was flushed and she was looking around. She flagged down a houseboy for another refill of wine and took a deep swallow.

Conversation in the women's cluster had taken on the hushed tone that signals juicy gossip. Heads were leaned in, ears perked, eyes bright. Nostrils seemed to flair, picking up the heady scent of prey.

"Poor thing, only back a week and already wearing those huge sunglasses, like no one can tell." The woman smiled and shook her head— insincerity resonated.

"Have ya'll heard about Dr. Phillips?" Bobbi asked, holding her cigarette high. "Smoke was billowing from his house last night and when security showed up he was passed out drunk on the sofa. His cigarette started a fire." Bobbi smiled. "He was arrested and Rebecca is being deported next week."

Rebecca? My Rebecca? I was surprised by my strong feeling of kinship.

There were horrified gasps. "The house was on fire? Where was Rebecca?"

"Upstairs in their bedroom, sound asleep." Bobbi raised an eyebrow. "Or maybe she was passed out, too." Bobbi took a long drag and, as the smoke slowly escaped through her smirk, I suddenly detested her.

"He's my doctor! They can't arrest a doctor!" This woman was genuinely upset.

Bobbi tapped the ash from her cigarette. "Doesn't matter. Not even Mohammed can fix this."

The murmurs were concerned. Hushed.

"So, where the fuck is Mohammed?" Jennifer's voice was loud and slurred. The room quieted as everyone turned to stare. Jennifer looked around with a puzzled expression. "We're in fucking Saudi Arabia and there's not a single fucking Arab at this party."

"Oh, honey." Bobbi smiled, shaking her head. "We never socialize with them."

Across the room, Ben looked stricken and Max signaled me with an alarmed expression. I put my arm around Jennifer. "Come on, let's get you more food."

Jennifer took another gulp of wine then glared around the room. "It's like we're in some fucking bizarre Club Med," she yelled.

While other women exchanged glances, I suppressed a laugh. *Exactly!* Jennifer had put into words what I'd not been able to articulate.

When I got in bed that night, Max was staring at the ceiling. I was nude under my black silk abaya. After the evening's drama and all that wine, I was definitely in the mood.

"Hey." I smiled invitingly.

"You said Jennifer was nice," Max stated flatly.

I closed my eyes and sighed. "I said I like her."

"Do you still like her?" His tone told me the correct answer.

I looked at Max and shrugged playfully. "Well, she does have a point."

Max's rage was instantaneous. He sat up, face red and contorted. "If this project tanks I can kiss this promotion goodbye." Max jabbed his finger at me. "And it will be your fault." His eyes burned with hatred. "Is that what you want?"

It had been awhile since I'd seen the chilling change in Max's eyes. "No, baby, of course not." Heart racing, I touched his arm. "Of course that's not what I want."

Max yanked his arm away. "Jesus Christ! You said you'd take care of her."

"I'm sorry," I whispered.

Max lowered his voice to a menacing whisper. "She thinks she wants to see Arabs? Take her to see fucking Arabs."

I stared at him, breathing deeply, then smiled and reached out again. "I will," I whispered, rubbing his chest. "I promise. Sorry, baby." I kissed him. Only apologies and adoration worked.

Max didn't respond, but didn't pull away. I kissed him again and again. Finally, he rolled toward me. I wasn't in the mood anymore, but it felt the lesser of two evils.

Much later, in the deepest darkest part of the night, I was still awake. It had been years since Max was transformed by rage—and that familiar stranger caught me by surprise, leaving me unsettled. Eyes closed, I tried to match my breathing with Max's, but we were out of synch. *I've got to get out of here.* I pulled on my abaya and quietly padded downstairs.

Outside the back gate, I smoked a cigarette and stared up at the vast black sky. The night was balmy and I had just begun to relax when I heard rustling nearby. I froze, instinctively cupping the cigarette in my hand. My eyes searched the night.

Barely visible in the darkness, a veiled woman walked barefoot on the path leading to the beach. She moved slowly and I heard the faint chime of bells with each step. Suddenly she froze, as if she'd caught my scent. Standing stock-still, she turned her head and looked at me. It was an apparition so dark I felt chills. Sweat drenched my armpits and my mouth went dry. I stepped backwards into my yard and watched from inside the gate. The woman hesitated another moment before continuing down the path.

My heart raced as adrenaline flooded my body the second time that night. I leaned against the wall, catching my breath. I was positive it was the woman from the beach. After a moment's hesitation, I crushed out the smoldering cigarette and followed.

The path was smooth, but the soles of my bare feet were tender. I winced when I felt the occasional sharp stone, but resisted crying out. I knew I'd have to toughen up to do this again. Already, I knew I'd do it again.

Over the dunes, the water was so black the horizon was invisible. There was no moon, just a myriad of stars—pinpricks of light in the sky. Even the sand was a darker shade of gray. Scanning the beach, I saw the woman moving, like a shadow. I followed, feeling invisible in my abaya, except for my pale hair and skin.

When she stopped, I crouched in the darkness. She took off her abaya and veils, dropping them into an inky pile on the sand. Naked, she walked to the water's edge. Her body was slim, pale skin in vivid contrast to the black night. Her dark hair fell thick and wavy around her shoulders and I saw the long line of her back, the fullness of her hips. She waded into the water until it was waist deep, then she raised her arms and dove in—surfacing some distance away.

I sat hidden in the deepest shadows of the dunes, watching the woman swim. She swam with strong graceful strokes, arms flashing in pale arcs against the black sky. Back and forth, parallel to the beach, an even number of strokes each way. After a long while she waded out, bent over, and squeezed water from her hair. She dressed quickly then hurried down the beach, disappearing into the darkness.

After she left I stared at where she'd been swimming. It was as if I'd imagined her. I got up and walked to the water. There was an eerie luminescent neon-green ruffle along the water's edge. Gathering my abaya, I waded in. The warm water swirled around my calves, tugging, pushing. I planted my feet firmly and faced the invisible horizon. I wondered how it would feel to dive in, surrendering to the dark salty sea. I imagined the exhilaration of swimming under the blanket of stars. Suddenly, I felt a flash of fear. The air and water temperature were the same. The sand, sea, and sky a continuous black. I had no sense of north or south, up or down.

I turned and waded quickly back to the beach. It was then I saw her ankle-bracelet glistening dully in the sand. It was heavy and cool, the soft chime of tiny bells tangible evidence of the woman. I held the bracelet to my nose. The metallic scent smelled like fear.

I lay awake watching the clock until 4 a.m. With the tip of my tongue I licked the inside of my wrist, tasting salt. I felt the lightest dusting of sand between my toes. I'd left the ankle-bracelet tucked into one of my running shoes, not daring to risk bringing it upstairs and waking Max.

At daybreak, I jogged slowly down the beach, dizzy with fatigue and hope. I saw her in the distance—I knew she'd be there. She walked in tight circles, staring down, crouching and running her hands through the sand. She froze as I approached, then stood up.

I walked toward her, the ankle-bracelet in my upturned palm like an offering to a wild beast. She reached out and took it. "Thank you," she whispered.

"You're welcome." Neither of us moved for several moments. "My name is Sarah Hayes."

After another long silence the woman lifted her veil. Dark brown eyes were visible above her black mask. Her eyelids were swollen and there were dark circles under her eyes.

"I'm Yasmeen Ali." She glanced at the bracelet and back at me. "When did you find it?" Yasmeen had only the slightest hint of an accent.

"Last night."

Her eyes widened. "Please, promise you won't tell anyone. Not anyone." Yasmeen's tone was urgent. "My husband will kill me."

I smiled. "I understand. My husband would kill me if he knew I smoked."

Yasmeen grabbed one of my hands with both of hers. The ankle-bracelet cut into my palm as she squeezed my hand. She leaned close and gazed into my eyes with an intensity I'd never seen before. "You don't understand. It's not the same. Please, promise."

"I promise."

"Shukran." Yasmeen dropped my hand and pulled the veil over her face. "Thank you." She backed up, turned, and ran away. I watched as she disappeared down the beach.

"Yasmeen," I whispered, feeling the foreign name on my lips. "Yasmeen Ali." *My friend on the beach, Yasmeen Ali.* Exhausted and exhilarated, I began the slow run home.

22

Determined to regain my emotional and physical strength, I started going to bed early so I could run every day at dawn. I watched for Yasmeen, but she was never there. Some nights I startled awake at 3 or 4, as if from a dream or a beckoning. I slipped on my abaya, went outside, and waited. A few times I stepped outside the gate, summoning courage to go to the beach, but fear stopped me. It was black and still, and I was afraid to go alone.

On May 1st we had been in Saudi one year. Amy was due back the 7th. I'd missed her. On the 6th I left flowers, groceries, and cookies at Amy's—hoping to make her reentry as smooth as possible. On the 7th I waited for a call. On the 8th I called in the afternoon and left a message on the answering machine. That night my phone rang.

"Sarah? It's Mark, Amy's husband. Amy wanted me to call you."

I felt a twinge of apprehension. "Is everything okay?"

"Yes and no. Everyone's okay, but Amy and the kids are still in the States," he said.

"Oh," I said. "When are they coming back?"

"They're not." Mark's tone was clipped. "After your mother died Amy decided she didn't want to be away from her mom." The last was said with a hint of accusatory.

I remembered the first time we met. *Mark has wanted to come back to Saudi his whole life.* I felt Mark expected me to apologize for my mother's death.

"Anyway, I'm packing up the house," Mark continued. "Amy sent you a letter and wants me to give you some stuff. I'll drop it off soon."

After hanging up, I cried.

Several days later the doorbell rang and I found a box on the porch. Inside were a letter, three silver Christmas ornaments, and the blue silk comforter. Amy knew I loved it. Wrapping myself in the comforter, I read her letter. Amy apologized for not coming back, but knew I'd understand.

She hoped the comforter would "comfort" me and promised to keep in touch.

The last Wednesday in May I took Jennifer to Al Khobar on the Women's Club shopping trip. We'd already been to Rahima, where I introduced her to Arab bread and the produce market, but I knew Jennifer wouldn't really experience Saudi until she saw the souqs.

On the ride down, I pointed out the camels.

"I've never seen camels outside a zoo!" She smiled.

"We'll go to the camel market sometime. You'll love it."

I didn't point out the break in the fence, which still had the power to quicken my heartbeat and tighten my gut.

Temperatures were in the 90s, so we were assaulted by stifling heat when we got off the bus. But soon we entered the shady market and I felt a wave of pleasure at the potpourri of smells, Middle Eastern music, babble of voices, and buzz of excitement. The energy was especially high, being right after Ramadan. I hadn't been since December so it seemed new again. And, since meeting Yasmeen, I imagined the eyes and names of the veiled women we passed.

Jennifer was smiling. I was showing her the Arabia she wanted to see, and she looked around with all the wonder I remembered feeling my first time in the souqs. I pulled out my camera and took furtive shots as we walked through the crowded alleys. Our first stop was the abaya store.

Jennifer draped a hijab over her head and I took a picture. Then she looked through the rack of designer abayas. "Wow, these are silk."

"I use a silk one for my robe." It seemed so long ago I'd made that extravagant purchase. "Nylon is good for everyday."

Jennifer laughed. "Like a house dress?"

I couldn't talk her into silk. The abaya she chose was plain and inexpensive—the Middle Eastern equivalent to khaki slacks and a polo shirt.

At the gold souqs, Jennifer looked at me with a smirk. "Is this where the women of Al Hassa bejewel themselves?"

I laughed. "Come," I said. "I'll show you my favorite souq."

At the spice shop, the young Saudi man smiled when he saw me. "Marhaba."

"Marhaba," I answered. "I brought a new friend to show her your shop."

"Hello. Please look around." He smiled and gestured gracefully toward his colorful baskets.

"See this?" I tossed Jennifer a small, hard, greenish-black ball. "It's a lime."

Jennifer examined it. "Imagine this in a margarita!"

We laughed, and instantly I craved an icy-cold margarita with a wedge of lime—light salt.

"I'd kill for a margarita right now!" Jennifer said.

"You just read my mind." I widened my eyes. "Seriously."

As we fantasized about margaritas, two veiled, abaya-clad women stopped beside us. They chatted while filling paper bags with spices, paid the shopkeeper, and left.

Jennifer grimaced. "Jesus, how do they stand it in this heat?"

It was much cooler in the shady souqs than in the sunlight, but still uncomfortably hot. With no breeze and more shoppers than usual, it felt particularly stifling. As I watched the dark forms of the women I wondered how they stood it at all.

"I don't know." I shrugged.

Sweat slicked Jennifer's face and darkened the underarms of her long-sleeved denim shirt. She took off the shirt and tied it around her waist. Underneath, she wore a white T-shirt. Jennifer crouched to read the signs in the baskets.

"Cardamom, coriander, cumin. What do you make with this?" Jennifer asked.

"Different Arab dishes."

Jennifer scooped up a handful of amber nuggets. "Frankincense?"

"It's incense. Smell it." I snapped a shot as Jennifer smelled the frankincense with an expression of exaggerated delight. She laughed, dumped it back into the basket, and stood up. At that moment a man started shouting in Arabic.

The matawah appeared from nowhere, blindsiding us with his rage. His sandals slapped the ground as he rushed toward us, waving a whip. Indignation darkened his eyes. Spit spewed into the air with every angry word he screamed. He towered over Jennifer, viciously whipping her arms. Mouth open in a wordless scream, Jennifer was too stunned to move.

Without thinking, I rushed between them. "La! La!" I screamed at the matawah. "Stop!"

He did stop, for a split-second, before turning his wrath on me. The lash of his fury stung my face and arms. I screamed and raised my hands as the matawah's arm became a blur. Beating me fueled his rage. He yelled at male Saudi onlookers, as if to engage them in his battle.

It was the spice man who stepped forward, but his words were directed at the matawah. I couldn't understand him, but his tone was pleading and rational. As the matawah hesitated, several other Saudi men stepped forward. Their chorus of voices seemed to talk him down. Still, the matawah stood braced and irate, muttering loudly, pumped with indignation.

Within minutes, two Saudi policemen arrived and escorted me and Jennifer to the police station. They confiscated our shopping bags, backpacks, and IDs, then led us down a hallway.

"Wait here," a policeman said, ushering us into a room. He locked the door behind him.

The room was tiny, hot, and airless. There were four chairs and a table. On the table was a metal pitcher of water and two plastic glasses. Jennifer and I huddled together.

"What do you think is going to happen?" she whispered.

I cast a slow, meaningful glance toward the obvious two-way mirror. "I don't know."

"You think the room is bugged?" Jennifer mouthed.

I nodded.

We sat quietly, sweating and sipping water. Occasionally one of us started crying, but we'd stop ourselves. It didn't feel safe to talk or cry. Sweat stung my cuts and when I wiped my face, my hand came away bloodied. Angry welts crisscrossed Jennifer's arms. We dabbed our faces with her denim shirt until it was wet and bloodstained.

Over several hours, the door opened only once. We were led to a filthy hammam buzzing with flies, the floor slick with urine. There was no toilet paper. Jennifer and I took turns holding each other steady over the hole in the floor. The stench was unbearable and we were gagging before we were done.

"Can you tell us what's happening?" Jennifer asked the policeman taking us back to the room. He shut the door and locked it without answering.

The pitcher was refilled in our absence, but neither of us drank more. The trip to the hammam was too horrible to repeat. Eventually, there was commotion outside the door. We heard Max and Ben conferring with the police and the matawah. The door opened and our husbands walked in. The policemen and the matawah watched from the doorway.

Without making eye-contact, Max slid two pieces of paper and a pen in front of us. "Sign these and we can go." His expression told me nothing. I reached for the pen.

But Jennifer looked at the paper and grabbed my hand. "It's all in Arabic. What does it say?"

Ben sighed. "They're confessions to public indecency."

"What does that mean?" I asked.

"Jennifer's arms were bare. You resisted a matawah. They could have jailed you," Max said.

Jennifer and I looked at each other incredulously.

"Instead, they're releasing you into our custody," Ben said.

I picked up the pen, but Jennifer stopped me again. "Don't sign it," she hissed. "We don't know what it really says and what will happen if we sign."

Max leaned down and spoke in a quiet firm voice. "Here's what will happen if you don't. We'll all go to jail and Ben and I will lose our jobs."

I was tired, in pain, terrified, and had to pee again. I signed and gave Jennifer the pen. After she signed, Max grabbed the papers and gave them to the police. The matawah looked barely contained, as if he'd hoped we'd be jailed instead of confessing to unjust, arbitrary crimes.

I looked at Jennifer who surprised me by covering her face and sobbing. "It's all my fault. I'm so sorry." I knew nothing I said at that moment could change her mind.

Jennifer and I rode home in the backseat in dense silence. It was night, and I saw our dim reflections in the window. Leaning my head against the glass, I slept as the dark desert flew by.

When we got home I called the Al Hassa Clinic, but it was closing. They took my name and told me to come in the next morning at 8. So, I took a shower and washed my hair. I stood awhile letting a gentle cool spray bathe my face. But afterwards it was still red and swollen, and there was bruising on my forehead and cheeks. The matawah's whip had left angry, oozing lesions slashed across my face.

Later, we picked at leftovers I threw together for dinner. After briefly explaining what happened in Khobar, Max lapsed into stony silence and I had no energy for small talk. The kids cast frightened, furtive glances at me until Kate finally broke the silence.

"I don't understand. How could he beat you?" Her eyes filled with tears.

"Yeah, Mom, what did you do?" Sam looked scared and indignant.

I wanted to reassure them, but it hurt to smile. "Please don't worry. It's okay." My words sounded as hollow as I felt.

Max stabbed angrily at his food and the sharp sound of metal on porcelain startled us. "It's not okay." Max pointed his fork at me. "Your mom broke the rules and she got into trouble."

Stunned, I looked at Max. *He's afraid he's going to lose his engineer!* There had been no pretense of comfort since he picked us up at the police station—no hug, no touch—not even a glance. Another time I might have put up a fight, but I didn't have the strength. Bonita and Amy were gone, and now Jennifer would be gone, too. The only hope would be if she could get a job.

"Get her a work-permit," I said.

"What?" Max snapped, finally looking at me.

"Get Jennifer a work-permit. Then it might be okay."

Max stared at me.

"Talk to Mohammed," I said. "I'm sure he can make it happen."

Late that night, Max slept while I watched the clock. At 3, I slipped out of bed and into my abaya. I didn't stop for a cigarette and didn't let fear keep me cowering in the dark. Hurrying toward the beach, I wondered if Yasmeen was there, but it wouldn't have a made a difference— that night I was going to swim. Then I saw her. Yasmeen was swimming so far offshore if I hadn't been looking, I wouldn't have seen her.

I stood at the water's edge until Yasmeen noticed me. She was startled at first, her eyes as wide and wild as a panicked horse. Hugging her arms across her chest she looked frantically up and down the beach, then back at me. When I tried to smile it hurt so much I cried. I took off my abaya and waded into the black water.

Yasmeen swam toward me and we met where the sandbar ended and the ocean floor dropped off to unfathomable depths. Her eyes widened when she saw my swollen, lacerated face.

"Follow me," she said. "I'll show you how to do it."

A trance-like rhythm—twenty strokes one way, twenty strokes the other—was how Yasmeen kept the shore within reach, avoided the treacherous undertow, and resisted being swept to sea. It was how she kept track of where she was in total blackness. To lessen the risk of discovery, Yasmeen only swam during the new or crescent moons.

At first, the salt stung more than tears and sweat, but soon it stopped hurting. I took long, hard strokes, turning my head side to side. It had been years since I'd been swimming. I doggedly plowed through the water. Later, with practice, I would learn grace. Finally, exhausted, I stopped and floated on the surface. I looked at Yasmeen and smiled. Laughing quietly, Yasmeen grabbed one of my ankles and towed me to shore.

23

At 8 the next morning I was sitting in the women's waiting room of the Al Hassa Clinic, part of the compound hospital. Three Saudi women sat nearby, children playing at their feet. A tiny girl with a dark cloud of curls looked at me then climbed onto her mother's lap. Snuggled against her mom, she stuck her thumb into her mouth and stared curiously. I knew how scary I looked, my swollen face covered with bruises and lacerations. I wished I was wearing a veil.

"Mrs. Hayes?" A statuesque Sudanese woman about my age was smiling down at me. "I'm Dr. Kayra. Please come with me."

Even in sneakers, Dr. Kayra was taller than my 5-9, and her colorful turban added three more inches. I hurried to keep up as I followed her down the hall. Below the hem of her white lab-coat, a floral-printed skirt swirled around her calves.

The examination room was a long metal table walled with white curtains. Dr. Kayra put on glasses and gently examined me. She was striking, with finely sculpted features and inky-black skin. Her dark eyes exuded compassion, especially when I winced and pulled away.

"Sorry," I whispered.

"I understand you stepped in front of a matawah's whip," she said. "Very brave."

I felt embarrassed. Rumors had already spread around the compound. "Or very stupid."

The doctor patted my shoulder. "The cuts don't look too bad. What have you put on them?"

I thought of the warm heavy sea. "Saltwater."

Dr. Kayra looked curious, but only nodded. "Saltwater has healing properties, but I'm giving you ointment to prevent infection and reduce scarring." She made a notation in my chart then paused, removed her glasses, and looked at me. "I'm sure you've heard we are suddenly short-staffed. We had another physician, Dr. Phillips, who has recently left Ocmara."

Dr. Phillips? Suddenly I remembered Bobbi's words. *Not even Mohammed could fix this.*

"Rebecca Phillips was a valuable member of our volunteer staff. We need another brave woman." Dr. Kayra gave me a challenging look. "Are you interested?"

Her question surprised me. I had been afraid of becoming crazy like Rebecca, but I'd also experienced her kindness. I felt honored to be recognized as brave and valuable. "Yes, I am."

Dr. Kayra smiled and gave me her card. "Call me when you're feeling better."

"Thanks," I said. "I'll talk to my husband."

"As I said, this is a volunteer position." Dr. Kayra's posture was suddenly rigid. "You don't need your husband's permission."

Leaving the clinic, I felt hopeful for the first time in months.

That afternoon, my face greasy with ointment, I played loud music and made meatloaf and mashed potatoes for dinner. Although it still hurt to smile, I couldn't stop. Dr. Kayra's offer was a miracle in the wake of disaster. When Max got home, I greeted him with the news.

"Absolutely not," Max said.

Why was I surprised? "Why not?"

"You need to be home for the kids."

I brushed past him carrying food to the dining room. Kate was setting the table and Sam was already sitting down. Both were listening while pretending not to.

"It's just a few hours a week. I'll be here when the kids need me."

"Why don't you go back to the Women's Club? Bobbi and those gals wonder where you've been." Since the debacle at the Mitchell's party, Max was even more invested in my becoming one of the popular girls. I couldn't make him understand it was never going to happen. "Take Jennifer. It'll keep you two out of trouble." Max laughed, as if joking.

Jennifer had refused to go to the welcome coffee and the shopper's trip was the best I could do. *Look how well that turned out.* Suddenly I remembered Jennifer's words. "I need something more meaningful than going to teas and baking cookies," I said.

When we were seated, Max nodded at Sam. "Sam, say grace." Max bowed his head.

Sam looked startled—we hadn't said grace in years.

"God is great, God is good. Let us thank Him for our food," Sam mumbled.

"I just don't like it." Max reached for the meatloaf.

I smiled at the kids. "I've been asked to volunteer at the clinic."

"Nice," Kate said. "What would you do?"

"Help with the female patients. Be in the room when doctors examine them."

"Gross," Sam said. I gave him a tight warning look.

Max pointed at me with his fork. "Exactly. You don't need to be exposed to all that." He looked at the kids. "Besides, you guys need her too much for it to be okay. Right?"

"Would you still come to my soccer games?" Sam asked.

"Yep," I said. "Every one."

Sam shrugged. "Then I don't care." He shoveled in mashed potatoes.

Kate glanced at Max then smiled at me. "It's okay with me."

I tilted my head and gave Max a pleading smile, but I'd already made up my mind.

I was reading when Max came to bed. When I looked up, he was gazing at me.

"What?"

Max reached out and tenderly traced the cuts on my cheek with his fingertip. I felt the slip of ointment and a twinge of pain. "Do they hurt?"

I pulled away. "A little. The doctor doesn't think they'll leave many scars."

"You'll still be beautiful to me," Max said.

I took a deep breath. His words were so trite, so too-little-too-late. I looked at my book, trying to concentrate on the words. In the long silence, I felt Max staring at me.

"I'm sorry, babe. I've been such an ass," he said.

Yes, you have. I closed my eyes and sighed. Max fumbled for my hand and I looked at him.

"I could kill that bastard for what he did to you." Max looked small in that moment, helpless. Part of me understood he really meant it. Strangely, I didn't crumble, as I once might have. Instead, I thought about Dr. Kayra calling me "brave."

"I was so scared." Max hugged me. "I love you so much. I just want to keep you safe."

Even as I let Max hold me, I didn't reach back. There was nothing left in me to comfort or reassure him. I just wanted to read my book and go to sleep.

The next week I saw Jennifer for the first time since Khobar. There were scabs on her arms and faint pink slashes. I had scabs and slashes of my own, including a deep cut on my right cheekbone that was still sore and raw. Jennifer had come over because I refused to leave my house while I still looked like a freak.

She was studying the black and white photographs on the dining room wall when I walked in with iced tea. "I love these pictures. Where'd you get them?"

"I took them," I said.

"You're kidding!" Jennifer said. "You could be a professional."

I looked at the pictures. "I once was."

"And you gave it up?"

I sat on the sofa beside Mimi. "Only the professional part."

"I've always wanted to learn photography." Jennifer moved to the piano and looked at me with a grin. "Do you play the piano, too, oh woman of many talents?"

I laughed. "No, Kate plays. And Max, on occasion."

"Max? Really?" Her scornful expression was fleeting. She sat and started petting Mimi.

"I could teach you photography," I said.

"Sounds good, but I won't have time." Jennifer smiled. "I got a job. I start next week."

Once again I felt the pang of being left behind. Max had spoken to Mohammed and Jennifer's work-permit was issued without her even having to apply. This time I hoped I'd be working too, but Max was still resisting. "Congratulations."

Jennifer shrugged. "It's just a secretarial job, but it's in the engineering department. Thank God, it's mostly men. You're the only woman I like in the entire Kingdom."

"Even after I got you arrested?"

"You've got that backwards," she said quietly. "If I hadn't taken off my shirt." She shook her head. "The sight of all that flesh drove him wild."

"And there I was taking pictures of it." We laughed.

"God, that was awful," Jennifer said. "This place is fucking crazy." She studied my face. "Are you going to be okay?"

"I'm getting there."

"Thank you for saving me," Jennifer said. "I couldn't have stepped in front of that whip. I owe you big time." She smiled. "And thanks for making sure I got a job. Ben told me you had something to do with it. I couldn't have stayed here without one."

"Then I'm glad for you and I'm glad for me," I said.

After Jennifer left I made a double batch of chocolate-chip cookies. While the first baked, I shoveled raw dough into my mouth. When the timer rang, I had finished the remaining dough. The sweet dough gave me a momentary boost, but then I crashed and was left sick and filled with self-loathing. The rest of the day I felt lonely, edgy, and weepy. Max was working late, so the kids and I ate leftovers for dinner.

When Max got home I was in bed with my book. Maybe I was looking for a fight—mostly I was looking for the permission Dr. Kayra told me I didn't need. Whatever was driving me, I couldn't wait. Max barely got into bed before I started in.

"I'm taking that position at the clinic," I announced.

"Whoa, wait a minute." Max looked confused, but sounded angry. "Before Jennifer came along you never even mentioned getting a job."

"How can you say that? When we first got here I wanted a job. When we were home, I talked about it," I said. "Besides, this isn't really a job. It's volunteer."

"Why do you want to spend all that time with Saudis?" Max asked. "I do it every day and, believe me, it's no picnic."

"It's not just Saudis, everybody uses the clinic. I was just there, for God's sake," I said. "I really want to do this."

"We agreed," he said.

"I never agreed. I just gave up."

"None of the other wives work," Max said.

"Jennifer starts next week!" My voice rose in frustration. "What does it matter, anyway? It won't make you less of a man if I have a job."

"What do you mean by that?" Max asked.

"All this macho bullshit!" I gestured wildly. "Who has the biggest car, or the biggest Rolex, or the biggest belt buckle? When did you get so insecure?"

"Don't start that fucking psychobabble," Max said. "You don't know what the hell you're talking about."

"All I'm saying is my working never bothered you when I was paying all the bills."

"Goddamn it, I'm working my ass off to make it up to you," Max screamed. "What do you want from me?"

"What do you want from me?" I screamed back.

In the long burning silence we stared furiously at each other, locked in old battle. I closed my eyes and took a deep breath. *This isn't what I want to do.* "I'm sorry."

"Isn't it enough for you to stay home and take care of me and your family for once?" Max managed to sound both betrayed and angry.

No. It isn't enough. I felt like a trapped animal. I closed my eyes and didn't answer.

"Aren't you going to answer me?" Max asked.

I rolled on my side facing away. "Leave me alone."

"Don't turn away from me." Max pulled me onto my back and straddled me.

I opened my eyes. "Get off me."

Instead of moving, Max kissed me. When I didn't respond he kissed me harder.

"Don't." I pushed against his chest. "Let me go."

Max looked down with a mean grin. "Oh baby, I'll never let you go."

Holding my shoulders, Max kissed my forehead and cheeks. Each time I cringed, repulsed. When he kissed my mouth hard and I still didn't respond, he pinned my wrists over my head with one hand. Once, that would have made me gasp or moan. Now it scared me.

Breathing hard, Max caressed my body with his free hand. When he kissed me again I bit his lip so hard I tasted blood. "Ow!" Max let go of my wrists and grabbed his mouth.

That was all it took. I gave one powerful push and rolled out from under him. "Goddamn it, leave me the fuck alone!" I screamed, jumping out of bed.

Max looked at me in disbelief. I'd never resisted him before. I locked myself in the bathroom, turned on the shower, and let hot water beat down on me until it ran tepid. When I finally went back to bed, Max was asleep.

I rarely remember my dreams, but have never forgotten the one I had that night. Wearing my abaya, I lay in the middle of the floor in an all-white room, arms stretched out at my sides. A door opened, closed, and footsteps approached. Turning my head, I saw a man's legs and feet, but couldn't see his face.

"Why did you do it?" It was a familiar voice I didn't recognize.

I wasn't tethered, but I couldn't move.

The man placed a shapeless gray bag on the floor beside me. "You knew it wasn't right," he said, pulling a pair of pruning shears from the bag.

"I didn't want to have to do this," he said, calmly. "But you made me." He cut off my right hand at the wrist.

Horrified, I watched as blood flowed, but felt no pain. I never moved or cried out.

"It's the only way I can trust you." He cut off my left hand.

Wide-eyed, frozen, I watched the blood flow from my body.

Heart racing, I sat up wide awake. Max slept as I crept out of bed. In the bathroom I locked the door and turned on the fan. My hands shook violently as I lit a cigarette and took a deep drag. I stared at my reflection in the mirror—the marks on my face, my bruised, swollen lips.

I looked at the scab on my right cheekbone and imagined it was the first place the matawah hit me. I dug my fingernail under the edge of the scab and ripped it off, gasping in pain. The cut bled and I blotted it until it was just a white crescent-shaped crevasse. *This, I have chosen to be my scar. I will do whatever I need to do to make sure I carry this scar forever.*

Sheila Flaherty

Leaning against the wall, I studied my reflection as I smoked the cigarette. *Friends and grandchildren will ask me about this scar and I will have a story to tell. Someday a man might run a finger across this scar and kiss it gently.* In my imagination that man wasn't Max.

24

At dawn I was running on the beach. Staring straight ahead, my soles hit the sand, jarring my legs and body. Rounding a curve, I was startled by a group of men with rakes and brooms. They wore long pants, long-sleeved shirts, gloves, hats, and sunglasses. Scarves covered the bottom of their faces. They were tall and thin, so I imagined them to be Pakistani or Sri Lankan. But there was no way to be sure. With all their skin covered, they were as invisible as Saudi women.

I felt a rush of fear, but kept my expression neutral. *Never show fear.* The men stood motionless, watching as I ran. I felt their eyes on me. Any movement in my direction and I would have surged ahead. I would have flown and they never would have caught me.

Finally, I slowed down and glanced back over my shoulder. And in that moment I tripped. Momentum kept me moving forward, and I fell hard on my hands and knees. My face hit the sand, then my chest and elbows. I rolled over, sat up, and screamed. I'd tripped on a dead sheep lying at the water's edge—its head almost completely severed from its bloated body.

I struggled to my feet, brushing sand from my face and hands as I ran. At the outcropping of rock, I scrambled up the path to the top. There I sat, panting and staring at the rising sun reflected in the flat water. I tried slowing my racing heart, catching my breath, and concentrating on the sun and the water, but I kept seeing the sheep's head—hollows where eyes had been, black swollen tongue. Gentle waves made the floating, bobbing head move like it was alive. But the smell of decaying flesh stayed with me and I gagged. Wrapping my raw arms around my bloody skinned knees, I put my head down and wept.

Call to prayer began and ended. Too much time passed, but I couldn't move. I wondered if the kids got themselves up and to school. I worried, but in an abstract, disconnected way. When I finally stood, my legs were stiff and sore. I no longer felt like I could fly.

Once home, I left my shoes outside the sliding doors. The house was empty and quiet, dirty bowls on the table. I limped into the laundry room, stripped off all my clothes, and stuffed them into the washer. Doubling the amount of detergent, I set the dials for the hottest water and longest cycle. I wanted to wash away the blood, sweat, sand, and smell of rotting sheep. Naked and chilled, I slowly, painfully, climbed the stairs.

The hot water stung the new abrasions on my body. After soaping and shampooing, I leaned against the wall, letting water beat down on my back. Slowly, pain and tension were replaced by waves of exhaustion. Sleep would come easily. Since I had nothing else to do, I planned to sleep the rest of the day. As I turned off the shower, I heard the doorbell ring. I pushed open the curtain as it rang again.

I put on my abaya and wrapped my hair in a towel. Downstairs, I tiptoed to the front door. Through the peephole I saw a woman covered in veils. I opened the door and stared, vaguely aware of the rivulets of water running down my cheeks.

Yasmeen lifted her veil. "May I come in?"

I stepped back and she hurried inside. After slipping off her sandals, she followed me into the living room. Yasmeen sat on the sofa and took off her hijab, veil, and mask. It was the first time I'd seen her entire face in the light.

Yasmeen was pretty in a plain, natural way, with pale skin and high cheekbones. Her serious dark eyes were punctuated with thick, untamed eyebrows, and her black wavy hair fell just below her shoulders. She appeared in her early thirties.

I sat on the chair, pulled off the towel, and blotted my face. Then I tucked my hair behind my ears. Yasmeen watched with a smile, studying my face as well. It occurred to me that whenever she'd seen me on the beach, I'd worn a baseball cap and sunglasses, my hair in a ponytail.

"Sorry." I tightened my robe. "I was in the shower."

"You think modesty is necessary? Considering?" Yasmeen laughed, and in that moment she came alive. While pretty in repose, when Yasmeen laughed she became animated and beautiful. She had a wide smile, with slightly crooked white teeth that looked too big for her mouth. A deep dimple appeared in her left cheek, and her eyes instantly went from soulfully sad to mischievously lively. Yasmeen's beauty was not so much in her features as in her energy.

I laughed, too. We'd already been skinny dipping! I felt a flush of embarrassment, but also a surge of happiness. Both times together we had laughed.

Although still smiling, Yasmeen's eyes were suddenly serious. "I came to make sure you're okay. You took a bad fall." Yasmeen grimaced as she glanced at my knees. The skin was tight and shiny. Bright red abrasions oozed blood and fluid.

"I'll be okay." *Where was she? If she saw me fall, did she see me break down?*

"It was that damn sheep, wasn't it? I almost tripped on it myself," Yasmeen said. "Too bad they hadn't gotten there yet." Her English was perfect, with the slightest melodic nuance.

"Who?" I asked.

"The beach sweepers. That's their job, collecting carcasses after Ramadan," Yasmeen said. "Was that the first time you'd seen them?"

"Yes. They scared me." I felt guilty admitting it. "That's why I fell. I didn't see the sheep."

"The men are Pakistanis, a frightened, gentle people. They work and live in appalling conditions to feed their families back home." Yasmeen smiled. "Don't be afraid of the beach sweepers. They aren't the ones you should fear."

There was an undercurrent in her tone, a message given in code. I was about to ask what she meant when she shifted and I heard her ankle-bracelet. I glanced down and Yasmeen jiggled her foot to make it jingle even more. She unfastened the ankle-bracelet and handed it to me.

"It's called a khalakhil. This kind with bells is for dancing," Yasmeen said.

I held one end of the bracelet in each hand. It was made of dull silver metal, more pewter than sterling. A hundred tiny silver bells were fastened in clusters of two or three. It looked old and handcrafted. I shook it and smiled at the soft sweet chime.

"It's beautiful." I reached to give it back.

"Keep it," Yasmeen said.

"Oh, no, I can't." But I felt torn. I did love it.

"Please, I want you to have it. I have several." Yasmeen smiled. "It would mean a lot to me." She gestured toward my ankle with long, elegant fingers. "Put it on. Let's see how it looks."

I fastened it around my ankle, feeling the weight. It didn't look as exotic on me, especially with my skinned knee. Still, I shook my foot and made it jingle.

"It's beautiful." I smiled. "Shukran."

Yasmeen's face lit up with her killer smile. "Now you can belly dance!"

The only belly dancers I'd ever seen were in movies or on TV. The thought of doing anything that exotic made me blush. I touched my stomach. "I've had two kids. I can't even wear a bikini anymore. I could never belly dance."

"Oh, I think you can." Yasmeen tilted her head and smiled mischievously. "You went skinny dipping. That was brave."

"That was desperate." I was surprised how quickly those words came out. But she'd seen me that night, beaten and crying.

"Well, then. Be brave." When I hesitated, Yasmeen said, "Or just wear it for fun." She smiled, but I thought she looked disappointed. I jiggled my foot again. *Maybe.*

Yasmeen pointed toward my neck. "Your necklace is beautiful."

"Thank you." I touched my cross.

"Keep it covered when you're not on the compound. As you know, the Saudis are not tolerant of any religion outside of Islam. And they're becoming more vigilant." Yasmeen smiled. "You don't want another run-in with a matawah."

There was something about her wording. "Aren't you Saudi?" I glanced at her abaya, the pile of veils by her side.

Yasmeen followed my gaze. "My abaya, of course!" She unzipped her abaya and took it off to reveal a white T-shirt, khaki shorts, and a black leather fanny pack. A gold and diamond Rolex watch encircled her wrist. "Mohammed insists on my being veiled."

"Mohammed?"

"My husband, Mohammed." Yasmeen grinned. "Not the prophet."

"My husband's boss is named Mohammed," I said.

"It's a popular name in Saudi." Yasmeen shrugged.

There I was, wearing an abaya with a khalakhil on my ankle and she wore T-shirt and shorts. It was disorienting. "Are you saying you're not Saudi?"

"My mother is Saudi, so to the Saudis I'm Saudi. But my father was an American. I was born in the States and grew up there." Sadness mixed with anger in her tone. Yasmeen abruptly stood and walked to the piano. "Do you mind?"

I shook my head, but wasn't sure what she meant. *Is she going to play?* I joined her as she examined the photographs lining the top of the piano. She pointed toward a picture of me and Max. "Your husband is very handsome."

"Thank you," I whispered.

Yasmeen picked up a picture of me and my mom and studied it with a smile.

"Your mother?" When I nodded, she looked at me. "You miss her." It wasn't a question.

I suddenly felt uneasy. "Yes, I do." I took the picture and put it back on the piano. "Do you have pictures of your family?"

"No, no pictures," she answered quickly. Yasmeen pointed to a photograph of Kate and Sam. "Whose babies are those?"

"Mine, when they were babies. Sam is ten now and Kate's almost 13."

Yasmeen looked alarmed. "She'll have to go to boarding school soon."

"No. We'll be going back to the States before then."

Yasmeen glanced around and saw the pictures on the dining room wall. She pointed. "That's Mias, my cousin's horse. How did you get that picture?"

"I took it," I said. "At the stables."

"Do you ride?"

"Oh, God, no. I've tried, but I'm terrified. Kate rides, she loves horses. You know, girls and horses." I smiled.

Yasmeen raised her eyebrows and smiled knowingly, then glanced at her watch. "I must go." She hastily pulled on her abaya and hijab and got her sandals. "May I leave by the back door?"

"Of course." At the sliding doors, I said, "Thank you for coming, and for the khalakhil." The word was awkward on my tongue.

"*Afwan.* You're welcome." Suddenly serious, Yasmeen took my hand. "I'm sorry I couldn't help you on the beach this morning. Forgive me, it was impossible."

I didn't understand, but I nodded.

"And please, promise again you will never tell anyone about me. Especially not your husband."

"I promise." Yasmeen had no idea how easy that was.

I opened the drapes and sunlight flooded the room. Yasmeen slipped on her mask and veil. She was across the yard when I called out, "Yasmeen?" She turned. "Will you teach me to belly dance?" I heard her laugh and saw her nod. Then she was gone.

"Be brave," I whispered. "Be brave."

25

Every examination room was full and the waiting room overflowed. Women's voices and children's cries created an energetic babble. It was my first day as a volunteer and Dr. Kayra explained procedures as we rushed down the corridor.

"A woman must always be present when the patient is Arab. Male doctors are forbidden to see her body," Dr. Kayra said.

"How can he treat her?" I knew I sounded naïve.

"That's why you're there, to interpret her body to him." We stopped outside an examination room. "I'll be back as soon as I can." Dr. Kayra smiled. "Ready?"

I nodded, hoping I looked more confident than I felt. The doctor opened a discreet crack in the curtains and motioned me through. Inside, one Saudi woman sat on the table while two others stood touching her, murmuring in Arabic. The patient saw me and began rocking and sobbing.

The shorter, rounder of the other women lifted her veil to reveal dark eyes filled with tears and desperation. Her English was heavily accented. "Please help my daughter. She can't sleep and won't eat. She cries all the time." The other woman spoke urgently in Arabic and the mother continued, "She won't feed her baby."

I took the patient's hands and smiled at her. Gazing where I knew her eyes to be, I asked, "How old is your baby?"

"Two months," her mother answered. There was another rush of Arabic from the third woman. "She says their husband is very angry."

Their husband? "Are they married to the same man?"

"Yes," the mother nodded. "They are both his wives. Please, you must help my daughter."

"I'm not the doctor," I said. "She'll be here soon. But it sounds like your daughter is depressed. It happens to some women after their babies are born." Even under her veils the patient appeared depressed. Her back was rounded, shoulders forward, head hanging low.

"What should we do?"

"First, the doctor must examine her." After my words were translated, the patient yanked her hands from mine and got off the table. When the two restrained her, she fought, wailing loudly.

"Tell her to please wait," I said, feeling incompetent.

"She's scared," the mother said. "Please, her husband will kill her if his son dies."

Suddenly the patient stopped struggling, lifted her veil, and leaned close to me. Her eyes were wild and imploring. She whispered something in Arabic. Even through the mask, her breath was hot against my cheek.

"She wants to kill her baby," the mother translated, sobbing while the patient was eerily calm. The mother grabbed me, "Please, you have to help."

Parting the curtains, I looked into the hallway. "Where is Dr. Kayra?" I asked a passing nurse. When she shrugged I turned back into the room. The patient had resumed struggling with the others. I didn't have much time.

"Listen," I said, thinking frantically. "Your daughter is not a bad mother. She's sick. Like if she lost too much blood in childbirth and she's weak." The mother translated. "You have to take care of her. Feed her, take her for walks. Let her rest and sleep as much as possible." I pointed at the mother and other wife. "Take care of the baby. Feed him, change him." I stood tall and spoke sternly, "Do not leave her alone with the baby."

The mother translated, both women nodded solemnly, and they all moved to the curtains.

"If she's not better in a few days, you have to bring her back to see the doctor!" I said.

As the mother was about to leave, she turned, took my hands in hers, and kissed the back of one then the other. "Shukran." Her eyes were warm with gratitude. "Thank you." She squeezed my hands before dropping them. Pulling her veil over her face, she slipped from the room.

The curtain dropped behind her, leaving me shaken—already exhausted and I'd just begun. Stepping out, I watched the women disappear around a corner. I had only a moment to wonder if I'd been wrong and Max had been right, before Dr. Kayra swooped by, grabbing my arm. While we rushed down the hallway, I told Dr. Kayra what had happened.

"I hope I did the right thing," I said.

Dr. Kayra stopped and smiled. "You did exactly the right thing. That's why I need you here."

She left me at another room and was gone. By day's end we'd seen thirty women, Arab and Western. Many were frightened and abused, resistant and angry. I understood why Dr. Kayra needed a brave woman to replace Rebecca, and I was determined to be the one.

But I was not brave at home. I longed to tell Max about my day at the clinic, but didn't dare. I was too afraid of his rage. There were 21 months left on Max's contract—nine months until his next repat. Without Max's permission, that would be the earliest I'd have my passport and exit-visa. Throughout our marriage, I'd chosen to stay when times were tough. Now, I had no choice but to stay. So I had to protect my sanity.

That day in the clinic I felt alive again—needed, appreciated, recognized. I knew the precarious line I was walking, but couldn't chance going back into battle. I might lose. If Mohammed could get Jennifer a work-permit, couldn't he take away my lifeline? Without it, I'd fall back into the abyss of depression. In the end, I made the soul-shattering decision to keep another secret from Max.

That night I'd finally found sleep when Kate shook me awake. I saw her pale face and sat up.

"What's wrong?"

After Kate led me to her room and showed me the blood on her sheets I gave her a long hug. While she took a bath, I threw her sheets and pajamas in the wash and gathered what she'd need for the night. Later, Kate hugged her sock-monkey as I made her bed. Pulling back the sheet, I patted the pillow.

"Hop in."

As Kate snuggled under the covers, I sat on the side of her bed. Still holding her monkey, Kate looked at me. "Does this make me a woman?"

"Yes, sweetie, I guess it does." I kissed Kate's forehead and turned off the lamp. At the doorway I looked back at her. Illuminated by the hall light, Kate was beaming with pride.

Near the end of June, Max and I were invited to Jennifer and Ben's house for dinner. I hadn't seen Jennifer since the day she told me about her job. They'd recently received their shipment and were ready for company.

"Welcome!" Ben greeted us exuberantly. "Come in!" While the guys went to the living room, Jennifer hugged me.

"It's so good to see you," she said quietly. Jennifer had been working a month and looked happier than I'd ever seen her.

"Good to see you, too."

After serving cheese and cracker appetizers and homemade red wine, Jennifer went into the kitchen. When I noticed the table was set with candles, flowers, and good china, I suddenly realized the dinner was to impress us. After all, Max was Ben's boss. Watching Ben fawn over Max, I knew he was unaware of how desperate Max was to keep him. While the men drank and watched TV, I took my wine and went to help Jennifer.

"It's only spaghetti and meatballs, but it's the best I can do." Jennifer grinned. Sauce bubbled on the stove and the kitchen looked like a disaster area. Jennifer was making a salad.

"We love spaghetti and meatballs." I got a sponge and began wiping up red splatters.

Working side-by-side, Jennifer cooked and I cleaned. She chatted about work and I confided about the clinic.

"I'm so much happier," I said. "Every morning I run at dawn then get the kids off. Two or three days a week I go to the clinic, work until one or two, then rush home to start dinner."

"Sounds exhausting," Jennifer said.

"Yes, but I love it."

"And Max has no idea?" Jennifer asked.

"Not yet," I said. "But being Al Hassa, it's only a matter of time."

"And when he does?"

"I'll have proven that I can do it all!"

Jennifer lifted her wine glass to mine. "Superwoman lives!"

I longed to tell Jennifer about Yasmeen, but kept my vow of secrecy. Yasmeen had visited two more times and on three dark nights I'd met her at the beach. I teetered on the razor's edge of reckless, and the possibility of a fall was intoxicating. Like an exhilarating addiction to an extreme sport, every victory left me hungry for more.

"We're done," Jennifer said, pouring sauce over a bowl of pasta and meatballs.

By the time dinner was served it felt like a team effort and we were close again. Afterwards, we cleaned up while the men watched TV. When we joined them, Max draped his arm across my shoulders. *I Love Lucy* was on in black and white with a loud, forced laugh-track. The show was abruptly replaced with a photograph of a mosque as the nightfall call to prayer began.

Ben got up and turned off the TV. "More wine while I'm up?"

"Sure," Max said. He'd been drinking steadily all evening and I was worried.

"Not for me, thanks." I looked at Max. "Shouldn't we be getting home to the kids?"

Max stiffened and shot me an irritated look. "It's just nightfall. They'll be fine."

Embarrassed, I looked down with a smile.

"Jennifer makes a mighty fine wine," Ben said, refilling everyone's glass. He sounded looped himself. "You have to visit her cellar."

Clearly uncomfortable with the tension, Jennifer spoke in a light tone. "Wine is easy—grape juice, sugar, yeast—in a month or so, *voila!*" She held up her glass. "For sid you need a still. I'm building one in the storage room in the garage. That may be the only advantage of being a chemical engineer in this godforsaken place."

Max took another sip. "If you didn't have a job you could open your own bar."

Jennifer and Ben laughed heartily at Max's lame joke, but I still felt uncomfortable.

"Just don't get caught!" Ben said, grinning at Max. "Don't want you to be arrested!"

Max studied his wine, swirling it in the glass like it was some fine vintage. He sniffed it then took a big swallow. "We've got to be especially careful since our girls already have a record."

Ben and Max laughed even more heartily, sounding remarkably like the TV laugh-track. Jennifer and I just looked at each other with weary, wary expressions.

The following Wednesday, the kids were off school so I took them with me on the Rahima shopper's bus. It was brutally hot, so I wore my lightest baggy clothes. Sam wore a T-shirt and long shorts, but I made Kate wear pants and a long-sleeved T-shirt.

"It's so hot," she said as I handed her a scarf. Mine was looped loosely around my neck.

"I know, I'm sorry," I said. "Put your scarf in your backpack so you have it just in case."

First stop was the bakery. Tearing into the warm chewy bread was always heavenly. Next was my favorite produce stand, owned by a gruff old Saudi man who kept watch from a stool in the back. The young Pakistani clerk greeted me with an eager smile.

"Good morning, sir."

"Marhaba," I said. "I need lettuce, tomatoes, and oranges, please."

"No oranges today," he said, apologetically. "Saturday, Enshallah."

"What's Enshallah?" Kate whispered.

"It means God willing."

The old man watched as I filled bags with firm ripe tomatoes and fresh lettuce. Then he stood, walked slowly over to us, and pointed at Sam. "Is this your son?" He had a heavy accent.

"Yes." I smiled proudly, and put my arm around Kate. "And this is my daughter."

The man looked only at Sam. Grinning, he pointed first at me then at Sam. "Same, same. It is good." He touched Sam's shoulder then slowly walked back to the stool.

My smile faded when I glanced at Kate, who stared down looking embarrassed. Meanwhile, the clerk had weighed my produce. "Fourteen riyals, sir." As I counted riyals, he put two bananas into my bag, making sure I saw.

"Shukran," I said.

As we walked away, Sam looked at me. "Why did he call you sir?"

"I don't know, but he always does." I laughed.

"Maybe for the same reason I'm suddenly invisible." Kate's tone was light, but she looked upset. I reached for her, but she pulled away.

"There's the mosque," I said, hoping to distract her. The shiny gold crescent at the top of the minaret was the same shape as the shiny pink scar on my cheek.

A Baskin Robbins had just opened and I could see it ahead. "Anybody want ice cream?"

Sam grinned and Kate nodded.

Outside, a Saudi woman discreetly lifted her veil to lick her cone while ice cream dripped down her arm. Inside, it was like the Baskin Robbins back home—except the clerk wore a thobe and gutra. Only one of the four booths was occupied by a Saudi man and two adolescent boys. My kids got their cones and settled into a booth. Waiting for change, I saw a sign on the counter printed in Arabic and English: As per the Law, Ladies are NOT allowed to sit in the Parlor.

I beckoned the kids and pointed to the sign. As we headed for the door, the Saudi man and boys were also leaving. The boys stared openly at Kate's chest and one made a remark in Arabic. They all laughed, looking back at Kate as they left.

Kate glanced at her chest with a mortified expression then hunched forward to conceal her budding breasts. Feeling a surge of rage, I pulled her close. By this time, the Saudi males were walking down the street, the veiled woman following behind.

"I hate it here," Sam said, with rage I hadn't seen since the amusement park.

"Katie and I thank you for that, don't we?" Kate nodded tearfully.

"Here, sweetie, let's do this." I looped her scarf around her neck so the ends dangled in front of her chest. Then I put an arm around each of my children and we walked to the bus.

At dinner that night, Sam blurted, "Hey, Dad, we went to Baskin Robbins today."

"Where was this?" Max said.

"Rahima," I said.

"Was it just like home?" Max asked.

"Not exactly." Kate, wearing a blouse over her T-shirt, stared at her plate.

"They don't have a family section," I said, hoping that would be enough.

Max looked at me then back at Kate. "Did something else happen?"

"I don't want to talk about it." Kate glanced at me, shaking her head.

I signaled Max to drop it, but he looked at Sam. "Hey, buddy, what happened in Rahima?"

Sam shrugged. "Some Saudi guys stared at Kate's boobies."

Kate gave me an exasperated look. "Mom!"

"What the hell?" Max said, reflexively looking at Kate's chest.

"Dad!" Kate jumped up and ran upstairs.

"Jesus, Max." I glared at him.

"What?" Max looked clueless.

Sam continued eating as if unaware of what he'd set in motion. But remembering his rage in Rahima, I knew he'd deliberately stirred it up.

"Goddamn it." I went upstairs to comfort Kate.

Kate cried inconsolably, refusing to leave her room all night. I felt sorry for her. And, as is often the case, her dad was suddenly the target for all the embarrassment she felt about her changing body—made worse by the incident in Rahima.

26

My relationship with Yasmeen continued to have an elusive quality. She disappeared for weeks then suddenly reappeared. She knew my schedule. Sometimes when I was alone, I'd hear tapping on the sliding doors. But her visits were always brief, conversations superficial. She was skittish, on guard. The relationship felt so tenuous I feared someday Yasmeen would disappear forever.

Then, one day, Yasmeen appeared soon after the kids left. I was in the kitchen when I heard the tap. Crossing the room I saw her dark form. She slipped inside and kicked off her sandals.

"I've got lots of time, today." The dimple appeared with her grin. "Is this good for you?"

"Perfect. I'll make coffee."

We settled on the sofa, her abaya piled between us. Yasmeen held her mug in both hands, took a sip, and smiled. I knew she hated the strong black coffee that was the Arab staple. She liked lots of cream and sugar, the way I like mine. "Delicious. Thank you."

"You're welcome."

Yasmeen peered at me over her mug. "I want to take you to my house soon. Will you come?"

"I'd love to." I felt surprised and pleased.

"Good. I'll let you know when."

We drank our coffee in silence. It wasn't awkward, but not as comfortable as with an old friend. We were clearly still easing into this friendship.

"How long have you been back in Saudi?" I asked.

"Four years," Yasmeen said. "After Daddy died, my mother was devastated and wanted to be with her family." There was suddenly raw grief in Yasmeen's eyes.

"What made you decide to stay?"

"I was married to Mohammed," she said.

That name again. *Could it be the same Mohammed?*

Yasmeen smiled. "It's been wonderful being with my family. Before my dad died, I only knew my cousin, Jamal. He went to boarding school in Virginia, so he spent lots of time with us. He's like my big brother."

I'd been given another clue. "You grew up in Virginia?"

"Georgetown," she said.

"Is Jamal the one who owns the horse?"

Yasmeen nodded and glanced down at her abaya. I couldn't resist touching it—silk. That and her Rolex were adding up.

"Did your mom wear an abaya in the States?" I asked.

Yasmeen looked at me. "Never. Mother was a concert pianist and totally westernized. But Daddy was a professor of Arabic studies, so we spent time with Arab women and they were often veiled." Yasmeen's expression grew pensive. "I'm comfortable in both Arab and Western cultures, but at home in neither. Here, I have no Western friends at all."

I froze.

Yasmeen laughed. "Except you, of course. Actually you're my only friend."

"Why me?"

Yasmeen smiled, but her eyes were serious. "You spoke to me on the beach. Even when I didn't answer, you never gave up. Nobody speaks to us when we're under the veils."

I knew why and wondered how it felt on the other side. "Is it hard to be veiled?"

"Western women always think the abaya and veils are oppressive, but they're not supposed to be. Islam mandates Arab women are protected from men outside their family. Veils help provide that protection." Yasmeen leaned forward. "I'd never worn veils in the States, but here in Saudi I feel safer covered up. Anonymous."

"Being anonymous makes you feel safe?" I asked.

"Don't you feel it?" Yasmeen asked. "There's a constant vigilance in the Kingdom. A veil gives me freedom and protects me from scrutiny. To a certain extent, I'm invisible."

I remembered the first night on the beach and nodded.

"Don't you feel exposed?" Yasmeen continued insistently. "There's not a single move you make that isn't observed and noted."

Suddenly I felt uneasy, but I shook my head. "I haven't thought about it," I lied, not wanting to go back to that crazy place.

Yasmeen stared into my eyes. "You should."

I felt chilled from what seemed like a warning. As we stared at each other, a strange tension built. Then Yasmeen leapt up with a laugh, holding out her hands to me. "Except, of course, behind the walls. Anything and everything goes on behind the walls."

I took Yasmeen's hands and she pulled me off the sofa.

"I'm going to teach you to belly dance," Yasmeen said. "I'm going to show you how we live beneath the veils and behind the walls."

Yasmeen had brought a tape of Middle Eastern music for me to keep. "Belly" was written on the case in black ink. We stood facing each other as the music began.

"Do what I do," Yasmeen said, moving in time with the music.

With slow self-conscious steps, I tried to imitate Yasmeen's graceful dancing, but felt like an idiot. Exasperated, I covered my face. "I look ridiculous."

Yasmeen pulled my hands from my face. "Don't worry about how you look. Think about how you feel." Holding my hands, Yasmeen wove sensually around me—smiling, flirting, shaking her hips in time to the music.

"Now you're just showing off," I said.

She laughed. "Let the music guide you. Have fun. Let go."

I swayed stiffly. "I can't let go."

Yasmeen laced her fingers though mine. "You can, I promise." She locked eyes with me and moved her arms. "Relax your arms!"

Slowly, she coaxed me into a rhythm, turning us in a tight circle. When she let go of my hands, we continued to circle each other, moving our arms and bodies to the beat. Soon we were sweating. Yasmeen's sweat had the tart-sweet smell of Clementine oranges.

When the tape finished, Yasmeen looked at her watch. "Got to go. Practice!" She slipped on her things and disappeared through the gate.

Breathless and exhilarated, I rewound the tape then pushed play. As music filled the room I closed my eyes, lost myself in the rhythm, and danced.

When Max got home it was hard to contain my excitement. With Middle Eastern music running through my head, I wanted to shimmy and shake and show him what I'd learned.

"Let's take a walk before dinner," I said. The kids were out and wouldn't be home for hours.

At the beach, the sun was sinking toward the horizon and there was a lovely breeze off the Gulf, but it was still hot. Max held my hand, chatting vaguely about work.

"Ben's a real genius and Ray is happy." Max beamed. "Even Mohammed is pleased."

We passed three Saudi women sitting on a blanket, no doubt sweltering under their black. A Saudi man and three boys wearing bathing suits frolicked in the water nearby. The man was probably their husband. I looked for a khalakhil.

Max tugged my hand. "Are you listening to me?"

"Yes." Something nagged me. "Speaking of Mohammed, what's his last name?"

"It's Zamil. Mohammed Zamil. Why?" Max asked.

"No reason, just wondering." I shrugged, feeling relieved.

But now Max was distracted. "Is that Kate?"

Following his gaze, I saw Kate with a group of boys and girls. Amanda, Lizzie, and a girl named Nadia were there. Music played on a boom-box and the kids were talking and laughing. Kate wore her one-piece bathing suit, and a few girls wore bikinis. They were all slick with suntan oil and sweat. I was happy to see Kate laughing and having fun with her friends.

Near the kids, three Saudi men sat with their veiled women—openly watching the girls.

"What the hell?" Max dropped my hand. In seconds, he was looming over the men. "What are you staring at?" Max screamed. "They're twelve year old girls!"

The Saudis smiled uncomfortably and muttered to each other.

Then Max moved toward the kids. "Kate! Cover yourself. What are you thinking?" Kate flushed with embarrassment and pulled on a blouse. The other kids exchanged smirks.

I touched Max's shoulder and spoke quietly, "Honey, it's the beach. She's fine."

Max whirled about and screamed at me, "She's half-naked!" Max beckoned to Kate. "Come with me. Right now," he said, stalking off toward home.

Eyes lowered, Kate followed Max. I smiled apologetically at the other kids before running after her. I gently touched Kate's arm. "I'm so sorry, sweetie. He's just worried about you."

Kate wrenched her arm away, glared at me, and screamed, "Why do you always make excuses for him? He's an asshole!" She took off running.

I froze, stunned and embarrassed for both of us. That night Kate locked her door, refusing to let anyone in. I felt sorrow like a dagger, and resolved to do whatever needed to repair my relationship with my daughter.

27

When Yasmeen arrived at my house at noon, I was wearing a knit blouse and skirt and had my everyday abaya ready to go.

"Let me show you how it's done," Yasmeen said.

I watched in the mirror as Yasmeen snuggly tied the hijab, concealing every wisp of blonde hair. The mask was a rectangular layer of black gauze attached to an elastic band. Yasmeen positioned it on the bridge of my nose, leaving only my eyes and forehead exposed. Already it was difficult to breathe. Next, Yasmeen put the final layer of veils over my head, zipped my abaya, and I disappeared.

"You okay?" she asked.

I nodded, pushing back panic.

"Let's go," Yasmeen said.

I picked up my backpack and the cookies I'd baked for the occasion. We slipped on our sandals and out the sliding doors.

As Yasmeen looped her arm through mine and led me through the compound, I felt the sun's heat. It was hard to see and hard to breathe. The more I gasped for breath, the more the mask stuck to my sweaty face. It covered my nose and mouth like a hand, and I had to concentrate on the pressure of Yasmeen's arm to keep from screaming and ripping the cloth from my face.

Yasmeen's house was on the other side of Al Hassa, and part of a complex of attached houses—a compound within the compound. We entered through a courtyard. Women's sandals and shoes were piled outside the front door. Inside, abayas hung from hooks lining the wall. Yasmeen slipped off her things then helped me. When I took off my layers, Yasmeen laughed and pointed to a mirror.

"Oh, God!" I said. My face was scarlet, my hair matted. I ran my fingers through my damp hair. "Do I look okay?"

"You look fine," she smiled. "Come in. Welcome to the women's quarters."

In the living room, drapes were drawn and women and children milled about or lounged on sofas and cushions. The women wore colorful dressy clothing, make-up, and gold jewelry. Hair was loose or twisted into ponytails. Incense and cigarettes created a smoky blue haze and Middle Eastern music played softly under the hum of conversation and laughter.

Yasmeen took my hand, pulled me forward, and the room quieted. Women nudged each other and stared. I glanced nervously at Yasmeen as she put one hand on her heart and gestured toward me with the other.

"This is my *sadeek*, Sarah." Yasmeen smiled at me then gestured toward the women and children. "Sarah, this is my family."

In the long silence that followed, I fought the urge to flee. Suddenly there was a joyous shriek and a woman rushed toward me, arms outstretched.

"*Assalam alaykum*! Welcome! I am Huda." Huda grabbed my hands, kissed one then the other, then hugged me to her ample bosom. When she stepped back and held me at arm's length, I recognized her eyes. Huda was the mother of the first patient I'd seen at the clinic.

Beaming, Huda pointed to an achingly young woman nursing a chubby baby. "There is my daughter Zahra, and my grandson!" Embracing me again, she whispered, "Shukran."

Zahra smiled shyly at me over her baby's head. I glanced at Yasmeen. "Yes, the clinic." Yasmeen smiled.

Looking at Zahra and her son, I felt a well of emotion. She sat tall and proud, so unlike the huddled form on the examination table. I suddenly realized this gathering was in my honor.

"Huda is my aunt," Yasmeen said. "Jamal's mom."

Another woman stepped forward. "This is Shadan, Jamal's wife."

"Nice to meet you," Shadan said.

"Nice to meet you, too," I said.

Yasmeen took my hand and turned toward an elegant older woman. "Sarah, this is my mother." The resemblance was unmistakable.

"I am Leila." Yasmeen's mother held out her hand, but her eyes were guarded.

"I'm so happy to meet you." I shook her hand enthusiastically.

"Thank you." Leila smiled, but pulled her hand away and cast a worried glance at Yasmeen.

Yasmeen looked annoyed, but I had only a moment to wonder about the exchange when a girl about Kate's age came running into the room.

"Auntie!" she shrieked with joy.

Yasmeen laughed as the girl hugged her. Even after she let go, the girl stayed close, resting her head on Yasmeen's shoulder.

"This is Nora, my favorite niece." Yasmeen looked lovingly at Nora.

"Your only niece!" Nora laughed. She wore a pink dress with a chiffon skirt. Nora was tall and gangly, with brown eyes and a mass of long, wavy black hair.

"If I had a million nieces you'd still be my favorite," Yasmeen said. "Say hello to my friend."

"Hello." Nora shyly shook my hand. She looked like the daughter Yasmeen didn't have.

"Nora is your niece?" I asked. "I thought you were an only child."

"I am." Yasmeen smiled. "But since Jamal is more like a brother, I'm more like her aunt."

A tiny girl in a frilly dress toddled up to me. Her ears were pierced with minute gold studs. I squatted and she shyly touched my hair. When I reached out to her, she squealed and ran away.

Huda laughed then clapped her hands. "Come, let's eat! *Bismallah!*"

A lavish feast was spread across copper trays—Arab bread, hummus, tabbouli, olives, sliced tomatoes, and cucumber with yoghurt. There were fava beans, and "lady fingers," which I recognized as okra. Lentils with chicken or lamb were accompanied by bowls of rice. Dessert was fresh fruit, dates, nuts, pastries, and my cookies.

I wanted to taste everything, so I was taking tiny portions when Huda took my plate.

"Let me." Huda filled my plate with generous servings of several dishes, topped with a piece of Arab bread. "Finish this. Then come back for more!"

That was how it was done. Women piled their plates high then returned for seconds and thirds. Colorful glasses of sweet mint tea and tiny cups of coffee were served with dessert.

Afterwards, the party was alive with conversation and laughter. Little girls in dresses and tiny boys in miniature thobes toddled around. The women smoked cigarettes or took long draws from a brass *hookah*.

"Try it," Yasmeen said.

"I don't know." It had the feel of an opium den—foreign and dangerous.

"Come on, be brave! I know you smoke." Yasmeen grinned. "It's just flavored tobacco." Yasmeen closed her lips over the mouthpiece at the end of a hose and took a long pull. She inhaled deeply then blew the smoke out in a fragrant stream. "Your turn."

I took a tentative draw and was surprised when thick cool smoke filled my mouth and lungs. I tasted a sweet blend of apples and mint. "Wow," I said. "What is that?"

"*Shisha*," she said.

Remembering that Yasmeen had no family pictures, I'd brought my Nikon. Two hours into the gathering women were eagerly posing for the camera. While most the women were relaxed in my presence, some watched me warily, whispering behind their hands. Leila remained cordial, but not warm.

"Huda and your mom seem so different. Are they sisters?" I asked.

"No, Huda is married to my mother's brother, Abdul." Yasmeen gazed at Huda who sat beside Zahra and the baby. "You're right. They couldn't be more different."

Suddenly there were peals of laughter as the baby sprayed Zahra while she changed his diaper. Remembering the day in the clinic, I wondered which woman was the other wife. I needed a chart to map all the relationships.

The women were clustered in small groups, sitting close or leaning against each other. Unlike American women, the Saudi women held hands or casually touched, rubbed, or massaged each other—comfortable with physical closeness. Suddenly I understood the ease with which Yasmeen took my arm or my hands.

Yasmeen and I eventually sat on floor-pillows with Nora and Huda. Nora nestled against Yasmeen and the tiny toddler lounged on my lap. Her dark soft curls smelled sweet. Huda leaned against me and, as I felt myself pulling back, I rocked the little girl to cover my discomfort. Then I relaxed into Huda, taking comfort from her soft fragrant warmth.

When the party ended there were hugs, kisses, and invitations for me to return soon. I happily agreed. In the entryway I zipped my abaya and Yasmeen tucked my hair under my hijab. She positioned my mask and draped me with a veil. We were laughing as we walked out the door.

"Uncle." Yasmeen's voice was suddenly subdued.

An older Saudi man stood in our path watching us and frowning. "Who is this woman?"

Huda burst out the door with the baby. "Abdul! Take your grandson. He is crying for you!"

As Abdul turned, Huda thrust the baby into his arms and shooed Yasmeen and me away—in one fluid motion.

That night I could barely contain myself. It was the most joyous secret I'd ever kept. I wished I could call Jennifer. *I'll write to Lara! She can keep my secret!*

While I cooked dinner and washed dishes, the music I'd heard that day played through my head like an old familiar tune. I found myself humming and swaying. I didn't have to lie about my day, since no one ever asked. Months of monotony suddenly paid off—an alibi for an afternoon spent in a harem!

28

The next day I awoke before dawn, arms wrapped hard around my pillow. Wailing wind had invaded my dreams, leaving me uneasy. A *shamaal* blew in from the Empty Quarter during the night—by morning, winds were at gale-force strength. The desert storm pushed the temperature over 100 degrees and darkened the sky with a cloud of sand. At high noon the sun was only dimly visible through the red haze.

School closed, but Max had to go to work. Since walking outside was literally to be sandblasted, the shamaal imprisoned me and the kids for four days. The constant drumming of wind and sand against the windows made me crazy. Dust invaded the house through every crack and covered every surface.

The fifth night I was jarred awake by abrupt silence. In the morning we blinked in the sunlight and breathed fresh air. Throughout the compound trees were uprooted, roof-tiles had gone missing, palm fronds littered the ground, and drifts of sand had accumulated against buildings. It was like a bomb had gone off.

Yasmeen reappeared the week after the shamaal, slipping through the sliding doors.

"Ready to dance?" She took off her veil.

It was only my third lesson, but I felt much more fluid. I'd danced every day except during the shamaal. I practiced with different kinds of music and loved dancing to *Faith,* by George Michael. It had a seductive beat—fast and slow, playful and sensual—lyrics that felt forbidden.

After dancing, Yasmeen and I drank tea and smoked. Yasmeen brought me a burgundy and gold box of Dunhill cigarettes imported from England. I loved the exotic look and feel of the cigarettes—the heft, the thin gold band wedding the paper and filter.

"How did your parents meet?" I took a drag, remembering the awkward exchange between Leila and Yasmeen in the women's quarters.

"They met on the slopes at a ski resort in Switzerland. Daddy was vacationing with his family and Mother was on a day trip from her all-girl boarding school. It was love at first sight." Yasmeen looked pensive. "She had a lot of spunk back then. They exchanged addresses and corresponded. Within months Mother convinced her parents she should apply to Wellesley."

"Why Wellesley?"

"It's a prestigious woman's college close to Boston where Daddy lived." Yasmeen smiled.

"Clever!" I tapped the ash from my cigarette. The Dunhills were stronger than I was used to, with dense smoke. I'd have to air out the house and sauté onions to cover any lingering scent.

We sat quietly. Yasmeen was probably thinking about her parents. I was picturing the kind of foreign and elegant lifestyle where one vacationed in Switzerland and attended boarding school.

Putting down my cigarette, I twisted my ponytail into a Grace Kelly-type chignon and imagined belonging in that world. *Nope. This is the closest I'll ever get to elegant.* I let my ponytail fall and studied the split ends.

"Olive oil," Yasmeen said.

"What?"

"For your hair," Yasmeen said. "For skin, too. Combats sun damage."

I laughed. "Like you would know about sun damage!"

"True." Yasmeen smiled. "But it works. Saudi women have to be especially beauty conscious when four of us compete for our husband's attention."

Intriguing.

Yasmeen touched my hair. "I could give you a henna rinse. How would your husband like you as a redhead?" She smiled suggestively. "He's a very handsome man. You'll make him feel like he's with another woman."

"I don't want him to feel like he's with another woman." Her teasing embarrassed me.

Yasmeen took a long, slow drag from her cigarette and studied me seriously. I knew I was blushing. The last passionate lovemaking I'd had with Max was during the storm. *A lifetime ago.*

She blew the smoke out in a slow, steady stream. "Have you ever even been with a man besides your husband?"

"No." Her question astonished me and I snapped back. "Have you?"

Yasmeen's worldly façade immediately cracked like cheap veneer, leaving her looking bare and vulnerable. She closed her eyes. "His name is Omar."

I waited.

"He was Jamal's best friend in boarding school." Yasmeen looked at me. "And my childhood sweetheart." She crushed out her cigarette with an angry twist of her wrist and lit a new one. "We were planning our wedding when Daddy died."

"What happened?"

"I came back to Saudi," she said flatly. "Eventually I was married to Mohammed."

I had no sense of how Yasmeen felt about Mohammed. *Why hadn't she left Saudi and gone back to Omar?*

Yasmeen took another drag and stared at a point across the room. After exhaling she hesitated, as though weighing the wisdom of what she was about to say. "Omar and I are still in touch."

"Oh, that's good." I smiled. "How do you do that? Not phone calls."

"Oh God, no!" Yasmeen shook her head. "I never talk on the phone. You never know who's listening in Al Hassa."

I wondered if she knew about me and Bonita.

"Letters, mostly," Yasmeen said. "Sent through Jamal or my mother."

I thought about how I'd loved Max. How I loved him still, in spite of everything. "You must miss him."

"Terribly," Yasmeen said. "Want to see pictures?" She unzipped her fanny pack, took out a small wallet, and set it on the sofa. I saw her Ocmara ID, her face above Mohammed's employee number, "Yasmeen Ali" in bold print. She pulled pictures from a secret compartment in her fanny pack. "Omar has the other two."

They were the top two photos from a black-and-white photo-booth strip. In the first, a young Yasmeen and a beautiful boy stared into the camera. Yasmeen was in full, deep-dimple grin. Omar's skin was smooth and tan. He had a wide smile and even white teeth. I was surprised by his light eyes and curly blonde hair. In the bottom photo they were kissing.

"He's a mutt like me! His mom is German and his father's Egyptian." Yasmeen leaned close, smiling at the pictures.

In the top picture, Yasmeen's eyes had more life than I'd ever seen. "Yasmeen, what happened? Why didn't you go back and marry Omar?"

Yasmeen took a deep breath. She started to speak, but suddenly looked terrified, as though she'd already said too much. She grabbed my hand. "Please, you must promise never to tell anyone about Omar."

"Of course not," I said. "I've never told anyone about you."

Yasmeen quickly stood—putting the photos and wallet away, pulling on her abaya. "You don't know how lucky you are to have a perfect marriage and family."

"Are you okay?" I said, knowing she wasn't. I heard her sob as she fled across the yard.

At the clinic the next day, I held the hand of Tracy Nash, an American woman in her late thirties. Instinctively, I knew she was the one who'd been gossiped about at the Mitchell's party. The one behind sunglasses whose drama had been out-staged by Rebecca's husband's fall from grace and Jennifer's drunken tirade.

Tracy was a beautiful woman with thick blonde hair and clear grey eyes. She had delicate features and skin pale as death. Dr. Kayra was suturing a gash on Tracy's face. She worked with a tight-lipped, angry expression.

"You have left Saudi three times, Mrs. Nash, and you have come back three times. Every time is the same." Her tone was not compassionate. Dr. Kayra saw me give Tracy a gentle smile and she wasn't happy.

"Did you know insanity is sometimes defined as repeating the same action time after time, always expecting a different result?" Tracy winced as the sutures were snipped. "Soon I will have to admit you to psychiatric."

Tears filled Tracy's eyes. "It's different this time. John's really sorry."

"He is always sorry," Dr. Kayra said in a clipped tone, gently sponging the wound.

"I need him. I can't do it alone." Tracy's voice was small and whispery, like a young girl's.

Once again, the doctor caught my compassionate expression and it increased her ire. "You have no idea how frustrating it is to know you actually believe that." Dr. Kayra included me in her gaze, and I wondered what she knew.

Later that day, I was in an examination room with two Saudi women. One whispered in broken, heavily accented English. "Her husband," the woman said. "He did it."

The other woman faced away from me and lifted her abaya. Her skirt was dark with blood. She had been anally raped. As fresh blood pooled on the floor, I felt faint.

"It's Dr. Abut, may I come in?" At the man's voice, the patient shrieked in protest.

I peeked out the curtains. "Get a female doctor. Stat!"

At the end of a brutal day Dr. Kayra saw my face as I was leaving. All the violence, ripped flesh, blood, and tears had been too much for me. She took me to her office where we drank heavily sweetened tea from cracked porcelain cups. I could have used bourbon.

Dr. Kayra peered at me over the rim of her cup. "Today you have seen some of the worst that comes with money and power."

I shook my head. "How do they get away with it?"

"Who is to stop them?" Dr. Kayra finished her tea, set down her cup, and stood with a weary sigh. It was the first time I'd seen her impacted by the tragedy of her job.

"A man uses his wife as he wishes, for his pleasure or his rage," she continued. "This is the world we live in." Dr. Kayra gently touched my shoulder. "You and I, we do what we can."

I recognized her entreaty that I remain at the clinic and continue to be brave. I nodded.

"Enough, Sarah Hayes. Go home," she said.

Spaghetti sauce simmered as I cut vegetables for salad. I was barefoot and still wearing the skirt and blouse I'd worn to the clinic. The front door slammed and Max stormed into the kitchen.

"What the hell is going on?" he yelled.

My welcome smile faded as I froze.

"John Nash told me his wife went to the clinic today. She said you work there."

Of course he found out today. I took a breath and nodded. "Yes, I volunteer at the clinic."

Max slammed his hand on the counter and I jumped, clutching the knife to my chest. "Jesus, Sarah, we agreed on this."

I felt a surge of fear, but stood tall. "No, we didn't."

"We are now," Max said.

I took another breath. "Did John Nash tell you why his wife was at the clinic?"

"No, he didn't. But that's beside the point."

"It isn't beside the point," I said.

Max stepped closer. "You're going to quit."

"No, I'm not."

"Goddamn it. You'll do what I say!" Max jabbed his finger at me, his face red and contorted.

"I'm not quitting."

Max stepped toward me with his hands raised and I stepped back, holding out the knife. Frozen, we stared at the knife, then I threw it on the counter and pushed past Max to leave the kitchen. He grabbed the back of my blouse.

"Don't you walk out on me," he bellowed.

When I turned around, he slapped me.

Stunned, I held my face. No one but the matawah had ever hit me, and I'd always sworn no one ever would. I slapped Max as hard as I could.

"Your buddy Nash is beating his wife," I screamed, running from the house.

I was crying openly when I reached the beach and felt Max's hand print scarlet on my cheek. Holding my skirt high, I ran hard and fast. When I was far past the houses, I finally stopped and bent over gasping for breath. Then I waded into the water.

My wet clothes were heavy, but I struggled toward the horizon. When I reached deep water I started swimming. Soon I'd hit currents that would pull me out to sea. Awash in pink rosy light I would sail effortlessly across the Gulf toward home—toward freedom. I'd managed a few hard strokes, before I felt myself caught. *So soon!* I was ready to fling out my arms in surrender.

"Sarah!" Max sounded anguished.

I kicked at him and pulled at the water, but he was stronger. I scratched and bit the arm he wrapped around my chest, but he held tight. I felt the motion of his other arm and his legs pumping as he pulled me back toward shore. I couldn't break his grasp.

"Oh, God, I'm sorry. I'm so sorry," was all Max could say.

Back in the shallows we stood, holding each other. The setting sun put on a riotous purple and pink lightshow with a soundtrack of call to prayer, but neither of us saw it. We were too lost in the undertow destroying our marriage.

Late that night, after lying to the kids about burned spaghetti, wet clothes, and swollen faces, Max and I made our peace. But it felt hollow. The unthinkable had happened. The air was thick with what wasn't said—secrets and hidden agendas. I begged to leave the place that had turned us into people we weren't, but Max only agreed to let me continue at the clinic and promised we'd leave at the end of his contract.

Sleep eluded me so I went outside, smoked a Dunhill, and blamed myself. *I should have told him. I held a knife.* But I knew it was crazy. Once the line was crossed it was likely to happen again. Another trust had been betrayed, another step taken away, more foundation crumbled.

29

Jennifer took off one day in early November to go to Rahima with me. As soon as we settled into our seats, she looked at me with concern. "Are you alright?"

"Why?" I tried to look alright.

"You seem subdued."

Maybe it was the comfortable intimacy of the bus, or because I had no one else to tell, but I broke the rule I'd been taught my whole life. "Max and I are having problems." I whispered.

"He found out about your job."

"Did you guess or did you hear about it?" For all I knew someone had seen us that day and the news had spread through Al Hassa like a virus.

"I guessed," Jennifer said. "What happened when he found out?"

"He went crazy. Demanded I quit," I said.

"Did you?"

"No," I said.

"Good for you," Jennifer said.

I smiled, but knew what this victory had cost me—the trophy was not so shiny. I gazed out the window a moment then looked back at Jennifer. "It got really ugly."

She narrowed her eyes. "How ugly?"

"Screaming, threatening."

"What else?"

"Nothing else," I said, looking out the window again. I couldn't look Jennifer in the eyes while I lied to her and I couldn't tell her the truth.

Jennifer was silent, but I felt her watching me. I knew she didn't believe me. And because Max was Ben's boss, I'd broken another rule. But I felt relief mingling with my discomfort.

"Thanks again for coming with me." I smiled. "I know how much you love gold souqs."

"I'm happy to do it."

Kate's thirteenth birthday was a week away and I was picking up her gifts. On a quiet street in Rahima, I'd found a small gold souq owned by a gracious Saudi man.

"Welcome, Mrs. Hayes, nice to see you again." The jeweler smiled. He went into a back room, reemerging with two boxes. Nestled inside a small square box were gold stud earrings. The second box was long and rectangular. The jeweler opened it proudly. "It came out nicely."

Cushioned on cotton was the 22-karat gold necklace I'd ordered for Kate—her name in Arab calligraphy. It was choker length, with delicate chains and a sturdy clasp. I had considered Kate, Katie, and Kathleen. The jeweler wrote down each name and Kathleen looked the most graceful looping backwards across the page. Kathleen had also been my mother's name. Since gold was priced by weight, the extra letters cost me, but it was worth it. I'd chosen the finest, most subtle lettering and it looked elegant.

"Wow. That's really beautiful," Jennifer said. When I'd told her about the necklace she'd looked skeptical, but wisely said nothing.

"Kate will be surprised," I said. "I always promised she could get her ears pierced at 13, but she doesn't expect the necklace."

I paid with riyals from a stash I had started after Max bought himself the Rolex. I'd created a budget and strictly adhered to it, buying all our fresh produce, rice, herbs, and spices in Rahima. Savings went into my stash. It felt good to be able to buy Kate a nice piece of jewelry to celebrate turning thirteen.

Jennifer and I wandered down the sidewalk, sharing a falafel and hummus pita. Baskin Robbins called, but we boycotted it. Instead, we stopped at a carpet store and sipped glasses of mint tea while kneeling to examine rugs. My favorite was an Afghani "war rug" in maroon, black, and beige. Woven into the design were grenades, rifles, planes, and helicopters—documentation of everyday life in Afghanistan. I checked the price so I could save for it.

Middle Eastern music played on the store radio and as we stood to go I recognized a familiar tune. I nudged Jennifer and moved to the beat. "Did I tell you I'm learning to belly dance?"

"No kidding? Is it fun?"

"I love it," I said. "I might have a new career when I go back to the States."

"You can dance in my bar," she laughed. "Who's teaching you?"

"A Saudi woman I met on the beach." I was afraid I'd said too much.

"Oh! What's she like?" Jennifer asked.

"Like us." I shrugged. "Women seem the same everywhere you go."

Walking back to the bus we passed the mosque, where several old Saudi men sat on the sidewalk chatting and fingering prayer beads. One called out to us in Arabic, the tone unmistakably suggestive. As we picked up our pace, we heard derisive laughter.

"Apparently men are the same everywhere, too," Jennifer said. We laughed as we boarded the bus—relieved we'd only been subjected to cat-calls and not a matawah's whip.

For Kate's birthday I made angel-food cake with chocolate frosting, and we sang "Happy Birthday" while she basked in the candles' blaze. She grinned when she saw the earrings.

"We'll get them pierced soon," I promised.

Kate examined the tiny studs.

"One more thing," I said, giving Kate the long box. I'd shown Max the necklace the night before and evaded questions about price by saying "I got a good deal."

Kate beamed as she lifted the necklace from the box.

"It's your name in Arabic," I said.

"I love it!" Kate squealed, bouncing in her chair.

Max stepped behind her. "Let me help you."

Kate lifted her hair while Max fastened the necklace. She traced the letters with her fingers then jumped up and hugged him. "Thanks, Dad."

Max smiled at me. "Thank your mom, Katie. She bought it for you."

I often saw Yasmeen on the beach at dawn and occasionally for late night swims. Sneaking out at night continued to stir up an addicting cock-tail of fear and excitement. I hadn't been back to the women's quarters, but Yasmeen frequently visited. We danced then smoked.

"Like after sex, only better!" Yasmeen said, laughing so hard tears streamed down her face. She ran to the bathroom and I heard water run-ning. When she came back, she was composed.

One day, she grinned as she left. "Meet me on the ledge tomorrow at dawn and bring your small camera. I have a surprise."

I was there when call to prayer began. Yasmeen was sitting on a boulder without her veil and mask. I'd run there in T-shirt, shorts, and running shoes, camera tucked in my backpack. After climbing the steep trail to the ledge, I sat panting. Since starting belly dancing I'd cut back on running. Dancing was more fun.

"What's up?"

"You'll see." She smiled mysteriously.

I took off my hat, loosened my ponytail, and ran my fingers through my hair. Pulling out my camera, I aimed at the horizon and captured another magnificent Saudi sunrise.

"There he is." Yasmeen stood.

"Who?" I felt a bolt of alarm.

"The surprise!" Yasmeen waved her arms. "Jamal! Here we are!"

It was like *Lawrence of Arabia* as Jamal galloped over the desert on his magnificent steed. Mias was bridled, but not wearing a saddle. Jamal wore a white long-sleeved shirt and khaki jodhpurs cut off below the knees. His legs dangled along the horse's side and he was barefoot.

Jamal glanced around to make sure no orange cars lurked nearby then stopped alongside the boulder. Yasmeen looked at him with adoring eyes. "Jamal, this is my friend Sarah."

Jamal reached up to shake my hand. He was a beautiful man—shoulder-length black hair, close-cropped beard, dark eyes, and Yasmeen's smile, including the dimple—they looked like siblings. Yasmeen shot me a mischievous grin. "I promised you'd give Sarah a ride on Mias."

I stared fearfully at the horse and nudged Yasmeen. "No," I whispered.

If Jamal heard, he didn't let on. "Take off your shoes," he said, smiling.

With a determined sigh, I gave Yasmeen the camera and took off my shoes and socks.

Jamal walked Mias closer to the boulder. "Climb on." When I was behind him, Jamal glanced over his shoulder. "Hold me with your arms and the horse with your legs."

Wrapping my arms around a strange man felt odd, but I was terrified of falling. I held tightly as Jamal guided Mias down the narrow trail leading to the beach. Yasmeen followed, surefooted as a goat. At the bottom,

Jamal wove Mias around the rocks. Once on the beach, Jamal nudged the horse with his heels and we trotted along the water's edge.

After a few yards, Jamal turned Mias toward the horizon. Slowly we moved into the water, going deeper and deeper. The familiar warmth rose from my feet to my knees. I felt Mias stepping, finding footing in the sand, and suddenly we were gliding. Then I felt the strong rhythmic paddling of all four legs as water crested over the horse's back onto my thighs.

"Oh, my God, we're swimming!" I laughed as Mias moved gracefully through the calm water. The sun hovered just above the horizon, reflected in the gulf. It was one of those rare perfect times when nothing exists but the moment. On the back of that horse, my arms wrapped around that gorgeous man, I was lost in unexpected joy. I forgot to be afraid.

As Mias swam parallel to the shore, Yasmeen ran along the beach, taking pictures and waving. I laughed as I held onto Jamal, our legs thigh deep in water, pressed together against the horse's sides. Slowly we moved toward shore. In the shallow surf, Mias's hooves kicked up a spray of foam. Then we were back on the beach.

"Ready to run?" Jamal asked.

"Go!" I said.

Jamal nudged Mias and we took off, galloping down the beach. I held tight, laughing all the way. Midway down the beach we turned and raced back to Yasmeen, who was clapping, laughing, and jumping up and down like a delighted child.

As I started to slide off, Jamal said, "Wait." He jumped down and held the reins. "Take another picture." Yasmeen took a shot of me on top of Mias, Arabian Gulf in the background. After Jamal helped me down, he remounted in one swift graceful movement.

I stood, flushed and breathless, looking up at Jamal silhouetted against the sky. "Shukran!"

"You're welcome," Jamal said, grinning at Yasmeen. He guided Mias up the trail to the ledge, and they disappeared from sight.

30

During our second Christmas in Saudi, the religious reins tightened. Ocmara sent out a memo announcing zero tolerance for any kind of Christmas displays or celebrations on the compound. Security would be heightened, curfews rigidly enforced, and there would be severe penalties for disobedience. There was a constant parade of security cars and foot patrols. *Merry Christmas!*

For expats, this meant doors opened warily, drapes tightly drawn, silent nights. There was no Women's Club luncheon, no secret church service. Holiday gatherings were furtive and outlaw Santas had to remain sober. I was not unhappy about the sober Santa rule, but felt the razor edges of paranoia slicing into my wellbeing. The heightened tension in Al Hassa was palpable.

Andrea loaned us her tree again, while escaping to Greece. Setting up the tree, I felt the usual melancholy, heightened by missing Mom. We decorated with the handmade ornaments and gutra stockings, but hanging six silver balls also made me sad.

Christmas fell on Sunday, a work day. It couldn't be official, but Mohammed told his team to be "sick" on Sunday. "Consider it my Christmas bonus," Max joked. "Instead of a ham."

"Funny," Kate uttered, not looking up from her book.

Thursday night before Christmas, Kate disappeared after dinner. Sam and Max watched TV and I sat down with a cup of tea and a book, looking forward to a quiet evening lost in the lives of strangers.

After awhile, Kate came downstairs wearing a short skirt and a T-shirt that showed off her necklace. Her hair was parted in the middle and brushed into shiny waves and she had on lip-gloss. Kate leaned against my chair.

"You look cute," I said. "Where are you going?"

"Nadia's. Her sister's home for Christmas and a bunch of high school girls are going to be there." I liked Nadia. She was smart, sweet, and good to Kate. After the day Max acted so outrageously on the beach, Nadia made sure Kate didn't pay the social price for his behavior.

Max frowned. "Is it a party?"

Kate looked at Max with her recently perfected expression of scorn. "No, just hanging out."

Max went back to watching TV.

"Be home before 10," I said.

"Nadia wants to know if I can spend the night." Kate smiled. "Please, Mom?"

"Sure, if it's okay with her parents."

"Thanks! I'll see you tomorrow." Kate hugged me and was gone before Max could object.

It was the middle of the night when I felt Sam shaking my shoulder. "Mom, wake up," he whispered urgently. I followed Sam to the bathroom where Kate knelt in front of the toilet. Tears, sweat, and black mascara streamed down her pale face.

Sam watched from the doorway while I held Kate's hair as she vomited. Cold water ran over a washrag in the sink. Kate sat back on her heels, mouth open, panting. In one swift motion I flushed the toilet, squeezed the washrag, and wiped Kate's face. When Kate gagged noisily and vomited again, hot liquid spewed into the toilet. I wiped her face, but before flushing I was startled by the smell of booze.

After she finished, I lowered the lid and helped her sit. Her T-shirt was wet and filthy and when I pulled it over her head, I realized it was torn and inside-out. Kate sat in her training bra, shivering, sobbing, and babbling incoherently. There were scratches and red pressure marks on her arms and chest. Her right hand was clenched in a fist. When I gently opened Kate's hand, her broken necklace fell to the floor. I looked at Sam. "Go get your dad."

A half-hour later we were at the clinic. Kate sat wrapped in a blanket on an examination table. She leaned into me, her head heavy on my shoulder. Max stood looking angry and helpless. Sam waited in the hall where Max and I had also waited while Dr. Kayra examined Kate.

Dr. Kayra had responded immediately to my phone call, and I saw the hem of her nightgown under her lab-coat. Her hair was hastily tucked beneath a scarf and she wore sandals, but she was still an imposing presence. She was clearly worried and I recognized the outrage in her voice.

"Your daughter will be okay, but she is very lucky. Sidiqui is almost 100 proof alcohol." Dr. Kayra's eyes went damp. "I've seen many cases of alcohol poisoning and a number of deaths from far less than Kate consumed."

I felt the sensation of falling and pulled Kate closer.

Max took a breath, but before he could speak Dr. Kayra continued. "No need to fear, Mr. Hayes, I won't report this to security." The doctor smiled gently at Kate. "We must talk about the sexual assault. Kate was not raped, but she was physically attacked."

Oh, God, oh, God, oh, God. I squeezed Kate. Max leaned on the table looking like he was going to faint. The doctor looked into Kate's eyes with radiant compassion.

"Who did this to you?"

Kate's chin trembled. She looked away and started crying. Finally, she looked at the doctor. "Billy did it. Billy Mitchell," she said in a hoarse whisper.

I closed my eyes and felt the room spin. Now I thought I was going to faint.

After we got home, I tucked Sam in bed while Kate showered. When she finished, I toweled her dry like I had when she was a toddler then pulled a nightgown over her head. In her dark bedroom, I leaned against the headboard, while Kate curled against me.

"Mommy, I'm so sorry." She looked at me with such anguish.

"Ssshhh, sweetie, go to sleep." I stroked her hair. Now was not the time to tell her it wasn't her fault—no matter what happened. But tomorrow would be, and the day after that. I'd tell her until she finally believed me. Kate closed her eyes and I stroked her until she fell asleep. I sat watch over my child until call to prayer began then went downstairs to talk to Max.

Because Kate was a juvenile, Dr. Kayra left it to us to handle the assault, but urged us not to involve Ocmara. Katie would come under scrutiny for drinking and sexual behavior, even when she'd been attacked. In the Kingdom, either activity was punishable by flogging, jail, or death.

I was out of my mind with rage and my immediate impulse was to pull Billy from his bed and beat him to death with my bare hands. But I didn't want to wind up in jail in Saudi Arabia. Max and I fought in hushed tones—the unlit Christmas tree silent witness to our battle.

"If you don't tell them, I will," I said.

"No, you won't," Max said. "We've got to think this through."

"What's there to think through?"

Max took a deep breath. "Look, Kate lied about everything. She got dressed up, went to the party knowing boys would be there, and drank the sid. She was asking for trouble."

His words made me crazy. I covered my face with my hands, resisting the powerful urge to beat the hell out of Max. I looked at him through my fingers, clawing my face in frustration. "Jesus, Max, listen to yourself. Nothing gave Billy the right to rape her."

"He didn't rape her." Max sighed.

Why was I the only one who wanted to kill Billy Mitchell? Wasn't this what fathers were for? "He tried! Thank God she got sick." As Kate's story unfolded, it was clear Billy's intentions were wrecked by his friend sid. I gestured frantically. "She's thirteen. Billy is seventeen."

When Max didn't respond it made me crazier. "We've got to get out of Saudi." If I couldn't tear flesh and break bones, my restless hands were ready to start packing.

Max took on a low, condescending tone. "You don't think kids drink in the States?"

"They don't drink 100 proof moonshine their parents made in the garage." I clenched my fists. "This is a crazy fucked up place and it's destroying us. I want to go home."

"Quit my job, just like that?" Max said.

"You can find another job. I'll go back to work."

Max leaned close, narrowed his eyes, and pointed his finger in my face. "I'm not quitting my job. That's final. And maybe Kate has learned something from all this."

I froze. "Learned what? Not to ask for it?" I spoke quietly. "You fucking bastard. You better hope your children never learn what a coward you are. Now, I'm telling you what's going to happen. The kids and I are going back to the States, with or without you."

Max went white with rage. "Are you threatening me?"

"I'm promising you," I said.

We stood, eyes locked. Finally, Max shook his head and rubbed his face. When he took his hands away his eyes were full of tears. He looked defeated. "Okay."

"Okay, what?" I squinted warily, hands still in fists.

"Whatever it takes to keep us together."

Later, we talked strategy. Our renters' lease would be up mid-May, but if we stayed until the end of July, the kids could finish the school year in Saudi. After contemplating what Dr. Kayra told us, I reconsidered telling Bobbi and Ray. I was afraid for Kate. Billy would be gone in a week and we'd leave soon after he returned for summer. We'd keep Kate safe during any overlap.

"I'll start sending out resumes and maybe go on interviews during repat in February," I said.

Max nodded thoughtfully. "I've got another idea. Why don't I ask Mohammed if I can postpone repat until August? That way we'll save all the money we'd be spending in February and vacation in Europe on the way home."

I thought about it. Repat in February meant we'd be nomads in the Chicago winter and the kids would miss a month of school. After awhile, I sighed. "That makes sense. I can make it seven months if I know we're leaving for good in August."

I didn't know I would regret this decision for the rest of my life.

31

January 2nd the kids went back to school and an hour later Yasmeen was at my door.

"Merry Christmas!" Yasmeen handed me a package.

Inside was a black triangular-shaped scarf. Along the edges were dozens of silver coin-like discs that jingled like a tambourine. "It's for dancing." Yasmeen tied the scarf around my hips.

"It's beautiful! Thank you." I hugged her.

That day we belly danced to Middle Eastern music in the light of the Christmas tree. I liked the weight of the scarf on my hips, how it chimed along with my khalakhil. We circled each other, moving together and apart. Yasmeen was a good teacher, always helping me master more intricate movements. I could shimmy my shoulders and hips and almost undulate my belly.

"It's easy," Yasmeen said. "Once you know the secret."

The secret is to simultaneously suck in your belly and round your back on one movement, push your belly out and arch your back on the next—all while rocking your pelvis in a subtle humping motion that starts slow and gets faster. It takes killer abs and can look very sexy.

After working up a sweat, I poured us iced tea. When I came back from the kitchen Yasmeen was standing by the Christmas tree. The scarf clinked as I walked. I loved it.

"Are these ornaments homemade?" Yasmeen asked.

"All but the silver balls. Ours didn't make it through customs, so we made them last year. Guess which ones are Sam's!" I pointed to the gingerbread man.

She laughed.

"The others are mostly Kate's."

Yasmeen smiled at me. "I'd like to meet your Kate."

I was surprised, but pleased. "I'd like her to meet you, too."

Yasmeen touched a seashell dangling from a red ribbon. "My mother is Muslim, of course. Daddy called himself agnostic." Yasmeen smiled. "I've never celebrated Christmas."

"Time to start," I said, reaching for the present I'd hidden under the tree.

Yasmeen looked delighted.

We sat on the sofa as Yasmeen slowly leafed through the album I'd created after spending hours in the photo-lab. There were pictures I'd taken of her family in the women's quarters and those she'd taken of me, Jamal, and Mias on the beach. There were shots we'd posed for in my living room using the timer—silly pictures where we grinned and smoked Dunhills while wearing veils and hijabs. In the final photograph our heads were together and we simply smiled into the camera.

"You can't know how much this means to me." Yasmeen had tears in her eyes.

"I know what your friendship has meant to me," I said. "I made duplicates of these, to help me remember."

"Remember?" Yasmeen asked.

I hesitated. "We're going home early. We're leaving in August."

Yasmeen froze, took a deep breath and frantically looked around the room. When she covered her face with her hands and broke down, I put my arms around her.

"We have seven more months," I said. "Maybe you can visit me in Chicago."

Yasmeen leaned into me and wept. Stroking Yasmeen's hair felt like I was holding an older Kate. I had to save my daughter's life, but was so eager to leave Saudi I hadn't thought about what I'd be leaving behind. Or that I would devastate anyone in the leaving.

Finally, with a deep shuddering sigh, Yasmeen sat up and wiped her face. She pulled out a Dunhill and offered me the box. After we lit up, Yasmeen leafed through the album again.

"Before you go I want you to see more of Saudi than just the souqs. I want to show you the real Saudi." She frowned.

"What?" I asked.

"I think it'll work, but I have to make sure."

I was intrigued. "Make sure of what?"

Yasmeen spoke as if thinking aloud. "Jamal drives us different places, me, Shadan, my mother. I'd love to show you Qatif. It's my favorite place in Saudi."

"Where is it?"

"An hour south on the coast," Yasmeen said.

"How would we do it?" I asked.

"We would borrow Shadan's ID, in case we're stopped. You would be veiled, but it'll be risky because you're not related to Jamal."

I thought about the guardhouses, the rules against unmarried people being together. *What are the rules about impersonating a Saudi woman?*

"Jamal will have to agree and you'll have to stay veiled all day." She looked doubtful.

Being winter, it was cooler. I sometimes needed a light jacket at night. It would be the veiling—I wasn't sure I could do it.

Yasmeen read my expression. "Never mind," she said quickly. "I don't even know if Jamal would do it." She looked at the Christmas tree. "I'm sorry they took your ornaments. You shouldn't have to hide your religion."

Yasmeen was deliberately changing the subject, but I carefully considered her words. "We're guests here in the Kingdom. It should be more about our respecting Saudi traditions than expecting Saudi to embrace ours."

Yasmeen's eyes burned intensely, like she was struggling with something deep and dark. "Guests should be made to feel welcome, not persecuted for their religious beliefs."

It felt like she was trying to tell me something else. "But that's not just Saudi or Islam," I said. "There are fundamentalists and fanatics everywhere. They're the problem. Christianity isn't exactly known for tolerance. 'Jesus, the one and only way?' I don't believe that."

Yasmeen looked at my cross. "You don't? And you're Christian?"

I shrugged. "Not a good one."

"Do you pray?" Yasmeen asked.

"All the time," I said. "Do you?"

"Not as much as a good Muslim, but at least three times a day."

"Okay." I stood and held out my hands to her. "You've taught me belly dancing, now teach me how you pray."

Yasmeen set the album aside, stood, and turned me to face the direction she knew by heart. "First, we face Mecca."

In the light of the Christmas tree, Yasmeen showed me the positions of Islamic prayer. I never learned them all, or the prayers chanted with them, but it was beautiful to see her pray. I followed her movements as best I could, my scarf chiming along.

A week later I spooned cookie dough onto a baking sheet while Kate watched. She held a bowl and listlessly shoveled dough into her mouth with a wooden spoon. It was almost noon and she was still in pajamas. Kate came home sick the second day back from break and had been "sick" ever since. I knew it was emotional. Kate wasn't the same since the attack.

After sliding the cookies into the oven, I looked at her.

"What?" She looked annoyed.

"Are you really sick or just don't want to go to school?"

When she just shrugged and took another bite of dough, I grabbed the bowl and spoon from her hands. "Go shower and get dressed."

"Why?"

"Because I said so." I smiled. "Don't worry. You're not going to school."

"Where am I going?"

"It's a surprise. Go. Hurry up."

Kate looked suspicious. "What should I wear?"

"Shorts and a T-shirt." I'd been invited back to the women's quarters that afternoon, but with Kate home I was afraid I couldn't go. Then I remembered Yasmeen saying she wanted to meet Kate. *What better time?*

Kate was a good sport about being cloaked in black and led across the compound in the midday heat. I guess she figured anything was better than school. Shadan greeted us at the door with a smile. I couldn't let Yasmeen know I was bringing Kate, but needn't have worried. Everyone was warm and welcoming and I loved Kate's reaction.

"Oh, wow," Kate said, blue eyes huge as she gazed about.

The room was lit with small lamps and candles, music played softly, and incense perfumed the air. It was a smaller gathering and everyone was dressed casually. Women talked and laughed. The baby cried and was fastened to Zahra's heavy breast without interrupting her conversation. When the tiny girl shrieked with pleasure, toddled up to me, and hugged my legs, I scooped her up.

Yasmeen rushed in. "You brought Kate! I'm so happy." Yasmeen hugged me then Kate.

"Sweetie, this is my friend, Yasmeen," I said. Kate looked astonished.

"Come to the kitchen," Yasmeen said. "We're making lunch."

The kitchen was enormous. Shelves held everything from dishes to colorful tins of tea and olive oil. Herbs and spices crowded a narrow ledge. Crocks of wooden spoons lined the counters. Pots and pans hung from hooks on the wall. It was Julia Child's kitchen gone Middle Eastern.

Huda rushed over, hugged me then looked at Kate. "You are beautiful, like your mother." Laughing, she touched Kate's hair. "But you look more like Yasmeen, except your eyes."

"Thank you." Kate flushed with embarrassment. It was true—with Kate's wide grin, thick dark hair, and pale skin, she and Yasmeen could easily have been related—only Kate's clear blue eyes made it improbable.

Leila smiled and nodded from the stove, but didn't come to us.

"Kate, I want you to meet Nora," Yasmeen said. Nora sat on a stool at the counter wearing shorts and a sleeveless blouse that revealed long skinny arms and legs. The girls were the same height and almost exactly the same age. They looked at each other and giggled.

"Put us to work," I said.

Huda pulled up another stool. "Hop up, Kate. You can help Nora."

"What can I do?" I asked.

"Help me make salad," Yasmeen said. We sat at a table in the middle of the room and I watched Kate and Nora interact.

One bowl on the counter contained dough and another held a paste made from dates. Nora took a handful of dough. "First you roll it into a ball." She demonstrated and Kate did the same.

"Now poke a hole." Nora pushed her finger into the dough. "And put the filling in." She stuffed a spoonful of the paste into the hole. "Then close it." Nora pinched the dough together. Kate carefully followed every step.

Nora picked up a utensil like a wooden spoon, except the top had an intricately carved design. "Here's yours." Nora gave Kate one with a different design.

"This is the best part," Nora said, pressing the ball of dough into the mold. When she flipped it out, the dough had a deeply imprinted design. Nora set it on a cookie sheet, design side up.

Kate pressed her dough into the mold and turned it out into her hand. She looked at the design, smiled at Nora, and put it on the cookie sheet. Both reached for more dough.

"What are these called?" Kate asked.

"Mamool," Nora replied.

Kate seriously repeated the word. "Mamool."

Both girls burst into giggles. I suddenly remembered seeing mamool molds my very first time at the souq with Amy and Bonita. I watched a few more minutes then smiled at Yasmeen.

"Thank you," I whispered. Yasmeen knew about the attack and that I worried about Kate.

"You're welcome."

Later, the living room had the same smoky blue haze as last time. We'd eaten bowls of goat stew, cucumber and tomato salad, and Arab bread. Kate dug into her stew without a word about not eating goat and actually finished it. Afterwards everyone enjoyed mamool and cookies. Throughout the afternoon, conversation became loose with laughter. Music was loud and some women were dancing.

At some point, Kate admired Nora's small gold hoop earrings and talked about getting her ears pierced. Now, Kate sat bravely on a stool, surrounded by Nora, Shadan, Yasmeen, and me. Huda bent over Kate then gave her a mirror. We applauded as Kate examined her newly pierced ears. Kate's ears held tiny gold hoops instead of studs, and she was ecstatic with the substitution.

The applause became rhythmic clapping as we filed into the living room and joined the circle around two women who were dancing. Their bellies undulated and they waved colorful scarves while calling out in high-pitched trills. The dancers passed their scarves to others who stepped inside the circle. Women of all shapes, sizes, and ages danced.

Nora stepped into the circle and beckoned Kate to join her. When Kate giggled and shyly refused, Yasmeen stepped in. The two were a beautiful contrast—Yasmeen all lush hips and belly, Nora with her thin childish form. Eventually, Nora stepped out flushed and breathless.

Yasmeen held out her hands to me. Like Kate, I laughed shyly, but the others loudly encouraged me. To Kate's amazement, I stepped inside the circle. Then Huda rushed in, adjusting my blouse and skirt so my pale belly was exposed. Self-conscious and aware of Kate, I couldn't relax, but Yasmeen was relentless. She circled me, shaking her shoulders and hips, belly moving to the beat.

Finally, Yasmeen locked eyes with me and I forgot about the others, losing myself in the music and movement. As we danced—circling each other, moving together and apart—I began to have fun. Kate watched with wide-eyed surprise and I grinned at her. The circle of women swayed and clapped and I felt the communal energy. When the music ended, the women applauded and trilled. Yasmeen and I rejoined the circle while others took our places.

"Wow, Mom," Kate said. "You were great! Will you teach me?" I hugged her and we turned to clap for the new dancers.

When it was time to go, we put on our abayas and hijabs. Before the final veils we said our goodbyes. Kate's face was just a pale oval framed by her hijab, but she looked the happiest I'd seen her since the attack.

Shadan, Nora, Huda, and Leila watched as Yasmeen tucked away a stray lock of my hair and made sure my cross was covered. She hugged me, then Kate. "It was lovely to have you. I hope you'll come back."

"I'd like to," Kate said.

"Oh! The wedding!" Shadan beamed. "You must come to Nora's wedding!"

Nora? I thought I'd misunderstood, but then Huda proudly threw her arms around Nora.

"Nora has begun to menstruate," Huda said. "We celebrated her introduction to the veil and now we are planning her marriage. You would both honor us with your presence."

I felt the blood leave my face. In the ensuing silence, Kate looked at me with confusion. Nora flushed with what could have been shame or pride. Leila covered her mouth and turned away, but not before I saw the tears in her eyes. I looked at Yasmeen, but she wouldn't meet my eyes. Her expression was unreadable. It was as if a veil had fallen across her face.

Shadan pressed a note into Kate's hand. "Nora is marrying a Saudi prince! Here is the date and time. We're having it here." Shadan smiled. "Please come."

"Can we, Mom?" Kate gave me a pleading smile. "Please?"

In the long moment that followed, I felt the pressure of six pairs of watchful eyes, and was in the intensely awkward position of having to make an appropriate response.

"Sure," I said, with a smile. "We'd be happy to."

Kate and I barely made it home before Sam. We still shared a giddy energy, but for me it was muted by the news of Nora's wedding. The idea of that child being married felt so alarming I had to hold it at arm's length.

"This has to be our secret." I looked into Kate's eyes. "Today. All of this."

Kate nodded, her cheeks pink with heat and excitement. "I know. I can't wait for the wedding! Nora's marrying a prince! It's going to be so romantic. Like a fairytale!"

That night, Kate caught up on homework while I made dinner. She'd pinned up her hair to show off her earrings. Max stood in the doorway between us. He wasn't happy.

"Let me get this straight. Too sick to go to school, but not too sick to get her ears pierced?"

Kate froze, staring at her books.

"Blame me," I said. "I didn't want to leave her home alone, so I made her go with me." I was careful with my wording, so I didn't have to lie. Max assumed we'd gone to Rahima.

"Why didn't you use the earrings we bought her?" Max asked.

"Because it was spontaneous," I said.

"Well, I hope those earrings weren't expensive," Max said.

A ridiculous assertion from a man wearing a Rolex. "Not at all."

Before Max could ask another question I wrapped my arms around his neck and smiled at him. "I wanted some company. I've been feeling lonely."

Max smiled and whispered in my ear. "Why don't we do something about that later?"

I kissed him then Max smacked my butt and walked away smiling, the earrings forgotten. I winked at Kate who gave me an affectionately disgusted look.

Later, I lay with my head on Max's chest. He nuzzled my hair and I shifted closer. It had been a confusing day and I wished I could share it with him. But in the absence of truth, the closeness of his body had almost been enough. Max looked into my eyes and whispered, "I love you."

"I love you, too."

While I rubbed his chest, Max stroked my back and hips. It felt good to be touched. His hand stopped on my butt. "Hey, babe?" he whispered.

"Uh huh?" I smiled dreamily.

"Have you stopped running?"

I lifted my head and looked at him. "I'm not running every day. Why?"

Max smiled and grabbed a handful of my butt. "You're just getting a little fat."

Don't ask me why, I disgust myself. The next morning I was running on the beach. I thought about the day before—the abundance of flesh without the curse of self-consciousness—reveling in the female body in its natural state. I hated myself for caring enough about what Max thought to go back to running every day. But there I was.

32

Yasmeen's doubts about my ability to stay veiled all day had become a challenge. At home, I layered on an abaya, hijab, mask, and veil for increasing lengths of time. I stood in the backyard under the hot midday sun, sweat matting my hair and running down my neck. I practiced taking deep, even breaths as I fought panic and the urge to rip the cloth from my face.

Showing me Qatif seemed so important to Yasmeen that I wanted to do it for her. Especially because I sensed she was avoiding me. A month had passed since the day in the women's quarters when we learned of Nora's wedding. It was the last time I'd seen Yasmeen.

One morning, I went to the beach before daybreak and found Yasmeen standing on the ledge where I'd first seen her. "Ask Jamal to drive us to Qatif," I said.

"Are you sure?" Yasmeen said.

"I'm sure."

Yasmeen hugged me. "You're going to love it."

There was no mention of where she'd been the past month, and I didn't ask.

The day of our trip, I veiled and met Yasmeen at her house at 9 a.m. We'd planned it carefully—drive an hour, spend two hours in Qatif, drive back during noon call to prayer. Our schedule coincided with a shopper's bus to Dammam. I'd say I'd taken that bus if anyone asked, but no one ever did.

Yasmeen inspected me, eyes searching. "You're absolutely sure?"

"Yes."

"Put this in your backpack." Yasmeen gave me Shadan's ID then dropped her veil over her face. "Follow me." Yasmeen led me down a hall, through a door, and into a garage where Jamal waited behind the wheel of a white Mercedes.

When we got into the backseat I was relieved to feel a rush of cool air. Jamal's eyes were reflected in the rearview mirror. "All set?"

We nodded and Jamal backed the car out and drove toward the compound gates. At the first guardhouse, the guard glanced at Jamal and lazily waved us through. But at the second, the guard held up his hand.

"Sit still. Don't say a word," Jamal said quietly. He lowered the window and flashed his ID.

The guard examined Jamal's ID then looked at me and Yasmeen. My mouth went dry and my heart raced. Sweat trickled down my sides. I knew I was completely covered, but fear made me feel exposed. I resisted the urge to grab Yasmeen's hand.

"*Bes! Bes!*" Jamal indignantly barked at the guard, who backed away and waved us through.

As we turned onto the highway, I let out the breath I'd been holding and heard Yasmeen do the same. Outside the windows, the desert flew by through a dark film. As long as I didn't think about being covered, I was okay. But whenever awareness slipped in, I had to fight anxiety. At one point a wave of panic washed over me, and suddenly I couldn't breathe.

Yasmeen tuned in immediately. "Lean forward." As I did, the veil and mask fell away from my mouth. I took deep gulps of cool air, embarrassed at my inability to stay calm.

"If you can't do it we have to turn back," Jamal said.

I saw his worried eyes and hesitated, struggling against defeat. After another deep breath, I nodded. "I'm okay."

Yasmeen touched Jamal's shoulder. "She'll be alright." Her voice sounded more confident than I felt, but her conviction strengthened my resolve.

Jamal was a skillful driver, even at breakneck speeds. The size of the Mercedes made it feel like we weren't going as fast as we were, except when flying by smaller vehicles. The smooth ride and plush luxury of the Mercedes put the Land Rover to shame.

After awhile I relaxed. Beneath the darkness of my veil, I felt closed off and safe. It was quiet, and the gentle motion began to lull me to sleep. Unwilling to succumb, I straightened and looked at Yasmeen. She was staring out her window.

"Tell me about Qatif." My voice sounded too loud.

Yasmeen turned toward me. "It's a small Shiite village and the oldest town in Saudi."

"Tell her why it's our favorite," Jamal said. I could tell by his eyes he was smiling.

"My mother and uncle grew up in Qatif," Yasmeen said.

"It feels like home to us," Jamal said. "Our Saudi home."

"Look, the oasis." Yasmeen pointed at groves of date palms and canals of flowing water. "We're here."

We drove slowly down narrow streets lined with ancient two- and three-story houses made of crumbling adobe. All had ornately carved wooden doors and some had balconies jutting from the upper floors. The houses resembled fortresses—windows on the first floors were high, long, and narrow, like in a bunker. Many had minaret-like structures on the roof.

"What are those things on top?" I asked.

"Wind towers," Jamal said. "They catch the ocean breezes and cool the house." Jamal parked in front of a house. He and Yasmeen silently gazed at it.

"This is our grandmother's house," Yasmeen finally said. "Where our parents grew up."

The house was a two-story adobe with a balcony on the second floor and weathered wooden doors. "Is she expecting us?"

"She died a year ago." Jamal's voice had a catch.

"We miss her so much." Yasmeen squeezed my hand. "I wish you two could have met. You would have loved each other. She was brave, like you."

I felt a flush of pleasure. "How so?"

"Grandmother was ahead of her time. She insisted my mother leave the Kingdom to be educated," Yasmeen said. "If she hadn't, my parents would never have met."

"She caught hell for that, too," Jamal said. "My father has never left Saudi. After college, he went to work for Ocmara. But when it was time for me to go to school, Grandmother made sure I went abroad, paying for it with her own money when my father refused to."

"If she hadn't fought the system our lives would be completely different," Yasmeen said. "We owe her everything."

I remembered Yasmeen's Uncle Abdul in the doorway of the women's quarters. Jamal seemed so different from his father, but Jamal's daughter was about to be married at thirteen. I wondered how he felt about that, and if Yasmeen would ever be willing to discuss it.

We sat staring at the house a few more minutes. The air was heavy with their sadness.

"Ready?" Jamal looked back at Yasmeen.

She nodded and Jamal began to drive. We crossed a causeway, stopping beside a harbor. Jamal parked in a shady lot and we got out. I stood a moment, gathering my courage. It was hotter than Al Hassa, but with an occasional gust of sea-breeze. Jamal and Yasmeen examined me, making sure I'd pass for a Saudi woman.

"You're sure you're okay?" Yasmeen asked.

"I'm sure." I knew this would be my only chance. *Be brave.*

"From this point on, don't speak out loud. Whisper if you need anything." Jamal took off, Yasmeen and I trailing behind.

As we walked down the narrow street I wished I had my camera. There were so many great pictures I would have taken—a tiny mosque, a white donkey peering from behind a palm tree, ruins of a Turkish fort on a hill overlooking the harbor. Everything looked hazy through my veil.

We climbed to the top of the hill and looked down. Offshore, a large wooden boat floated in the water, a single triangular sail flapping in the breeze.

"That boat is called a *dhow*," Yasmeen whispered. As we stood looking out to sea, our abayas and veils blew gently in the breeze.

"If we're going to the market, we have to hurry," Jamal said.

Down the street we passed a group of Arab boys shabbily dressed in T-shirts and ripped jeans, barefoot or wearing sandals. One wore a Mickey Mouse T-shirt, and I smiled thinking of Sam's Goofy hat. The boys squatted around a pile of oysters, prying open the shells before tossing them into a bucket.

Once past, Yasmeen spoke, "They're looking for pearls. Qatif used to be famous for pearls before oil-pollution destroyed the oyster beds."

At the market Yasmeen bought dates and mamool molds. Several shops were filled with sandals, swords, incense burners, and dellas. In one tiny shop, the owner was carving a piece of wood. Lining the walls was an armada of miniature wooden dhows. Max had always wanted a sailboat and I decided to buy him one. I whispered to Yasmeen and she told Jamal.

"Bi kam?" Jamal pointed to a ship. After several minutes of haggling they agreed on a price and we walked out with the dhow.

Throughout, I remained silent and invisible under my veils. It was true what Yasmeen had said. No one looked at us or spoke to us as we floated behind Jamal like dark shadows.

The ride back to Al Hassa was quiet, each of us lost in our own thoughts. Driving back through the gates, Yasmeen and I didn't even warrant a cursory glance. Once in the garage, Yasmeen and I hurried to the women's quarters. I gave her Shadan's ID and rushed home.

As I walked through my gate and took off my veil and abaya, I blinked in the bright light. Some point in the day I'd become accustomed to seeing everything through a haze. Suddenly, I had a new appreciation of how clear and sharp everything looks without dark filters.

That night at dinner, I grinned excitedly. "Today when I was shopping I bought everyone presents." I felt like I'd taken a trip and brought back souvenirs. I gave Max the boat.

"It's called a dhow. Like it?"

"It's nice. Thanks, babe."

As Max examined the finely carved mast and riggings made of string, I gave Sam a bag containing a small curved dagger. I'd struggled with the idea of buying Sam a knife, but the one I chose was clearly just a souvenir. Sam wouldn't know the difference, and I didn't have to feel I'd given him a weapon.

"Cool!" Sam unsheathed the dagger and waved it around. "Thanks, Mom!"

"Let me see that, buddy." Max's expression told me he liked the dagger better than the dhow.

"Careful. It's sharp," Sam said.

"And for you." Kate's bag held a gauzy black scarf embroidered with red and gold thread. Green and red sequins formed the shapes of flowers. Kate put the scarf on her head like a hijab, wrapping the ends with surprising skill. "Thanks, Mom. It's beautiful. What'd you get yourself?" When I pulled out mamool molds, Kate lit up. "Mamool!"

"What?" Max looked up.

Kate covered her mouth and looked flustered.

I smiled at Max. "Mamool is an Arab cookie. Kate and I were going to surprise you."

But Kate surprised me by pulling the scarf across the lower half of her face and blinking coquettishly at Max. He laughed, but I was disturbed by the seductive image. I worried what I was teaching her. I knew I'd given Kate an amazing experience in the women's quarters, but feared I had entrusted her with the burden of a secret she was far too young to keep.

33

I began sending out queries for jobs in Chicago that would start in the fall, and updated my résumé to include the clinic. Now that it was no longer a secret, I put in as many hours as possible. I was there at least three days a week, on call whenever Dr. Kayra needed me. She had been a godsend to me and Kate, and I was happy to be there for her.

I had regulars at the clinic, American and British women who had been close to Rebecca and knew she liked me. There were Saudi women whose names I knew, though I rarely saw their faces. I recognized them by their shoes, height and shape, the way they walked or carried their bodies. They asked for me and readily disclosed their problems. It made Dr. Kayra's job easier.

Most of the Saudi women appeared in clusters with family or close friends—a community missing among Western women. Rarely would an Arab woman arrive alone, while Americans and Brits were rarely accompanied. I had finally found my community at the clinic and with Yasmeen and her family.

It felt unsettling to be planning to leave at the very time I'd begun to thrive and feel like I had purpose. I was straddling two worlds and, like Yasmeen, was "truly at home in neither." I didn't dare share this with Max, afraid it would give him an excuse to stay and I'd lose control. I still had to do what was best for my family.

One day, the first week of March, I'd just said goodbye to three Saudi women and moved to the next examination room. I paused at the curtain.

"Hello. Marhaba. May I come in?" I took the muffled response as permission.

A frail woman with faded red hair was sitting on the table. Her head was bowed and her body shook. When she lifted her head and looked at me, I resisted the impulse to cry out.

One of Bobbi's eyes was swollen shut, the other bloodshot and bruised. Her lips were split and bloody, and her neck red with hand-shaped bruises.

When Bobbi saw me, she covered her face and began to cry. I winced as much at her broken spirit as I did at the evidence of brutality on her body. Moving close, I opened my arms and Bobbi leaned into me, crying while I held her.

Immediately everything slid into place—Bobbi's fragility, Ray's drunkenness, Billy's attack on Kate. I was thankful we'd never told them. There was no telling where that confrontation would have led, but I was certain it would have involved violence. Again, I was grateful we'd be leaving Saudi within months.

As Nora's wedding approached, I struggled with whether to take Kate. Yasmeen and I hadn't talked about it, so I didn't know what to expect. Many cultures arranged marriages and I wondered if this was just a formalization of such an arrangement—rather than an actual wedding with a child-bride. Because of Kate's dreamy reaction to Nora marrying a prince, I knew she was imagining something out of a Disney movie. But Leila's tears at the announcement and Yasmeen's subsequent silence had triggered an uneasiness I couldn't ignore. I decided not to take Kate. We'd never discussed it and I hoped she had forgotten.

The afternoon of Nora's wedding I said I was attending a Women's Club event that night. After dinner, I went upstairs, put on a nice dress, and stuffed my abaya into my backpack. When I walked out of my bedroom, Kate was in the hallway. She too, was in a nice dress, backpack slung on one shoulder.

"Where are you going?" I said, quietly.

"With you," she said. "To Nora's wedding."

"Oh, sweetie." I touched her arm. "I don't think that's a good idea."

Kate shrugged away. "Why not? I was invited."

"I just don't think it's appropriate for you."

"But I want to go," Kate whined. "Please?"

"I'm sorry." I shook my head.

"I'm going." Kate's voice edged toward loud.

"No, you're not." I tried to sound quietly firm.

An angry flush crept up her neck. "Then I'm telling Dad."

I wanted to slap her. Instead, I covered my face with my hands and tried to stay composed. When I looked at Kate she was smirking. "You can't do that, Katie. You promised me."

"Take me to the wedding," she said.

"No."

"Dad?" Kate yelled.

"What?" Max answered from downstairs.

"Jesus, Kate." I grabbed her shoulders.

"Are you taking me with you?" she whispered, squinty angrily.

"Kate? Did you call me?" Max yelled.

"Okay, dammit," I hissed, furious at her and myself for having created this monster.

"Nothing, Dad." Kate smiled smugly and started downstairs. I followed, shaking with rage. In the living room, Kate gave Max a hug. "Guess what! Mom's taking me with her."

"That's nice," Max said. "You girls have fun."

Crossing the compound, I held Kate's arm, resisting the urge to pinch her. Women were still arriving when we got there. High heels were lined neatly beside the usual pile of sandals and shoes. Inside, the row of hooks was completely full. Yasmeen was waiting when we walked in. Her smile didn't reach her eyes.

"Don't take off your veils," Yasmeen whispered. "Men will be in and out all night. I don't want anyone to see you."

Yasmeen's abaya was open over her green silk sheath. Her hair was uncovered, but her hijab was draped over her shoulders. Many women were finely dressed, bejeweled, and made-up. But all had hijabs close by and some were completely veiled.

There was a buffet, but I had no appetite. When I saw a plate of mamool, I flashed to Kate and Nora sitting on their stools—innocent, gawky, giggling girls. I glanced at Kate's veiled form, wishing to God I'd been able to leave her at home. *What happens at the wedding of a thirteen year old girl?*

I tried to pick up clues from the other women. Most talked and laughed. Music played loudly and some women sang and danced. Incense smoldered and Dunhills smoked. Sweetly fragrant tobacco burned in the hookah. On the surface it appeared nothing more than a joyous occasion.

"Come," Yasmeen whispered. "There's something I want you to see."

Yasmeen led us down a hallway and up a flight of stairs, then opened the door to a closet and beckoned us inside. The closet held an air-conditioning unit—one duct went into a wall and one into the floor. Signaling quiet, Yasmeen kneeled and moved the one on the floor. We lifted our veils and looked down.

Below us men laughed and yelped and spun around swinging curved daggers. All the men wore thobes and gutras, so we saw a red-and-white swirl and couldn't distinguish faces. It was a Middle Eastern bachelor party.

Back downstairs, we were standing beside Leila when we heard excited voices, spattered applause, and trilling. Huda and Shadan, festively dressed and beaming, slowly led Nora into the room. Nora wore a frilly purple dress and the palms of her hands were decorated with henna. But her face was pale and expressionless, her eyes glassy. When Nora's knees buckled, Shadan and Huda held her steady until she regained her footing. With a shock, I realized Nora was drugged.

Next, a group of Saudi men entered the room. I saw Jamal and Yasmeen's uncle. In a flurry of activity, women covered their hair and faces and pulled on abayas. Kate took my hand.

"Where's the prince?" she said.

Yasmeen leaned close and whispered. "The man on the far right."

I felt immediate revulsion. Unlike a young, handsome, Disneyland-version of a prince, Nora's groom was a bearded man in his mid-forties. His belly filled the front of his thobe like the bow of a ship as he grinned and swaggered. Beside me, I heard Leila hiss quietly under her veil.

"That's the prince?" Kate said, incredulously. "That's Nora's husband?"

"Shhh," I hushed her.

"No!" Kate said loudly, her voice filled with indignation. "No!"

Yasmeen's uncle stared at us with a questioning frown. *This can't be happening. How is this happening?* I looked at Nora's pale young face, her blank eyes, and I felt sick.

"We have to go," I whispered to Yasmeen as I pulled Kate toward the door. Yasmeen nodded. Her expression was impassive, but sorrow filled her eyes.

I backed out of the room, pulling Kate with me. We found our sandals and fled. Behind us, music and laughter filled the night air with tragedy.

"How can she marry him? Why isn't anybody stopping this?" Kate's voice was thick with rage. She ripped the veil from her head. "I hate this," she screamed.

"Run!" I said, stooping to grab Kate's veil as I pulled her through the darkness. I kept glancing behind us, afraid we'd be discovered. Not knowing what would happen.

We ran long enough to feel safe then stopped to catch our breath. It was hot and muggy and we were soaked with sweat. I pulled the veil and hijab from my head and slipped off my abaya.

"Give me yours." Kate's hands trembled as she fumbled with the zipper. I stuffed everything into our backpacks while Kate wept, her fists clenched in helpless fury.

Instead of going home, I led Kate to the beach. The Gulf stretched blackly under the star-studded sky and lapped quietly on the shore. I pulled Kate into the deepest shadows between sand dunes. There, with a thin crescent moon our only witness, I held Kate while she cried.

"He's an old man." Kate's voice was pleading and hoarse. "How can Nora marry him?"

"I don't think she has a choice," I said quietly.

"Why not?"

"In some cultures marriages are arranged by the parents," I said.

"Well, she just needs to say *no*," Kate said. "She needs to tell her mom and dad that she wants someone else to marry."

I leaned my head against Kate's and held her until she finally stopped crying. Her breathing slowed and she leaned heavily against me. She sighed, shifted, and looked at me. Her eyes were swollen and bright, her face still wet with tears.

"I'm sorry, Mommy," she whispered. "About earlier." Her face crumbled.

I brushed the hair off her forehead and kissed her brow. It felt damp and feverish. "It's okay, sweetie," I whispered. "I'm sorry, too."

The house was dark and quiet when we got home. Kate and I tiptoed upstairs. I waited while she got ready for bed and stayed until she fell asleep, sock-monkey clutched in one arm. After checking on Sam, I went to bed. Max was asleep so I was able to slip in quietly.

The chaos of the evening looped through my head, but I finally slept. Deep in the night, I awakened to the wailing of a shamaal. I got up, opened the curtains, and looked out the window. The night was still and quiet. Confused, I lay back down. It was only then I realized tears were streaming down my face. The wailing had been my own.

I found Yasmeen a week later at dawn. She stood on the ledge staring out to sea. I climbed the path, calling out quietly so I wouldn't startle her. As I reached the top, she turned toward me, but didn't speak. My eyes darted to her khalakhil, just to make sure.

When I walked toward her, she bent forward and started to cry. When I reached out to hold her, she was shaking and making a howling noise more animal than human. Yasmeen dropped to her knees pulling me with her. Jagged stone bit into my skin and I knew I'd be bleeding soon, but I didn't let go. Slowly, she exhausted herself.

We'd settled onto the ground when she let out a shuddering sigh. With one swift motion she pulled off her veil and mask and threw them to the ground. I waited.

"Nora's husband has taken her to Riyadh," Yasmeen said. "She is lost to me." Tears slipped down her face while she gazed out to sea. She looked defeated.

"How does Jamal feel about this?" I asked, tentatively.

"Jamal hates it, but he's powerless against tradition," Yasmeen said flatly. Her hands lay motionless in her lap. I took one. There was nothing I could say that would make it better. We sat like that for the longest time, holding hands and grieving for the child who'd been sacrificed.

34

Max worked late on Saturday, and since I'd spent the day at the clinic, I fed the kids leftovers then went to bed early. I was reading when Max came in.

"Close your eyes and hold out your hands," he said, sitting down.

With a sigh, I put down my book, closed my eyes, and held out my hands. I felt the small booklet, ran my thumb over the pebbly texture, and opened my eyes. *My passport!*

"I didn't say open them!" Max was smiling.

Opening the front page, I saw myself looking up. "Are we leaving?"

"For the weekend." Max waved a travel brochure for Bahrain. "Just you and me."

"We can't leave the kids alone in Saudi," I said, immediately alarmed.

"It's just two nights," Max said. "It's only a few hours away by car. Ben and Jennifer are staying here and watching the kids. They'll be fine."

Max opened the brochure in which swimming pools glistened and restaurants enticed with international cuisine, wine, and liquor. A causeway crossing the Gulf connected Saudi with the island of Bahrain, making the liberal kingdom a popular getaway for expats and Saudis.

"Come on, babe, it's been two years since we've been away alone together," Max said. "And we might never have the chance to explore another Arab country." He opened my passport. "Look, an exit-visa!"

I stared at the Arabic writing, the stamps in red ink. *An exit-visa!* Still, I couldn't imagine leaving my kids in Saudi, even for a weekend. "What if something happens?"

"Jennifer and Ben will make sure nothing happens," Max said.

"What if something happens to us?" I imagined a fiery crash.

"If anything happens to us, the kids will be sent right home." That was small comfort, but the part of me that wanted to see another Arab country won out.

Monday night, Jennifer and Ben came for dinner. I showed them where we kept our personal papers and contacts in the States, and gave them Dr. Kayra's numbers. After dinner, the kids went off and Jennifer, Ben, Max and I had coffee and dessert.

"I've heard anything goes in Bahrain," Ben said. "Like Vegas, with call to prayer."

"Yeah, but after living here I think it would be hard to relax in any Arab country," Jennifer said. We exchanged a look. Neither of us would ever forget that terrible day in Khobar. I still carried the scar on my cheek.

"Whatever," Max said, with a twinge of impatience. "It'll be good for us to get out of here." He smiled at Jennifer, as if to soften his tone. "Thanks for watching the kids."

"No problem," Ben said.

Jennifer raised her coffee mug. "To a romantic weekend in Bahrain!" She looked at me. "Have you gotten your passports yet?"

I smiled. "Complete with exit-visas."

"Watch out," Jennifer said. "I might go bottle-blonde and make my great escape."

It was late when they left. Max and Ben had stepped outside when Jennifer pulled a bottle of red wine from her backpack. "Just for you! Quick, hide it."

I grinned as I opened one of the top cabinets and hid the bottle behind baking supplies.

The next morning I kept hitting snooze, getting up just in time to make the kids' breakfast. I longed to go back to bed, but felt I had to run off dessert from the night before. I'd be wearing a bathing suit in a couple days. By the time I hit the beach it was too hot to run. I made a half-hearted effort then slowed to a walk. The water was glassy, no breeze at all. When my skin began to burn, I headed home.

Just inside the sliding doors, I kicked off my shoes then padded to the kitchen for water. I was standing with the refrigerator door open, when I heard a noise upstairs. I froze, listening. It was faint, but definitely something. The kids were in school, Max was at work, and Mimi was asleep on the sofa. My heart pounded as I quietly closed the refrigerator.

Listening at the bottom of the stairs, I heard nothing. For a moment I wondered if I should leave or call security, but there was only silence. I took a deep breath then stealthily climbed the stairs. Tiptoeing past the kids' empty rooms, I began to think I'd imagined the noise when I heard rustling inside my bedroom. I felt trapped. If someone was in there, I wouldn't make it downstairs without being heard. Heart thudding, I pushed the door open.

Across the room a veiled woman was digging through my dresser drawers. As I stepped into the room, she tucked something under her abaya. "Who are you?"

Startled, the woman froze then ran toward the door. I blocked her escape and tackled her onto the bed. As we struggled, her hijab slipped, revealing dark wavy hair. I smelled Clementines.

"Yasmeen?"

With a powerful shove, she pushed me off the bed and ran. I scrambled up and caught her at the top of the stairs. In the struggle, she lost her balance and took me with her. Together we rolled down the stairs, slammed against the floor at the bottom, and lay stunned and breathless.

When the woman started to cry, I painfully rose up, lifted her veil, and uncovered Yasmeen's bloodied, beaten face. "Jesus!"

After helping Yasmeen to the sofa, I filled a bowl with water and ice and dampened a dishtowel. When I walked back into the living room, my passport was on the coffee table. I pushed it aside and set the bowl down. "Let me see your face."

Bruises and cuts covered her face. Her mouth was swollen, lips split and bloody. I winced, knowing I'd never get used to seeing a woman's torn flesh. When I gently blotted Yasmeen's face, she gasped.

"I'm sorry," I whispered. Yasmeen stoically submitted to my touch, while looking directly into my eyes. Seeing the anguish there was more painful than seeing her battered face.

As I dipped the cloth into the bowl, a red cloud spread through the water. I glanced at the passport. Dabbing her face, I tilted my head in silent question. Yasmeen looked at the passport. When she looked at me again new tears filled her eyes. After I'd done all I could, I dropped the bloody cloth into the water and sat silently, waiting.

Finally, Yasmeen took a deep breath and let it out with a long ragged sigh. "When Mother and I came back to Saudi after Daddy died, my uncle made sure we could never leave again."

"What did he do?"

"He took our passports and arranged my marriage to Mohammed." Yasmeen's eyes were full of misery and shame. "Mohammed is an old man. I'm his fourth wife."

"Why didn't you tell me?"

"I was afraid and ashamed." Yasmeen looked down at her hands.

I wrung out the cloth and gently dabbed where blood was oozing again.

"Did Mohammed do this to you?"

"No. It was my uncle," she said.

I remembered her uncle looking at my hands and feet the first time I was in the women's quarters. Staring at me and Kate during Nora's wedding. Suddenly I felt nauseous with remorse. "Oh, my God, I've gotten you into trouble."

"No, it wasn't you," she said quickly. "He suspects I've been with Omar."

For a split-second I was confused—then I knew. "Omar is in Saudi?"

She nodded. "It's too bad Uncle didn't finish the job." Yasmeen put her hands on her stomach. "I'm pregnant with Omar's baby. Mohammed will kill me when he finds out."

"That's crazy," I said. "He can't kill you."

Yasmeen uttered a quick, ugly laugh. "Are you still so naïve? Of course he can. In Saudi the punishment for adultery is death."

"But what about your family? Jamal? Can't they protect you?"

Yasmeen shook her head.

My mind was racing. "You're a US citizen. We'll go to the Embassy."

"I already have. They can't help," she said. "The US has no jurisdiction in Saudi."

"Did you tell them you could die?" I whispered hoarsely.

Yasmeen nodded as tears and blood streamed down her face. She winced as I blotted her face again, helpless to do anything else. "How far along are you?"

"Three months." Yasmeen hugged her abdomen. "I have to save my baby."

I took her hand, closed my eyes, and tried to think. When I opened my eyes, I looked at my passport then at Yasmeen. My first impulse was to give it to her, but fear held me back. *What would happen to me?* I thought about her baby and knew I had no choice.

"I can help you." As I reached for my passport, it occurred to me. "How did you know I had my passport?"

"Mohammed was bragging about how much power he has. Your husband is very valuable to Ocmara. Mohammed almost didn't okay your exit-visas because he was afraid your husband wouldn't come back. He only allowed it because your children weren't leaving." Yasmeen nodded. "Mohammed has that kind of power."

"I don't understand. Your husband isn't Max's boss. Your last name is Ali. Mohammed's name is..." I tried to remember.

"Zamil," Yasmeen said. "Ali is my mother's maiden name. When I came back to Saudi I was only permitted to use Ali, not my American name."

"But when you got married to Mohammed?"

Yasmeen's smile was sad and bitter. "Ironic, isn't it? When Saudi women marry, we keep our maiden names, but lose everything else."

"Why didn't you tell me Mohammed is Max's boss?" I asked.

"I didn't know for awhile. By the time I realized it we were friends," Yasmeen said. "Then I was afraid to tell you. I didn't want to lose you."

Reassuring Yasmeen we would have still been friends was pointless. I wanted to believe it wouldn't have made a difference, but I couldn't be sure. "How can you use my passport? We look nothing alike."

Yasmeen took my hands and spoke quickly. "Jamal knows someone in Dhahran who alters passports. He'll change the name and put my picture in as a precaution. But I'll be veiled at the airport, and they can't make me lift my veil."

"Why didn't you just tell me you needed it? Why did you feel you had to steal it?"

"To keep you safe." Yasmeen stared into my eyes. "I wanted to protect you. If you weren't involved, you couldn't get in trouble."

"Were you going to leave without saying goodbye?"

"Only if I had to," she whispered. "But I would have left you a letter."

We were silent a moment before I remembered. "We leave for Bahrain tomorrow. If I give you my passport now, Max will find out."

"That's alright," Yasmeen said. "It will take a few days to put in place. Omar is working on getting us tickets. Give it to me when you get back."

Something else occurred to me. "Do you have a passport photo?"

"Not yet," Yasmeen said. "We still have to figure that out."

"Come with me. I'll take care of it." As I started to stand, Yasmeen grabbed my hand.

"I'm so sorry," she whispered. "I'm so ashamed."

I hugged her tightly. "There's no time for that. We have to hurry."

The photography lab was empty as usual. I brought my Nikon loaded with black and white film. There were five shots left on the roll. I also brought cosmetics and a hairdryer to speed the process. Yasmeen sat on a stool while I covered her bruises with a thick layer of foundation and brushed her hair to frame her face. Her swollen mouth needed no lipstick. After finishing the roll, I took a deep breath. There was only one chance to get it right.

"This will take awhile," I said. "Go home and take care of yourself."

"When will I see you again?"

"Saturday morning," I said. "I'll meet you on the beach at sunrise, under the ledge. I'll bring the pictures and my passport."

Yasmeen hugged me tightly for a long moment.

"Go," I said. "I'll see you then."

After she left I took deep breaths to push away panic, fear, and sorrow. I couldn't afford emotions just yet. I had a long afternoon ahead. After developing the film, I checked the negatives, relieved to see shadowy images of pictures I'd taken over the last few months. I moved down the strip until I reached the last five frames—the only ones that mattered—five shots of Yasmeen looking straight into the camera. In the end, I had four passable passport-sized prints. I stowed them in my backpack and went home.

35

Although I fought panic the whole trip, our drive to Bahrain was uneventful. The only traffic was at the border between the two Kingdoms, in the middle of the King Fahd Causeway. It slowed going into Bahrain and stopped entering Saudi.

"We're almost there," Max said.

The hotel in Bahrain exemplified what constitutes luxury in Arab nations. Within minutes of being escorted across the marble-floored lobby to the reception desk, we were in the most glorious room I'd ever seen.

It had plush white carpeting, ivory wallpaper, and real oil paintings. A silk duvet blanketed the king-size bed and a ceiling fan gently stirred the air. The marble bathroom had a whirlpool for two, Egyptian-cotton bath sheets, and two white terrycloth robes. Imported toiletries were laid out on a silver tray. The sitting area held a welcome-basket of fresh fruit and chocolates, and a split of Moët in an ice bucket beside two crystal champagne flutes.

I opened drapes and gauzy white sheers. "Come look." French doors led to a balcony overlooking the city. Dusk was falling and the view was breathtaking. Max put his arm around me as we gazed out.

"Everything's perfect." I didn't ask what it cost. Money suddenly seemed beside the point.

"What do you want to do now?" Max smiled seductively.

"Want to explore the rest of the hotel then walk around a bit?" I suggested.

We looked at the menu for the breakfast café and tested the pool's water temperature—cooler than the Gulf, but not frigid. "Want to swim after dinner?" I asked.

"Sure," Max said. "It'll be fun to swim at night."

I thought of my secret swims with Yasmeen and felt a pang. *Those times are over.*

The streets of Bahrain contained more Westerners than I'd ever seen in Saudi. Some Arab women wore abayas, but most wore dresses or pants and blouses, heads uncovered. When Max took my hand, I pulled away.

"Relax," he said. "It's legal here."

In a small Greek restaurant, we were given the best table in the house. "By the fireplace," the host said. "Very romantic."

An appetizer of flaming *saganaki* doused with Ouzo was delivered with a hearty *"Oopa!"* Max and I ordered red snapper and a bottle of *roditis*. The surreal feeling of being in a different place and time kept me present whenever I drifted toward darker thoughts.

After dinner we were both tipsy, but I insisted on going swimming. We were the only ones. There were city lights and pool lights, but stars were still visible overhead.

"I didn't know you were such a strong swimmer," Max said, as I swam laps.

After fighting Gulf currents, swimming in the pool seemed effortless. Like a runner's high, I felt I could go on forever—until I was suddenly exhausted. Back in our room, we luxuriated in a bubble bath while drinking champagne. When I slipped between the soft linen sheets I was out. It wasn't Max's idea of the perfect ending, but it was mine.

The next morning we had coffee and croissants in the hotel café before heading out. I wore a sleeveless sundress that had languished in my closet for two years, and felt both liberated and uncomfortable exposing so much skin.

Bahrain was a Kingdom of contrasts—ancient adobe buildings reflected in the glass windows of financial institutions— traditional souqs beside Chanel, Tiffany, and jewelers specializing in Bahrain's pearls— donkey-pulled carts parked next to Ferraris and Rolls-Royces.

"I wonder what that is." Max pointed to the top of a building.

"A wind tower," I said. "Keeps the inside cool."

"How'd you know that?" Max asked.

I shrugged, remembering Qatif. Had it thrived, Qatif might have looked like Bahrain.

At noontime call to prayer, we ate in an Italian restaurant decorated with travel posters and wicker-bottomed candle-holders. Shakers of cheese, pepper flakes, and oregano sat on top of red-and-white checked tablecloths. I realized I'd never again see red-and-white checks without thinking of Saudi. Max ordered beers then opened his menu.

"Let's have pepperoni pizza. I can't remember the last time we had pork." He took my hand.

I could. The last time was on the pizza we shared in Evanston the night we fought about my mother's money. I didn't remind him.

The waitress brought our beer and took our order. Holding his mug, Max toasted, "Pizza, beer, and you in that sundress. Life is good." The beer was icy-cold and delicious.

Max was trying so hard, at another time it would have been wonderful. I looked around and saw four young Arab women in a nearby booth. Their hair was loose and the palms of their hands were painted with henna. I remembered Nora at her wedding.

"What are you looking at?" Max asked.

"Those women," I whispered. "Aren't they beautiful?"

Max glanced at the women. "Sure are. No wonder their men keep them covered up."

I was stunned by Max's lack of awareness and felt the real loss I'd held at bay for two years. I missed the man with whom I'd shared so much. In Saudi I had lost the love of my life.

The pizza arrived so Max didn't see my tears. He took a bite and smiled—oblivious to the storm raging inside me. "Good, huh?" Hot cheese strung from his mouth.

"Very good." I ate pizza and sipped beer, pretending everything was fine. Between pangs of loss, I was acutely aware of the passport in my backpack. And more pain on the horizon.

After lunch we visited the harbor then walked through the souqs. We bought T-shirts for the kids and a "Bahrain chest" crafted of dark wood and ornately designed with brass. When sunset call to prayer began, we started back to our hotel.

Movement caught my eye while passing between two tall buildings. Threading through the alley was a row of men bowing in prayer. Each kneeled on his own small rug, bowing, raising up, bowing again—movements synchronized as a dance.

I watched, remembering Yasmeen praying in the light of the Christmas tree. Suddenly I was slammed with the reality of her leaving. Sadness washed over me and I was lost in the undertow.

"Come on, babe, this chest is heavy," Max said. I followed quickly, head bowed so he couldn't see my face. Wishing I was veiled.

At the hotel, I went in the bathroom and put on my bathing suit. When I came out Max was lying on the bed. He smiled and patted the space beside him.

"I need a swim before dinner. That pork is still sitting in my stomach." When Max looked disappointed, I smiled. "Later. I promise."

The pool was empty and I dove in. Swimming laps, the water soothed me and the movement took me out of my head. After an hour, we dressed and went to dinner. I wore another sundress, bringing a sweater in case of chill or discomfort.

We chose a Mexican restaurant lit with neon and candles. A bar lined one wall and there was a small dance floor. Throughout the night an Australian couple wearing fringe, cowboy hats, and boots, played guitars and sang country-western songs.

Chips and salsa were delivered after we were seated at a small round table. "Two margaritas, please," Max told the waitress. "And guacamole." He turned to me. "Having a good time?'

"I am." I smiled.

"You seem distant," Max said. "Are you worried about the kids?"

"A little," I admitted.

Max touched my cheek. "They'll be fine."

But will we be fine?

The margaritas came in enormous glasses—icy goodness with a perfect rim of salt and wedge of lime. The kind of margaritas Jennifer and I'd been longing for just before we were beaten by the matawah.

After we toasted, Max smiled. "You know, the kids would enjoy Bahrain. If we decided to stay in Saudi awhile longer we could get away more often. Come here for long weekends."

I took a swallow of my margarita and looked at Max over the rim. There was nothing I could say that wouldn't be reentering negotiations or starting a fight. So I glanced at the couple singing, as though they'd distracted me.

When our food came Max dug into enchiladas and I picked at my taco salad. After almost no choices in Saudi, having so many in Bahrain was overwhelming. I felt besieged and longed to be walking the beach or inside the walls of our quiet home. I sipped my drink.

After dinner we had a second round of margaritas and I felt myself loosening up. It had been a long time since tequila and I liked the wash of relaxation. After the couple sang something heartbreaking by Patsy Cline, I felt intoxicated with that lethal cocktail of tequila, mellow, and melancholy. The song ended to scattered applause and they began another slow sad song.

"Come on, babe, let's dance," Max said.

We were the only couple on the dance floor. All the stools at the bar were filled with Arab men in thobes and gutras. There were no wives. The men turned to watch us dance and I felt their eyes on my arms, neck, and legs.

Max held me tight. When I pushed away, he pulled me close again. "Relax," he whispered. "Why are you so tense?"

I took a deep breath and pretended to relax.

As we turned on the dance floor the men kept watch. Two lifted their glasses. *Were they toasting us or toasting Max?* Several whispered to each other and they all laughed. I felt embarrassed, but Max grinned at the men, pleased with their attention. I felt naked and gazed longingly at my sweater hanging on the back of my chair. Glancing again at the men at the bar, Max pulled me even closer.

I awoke early the next morning. We'd left the French doors open during the night, allowing ocean breezes to lull us to sleep. The room was dimly lit with predawn light. I got out of bed, pulled on my nightgown, and walked to the window. My nightgown blew gently around me as I leaned on the balcony railing, looking down at the Arab city.

The mournful sound of call to prayer was just beginning. A second call to prayer began at a more distant mosque and echoed the first, which continued softly. In a moment, yet another call began from another mosque. I watched and listened as pale light spread across the horizon. Soon, the city below me was bathed in pink. It was beautiful beyond words.

After watching the sunrise I closed the drapes and went back to bed. We slept until ten then went downstairs for the sumptuous breakfast buffet.

"I've eaten so much this weekend," I said. "Tomorrow morning I'm going for a long run."

"You look great." Max glanced at his watch. "We'd better get going. Checkout's at noon."

"This has been so nice I wish we could stay longer. Could you try to get us a late checkout?"

Deep in the night I'd realized I had to make sure Max didn't take my passport when he left for work on Saturday. It was a simple plan. I would stay awake all night and leave the house before he woke up. The later we got home, the fewer hours I'd have to fight to stay awake.

We stopped at the front desk and they graciously allowed us to stay until three.

"Thanks, sweetie." I hugged him. "Let's go to the pool."

Shops were closed on Friday, so there were other people at the pool. Oil-slicked bodies soaked up sun and kids splashed in the kiddy pool. Max sunbathed while I swam. I was drying off when I saw her. I put on my sunglasses so I could watch discreetly.

The woman was in her thirties with long, wavy black hair. She and her husband were Arab and their baby was three or four months old. After removing their hotel robes, the couple waded down the steps into the pool. The baby squealed with shock and pleasure as cool water crept up its body. The parents laughed and cooed, while the baby kicked its chubby legs in delight.

As I watched, I imagined Yasmeen laughing with the love of her life, playing with her happy, healthy baby. The image alleviated some of my pain and strengthened my resolve. I pushed away my lingering fears. *She will make it!*

Watching the young family, I also remembered vacationing somewhere with Max when Katie was a baby. We'd played with her in the hotel pool while she shrieked with joy, and laughed as she frog-kicked, instinctively trying to swim. I looked at Max and he was also watching the family. Feeling my gaze, Max gave me a smile that told me he also remembered. We reached out to each other at the same time.

Back in the room we made love. It was different from the night before when Max was driven by alcohol and lust and I was numbed by tequila and obligation. This was slow, tender, and intense—driven by history and the desperate need to reconnect.

Driving back over the causeway took hours. We were caught on the Bahrain side of the border at sunset, when everything shut down for prayer and there was a long delay at Saudi customs because of the extensive search of vehicles. When we reached the Saudi checkpoint, the evening call began and we had another thirty minute delay. Finally, Max and I were ordered to stand outside the Land Rover while it was searched.

Max tucked both passports into his flight bag after we got through passport control. We drove the rest of the way in the black Saudi night, arriving home after midnight. The kids were asleep and we apologized to Jennifer and Ben for keeping them up so late.

While Max was in the bathroom, I put my passport in my backpack, along with a blue airmail envelope holding Yasmeen's pictures. I hid the flight bag under the bed. When Max came to bed I snuggled close while he held me. I wished I could tell him everything, but knew I didn't dare. Soon he was asleep. I focused on the memory of the happy Arab family in the pool and the numbers on the clock— willing myself to stay awake.

36

It was dark when I went to the beach. I was so terrified of falling asleep, I got up at 4, dressed quietly, and left Max a note. By the time his alarm went off, it would be past daybreak. Unless he woke before then, he'd never know I'd left in the darkness before the dawn.

I moved stealthily down the path feeling vulnerable in my running clothes—arms and legs bare in the cool night air. Before, I'd always worn my abaya, disappearing into the shadows. Now, I felt perilously visible. I shivered and quickened my pace so if some other early riser were to glance out a window, all they'd see would be a fleeting white shadow.

Once on the beach I felt safe. I walked barefoot along the shoreline, climbed onto the big flat stone, and waited for the muezzin's wail. When the sky and beach came into focus, the sea was smooth as pewter. I felt sad, but calmly resolute—clinging to the vision of being with Yasmeen in the future, holding her child, laughing and belly dancing. I was smiling at that image when I saw her walking toward me.

As I watched, she picked something up and examined it. Then she continued to walk as foamy waves washed over her bare feet. I slid off the rock and went to meet her. She gave no indication of surprise or relief when she saw me. She'd known I would be there.

"For your collection." Yasmeen held out her hand. Cupped in her palm was a cowry shell.

I took the shell. "It's beautiful. Thank you."

Yasmeen lifted her veil. She was not wearing a mask and her face was covered with fresh bruises and newly torn flesh. I hugged her. We held each other tightly for a long while, rocking gently. The scent of Clementines mingled with the stench of fear. We pulled back and stared into each other's eyes. After another long moment we stepped apart. I gave Yasmeen my passport and the blue envelope and they disappeared under her abaya.

"What are your plans?" My voice sounded hoarse and foreign.

"Jamal is giving us his car. He'll report it stolen tomorrow, after we're gone."

"You're leaving today?"

"We leave the compound tonight at ten, and meet the man in Dhahran at midnight. Our flight is on British Airways tomorrow morning at two. We connect for the States in London."

"We'll be home in August, that's just four months." I smiled, feeling a rush of hope. "I'll be there when your baby's born."

Yasmeen nodded, but her eyes were wide with fear. "We just have to make it through the night. Tomorrow we'll be safe. Enshallah."

"Enshallah," I repeated. *Please, God, please.*

"Thank you for everything," she whispered. "I'll send word how you can reach me."

My face crumbled and I reached out. We held each other and sobbed. Then Yasmeen backed away, lowered her veil, and climbed the path to the ledge. At the top, where I'd first seen her, she gave me one last wave and was gone. I stood awhile, watching—in case she reappeared.

Opening my hand, I looked at the shell. Tiny pink speckles dotted the rounded top. The bottom was flat and white, a tiny stone caught between the serrated edges of the opening, as if held between tightly clenched teeth. I closed my fist over the shell and slowly walked home.

Max was gone when I got home and the kids greeted me exuberantly. I held them until they squirmed away. After they left for school, I closed the drapes and put on the belly dancing tape. Holding the shell, I sat on the sofa staring into space, already waiting for word to arrive.

Mid-afternoon I opened the bottle of wine Jennifer had given me, poured a glass, and hid the bottle again. I restarted the tape and lit a Dunhill, smoked the cigarette and drank the wine. Then slowly belly danced with my eyes closed—imagining a future time and place.

That night after dinner I sat at the table pretending to read a cookbook while Max watched TV. Wearing their new T-shirts, the kids were off to a movie with friends. When nightfall call to prayer froze the screen Max turned off the TV, walked over, and nuzzled my neck.

"Tickles," I said, pulling away.

"Is my flight bag upstairs?" Max asked.

My mouth went dry. "It's wherever you left it." I smiled. "Hey, do that neck thing again."

Max kissed my neck and I leaned into him. Then he straightened up. "I'm tired, babe. I want to get ready for bed."

"But it's only nine. The kids won't be home for another half hour. There's time for a quickie!" It was so ridiculously out of character that Max only laughed and started upstairs.

I stared blindly at the cookbook until Max returned with the flight bag I'd retrieved from under the bed and tossed in a corner. Max pulled out a passport, opened it then looked at me. "Where's your passport?"

"How should I know?" My hand trembled as I turned a page. "You had the passports."

"Come on, I'm tired, stop fooling around. It was in here last night. Where'd you put it?"

I stared at him with an innocent expression. "I don't have it."

Max looked around the room and saw my backpack. After rummaging through it he looked at me. "Damn it, Sarah, why are you doing this?" He dropped the backpack and went upstairs.

I heard Max banging around and looked at my watch—9:10. I had to calm him down before the kids came home. I ran upstairs. Max was digging through my dresser drawers. He yanked out the top drawer, shook out the contents, and lining-paper and an envelope fell to the floor.

Max picked up the envelope. "What's this?" Frozen, I couldn't reply. Max opened the envelope and looked at the pictures of me and Yasmeen and Yasmeen's family. "Who're all these people?" Max held up the picture of me and Jamal on Mias. Water is spraying our thighs and my head is thrown back in laughter. "Who the hell is this?"

"He's a friend. The cousin of a friend." I sounded like I was lying.

Max examined the picture. "A friend?" A maniacal expression crossed his face. "You're leaving me!" Max dropped the envelope and lunged toward me.

I turned to run, but he leapt across the room, slammed the door, and locked it. Then he grabbed me, pushed me onto the bed, and held me down. "Where is your goddamn passport?"

Despite my panic, I spoke slowly and calmly like I was reasoning with a crazy person. "Look, I'm not leaving."

Max's hands were on my neck. "You're lying! Where is it?"

"I don't have it." I pulled at his hands. He wasn't letting go and I could barely speak. "I gave it to someone." It was just a gasp, all I had.

Max loosened his grip and I gulped in air. After a moment he reached out his hand. I couldn't read his expression. He was like someone I'd never seen before. I cringed as he gently smoothed the hair from my face. Then he slapped me hard. I moaned and curled into a fetal position.

Breathing heavily, Max picked up the pictures. I watched through my fingers as he leafed through them. When he found the one with Jamal he studied it then looked at me with a horrified expression. "He's a fucking Arab! Goddamn it, tell me who he is."

"He's the cousin of a friend," I said. "That's all."

"You're lying. You don't have any Arab friends." Max stared at the picture, taking in every detail. Color rose in his face until, with an inhuman roar, he threw the picture down and reached for me again. I shrieked as he grabbed my hair in his left hand and drew back his right fist.

"Mom!" Sam screamed and banged on the bedroom door. The doorknob jiggled. "Mom! Are you okay?" Max froze. I looked at his fist hovering above me, poised to strike.

I heard panic in Kate's voice as the doorknob rattled again. "Mom?" Max looked at his fist like he'd never seen it before then let go of my hair like it had burned his hand.

"I'm okay," I called, hoarsely. I felt their presence behind the door, testing the knob, whispering. "Go get ready for bed." After a long silence, reluctant footsteps shuffled away.

Max was sitting on the side of the bed, face in hands, as I painfully struggled to sit. I picked up the envelope and found a picture of me and Yasmeen in abayas and hijabs, smoking Dunhills. We'd taken it in the living room, mugging into the camera as the timer ticked off. It was a silly picture taken one giddily happy afternoon.

Keeping my distance, I slid it in front of Max. "This is my friend," I whispered. "This is who has my passport."

Max sighed and lowered his hands. He stared at the picture. "Who is she?"

"A woman I met on the beach."

He looked at me with an expression of loathing. "I don't even know who you are."

"I'm who I've always been. I gave her my passport because she's my friend and needs help." I touched his hand. "I'm not going anywhere."

Max studied the picture awhile then picked up the others. As he tucked them all back into the envelope, his fingers trembled and he took deep shuddering breaths. The last one was of me and Jamal. When they were all back in the envelope he sat holding it in his lap.

I stayed in the center of the bed. Gradually, my heartbeat slowed and my breathing returned to normal. I desperately wanted to take the envelope from Max, but remained still—not wanting to startle the beast and unleash more fury.

"I have to report this to security," Max finally said, and stood up.

Stark terror rushed in, but this time I wasn't frozen. I crawled across the bed and grabbed his shirt. "Oh, God, no! She'll die if she's caught."

When Max pulled away, I jumped up and ran past him to the door. I fell against it, arms spread, talking fast. "Just wait. Please wait. You can report it tomorrow. Report it missing or lost or stolen. It won't matter tomorrow. Whatever you do, just don't do it now."

Max reached for the doorknob, but I held fast. "Please, baby, please. I beg you." I was crying now. I smelled my own fear and sweat. I touched his face. "I love you, you know that. I'd never leave you. This isn't about us."

Max still had his hand on the knob, but wasn't moving. I knew he wanted to believe me. I wrapped my arms around his neck and pressed my body against his. "I'm sorry, baby. I'm so sorry. I should have told you. I'll do anything." Feverishly, I pushed against him. "Anything you want. You know I'll do anything for you. Please stay here with me. Please."

Max looked confused. We'd known each other forever and at this moment we were strangers. He put his hands on my waist.

"I love you, baby. I love you." I held his neck and kissed him. I pulled his shirt loose and put my hand under it. I bit his mouth, tugged at his belt buckle, his fly, reaching, touching, grabbing. Finally, I heard the envelope drop to the floor as Max responded with a groan. He kissed me hard and pushed me toward the bed. I pulled him down on me and rolled up over him. In frenzied desperation, I used my hands, my mouth, and my body to convince him to stay. Even if I couldn't save our marriage, I could buy time to save Yasmeen's life.

After, I held Max until he slept. I waited, not daring to move, watching the clock—willing time to pass. At 10:30 I allowed myself to relax. *She's gone. Safely on the highway to Dhahran.* I untangled myself and put on my abaya. At the door I picked up the envelope and hurried downstairs. For a few heart-pounding moments I stood in the darkness then stashed the envelope in the highest cabinet in the kitchen, behind the red wine and baking supplies.

Back upstairs, I looked in Sam's room but his bed was empty. I found him in Kate's bed. The sight of the two of them sleeping huddled together shamed me to my soul.

I wanted to keep watch until two when Yasmeen's plane was taking off. I stared at the clock, but the numbers blurred. It was my second night without sleep. At 11 I closed my eyes for a moment and fell asleep. I never felt or heard Max get up, but in the morning he was gone.

I awoke with a start at seven. My entire body felt sore, and my neck and chest wore the red marks of Max's rage. I took a long shower then dressed accordingly. *Crazy husband casual.* I laughed aloud. My laughter had a maniacal quality. I sounded unhinged, even to myself.

The kids picked at their breakfast, eyes darting furtively to me and each other. They appeared torn between reluctant and eager when it was time for them to leave for school. That morning when I held them a little too long, neither pulled away.

I stayed inside all day, pacing, doing the countdown in my mind. Flight out at 2 a.m. would mean London by now. What time was the connection? Were they on their way to the States? There was no one to ask, no way to know.

The kids came home, touched base then fled. Late afternoon, when I imagined Yasmeen's plane in the mid-Atlantic, I began to relax. *Surely by now.* I was in the kitchen chopping vegetables for dinner when I heard Max come in. There was music on the stereo. I'd been keeping time to the beat trying not to think. The music stopped.

Max appeared in the doorway, his face pale and somber. "There are rumors that Mohammed's wife tried to leave the Kingdom last night." Max took a breath and let it out. "Was that who she was?"

I stared at him. All I heard was "tried."

"Rumor is they caught her and the man she was with," Max said.

I turned back to the counter and resumed chopping. *Oh, God, Yasmeen.*

"They were waiting for her at the airport at passport control." Max cleared his throat. "Security had tapped her phone. They heard it all and notified Mohammed."

My eyes filled with tears and I hacked blindly. *Oh, God, oh, God, oh, God.* I heard Yasmeen's voice. *Enshallah.*

"Stop it." Max's voice was loud and sharp. "We have to talk."

I froze, wanting to sink to my knees, fall forward on the knife, and never get up again.

"They're looking for accomplices," Max said. "Did you ever think about what would happen to the kids if you went to jail?"

I never thought about the kids. I never thought about jail. I thought she could make it. Horrified and lightheaded with fear I stared at Max. He took the knife, tossed it into the sink, and gently gathered me into his arms.

"It's okay, baby," Max crooned. "We don't have to worry. I turned in my passport today and reported yours stolen." Max stroked my hair. "I lied for you, baby. I told them someone broke into the house and took it from your dresser while you were out."

Instantly I had the image of someone going through the dresser, holding my passport. *I remember that part.* But I was confused, losing touch.

"You're safe." His breath was hot against my ear. "I'd never let anything happen to you."

I briefly wondered if Max thought I was crying out of gratitude or relief. As I went limp, he held me like a ragdoll. But the weight of sorrow is great and I finally made it to the floor—onto my knees, rocking and howling as everything flowed from me.

37

The next morning I was up before dawn looking for Yasmeen, but the beach was empty. I waited until after call to prayer before going home. For two days I numbly went through the motions. No one spoke of that terrible night. When the kids cast worried glances my way, I blamed a fall for my bruises, stiff movements, and faraway gaze. *A fall from grace.*

At night I waited in the backyard, smoking. Once I went to the beach searching for the flash of pale arms beyond the shallows, but there was only darkness. The quiet chill of the night sent me running home, shivering with fear.

During the day I sat on the sofa wrapped in Amy's blue silk comforter. I was always cold. There was no number to call even if I'd dared, and the few times my phone rang I stared at it in dark terror, unable to answer. I thought about going to the women's quarters, but was too afraid.

Early on the third day I was sitting on the sofa when the doorbell rang. Through the peephole, I saw a veiled figure and quickly opened the door. "Yasmeen?"

The lifted veil revealed a once-beautiful face now ravaged with tragedy. "Yasmeen has sent me for you," Leila said. A white Mercedes idled in the driveway.

I dressed hurriedly, throwing my silk abaya over my clothes, tying Kate's embroidered scarf on my head. Leila tucked a few wisps of stray hair beneath my scarf, put on her mask, and helped me with mine. As always, I felt a heartbeat of panic when the final veil was added.

And then we were in the backseat of the Mercedes heading toward the exit gates. The driver was Arab, but not wearing a thobe and gutra. I looked around the car, wondering if it was Jamal's, but I couldn't tell. Once on the highway, we rode for some time in heavy silence.

Leila cried quietly, lifting a handkerchief under her veil. Several times she started to speak then fell silent. Finally, she talked about the night of Yasmeen's arrest.

"At first all went according to plan." Leila spoke softly. "They left Al Hassa just before ten, headed toward Dhahran. She had everything she needed, everything was in place."

"What happened?" I whispered.

"They were stopped at a roadblock just outside the Dhahran Airport," Leila said.

Something dimly registered, but it was gone as Leila lifted her veil and looked at me. Her eyes were swollen, dark smudges like bruises under each one. I lifted my veil to meet her eyes.

"Do you understand where we're going?" Leila asked.

"To see Yasmeen." I nodded. "Is she in jail?"

Leila dropped her veil so I did too. She took my hands in hers. Her grip was strong, but I felt her trembling. "Yasmeen has been convicted of adultery."

The punishment for adultery is death. My lips went numb. A humming started in my ears. "But she was just arrested. Doesn't she get a trial?"

"This is not a legal matter." Leila sighed. "It is a family matter."

"So that means the family can decide?"

"It has been decided," Leila whispered.

I waited, unable to ask the next question.

Leila started talking and nothing she said made sense. She spoke in English, but it might as well have been Arabic or Latin or tongues. Words rushed from Leila's mouth under the veil. I couldn't see her face as she spoke what sounded like mouthfuls of obscenities. It felt like what I imagined confessional booths to be, faces behind screens, words pouring out. But there was no forgiveness. There was no grace given. There was no deliverance from this evil.

"The family has ordered she be stoned." Leila's words resonated with deafening clarity.

"No!" I screamed. "No!" Suddenly I couldn't breathe. I ripped my hands from hers and pulled the veils from my face. I tried to lower the window, but it wouldn't respond. Desperate for air I pounded the glass. The desert flew by as we raced toward the unthinkable.

Swallowed in complete panic, I felt my heart racing and was sure I was dying. I wanted to die. I reached for the door handle, but there wasn't one. As I began clawing my way over the front seat, Leila screamed at the driver. With a hard swerve, he crossed two lanes and pulled the car onto the shoulder. The sudden stop threw me into my seat.

I was stunned by the fall and sudden silence. In that moment Leila captured me in her arms, holding me with what felt like superhuman strength. Crooning my name she rocked me like a child. I struggled until, like a child, I gave in. I clung to her and sobbed until I exhausted myself.

I don't know how long we sat like that, but eventually we were back on the highway. The driver swerved between lanes, speeding to make up for lost time. Leila wiped my face with her sodden handkerchief. *This is Yasmeen's mother. I should comfort her.* But I couldn't move.

"Yasmeen knows you'll be beside me. You're not supposed to be there, so you must remain covered." She re-tied my scarf and mask. "Understand?" I nodded and she dropped the final veil.

"Something else you should know." Leila took a deep breath. "Omar has also been sentenced to death," she sobbed. "I've known Omar since he was 12."

I held her for the rest of the trip.

Soon we were in an area of Al Khobar I'd never been. A crowd gathered in a barren square the size of a city block—mostly Saudi men, but also small clusters of women. We sat in the idling car on the edge of the square.

"She needs to see you," Leila said. "But close your eyes after the first stone strikes."

I felt a surge of grief mixed with rage. "I won't close my eyes."

After the driver let us out, Leila took my hand and led me through the noisy crowd. At 10 a.m. the sun was so intense it burned the top of my head. We walked to where women stood weeping, holding each other. As Leila led me to the front of the crowd, hands touched me. Voices called my name. Shadan was there and, leaning into Huda, was Nora's slight form. I couldn't imagine Kate witnessing such a thing, but there was so much I couldn't imagine.

Moments later a police car escorted two black vans into the square. Cheers rose from an angry group of men standing near piles of small jagged stones. Matawain waved whips and screamed with indignation. I wondered if the matawah who'd attacked me and Jennifer was in the crowd. I saw Yasmeen's uncle in the group of men. Beside him was a man I imagined to be Mohammed. Jamal stood on the farthest edge of the crowd. As if sensing my gaze, Jamal turned toward me and stared at my pale hand in Leila's. Jamal's face was wrecked with grief and his dark eyes looked haunted. After a moment, he turned away.

Police opened the vans and Yasmeen, completely veiled, was pulled from one of them and led near where the men from her family stood. She was barefoot, a thick black cord looped around her ankles. Her hands were tied in front. Police stood on either side, holding her arms.

Omar was pulled from the second van, also barefoot with his ankles hobbled and hands tied. He wore a long-sleeved blue shirt and khaki pants. Over the blindfold covering his eyes, his curly blond hair gleamed in the cruel sunlight. The police half-led, half-dragged Omar into the clearing some distance from Yasmeen. He swayed and nodded as though drugged.

Suddenly, a cheer rose from the crowd as the executioner walked to where Omar stood. He was big and tall, wearing a black cloak with a scabbard strapped to his chest. A Saudi man stepped forward and read aloud from a piece of paper. When he finished reading, the police pushed Omar to his knees.

Leila squeezed my hand and I looked at her. Her head was bent forward and she was crying. The other women also cried in loud, tortured sobs. I was hot, desperately thirsty, and terrified. The humming in my ears had become a high steady ring.

A cheer arose and when I looked back, the executioner was holding his sword aloft. It was shiny, long, and narrow. With a dramatic sense of showmanship, the executioner twisted his wrist making the blade glint in the sunlight. The crowd went wild.

Suddenly, Yasmeen turned toward Omar and screamed, "Omar!"

It felt like time slowed as Omar blindly lifted his face toward Yasmeen. At that moment the executioner raised his sword with both hands, stepped forward, and swung it downward. There was the sound of metal meeting bone and the sword flashed as it arced back up. Blood showered the ground as Omar's headless body toppled forward. I closed my eyes, fighting nausea.

Yasmeen's screams were drowned by the crowd's roar. The women around me shrieked and wailed. Some dropped to their knees. I felt a well of nausea, gagged, and tasted bile. Lifting my mask from my face I bent over and threw up, feeling the hot spray on my feet. I vomited until there was nothing left then wiped my mouth on my sleeve.

It was so hot under the veils, I felt I was suffocating. My body was soaked and I could smell my own rankness. The stench of blood, sweat, and fear filled the air. I'd let go of Leila's hand, and hers found mine again. I focused on breathing and her painful grip.

Now, Yasmeen was led into the clearing. Left alone, she raised her hands and lifted her veil. Her dark eyes were visible over her mask as she desperately searched the crowd.

Huda rushed forward screaming, "Yasmeen! Here!"

Yasmeen looked our way and I lifted my veil so she could see my eyes. Leila did the same, as did Huda, Shadan, Nora, and others. As we locked eyes across the distance, another angry roar rose from male onlookers.

Again, the man read a proclamation, his voice drowned by the crowd. Yasmeen's uncle stepped forward, selected a stone from a pile and hurled it toward Yasmeen. The stone hit her in the forehead. For a split-second Yasmeen's stunned eyes were still visible, then she staggered and dropped her veil. Mohammed threw the next stone then more men rushed in. As they threw stones, the men taunted her, screaming in Arabic.

The stones tore Yasmeen's veil, exposing her pale skin. With each hit I imagined I heard her flesh tearing. Men shouted and women wailed and screamed her name. A chorus howled like sirens, my voice a part of it. Yasmeen raised her hands and they were bloodied. She dropped to her knees and the stones kept coming. Yasmeen's hijab and veils slipped revealing skin and hair shiny with blood. The men continued to hurl stones.

After a time that felt endless, Yasmeen crumbled to the ground. Still the stones hailed down, pummeling her body as she lay twitching. Yasmeen had long been still before the executioner approached her. The crowd quieted. The executioner touched Yasmeen's neck then raised his fist over his head. With a triumphant roar, the crowd surged toward the bodies.

As we were jostled and pushed, Leila's hand slipped from mine. I heard her screaming as she was lost to me. Crushed between bodies I was lifted forward. I was terrified of slipping under, being trampled. Panic swept over me like a wave and I lost all reason. Pushing against unyielding flesh around me, I gasped for breath.

Tearing the veil and mask from my face, I fought my way out of the crowd. Pulling with my arms, I moved across the flow as though swimming across currents in a turbulent sea. My scarf slipped and hair streamed across my face, but I pushed forward on my own course.

As I broke free, I saw a policeman swinging a stick as if herding crazed cattle. When he saw me he smashed his club down on my forehead. I felt a searing pain and blood streamed into my eyes. I stopped moving and he swung again, hitting the top of my head. I turned and was swept back into the crowd. Squinting through a stinging red film I fought against the bodies around me. Finally, losing all sense of direction, I closed my eyes and stood still. The ringing in my ears was now a vibrating roar. Lost inside myself I was only aware of my own screaming.

Suddenly strong hands grabbed my waist, lifting me into the air. I struggled, but couldn't escape as I was carried through the crowd. My face was draped with a veil and I fought for breath. As if from a distance, I heard a man's voice repeating my name. I opened my eyes enough to see Jamal's face through a red and black haze.

Closing my eyes, I surrendered to sensations. Doors slammed like gunshots, women wailed. There was movement and cool air, a water bottle tipped into my mouth, warm hands, murmuring, and another's tears dripping onto my face. I faded in and out. Movement slowed and I was pulled upright, draped in veils. The atmosphere became hushed and tense. There was stopping and starting and guttural men's voices. Then I was carried from the car.

I opened my eyes as I was being wrapped in blue silk and placed on my sofa. I saw Jamal's face and the shadows of veiled women. My feet were tenderly lifted. Somewhere I'd lost my sandals. My feet were bare, soles cut and bruised.

"We have to leave you," Jamal whispered, tears streaming down his face. "For your safety." The front of his thobe was soaked with my blood.

Jamal's grief-torn face was the last thing I saw before awakening in my living room. Head pounding, I sat up. I tried to stand, but the searing pain in my feet brought me to my knees. I crawled across the floor and painfully made it upstairs. In the bathroom I rested my cheek against the coolness of the white floor-tiles.

For hours, I lay in the dark as Yasmeen's slaughter replayed in a relentless, torturous loop. When I finally pushed myself into a seated position, the floor was slick with my blood. Huddled in the middle of the room, I cried and rocked myself into a stupor.

It was there Max found me after following the bloody trail up the stairs. When he turned on the light I cringed in the sudden harsh glare. "Oh, God, Sarah!" Max reached out and I shrieked and scrambled away. Covering my face with my scarf, I cowered in the corner. When Max tried to touch me, I batted at him with exhausted arms. When he lifted the scarf from my bloody face, I screamed and could not stop.

38

Time was lost to me for a while. The day of Yasmeen's stoning Max called Dr. Kayra. She came immediately, cleaned and stitched my wounds, and gave me antibiotics and tranquilizers. I stayed in the darkened bedroom for days, in the house for weeks. Dr. Kayra visited frequently and Jennifer came daily.

Although no one spoke about the stoning, Kate intuited it was about Yasmeen. I cried at the burden I'd placed on her. I cried about everything. I slept during the day and paced the house at night. Slowly, I began to resurface.

One night in early May, the four of us were quietly eating dinner. The wound on my forehead had shrunk to a dark scab, my bruises were fading. I pushed the food around my plate. Someone had brought us a casserole filled with ground beef, but I was too haunted by images of torn flesh to eat meat. I had no appetite and had grown gaunt and pale.

"Mom?" Sam spoke tentatively. "I need three dozen cookies for the school bake sale."

"Uh, me too," Kate said.

I used to know how to bake cookies. "When is it?"

"Thursday, but you can drop them off Wednesday before my soccer game." Sam's smile was clearly forced. "I said you'd make chocolate-chip."

I sighed. "What's today?

"Saturday," Kate answered.

It's time to come back. "Okay."

They exchanged relieved looks. I'd passed the test. Sam got up and hugged me. "Thanks, Mom. I knew you wouldn't let me down."

After Sam sat down Max cleared his throat. "Well, this family could use some good news. When school's out we're taking a vacation."

"Where are we going?" Sam asked.

Max smiled lovingly at me. "Someplace your mom has always wanted to go."

I knew I should smile back, but could only stare at him.

"We're spending three weeks in Europe doing everything we'd planned last year," Max said.

"On our way home?" Kate asked.

"No, for vacation," Max said.

"Then we're going home?" Kate looked suspicious.

"That's the rest of my news." Max beamed. "I've been promoted to lead engineer! I'm heading up the design and implementation of the new Jubail facility."

Max had mentioned Jubail. "But you said that refinery isn't opening for five years."

"That's start-up," Max said with exaggerated patience. "The design has already begun."

I closed my eyes. "You said implementation." I'd been in a fog, but it was lifting. I looked at Max. "That means you'll be there at start-up. In five years."

"It's an amazing opportunity with a huge raise." Max grinned.

"You haven't accepted," I said. "Not without talking to me."

"Of course I accepted," Max said. "You haven't exactly been present."

I felt like I'd been punched. I glanced at Sam and Kate who looked stunned.

"We'll see London and Paris, and when we get back we'll move into an oceanfront house." Max smiled at me. "You'll love that."

Kate threw her fork down. "You promised we'd go home."

"That was before my promotion," Max said.

Kate looked at me. "Mom, you promised."

These were conversations Max and I should have alone, but there wasn't time. All the rules had changed while I'd been lost. I looked at Max. "We're going home."

"No, we're not." Max's voice rose and I felt afraid.

"I want to go to high school with my friends," Kate said. "I'm not going to boarding school!"

"Yes, you are. In Switzerland! You'll love it," he smiled.

"I'll hate it and I hate you!" Kate ran upstairs and slammed her door.

"I don't want Katie to go away." Sam started to cry.

I reached for Sam, but Max just continued to smile—as if his family wasn't falling apart.

Later, after the kids were asleep, I took a long shower, washed my hair, and put on a fresh nightgown. Max was reading as I got into bed. He ignored me. I felt like I'd been asleep for years and awakened into a life that wasn't mine. "We have to talk."

"Nothing to talk about. I worked my ass off for this promotion." Max put his book down and glared at me. "You've always wanted money and travel. Now you're not happy."

It was crazy-making. "I want us to be a happy family. We need to go home. You promised."

Max's expression was chilling. "What about your promises? Remember? You promised to do anything I want." He smiled. "I want to stay here."

I'd made desperate promises and I was being held to them. *After all that happened?* I touched his arm. "Please, this place is destroying us."

Max yanked his arm away. "The only things destroying us are lies and bad decisions. This is the opportunity of a lifetime. Why should I have to pay the consequences for your mistakes?"

"What are you talking about?"

"Your secret life with that Arab woman," Max said.

It was the first we'd spoken of Yasmeen since Max came home with the news of her capture—even after the stoning. Immediately, I felt myself being pulled back into that place.

"Yasmeen was my friend," I said. "She was murdered. I saw it happen."

"She was punished," Max said flatly. "She broke the law."

"The laws are wrong," I said. "You don't even know the story."

"I know enough," Max said.

"Jesus Christ, listen to yourself!"

Max picked up his book. "All I'm saying is I'm not giving up this promotion."

The next day was Sunday—*Sunday morning coming down*—and I was on the beach at dawn for the first time since Yasmeen's stoning. I walked slowly, feeling soft, warm sand beneath my feet, a cool Gulf breeze against my skin. At our spot I sat on the large flat stone and closed my eyes.

It was then I felt it. A sensation of profound peace washed over me as if I'd been wrapped in a cloak of grace. I could breathe for the first time in a month. At that very moment I knew I was going to be okay. *Did I only imagine the sweet and bitter aroma of Clementines?*

Opening my eyes, I gazed at the spot where we had said goodbye. *We'll connect for the States in London.* Suddenly I knew how to do it. I watched the sun rise over calm water while call to prayer rang out across the desert.

The morning of Yasmeen's stoning I'd already been bundled into the car before midday call to prayer began. I was grateful call to prayer had not been part of the soundtrack of that long, horrifyingly brutal morning. Yasmeen was a devoted Muslim, and it would forever help me remember it was not *Islam* that killed her.

The kids were eating breakfast when I got home from the beach. Kate's hair was parted in the middle. She avoided eye-contact. I sat down and lifted her chin. Kate's blue eyes were lined with khol. She was back to her grieving Goth girl persona.

Kate stared at me as she tugged at the cuff of her long-sleeved blouse. I took her hand and pushed up her sleeve. Her forearm was crisscrossed with angry red cuts—a hatch-work of pain and betrayal.

"Oh, sweetie, don't do this." I hugged Kate. "Trust me, we're going home."

Maybe I still radiated peaceful energy from the beach. Maybe Kate was desperate to believe. She nodded and let me bandage her arm. As I wiped the eyeliner from her eyes, I suddenly saw Leila's face as she wiped tears from my face and made a vow. *Whatever it takes, I will not sacrifice my children to this godforsaken place.*

That morning I began formulating a plan. With less than three months, I couldn't afford the distraction of grief. First, I had to put away everything that would remind me of Yasmeen. The day Yasmeen was stoned Dr. Kayra had taken off my scarf and abaya, put the whole bloody mess into a plastic bag, and stuffed it under the bathroom sink.

That Sunday morning I ran cold water in the tub. The scarf and abaya had dried into a hard crumpled mass. When I dumped it into the tub, blood billowed like a red cloud. I swished the black silk around, pulled the plug, and watched a maroon river swirl down the drain. I refilled the tub and added soap. After three times, the water ran clear.

I draped the scarf and abaya on coat hangers hung from branches of the tree in the backyard. The scarf was ripped in several places and there was one small brown spot of blood left on the white label of the abaya. When they were dry I folded them and put them in my bottom drawer.

Monday morning I ran, saw the kids off, then gathered things together. I laid the abaya on the bed and wrapped my Nikon in the scarf. I collected photographs I'd taken in Saudi, and undeveloped rolls of film. I put the envelope with the pictures Max had seen on the bed without opening it. *No time to go there.* I added the belly dancing tape, khalakhil, and cowry shell to the pile. Last were a box of Dunhill cigarettes and book of matches.

As I pulled a small suitcase from the top shelf of the hall closet, I was surprised to see Max's briefcase hidden behind it. He always kept his briefcase in the bedroom closet. I carried the briefcase into the bedroom. I'd given it to him one Christmas, setting the combination for 714, our anniversary. *So you never forget.*

I spun the numbers and opened it. Inside was a manila envelope addressed to Max at his office. The return said: "Zamil." It had gone through intercompany mail, CONFIDENTIAL stamped in red letters across the bottom. It had been opened with a neat slice across the top.

My hands trembled as I carefully slipped my finger into the slit and shook the contents onto the bed. Out fell a US passport and a blue airmail envelope. When I opened the passport, my face stared up at me. My hands were shaking when I examined the airmail envelope. SHUKRAN was printed in red ink on the front. Inside was one of the passport photos I'd taken of Yasmeen.

"Jesus." I tapped a cigarette from the box of Dunhills, lit it, and inhaled deeply. I tried to make sense of it all. "Shukran," I whispered. *Why was Mohammed thanking Max?*

Other things were working at me, maddeningly just out of reach. Closing my eyes, I took another long drag. I remembered pleading and desperate promises. I remembered Max coming home with news of Yasmeen's capture. Suddenly I realized that's when the humming had begun—not in the Mercedes on the way to Al Khobar. It was the afternoon Max told me Yasmeen hadn't escaped. I'd gone numb with shock and fear and nothing made sense anymore.

Taking another long pull from the cigarette, I tried to hear Max's voice. What did he say? Passport control at the airport was waiting for her. *Security had tapped her phone.*

I blew out smoke and opened my eyes. That wasn't all. There was another piece. I took another drag, closed my eyes, and waited. This time it only took a moment and came in a woman's voice. *So close*, Leila whispered. I listened harder. *They were pulled over at a roadblock just outside the Dhahran Airport.*

Chills covered my arms, raised the hair on my scalp. I opened my eyes and I knew. With dead certainty, I knew. There is no such place as no more tears to cry, nowhere you are safe from the kind of betrayal that will kill your love in a heartbeat. But there is a place of clarity that will guide your steps—if you listen.

I quickly put the picture of Yasmeen back into the airmail envelope and slipped it, and my passport, back into the manila envelope. I put the manila envelope into the briefcase and put the briefcase on the closet shelf, behind the suitcase. I put everything I'd gathered into my bottom drawer, except my abaya. Then I crawled into bed and slept until the kids came home.

That night I pleaded a headache, hoping it would explain my inability to make eye-contact. When Max came to bed I laid as still as the dead, and he was careful not to wake me. Deep in the night I went to the beach wearing only my abaya. Naked, I waded into the warm black water and swam twenty laps before walking home.

Tuesday morning I went back to bed after the kids left. That afternoon I paced the house, beginning to unravel. Only constant motion allowed me to think, but it was a panicked energy. I was no closer to a plan and I'd never felt so alone. The razor sharp edges of paranoia were starting to fray my fragile sanity. I talked out loud and made no sense. Tuesday night I really had a headache, no need to pretend. I fell into bed and slept through the night.

Wednesday I woke exhausted. The kids left and I went back to bed. Violent dreams tossed me awake at noon. I got up, rummaged through the laundry basket, dressed in a wrinkled mismatched skirt and blouse, put my hair in a ponytail, and went downstairs to start dinner.

I was cutting vegetables, lost in thought, when the phone rang. It rang once, twice. On the third ring the answering machine picked up. I heard my own cheerful outgoing message.

"Mom!" As Sam's voice startled me from my reverie, the knife slipped and sliced my wrist.

"Shit!"

"I forgot my soccer shoes. Will you bring them when you bring the cookies? Thanks, Mom. I love you." He hung up.

I ran cold water on the cut, gasping in pain then wrapped a dishtowel tightly around my wrist. The sharp pain and cold water snapped me awake. "Oh, God, the cookies!"

Panicked, I rummaged in the freezer where I kept chocolate chips, found a bag, and shook three chips into my hand. I popped the chips into my mouth, and searched for more. The highest cabinet held the bottle of wine Jennifer had given me, but there were no more chips.

After moments of pondering, I ran upstairs for my backpack. In the garage, the Land Rover idled while I gathered courage for my first time driving in Saudi. At the commissary I rushed to the baking aisle, no chocolate chips. Back in the car I sat defeated then started home.

Driving past the beach I slowed to a stop. The sun was an intense white ball hanging at two o'clock in the cloudless sky. Water lapped sullenly on the deserted beach and the sand radiated heat like a mirage. *I knew you wouldn't let me down,* Sam's voice whispered.

I turned the car around and slowly navigated the maze of streets until reaching the compound exit. Armed guards stood at the gates where two cars were queued ahead of me. Heart pounding, I held back until both cars cleared the second checkpoint. Keeping my eyes on the guard, I rummaged in the glove-box for Max's black baseball cap and sunglasses. After carefully tucking my hair inside the hat and putting on the sunglasses, I slowly rolled forward.

The first guard chatted with someone in the guardhouse as I pulled alongside. I slowed, but didn't stop. The guard was absently waving me through as he glanced into the car. Seeing through my disguise, he jerked in surprise and raised his hand. "Stop!"

With a deep breath, I pushed on the gas. After the car sped past the astonished guard, he screamed and started pursuit. By then I'd raced through the second checkpoint past another guard. In the rearview mirror I saw them run toward a green jeep. I pushed harder on the gas.

At the highway I turned south toward Khobar. Tires squealed and for a second I felt a skid, then the car stabilized and I was off. Max was right, the Land Rover handled like a dream. As I pressed the accelerator and the turbo-engine responded with a roar, I felt a surge of power.

There were few vehicles on the highway and I wove back and forth, maneuvering around slower ones. Some hair blew wildly around my face. Pulling into the left lane, I flew past a Mercedes containing four Saudi men. They stared at me with stunned expressions.

When I passed the camels, the jeep was close behind. Max's hat was too big and all my hair was loose. I jerked the hat off and impatiently brushed hair from my face. Pain shot through my wrist. The dishtowel was soaked with blood. In the mirror, I saw a red smear on my cheek.

Ahead, a Toyota truck puttered along in the right lane. A Bedouin woman squatted in the back with several goats. Her dark eyes were visible over her mask and she watched me as I passed. I fought tears as I smiled at her.

At Safeway, I parked between two Ocmara buses, licked the palm of my hand and rubbed the bloody smudge from my cheek. I ran my fingers through my hair, leaving it loose around my shoulders, unwrapped the dishtowel, and pulled my sleeve over the cut. After grabbing my backpack, I ran into the store. Just inside, I caught my breath and tried not to look like the crazy woman I was. As I rolled my cart toward the baking aisle, I was aware of curious glances.

Breathing calmly I stopped in front of the chocolate chips. There were twenty or thirty bags. I marveled at the sheer abundance. I took one bag of the dark, bittersweet chips that made the best cookies then I took two more. I tossed in a bag of milk chocolate chips. But there were so many more bags. My cart was cavernous and suddenly I was so hungry. And I had my Visa card. I extended both arms and raked the rest of the chips into my cart.

At checkout, I wore my sunglasses and a stony expression. The cashier gave me the total and I gave him my Visa. The bagger filled four plastic bags with chips. At the exit, I carried two bags in each hand and walked calmly toward the car. Glancing around, I spotted the jeep across the lot. The guards stood talking to several Saudi police. I made it to the car without being noticed. They were watching for a black baseball cap—my long blonde hair gleamed in the sun.

Inside the car I sat breathing heavily, safely shielded by the two buses. Heart pounding, I slowly backed out and drove toward an exit, away from the jeep. Navigating the Land Rover across the lot, I remembered the last time I'd been in Khobar and fought to push back images of Yasmeen's bloody body.

I'd almost made it to the exit when a hand slapped my window. A matawah looked in at me and I shrieked. He hit the glass again and began screaming. I pushed on the gas and the car shot forward. For a second the matawah disappeared. *Jesus God, what do I get for killing a matawah?* But then I heard his angry shouts as he chased after me. I saw his screaming face in my rear-view mirror as I exited the parking lot.

Somehow, I made it through the streets of Khobar and back onto the highway, the green jeep and a Saudi police car following closely. Lights blinked furiously on top of the police car and sirens sounded, but I never slowed and they couldn't outrun me. For that hour on the highway I drove at breakneck speeds while blasting Bruce Springsteen and letting the wind whip my hair. I sang *Born in the USA* at the top of my lungs and pretended I was free. For that hour I was both truly out of my mind and more myself than I'd been in years.

After I turned into the compound the police car squealed past, forcing me to stop. I closed the windows, turned off the car, and sat with doors locked as the police and guards approached—weapons drawn. Hands gripping the steering wheel, I stared straight ahead, eyes veiled behind sunglasses. My heart rocketed and I could barely breathe. Sweat streamed down my face. I sat motionless, ignoring the shouts and commands. Angry intermittent knocks on the windows startled me, but I refused to respond.

After close to an hour, a key turned in the lock and my door was opened. I closed my eyes and resisted as my hands were pried from the steering wheel. I was pulled from the car and hands shook my shoulders. The sunglasses flew off and I heard them hit the asphalt.

"Sarah!" Max screamed. "Look at me."

I opened my eyes and Max hugged me. Once upon a time, I would have been comforted by his embrace, my cheek against the soft blue shirt I'd washed and ironed so many times. I felt his hard body, smelled his familiar scent and his fear. My arms hung loosely by my sides.

Max looked into my eyes. "Good God, baby. What the hell?" His worried expression was almost comical. I resisted the urge to laugh.

Tilting my head, I stared into his eyes and smiled. I shrugged as though I was as confused as he was. We were surrounded by onlookers—Saudi police, Ocmara security guards, expatriates. It was important to look as crazy as possible.

"I needed chocolate chips," I said, in what I hoped was a Southern accent.

Max looked stunned, but before he could react the guards grabbed my arms and pushed me into the backseat of the police car. As the car rolled away I looked through the rear window. Max stood watching as I disappeared.

39

I awakened slowly, brought to consciousness by an ache in my shoulder. My head pounded and I was cold and thirsty. But from some deep instinctive place I knew to lie perfectly still. Play dead. I kept my breath shallow as dread enshrouded me.

Slowly, I took an inventory. I was lying on my left side, arms locked around my torso in an awkward hug. My right wrist throbbed with pain. I was wearing loose pajamas and my feet were bare. My head rested on a pad, the waffle-weave embossing my cheek. Loose hair covered my face. Mouth parched, eye-lids stuck together.

Hearing nothing but my own shallow breathing, I carefully opened my eyes into a squint. Through my veil of hair I saw I was on the floor of a small unfurnished room. White vinyl covered the floor and padded the walls. Cold air blew from a vent near the ceiling. Above the vent, a camera lens was aimed at me like a gun. I closed my eyes, counted my breath, and tried to remember.

Silence hung heavy in the room and a wave of fatigue finally pulled me under. Time passed and a sharp pain jarred me awake. I gasped and rolled onto my back, opened my eyes, and stared at the camera—I remembered everything.

Soon, the door opened and two Filipino women in blue orderly uniforms lifted me to my feet. "Dr. Kayra is here," one said, brushing hair from my face. In the corridor we were confronted by the doctor's imposing form.

"Get her out of that thing!" Dr. Kayra pointed at the straitjacket binding my arms.

"Wait, I haven't given the order for her release." It was Dr. Abut, the male physician at the clinic. I'd interacted with him, but reported to Dr. Kayra.

"You are mistaken, Dr. Abut. Mrs. Hayes is my patient. I will determine when she is released." Dr. Kayra clutched my chart to her chest.

Dr. Abut looked uncertain, but nodded and walked away.

After being released from restraints, I was taken to a small room. Dr. Kayra and I sat across from each other at a table on which there was a glass of water. It reminded me of the police station in Khobar. I glanced at the two-way mirror then at Dr. Kayra. She nodded slightly.

"Let's see, Mrs. Hayes." Dr. Kayra looked my chart. "I've met with you on and off since the loss of your mother." She ran her pen down the page. "Struggles with depression, compounded with anxiety." When she leaned back and smiled, I understood there would be no mention of the visits she'd made after Yasmeen's stoning.

"You arrived in Saudi about this time two years ago. Right?"

"Yes." At that moment I would have failed an orientation test—I didn't know the date—I didn't know I'd been heavily sedated for almost 48 hours. But I knew it was mid-May.

"I'm thinking you had an anniversary reaction of some kind. Let's see." She wrote on a scrap of paper as if solving a problem. "It is two years since you last saw your mother. Might that be what prompted you to break down and drive off the compound?" She stared at me while tapping her pen on the paper.

Glancing down, I saw she'd written "YES."

"Yes." I drank some water.

She glanced at the bandage on my wrist. "Your wound is not consistent with a self-inflicted injury. How did it happen?"

"I was making dinner. Something startled me and the knife slipped."

Dr. Kayra made a notation with one hand while slipping the paper into her pocket with the other. "I'm giving you a prescription for a mild antidepressant. Looks like you have some personal supports." She smiled. "Your good friend, Jennifer."

"Yes."

"May I also say you've been terribly missed at the clinic? Quite a few women have asked after you, expressing concern." Dr. Kayra leaned forward and stared into my eyes. "Do you understand what I'm saying to you, Sarah? You are not alone."

Caught by surprise, I nodded tearfully.

"Good," Dr. Kayra said briskly. "I'm releasing you now, but I want you in my office Sunday morning at 9 sharp. After we meet, I'll determine if you're ready to go back to work."

Max hugged me at the hospital, but drove home in icy silence, clearly not happy I'd been released. Once home, I got a bottle of water from the refrigerator. Bags of chocolate chips covered the dining table. I hadn't eaten in three days so I sat down, ripped open a bittersweet bag, and started eating the chips, one by one.

"Why don't you go take a shower so we can talk," Max said.

My clothes were what I'd worn when I drove to Khobar. Wet with sweat and blood, they'd been stuffed in a plastic bag during my hospital stay. I couldn't remember my last shower. All in all, I was pretty foul. I looked at Max and shrugged. "We can talk now." I ate chips, one by one.

Max sat across from me looking irritated. "Stop eating those goddamned chips."

I stared at Max, poured myself a handful of chips, and slowly shoveled them into my mouth. Max angrily swung his arm, sweeping the chips off the table. Unflinching, I chewed then took a long swig of water.

"Where are the kids?" I glanced around as if they were hiding behind the sofa.

"Having dinner with Jennifer and Ben."

"Are they okay?" I asked.

"Not really. Your little adventure really upset them."

I sighed. *Was there no end to the pain I was causing my children?* "What's today?"

"Friday," Max said.

"They discharged me on a Friday?" Nobody worked on Friday. Suddenly I understood Dr. Kayra's rage. She must have discovered I was there while doing weekend rounds. Remembering Max's irritation at my discharge, I looked at him. *What other plans did you have for me?*

"I guess I missed the bake sale." I smiled. "Too bad, we've got all these chocolate chips."

"You know we're lucky they took you to the hospital," Max said, angrily. "If Mohammed hadn't intervened, you'd be in jail."

And if you hadn't intervened Yasmeen would be alive. "You're right. I could have jeopardized your job."

"No, you could have jeopardized everything," Max said.

It was then I remembered I had a plan. Driving off the compound had not been part of my plan, but might have worked, except for Mohammed.

With Mohammed on Max's team, I had to go back to my original plan. To get us out of Saudi I had to stay submissive and sane, or I'd jeopardize everything.

I covered my face and started to cry. It was easy to do—I had so much material to work with. "I've been such a mess," I said. "I've let everyone down." I heard Sam's voice and the tears started for real. I looked at Max. "Can you ever forgive me?"

Max hesitated then opened his arms. "Of course I can, baby. Come on, let's get you to bed."

I rose and stumbled into his arms.

After my shower I stood in my nightgown smoking a cigarette, blowing smoke toward the exhaust fan. I stared at my reflection, running my fingers over the scab on my forehead, the crescent-shaped scar on my cheek. I was startled by a sharp knock on the door and the knob rattling. Unlike usual, I'd locked the door.

"You okay?" Max called.

I ran water in the sink. "Out in a minute." I took final drag, doused the cigarette, and whispered to my reflection, "I'm just fine."

At dawn I was walking on the beach. The muezzin cried in the distance, but the water was still as glass. I kept hearing Dr. Kayra's voice. *You are not alone.* I just had to assemble my team.

When the kids came down, I was at the table holding Mimi.

"Mom!" Sam jumped on my lap, scaring the cat.

Kate hung back, eyes bruised with worry. I held out my hand. When she took it, I pulled her close. Kate buried her face in my neck. "I was so scared," she whispered.

"I'm sorry I scared you. It'll never happen again." I hugged them and kissed their heads. "I promise. Everything is going to be okay."

Sam smiled, but Kate stared at my bandaged wrist. "You promised that before."

I felt sick with fear as I pushed up her sleeve to reveal new cuts. "Jesus, Katie." I looked in her eyes. "I know I haven't been here for you, and I'm so, so sorry." When my eyes filled with tears, I took a breath. "Please trust me now. I promise we're going home."

She looked skeptical. "What, are you going to kidnap us?"

"Let's just say I have a plan." I'd already burdened Kate with heavy secrets—I wasn't going to make her carry any more. "All I ask of both of you is that you don't make waves." I looked at Kate. "Please hold it together. Don't hurt yourself again. We just have a couple months to go."

"What about Dad?" Sam looked worried.

I couldn't lie to Sam, but the truth would break his heart. "We'll see about Dad." Sam relaxed, choosing to be content with my answer.

"Hurry now or you'll be late." Already I was plotting ways to protect my children. I needed to catch Jennifer before she left for work. There was so much I wanted to tell her.

Jennifer pulled me into her house and into a hug. "You're back." Within minutes she'd called in sick and made a pot of coffee. Over the next hour I told her about my secret life with Yasmeen.

"You never told anyone?" Jennifer asked.

"No one but Kate," I said. "I promised Yasmeen."

Jennifer knew about the stoning from when she and Dr. Kayra had been at my house caring for me. "Dr. Kayra really respects you. And she's scared for you."

"I'm scared for me, too."

"What is it?" Jennifer asked. "What else?"

"Max thought I was leaving him when I refused to give him my passport." I flushed with shame. "When he got violent, I finally told him I'd given it to a woman to help her escape."

Jennifer sighed.

"Max told Mohammed that night," I said.

Jennifer was silent as I struggled with my own horrible truth—the crushing reality that would forever hover in the periphery of my mind—lying in wait to destroy me. For the rest of my life I'd replay that night looking for what I could've done differently.

"I killed her," I whispered. "If I hadn't told Max, Yasmeen would still be alive."

"Oh, God, no," Jennifer cried. "You had no choice. You can't blame yourself."

I wanted to believe her. It's what I would've told anyone else. But guilt has a life of its own, growing beyond the boundaries of reason. Guilt takes no prisoners.

We finished the coffee, so Jennifer brought out a bottle of wine, the only sensible next course. I confided my plans to lay low, get to London, and leave for the States from there.

"They'll be looking for you at the London airport," Jennifer said. "Take the train to Paris and fly out from there."

"Great idea." I touched my glass to hers.

"What are you going to do about Mimi?" Jennifer asked.

"Jesus, I haven't thought about the cat."

"Don't worry," Jennifer smiled. "I'm going home in August for a wedding. I'll bring her with me. We'll get together."

We sipped our wine, lost in thought.

"How did you find out that Max told Mohammed?" Jennifer asked.

I told her about the envelope in Max's briefcase.

"Son of a bitch," Jennifer said. "Goddamn fucking son of a bitch."

"Which one?" I asked.

"Both of them."

"Be careful," I said. "Remember Ben works for both Max and Mohammed."

Jennifer looked me in the eyes. "Not for long." It was good to have her on my team.

Dr. Kayra was waiting for me the next morning at 9. "Sarah Hayes," she said, shaking her head. "There's a difference between being brave and being stupid."

It was then I poured out my story to Dr. Kayra—the envelope addressed to Max, how he had brutalized me, how I blamed myself for Yasmeen's death. When I finished, Dr. Kayra studied me for several moments before speaking.

"There is plenty of blame to go around," she said quietly. "Most of it misplaced."

Worn out from talking, I just listened.

"I've spoken with Leila Ali," Dr. Kayra said. "She blames herself for bringing Yasmeen back to Saudi. How could Leila have known her own brother would turn on her and force them to stay? How could she have known Abdul would murder his own niece? Honor killings!" Dr. Kayra spat out the words with disgust. "They dishonor themselves and the name of Islam when they commit such shameful, barbaric acts."

There was a long silence and I wondered if she'd exhausted herself. But she took a deep breath and continued. "Jamal blames himself for helping Yasmeen try to escape. You blame yourself. Max, Mohammed, and Abdul blame Yasmeen." Dr. Kayra smiled sadly. "The truth is we are all victims." She slapped her chest with her hand.

"We?" I asked.

"I've been here for ten years," Dr. Kayra said. "I didn't come here to do good. I came because with what I make in Saudi I can support my entire family in the Sudan." She leaned forward, staring intently. "We are all the same, Sarah. All of us who come to Saudi are victims of desperation or greed. We sell our souls and become slaves to a god spelled O-I-L." She smiled. "Who is it that determines the price of a soul?"

I was stunned by her passion, her pain. For a long moment I just looked at her. "We did," I whispered. "We determined the price. Max and I sold our souls when he signed that contract." I examined my hands as if seeing blood on them then looked back at Dr. Kayra. "What's my penance for Yasmeen's death?"

Dr. Kayra sighed wearily. "You're not responsible for Yasmeen's death, but you are responsible for your life and the lives of your children. Saudi Arabia is a Kingdom of lost souls. You must get out however you can, and take your children with you."

40

The next two months, I practiced subterfuge—appearing resigned to staying in Saudi while preparing to escape. I wrote Lara, explaining everything, and telling her I'd be sending packages for safekeeping. Under no circumstances was she to call or write. Using the library machine, I copied vital documents and bank statements. Jennifer mailed everything for me, in case my outgoing mail was being monitored.

I made lists and sorted, deciding what needed to be sent back to the States. Jennifer would mail boxes of books, photographs, CDs, and personal mementos immediately after we left on vacation. I stashed riyals for her expenses. It was tricky, organizing stuff without boxing it up.

"What's different in here?" Max asked one night, looking around the living room.

"Oh, I've neatened up." I shrugged, heart pounding. "It'll make moving to the beach house so much easier when we get back."

"Makes sense," Max said. "You should box up what we're not using."

"Great idea!" I said.

I studied schedules for trains to Paris, and re-hung the bulletin board with information we'd collected for Europe. I stood beside Max as he examined the board.

"Oh, yeah," I said, as if having a revelation. "What do we need to do to replace my passport?"

Max froze before answering. "I'll check into it."

"We'll probably have to go to the Embassy," I said. "Let me know what you find out." There was no pleasure in my deceit, just pain at the thought of my passport hidden in his briefcase.

Following a Women's Club meeting, I carefully positioned a schedule of upcoming events on the coffee table—after circling trips and classes occurring in the fall. Later, I was pleased to see it had been leafed through and set back down.

Every morning I ran to stay focused and rebuild my stamina. After the kids left for school, I biked to the clinic where I spent as many hours as possible. The kids were doing well, I baked cookies and prepared nice dinners, everything was neat and tidy on the surface. It was surreal, as if our lives weren't really unraveling. Everything was going exactly as planned, until it fell apart.

It was a week before the last day of school, Max had said grace, and we were starting dinner.

"What's all this?" Max looked at the food.

"An Arab feast!" I'd set the table with a tablecloth and good china. "I took an Arab cooking class at the Women's Club today and we got to bring food home."

"What is it?" Sam asked.

I pointed. "Stuffed zucchini with lamb, rice, cucumber and yoghurt salad. And Arab bread, your favorite." As I dished up food, Sam reached for the bread.

"I hate lamb," Kate said.

"No you don't," Max said,

"Don't tell me what I like," Kate shot back.

"You don't have to eat it if you don't like it." I remembered the sheep trauma on the beach and understood her aversion to meat. I put a tiny piece of the stuffed zucchini on Kate's plate.

She stared at it. "I've tasted zucchini and know I don't like it."

"What's this stuff in the rice?" Sam asked.

"Raisins, cinnamon, and almonds. You like those, right?" I said.

"Not in my rice," Sam said.

When I saw Max pushing food around his plate, I gave up. It had been a mistake to even try.

"Fine," I said. "Tomorrow I'll make spaghetti."

Max took a bite. "It's good. I like it."

Kate just stared at her food.

"If you don't like it, I'll make you a sandwich." I said.

"That's not how it works," Max said. "Your mom went to all this trouble. You can eat your dinner or you can be hungry."

"Fine," Kate said. "I'll be hungry."

"Goddamn it, Kate," Max said. "Just eat your food."

"I don't have to listen to you," Kate said with a smirk.

My gut tightened. "It's okay, really." I smiled at Max. "It's not worth fighting over." As I stood to take Kate's plate, Max slammed his hand on the table.

"Sit down," he screamed at me.

"Don't talk to Mom like that," Sam said.

Max whipped around to look at Sam, who stared back with narrowed eyes.

"I'm going out." Kate stood up.

"You're not going anywhere," Max yelled.

"Fuck you!" Kate screamed. "I hate you!"

Max jumped up and lunged toward Kate who started to run. He grabbed her shirt, yanked her backwards, and spun her around. His face was livid when he raised his hand.

"Don't you touch her!" I screamed, thrusting myself between them. Never had I felt such fury. I was ready to take him down if he so much as moved toward me or the kids.

"Tell him, Mom," Kate yelled.

I shot her a warning look. For one crazy second, I hoped I could keep everything together.

"Tell him, he needs to know." Kate started crying.

"Know what?" Max screamed. "That I've got two spoiled brats for kids?"

I backed toward the kids and felt them grab me.

Kate was sobbing. "Tell him, Mommy. Tell him."

"Tell me what?" Max yelled.

Feeling real terror, I took a deep breath and tried to undo what I knew could not be undone. "Please, Max, just leave Kate alone."

"Tell him we're leaving, Mommy. Tell him we're going home," Kate cried.

In the ensuing silence, Max looked at Kate who clung to me exhausted and broken, and at Sam who stood rigid and furious. Max looked at me for a long tense moment then grabbed the tablecloth and yanked everything from the table.

"Forget about vacation. Forget about Switzerland." Max pointed at the kids. "There are plenty of boarding schools here in the Emirates, for both of you. You'll be nice and close to your mommy." He walked out of the house, slamming the door behind him.

Kate sank to the floor, sobbing loudly. Keeping one hand on Sam, I knelt to comfort her. As I did, I felt shards of china biting into my knees.

I was waiting when Max came home in the middle of the night reeking of sweat and alcohol. *Where had he been?* He stripped off his clothes and got into bed.

"Don't say a word." Max jabbed his finger at me. "I swear you'll be sorry. I gave you everything and you've even turned my kids against me."

Minutes passed before I dared speak. "The kids love you. They just want to go home," I whispered. "It's crazy over here, look what it's done to us."

"You're the one who's crazy," Max screamed. "Remember there's a confession out there with your signature. And with that last stunt everybody knows you're out of your fucking mind."

"Then why don't you let me and the kids go home?" I said calmly. "You stay here."

"No, babe, it doesn't work that way. You're my wife," Max smiled malevolently. "You're not leaving. After school's out, I'm taking the kids and enrolling them in boarding school. When I get back it will be just you and me."

I flinched as Max reached out, but he turned off my lamp and rolled over. I sat in the dark, my heart pounding so hard the bed trembled with each beat. An hour later I went to the beach.

The moon was full that night, bright enough to cast long shadows as I walked on the sand. I didn't care—I felt safer there than at home. I dropped my abaya and waded into the calm black water. I swam laps until I was exhausted then I floated on my back, stared up at the stars, and formulated plan B.

The next morning, in a brave but desperate act, I called Jennifer before the kids were up. Later, at her house, I told her what had happened.

"Son of a bitch," Jennifer hissed.

"The kids finish school in a week and I've got to get them out of Saudi." I stared at her. "Whatever I do, Max has got to be held responsible. Even if he blames me or I'm caught."

"Any ideas?" Jennifer asked.

"I keep thinking about Rebecca." I smiled. "She left just after you arrived. Her husband was arrested and she was deported when their house caught fire and security found his still."

"Was that the doctor they were talking about at that awful party?" Jennifer asked.

I nodded. "It has to be something like that, big enough that the kids and I will be deported."

"Why not do that?" Jennifer asked. "Set fire to the house."

"They wouldn't find anything incriminating. We don't have a still." I shrugged. "We don't even have wine."

"I do," Jennifer said. "I have both."

"I know." I nodded. "Can I borrow them?"

At that we laughed—hard laughter. I couldn't remember the last time I'd laughed. Much later, we resumed planning.

"Max has got Mohammed in his pocket," Jennifer said. "Are you sure they'll arrest him?"

"Pretty sure." *Not even Mohammed can fix this.*

"We have to make sure." After finding the employee handbook, Jennifer turned to the section on Saudi law and Ocmara jurisdiction. It confirmed that Max was responsible for anything his dependents did while on the compound—just like he'd told us that very first day.

"Let's do it," Jennifer said.

"We have to make sure no one gets hurt." I thought a moment. "There's an awards ceremony the last day of school. We'll be gone all evening."

"We'll get everything in place and I'll set the fire while you're gone." Jennifer smiled. "Our friend sidiqui is very flammable."

Stunned by the magnitude of her offer, I stared at her. "You would do that for me?"

"Yes." Jennifer nodded, her expression suddenly serious. "I would."

"What if you get caught?" I whispered, feeling my chest tighten. Tears filled my eyes.

"I won't get caught," she said. "I'll do it after dark."

"Wear an abaya and veil," I said.

"I'll be invisible."

"You can't tell Ben." I knew how close they were.

"Don't worry, I won't."

I felt a surge of fear. "What if Max denies it? What if he blames me?"

"There'll be a hundred witnesses that you were at the school when it happened. And it won't matter if he denies it. It says so in here." She slapped the handbook.

"You think he'll be arrested?" I asked.

"Probably." Jennifer stared hard at me. "You have to be okay with that."

"What do you think will happen to him?"

"Who the fuck cares?" Jennifer said.

The rest of the day we obsessed over details. I carried home a box of metal tubing and bottles of wine, stashing it in the garage storage room. Every day we smuggled more. Every day I worried. Jennifer could be impetuous. *What will happen if we're caught? Will we be stoned?* Images of Yasmeen's bloody body looped through my mind.

The afternoon of the last day of school I was mixing cookie dough when Max appeared in the doorway. I glanced at him then back at the bowl.

Max watched a minute before he spoke. "What are you doing?"

"Making cookies for tonight. I offered since I blew the bake sale." I began dropping spoonfuls of dough on cookie sheets. "And I had all these damn chips."

Max raised one hand and I saw the manila envelope from Mohammed. He began lightly smacking it against the palm of his other hand. "Did you see this?"

"What?" I glanced at the envelope then back at the dough. "No. What is it?" My heart began pounding and there was a low humming in my ears. *How does he know?* I continued dropping spoonfuls as Max watched.

"It's addressed to me," he finally said. "Did you open it?"

"I said I've never seen it." I slid the cookie sheets in the oven. *Shit, I never should have mentioned my passport.*

Max watched me as he smacked the envelope against his hand. "Are you sure?"

I looked Max in the eyes. "For the last time, I didn't see your damn envelope." *The lock! Did I screw up the numbers on the lock?*

Max stared at me until the front door slammed.

"Mom, I'm home," Sam yelled.

"We're in here, sweetie," I called.

Sam pushed past Max into the kitchen. "You're making cookies? Cool!"

As Sam hugged me, Max pointed at me with the envelope. "Later."

I listened to Max walk upstairs, following his footsteps, so I'd know where to look—later.

I was pulling cookies from the oven when Sam popped back in. "I can't find Mimi!"

"She's at the vet." I smiled before he could be alarmed. "Just for a checkup. The vet's keeping her overnight." This time I'd remembered the cat.

Two hours later, Max and the kids were waiting in the car when I walked out carrying the cookies. It was sunset and I heard call to prayer.

"We're going to be late!" Kate said.

Max threw the car in reverse and backed out of the driveway.

"We're fine." I smiled, trying to appear calm. "We have plenty of time."

At the school, Kate and Sam rushed to join their friends. All evening I was in a state of heightened vigilance, waiting for something to go terribly wrong. But the awards ceremony went well. Both kids got honor roll certificates and awards for participation in soccer. When Max was recognized for his contribution, I smiled and applauded—every bit the adoring wife.

When Sam was also awarded perfect attendance, Kate smiled at me and tugged her earlobe. I knew she was remembering the day in the women's quarters. I blew her a kiss. In that instant Kate and I were connected by a memory only we shared.

Following the ceremony, there was a reception. Parents, teachers, and students mingled. Graduating students said weepy goodbyes. I smiled and tried to look engaged as I pushed away fear. *Is Jennifer setting the fire?* Saudi champagne was served, along with desserts.

Max and I avoided conversation and eye-contact, as we chatted with other parents and teachers. His decision to transfer the kids to boarding school hadn't been made public, so it was easy to just smile and nod. Max was anxious to leave, but I encouraged the kids to keep mingling. The longer we stayed the better. I wandered through the crowd, making small-talk with everyone—greeting, chatting, stalling. That night *I* was the social butterfly.

It was dark when we drove home, long after the last call to prayer. Turning onto our street we saw fire trucks, security cars, jeeps. Sirens shrieked, lights flashed, the air was hazy with smoke.

"What's all this?" Max said.

Sam pointed. "That's our house!"

As Max maneuvered the Land Rover closer, red lights were reflected in his Rolex.

"I opened your envelope," I said calmly.

"What?" Max looked at me. "What are you talking about?"

"From Mohammed." I looked at him. "Was it worth it?"

The kids were leaning forward, listening to every word. "For God's sake, Sarah. Not now."

We could go no farther, so Max parked.

"Now is all we have left," I said, getting out of the car. Max and the kids followed as I pushed through the crowd. Thick smoke rolled from under our garage door.

"Mimi!" Sam started forward.

I grabbed him and whispered. "Remember! Mimi's not here."

An explosion sounded inside the garage, there was a powerful whoosh of wind, and we were bathed in the heat and glow of flames devouring the garage door. Firemen ran forward with hoses. When the flames subsided one fireman entered the garage. After a few tense moments, he ran out with coils of metal tubing and an armful of bottles. After conferring with several officials, two uniformed security officers broke from the crowd and walked our way.

"Are you Max Hayes?" one asked.

"Yes, I am," Max said.

They grabbed Max and handcuffed him. "We found your still. You're under arrest."

"What? I don't have a still." Max glanced around frantically. "Sarah, tell them. Tell them I don't have a still."

I stood holding my children, staring at the stranger who had been the love of my life. "I loved you," I said quietly.

Suddenly Max got it. "Wait a minute! She did it. Not me. Goddamn it, call my boss. Call Mohammed, he'll tell you." Max pulled against his restraints. "Arrest her!"

One of the officers walked over to me. "Mrs. Hayes, may I see your ID?" My chest tightened, but I calmly reached in my backpack and gave him my ID. He examined it briefly and gave it back. I put it in my backpack, beside my passport. "Thank you, you may go."

"You're letting her go?" Max screamed.

The officer gave Max a patient smile. "Mr. Hayes, is this your house and your wife?"

"Yes!"

"Then you are responsible." The officer nodded and they began leading Max away.

Max looked back with a panicked expression. "I didn't know who she was, I swear. I did it to save us." Max was crying and it *almost* broke my heart. "Tell them to let me go. Please!"

There was another explosion. New flames shot up and more smoke billowed out. Max looked at the house then at me. "Goddamn it, Sarah, you didn't have to blow up the whole house!"

There was much to say, but I didn't dare speak. I stood tall and silent, heartbroken and relieved. The kids sobbed as I held them. My face crumbled, but not my resolve. I watched through tears as Max was forced into the police car. Lights flashed, and the car drove away.

The fire was quickly brought under control and confined to the garage. The charred remains of a still and a dozen bottles of wine were found in the storage room. No one really knew how the fire started. But there was speculation. And, earlier that night, if anyone had been watching closely, they might have seen a small dark shadow leaving by the backyard gate.

For the next six nights the kids and I stayed with Jennifer and Ben. I collected Mimi from the vet where she'd gotten her checkup and all the necessary documents for travel back to the States. We were allowed into the house to gather whatever we wanted to take back in our luggage. Finally, the movers came for the rest of our belongings to ship back to Chicago.

Sheila Flaherty

On Sunday morning, the seventh day, I was on the beach before dawn. I watched the sky turn from black to gray to light enough to distinguish a black thread from a white thread. I sat on our stone listening to call to prayer and watching the pink sky show off for me as the sun rose on our last day in Saudi Arabia. Walking slowly back down the beach, I felt the cool sand under my feet. The heavy water caressed my legs, seducing me into one last swim. Walking into the warm embrace of the Arabian Gulf, I surrendered. Floating on my back, arms out at my sides, I stared up into the endless blue Saudi Arabian sky.

Late that night, Saudi Police drove us to the Dhahran Airport. As we were escorted through the airport we passed a group of Saudi men in thobes and gutras. They leaned their heads together and whispered. Their eyes followed us curiously. As we walked past a group of veiled Saudi women, one woman turned and watched me. I nodded at her and smiled. She nodded back.

Epilogue

It is freezing this morning—winter has Chicago in its firm, icy grip. But the sky is blue and the sun is shining for the first time in weeks. Even with sunglasses, I squint in the glare reflected off brilliant white snow. Fortified with gloves, scarf, hat, calf-length down coat, and tall boots, I slowly navigate sidewalks treacherous with ice. The lake beckons.

The park is deserted. No music and laughter, no aromatic smoke and women praying to the east. I wind my way between rocks and down a path. The beach is otherworldly—covered with layers of ice and snowdrifts resembling sand dunes. Subzero temperatures have tamed the mighty lake, capturing it like a tableau in a snow-globe. The silence is piercing.

Close to shore, a thick duvet of ice blankets the water. Underneath, is a slow rolling movement like breathing. Sun glints off water in the distance, gentle ripples evidence of wind and strong currents beneath the surface. Low on the eastern horizon a bank of pink clouds promises storms ahead. To the south, the Chicago skyline rises sharply.

Walking north, I follow the tracks of those who've already bravely ventured out. I crunch over frozen sand then step into snow so deep it swallows my boots. Each step takes a calculated effort and soon I'm sweating under all my layers. When I reach the northernmost point, only my face is cold. I brush snow from a flat stone and sit where I can see the entire beach stretching before me. Within this bleak glacial landscape, there is no pretending I'm on the beach in Saudi. But my thoughts quickly take me there.

There's more to the story of Saudi. Of course there's more. Even as I put the final words on the last page, another memory surfaced—I'm wearing an abaya, walking on the beach with Yasmeen. We laugh as we eat ripe mangos, juice running down our arms. Suddenly my mouth is filled with the taste of sweet orange flesh. That's the way of memories. Once one is unlocked, more flood out, like water through a dam. Fleeting images combine in the arbitrary fashion of dreams—or nightmares.

In the States, life went on. Sam was welcomed back by his pack of boys. Kate was once again a celebrity, exotic with her gold hoop earrings. Tears and sadness gave way to normalcy as laughter and energy filled the house. In the fall, when Kate and Sam went back to school, I did as well, using my inheritance to finally get my doctoral degree in psychology. Like most in my profession, I hoped what I learned would help make sense of my life.

Max was detained in a Saudi prison then released after a month with all charges dropped—thanks be to Mohammed, his friend in high places. Max stayed at Ocmara another year until late in 1990, when another kind of shamaal blew into Saudi Arabia.

Since that last night in Saudi I've seen Max only once, across a courtroom. Because he was careful to never let his eyes meet mine, I was able to study him. He was finely dressed, his Rolex gleaming subtly, the twitching muscle in his jaw his only acknowledgment of my presence. His black hair was streaked with gray, but he was still heartbreakingly handsome. The heart is a funny thing, not always connected to the head. As I watched Max, I felt a deep sadness. But the only tug I felt was to the distant past, and for the future lost to all of us.

After that day Max was gone. But despite the absence of their father, both my children have flourished. Kate channeled her creativity into a culinary career specializing in Middle Eastern cuisine. Sam got a law degree and turned his love of athletics into a lucrative career in sports management. He stills plays soccer with childhood friends. I am proud of them both.

I've developed a fulfilling private practice working with a diverse population of woman and girls. I guide them in finding their inner-strengths and truths and help them honor themselves in the living of their lives. And, I've written this book.

Telling the story of Saudi Arabia has not saved me, but I'm not surprised. Telling the story does not change the story, just the understanding. But it has lifted the veils and given a face, body, and voice to Yasmeen—and to all women shrouded in darkness.

Saudi Arabia and the Middle East are still not done with me. A fleeting glimpse of a black shadow, dark eyes above a mask, a story of yet another woman or girl sacrificed in the name of honor can haunt me for months.

And, because the head is not always connected to the heart, the sound of Middle Eastern music can still stop me in my tracks. Or make me shimmy to the beat as muscle-memory takes over. Those times, I feel Yasmeen's energy surrounding me and I smell the sweet and bitter scent of Clementines. Even though I've told our story, her spirit still haunts me—she is my familiar.

THE END

Author's Note

"Fiction is the lie through which we tell the truth." ~Albert Camus

I want to clarify that while *East of Mecca* is inspired by my personal experiences while living in Saudi Arabia and written in memoir format, it is a work of fiction. Aside from Mimi the cat, the names and characters portrayed in this novel are either products of my imagination, real people used fictitiously, or combinations of a number of people—real and fiction. This is also the case with places and incidents described.

Those who have lived in Saudi will note that I have taken great liberties with many details regarding geography and compound life. My own experiences were nowhere as dramatic as portrayed in my novel—in fact I met a number of lovely people there whom I remember fondly. You know who you are!

East of Mecca explores the dangers inherent in relationships where absolute power is awarded to only one entity—be it an ethnic group, a god, or a gender. Saudi Arabia is ranked among the world's worst human rights abusers and in 2012 was ranked 131st out of 135 countries in the World Economic Forum's Gender Gap Index.

But oppression and domestic abuse is not unique to Saudi Arabia—it is a universal tragedy. My goal is to lift the veils of those rendered invisible—whomever and wherever they are—and to give them a voice.

Second Edition Afterword

Since the publication of *East of Mecca,* it's been my honor to be invited to many books clubs, women's groups, and other author events. The question I have been asked more than any other is, "Haven't things improved for women in Saudi Arabia since the late 1980's when you were living there?" The simple and tragic answer is, "No." Circumstances have worsened for Saudi women—and for Muslim women and girls worldwide. Because of culturally sanctioned honor violence and radical Islamic terrorist groups, gender apartheid against women has reached epic proportions.

The following are facts about women in Saudi Arabia:

- Saudi Arabia is the only country in the world that prohibits women from driving. – *"World Report 2012: Saudi Arabia" Human Rights Watch (HRW), 2011*
- Under the Saudi guardianship system, women are treated as minors as well as forbidden from travel, studying or working without permission from male guardians –*"World Report 2012: Saudi Arabia" Human Rights Watch (HRW), 2011*
- Under Saudi law, all females must have a male guardian, typically a father, brother or husband. The guardian has duties to, and rights over, the woman in many aspects of civic life. - *Ertürk, Yakin (14 April 2009). Report of the Special Rapporteur on violence against women, its causes and consequences: Mission to Saudi Arabia. United Nations.*
- Women's freedom of movement is very limited in Saudi Arabia. They are not supposed to leave their houses or their local neighborhood without the permission of their male guardian. - *"Women's Rights in the Middle East and North Africa: Citizenship and Justice". Freedom House. 2005. p. 262*

- Traditionally, women's clothing must not reveal anything about her body. It is supposed to be thick, opaque, and loose. It should not resemble the clothing of men (or non-Muslims). In Saudi Arabia and some other Arab states, all of the body is expected to be covered except the hands and eyes. -"*Conditions of Muslim woman's hijaab*". Islam *Q&A. 3 October 2008. Retrieved 2 June 2008.*
- There are no laws defining the minimum age for marriage in Saudi Arabia. Most religious authorities have justified the marriage of girls as young as 9 and boys as young as 15. However, they believe a father can marry off his daughter at any age. - *Gender Equality in Saudi Arabia". Retrieved 21 September 2010.*

For more current information on global violence against women and girls, I recommend:

A Call to Action: Women, Religion, Violence, and Power. A book by President Jimmy Carter. Simon & Schuster, 2014

Honor Diaries: Culture is No Excuse for Abuse. A documentary written and produced by Paula Kweskin available on DVD or to download. Also see the *Honor Diaries* page on FaceBook.

Google the following terms: female genital mutilation, gender apartheid, honor violence, honor killings, sharia law.

Add Your Voice: Write A Reader Review

Writing a reader review on Amazon, Barnes & Noble and / or Goodreads will help support Sheila's mission to enlighten, inspire and empower others for the greater good. Visit SheilaFlaherty.com/readers for more information on how you can contribute your voice.

Subcribe To Sheila's Mailing List

For more of Sheila's writing, please sign up for her list to receive blog posts and updates via email by visiting SheilaFlaherty.com/subscribe.

Social Media

To interact with Sheila on social media, visit SheilaFlaherty.com/social to see a listing of her active social media profiles.

Acknowledgments

Since I have been telling the story of Saudi Arabia in one form or another for twenty-four years, writing my acknowledgments fills me with trepidation. I have been blessed with so many helpers along the way that I'm certain to leave someone out. So I will begin with a general thank you to all who have contributed in any way and a sincere apology to anyone I fail to name. Any contribution to my process in writing this book can be felt in the vibration of the words on the pages—and in my heart.

I will always be profoundly grateful to the two women most instrumental in the creation of *East of Mecca*. In 2004, when attention was drawn to the brutal treatment of women in the Middle East, Mary Siewert Scruggs remembered I had written a script ten years before and insisted I submit it to the Nicholl Fellowships in Screenwriting competition. To my surprise, it placed in the semi-finals. In 2005, as a CineStory finalist, I met Meg LeFauve (my "Hollywood producer") who generously devoted three years helping me develop my story. Meg pushed me to do what I never knew I could—and she taught me to be brave. Meg never stopped believing in the film, but continued her support when, in 2008, I decided to rewrite *East of Mecca* as a novel.

Once again, Mary Scruggs stepped in with loving and firm guidance. For over three years, she read and reread my manuscripts, continually making me go deeper—closer to the truth. Mary never stopped believing—right up to her sudden and untimely death in 2011. I will forever be missing Mary. One of my profound sorrows is that she is not here in the physical to help me celebrate—but I have never stopped feeling her presence in my life and in my process. I know she is watching, laughing, and saying, "I told you so."

This book could not have been written without the support and love of my friends. Most of all, I am grateful for those who tolerated my absences, unreturned phone calls, and my incessant talk about the book whenever I emerged—those who never stopped believing in my dream. Thank you for loving me anyway.

Many of my friends and family members have read the manuscript at various stages and I am indebted to them all. My deepest thanks goes to those who carefully considered draft after draft—Tanya Boaz, Tanya Sugarman, Ruth Firby, Dr. Sheila Culkin, Dr. Robbi Daiber, Avis Henkin, Paul and Becky Fields—and to Mark Bryan, Carl Ray Copeland, and Kristen and David Finch for their thoughtful endorsements. Thank you all.

I am also grateful for the gentle and insistent spiritual guidance of America Martinez. Over the past twenty years, your encouragement and wise words have often talked me off the ledge and taught me to trust divine timing. Thanks to Tia Griffith, for generosity of time and effort, and to Jillian Holly, for always believing, encouraging, and spreading the word. Much gratitude to Suzy Crawford, for keeping me physically strong and balanced and for the joy of Zumba!

Without my community of fellow writers, I would never have completed my novel. At Lakeside Writers, special thanks go to Nancy Beckett, who taught me to write memoir, and Laurie Cunningham for her careful editing, as well as Michael Tirrell, Kelly Kennoy, and Cathy Sherer for encouragement and feedback. Thanks to Write Club Fight Club members David Finch, Adina Kabaker, Ann Lammas, Cathy Postilion, Sylvie Sadarnac, and Jason Sarna who have kept me going through the home stretch. Special thanks to Cathy for also kicking my butt whenever I need it. Thank you all for your love and unwavering support.

I would like to thank the Ragdale Foundation for the generous gift of time and space provided during my two-week residency in 2010.

To be a psychologist is to be blessed with an awesome responsibility and a hug an hour. I am much indebted to all my patients over the years who have kept me grounded and gratified for having the best job in the world. To those who've known of my writing, thank you for your interest and inquiries. And to those who have read my book and/or essays—thanks for your love, support, and acceptance of my human frailties.

I am deeply in debt to my brilliant, creative, and devoted marketing team, all of whom have taken this introvert far beyond her comfort zone to make the dream of *East of Mecca* manifest in reality. I am grateful to Sandro Miller for the generous gift of his time and talents to take the photographs that make me look beautiful. And to Ron Gorny, for weaving my vague imaginings into a book cover that takes my breath away. Special thanks go to Harry Elliott for his meticulous creation of my beautiful websites, tireless efforts to get me out of my cave and connected to the world, and endless patience with my "mlm" questions. And to the beautiful, passionate, and gifted Diane Testa who helped me define my mission, create my vision— and whose gentle persistence has kept me moving ahead one step at a time. My everlasting love to you all.

Thank you to all the people I call "family" who have supported me, believed in me, loved me, and endured me all these years! Special thanks and love go out to my son Jeffrey, for all his encouragement and for allowing me to fictionalize much of his Saudi experience, and to his lovely, extraordinary wife Brianne, who has become the daughter I had to create in the book.

Finally, thank you, Barry. I am fortunate to have the love of a good man, who for years has tolerated my absence and divided attention and the soundtrack of *Babel* filling the night air while I wrote into the wee hours. You have always encouraged and never doubted. I love you.

Book Club Or Reading Group Questions And Discussion Topics

1. Where does the title "East of Mecca" originate?
2. Under the same or similar circumstances, would you have made the same choice as Sarah and Max when they moved their family to Saudi Arabia? Why or why not?
3. Did you like Sarah? Why or why not?
4. Which aspects of Sarah do you most and least identify with?
5. How did she change over the course of the story?
6. Did you like Max? Why or why not?
7. How did he change after moving to Saudi?
8. How do you feel the children adapted to living in Saudi?
9. The first day in Saudi, Sarah was fingerprinted, photographed holding Max's ID number, and her passport was confiscated—only to be released with her husband's permission. In what ways did Sarah's experience put her in the position of Saudi women in the Kingdom? How would YOU feel in Sarah's shoes?
10. What did you think of the Women's Club? Would you have joined?
11. In Chapter Twenty-Six, Yasmeen tells Sarah, "A veil gives me freedom." In what ways does Sarah come to personally understand this?
12. What range of emotions did you experience while reading East of Mecca? Which moments and particular scenes do you recall being most affected by? Which were the most compelling, painful, frightening, enlightening, and/or inspiring?
13. In Chapter One, Sarah tells us she blames herself for what happened to Yasmeen. Why? What else do you think Sarah blames herself for?
14. In Chapter Five, Sarah confesses to have kept her smoking a secret from Max. What does, "Maybe I just liked having a secret," reveal about Sarah's nature? What else might it suggest?

How do themes of secrecy, trust, and betrayal play out through the book?

15. What were signs that Sarah's marriage to Max was troubled before moving to Saudi? How did life in Saudi exacerbate these problems?

More discussion questions can be found on Sheila's website by visiting: SheilaFlaherty.com/discussion.

About The Author

Sheila Flaherty is an Army brat who grew up to be a writer and clinical psychologist. She earned her Ph.D. from Northwestern University Medical School in Chicago, and has had a thriving private practice in the Chicago area for the past 32 years, except for one year spent in the Kingdom of Saudi Arabia. While in Saudi, Sheila's compassion led her to practice counseling secretly with American and Saudi women. This experience inspired her to write *East of Mecca*, a story about women within the confines of a violent, oppressive, male-dominated society. Sheila has placed in several screenwriting competitions, including BlueCat, CineStory, and the Nicholl Fellowships. In 2010 and 2013, she was awarded residencies at the Ragdale Foundation in Lake Forest, IL for her work in fiction. Sheila's life mission is to enlighten, inspire, and empower others for the greater good. A majority of all profits from sales of *East of Mecca* will go toward providing funding for women and girls to meet their most profound needs. Sheila lives near Chicago with her husband and two cats. Visit Sheila's website at: www.SheilaFlaherty.com.

Made in the USA
Lexington, KY
19 May 2017